A Good Conviction   1

Lewis M. Weinstein

ALSO BY LEWIS M. WEINSTEIN

The Heretic (2000)
Case Closed (2009)
The Pope's Conspiracy (2012)

For the innocent prisoners
who live in unimaginable horror

Lewis M. Weinstein

A Good Conviction

Lewis M. Weinstein

Lewis M. Weinstein

PROLOGUE

Sing Sing Correctional Facility
Wednesday, January 21, 2004

Disjointed memories haunt me, as they do every night, shattering my once great expectations and leaving me to share a cold clammy cell listening to a guy named Spider jerk off.

The darkness emits a rumbling undercurrent of sounds, pierced randomly by eerie howls. Inmates yell obscenities to one another, or worse, to no one.

Doors clang, footsteps echo and fade away, angry music blares in short bursts. Odors of urine, decaying food, stale smoke, and sweaty unwashed bodies assault the air. Mice and roaches scurry.

The longer I'm here, the harder it is to imagine being anywhere else.

Giving in and allowing myself to cry would be suicidal. Others would observe my fear, and act on it. Predatory others. "Hey, white boy, they gonna' love you' ass in here."

How long before I lose my mind? And will that be better or worse? Is it already happening? Every day, the person who was Joshua Blake recedes further from reality. Is this process irreversible? Will there be a point when I can never again be who I was?

There's a sudden movement close to me and I cringe. I'm going to be hurt. Relief. It's just my cellmate, stirring in the bunk below me. The fact that his presence is actually comforting shows how much my life has changed.

Spider rolls out of his bunk and slides into view. In the dim light, I make out hairy legs, dark crotch, gray prison shirt. He settles his muscled bulk onto the toilet. More sounds and smells. When he's done, I roll off the upper bunk, take his place, feel his sweat. I remember what it used to be like in a bathroom with a door and a seat on the toilet.

I climb up, careful not to step on Spider's arm, crawl under my thin blanket, shiver in the chill. Spider's bulk shifts in the bunk below me. He settles into a slow steady rhythm which pulses my bunk as well as his. Spider is once again masturbating.

I strain for diversion.

A familiar burr grinds at the edges of my mind. I force myself to focus, visualizing each distinct moment of my arrest and trial.

I see a look in a man's eye. I grab for it, but once again it slips away, and I'm sinking, gasping, a deep eternal coldness filling my body.

Spider finishes with a grunt and a sudden lurch just as I slide into my personal bottomless lake of despair.

Deep in the murky water, the man's face reappears, staring at me intently, a puzzled expression in his eyes.

And - finally - I know the face.

ONE

Eight months earlier

"Next and last station stop, New York Penn Station."

I had been day dreaming. My friends were sitting around the table in Mom's house, always Mom's house even after she passed away, just another night like hundreds before it. But this time, we all knew it was the last time. Sure we'd always be friends and we'd get together now and then, but it would never be like it is right now, like it has always been.

I sold the house a month or so after Mom died. Closing was last Friday, the day after graduation. I spent the weekend with Tom and Barb before taking the train to New York.

At just past 5:00 pm the Amtrak regional train emerged from the Hudson River tunnel into the dim light of the underground approach yard and gradually slowed to a stop. Duffel on shoulder, suitcase in each hand, I followed the crowd up an escalator into a maelstrom of walking, running, and standing-still-looking-confused people. I joined the standing-still-looking-confused group and let it soak in.

My destination for the next three nights was the Broadway Big Apple Hotel, selected from the web as the least expensive choice near Penn Station, and also because of its magical name. What could be more New York?

I walked north on Seventh Avenue, maneuvering my way through the crowded sidewalks, dodged a hot dog cart flying across the sidewalk, and reached the corner of 38th Street and Seventh Avenue. There was no Broadway Big Apple Hotel. Another block. Nothing. Back to Thirty-eighth and east toward Broadway. Still nothing. Some hot stuff, can't even find your hotel.

Looking back the way I had come, I saw a tiny vertical sign hanging crookedly on the front of an undistinguished five-story graystone building. Broadway Hotel. An even smaller sign said Broadway Big Apple Hotel, and below that, a hand lettered piece of cardboard proclaimed an Internet Café. I peeked in. The description on the web was "charming boutique hotel." They lied.

Above the desk, taped to a column, a sign said "Directions for Showers," with a large arrow pointing to a diagram. While I was trying to guess why such directions might be needed, a round oriental face popped up from behind an ancient printer and stared at me.

On the train, I had allowed myself to fantasize a hotel desk clerk saying, in an elegant tone, "Welcome to the Broadway Big Apple. How may I help you?" But those words, or indeed any words, did not materialize.

"Uh, I have a reservation," I said.

The round face offered no sign of comprehension.

"My name is Joshua Blake," I said. After a pause, I asked, "Do you work here?"

There was some shuffling of paper, and a single page appeared on the counter between us. It had my name on it, which was encouraging. On the other hand, I glanced quickly at the stairs to my right - there was no elevator - and wondered if I really wanted to go any further into this not charming, not boutique, decidedly seedy place.

I signed my name and looked at the clerk for my next instruction. "Credit card," he said, wasting not a single word. I produced my Visa card, he took an imprint. He returned the card along with a key to room 301. He pointed to the stairs and promptly disappeared.

I had expected to feel important checking into my first New York hotel. On my own! Ready to conquer New York! I shuddered at my naiveté, forced down the panic, and unpacked.

I hung my blue blazer, pants and shirts, and threw the rest of the clothes in a drawer, wondering if I would ever see them again. The room was filthy. Was there maid service? Was there thief service?

No matter how nervous I felt about this disappointing hotel, I couldn't just stay in my room. I left my possessions to their fate and descended the stairs.

On Eighth Avenue, I passed a deli and a depressing place advertising "Girls, Girls, Girls." A bus pulled up next to me, and Michael Kay's smiling face on the side of the bus changed my mood. Remarkably, his picture made me feel I had a friend in New York. Michael had been the radio voice of the New York Yankees for several years, before switching to television, and I had listened to so many Yankee games I felt I knew him. I smiled at the bus, happy to be in Michael's city, and a little jauntiness returned to my stride.

At 42nd Street, I entered a different world. Long hailed as the worst and most dangerous street in "tourist" New York, it now proudly featured a new Disney Store, a huge 25 screen cinema, and Madame Toussaud's wax museum. I did a double-take when I saw Whoopi Goldberg standing near me on the sidewalk, but she wasn't moving and not likely to.

I chose a Mexican restaurant and ordered chicken quesadillas with a Corona. It cost $16.38, and I reminded myself I had to make my law school fund last for three years.

When I returned to the Broadway Big Apple, there were two women in the bar, obviously prostitutes. I hurried past, looking the other way.

Safe in my room, behind the double locked door, with all of my clothes still in place, I sat at a small table and reviewed a paper headed "Law Firms." I had contacted four firms, and sort of had appointments for summer job interviews at each. "Stop by, we'll see what we can do."

Referring to what the Metropolitan Transit Authority calls "The Map," I noted the locations already marked, and thought again how I would get to each. My plan was to visit all four firms the next day.

But it was still early, and I was fidgety. I decided to learn more about the law firms I was going to see the next day. I had started to study their web sites several weeks before, but then with finals and graduation and everything, I hadn't done the follow-up. My laptop was in the suitcase at Penn Station, so what good luck there was an Internet Café at the Broadway Big Apple. I pulled on a clean polo and headed downstairs.

"Hi, honey," one of the ladies said as I approached the bar.

Swiveling on the barstool and flashing an exciting expanse of inner thigh, she added, "Can we help you?"

She was blond, with long hair tied up in some sort of bun. Her breasts spilled over a tight orange wrap that left her flat belly exposed. Low cut white satin shorts and white high-heeled shoes with sequins completed the outfit. She looked to be in her early twenties, but it was hard to tell. The overall impact was flabbergasting, my life experience to date having given me no clue how to talk to such a person.

"I need to use the computer," I said. "Go on the internet."

"Ooh, a smart one," she said. "What's your name, honey?"

"Josh."

"I'm Darlene."

"Do you know about the computer?" I asked.

Darlene laughed and turned to her partner, "Do we know how to surf the web?"

They laughed together, and then Darlene said, "We are web surfers extraordinaire, honey, but you have to open an account first. The bartender will explain. He'll be back soon. This is my friend Annabelle."

Annabelle had dark hair and dark clothes, and looked Hispanic, despite her name. She was heavier and at least several years older than Darlene, and her ample bottom spilled out over both sides of the barstool.

"Hi, Josh," Annabelle said sweetly in a pleasantly accented voice.

"Hi, Annabelle," I said very cautiously.

"Where are you from?" Annabelle asked.

"Baltimore."

"What are you going to do on the computer?"

"I'm meeting with law firms tomorrow, about a job for the summer, and I want to learn more about the firms from their web sites." How weird was this, explaining my plans to the two prostitutes?

"We have a web site," said Darlene, her voice suddenly very businesslike.

"You have a web site?"

"How do you think we get business, honey?" asked Annabelle. "Since Mr. Gardino became mayor, certain marketing options are no longer available to us."

Before I could learn more about their web site, the bartender appeared, and Darlene asked him to set me up with a web account. Daryl was a small black man with slicked back hair and very large teeth, one of which was gold. He was wearing a shirt open in the front, with a heavy gold necklace on his skinny chest.

"That'll be ten bucks," Daryl mumbled.

"For what?" I asked.

"For one hour," he answered.

"How much for a half hour?"

"Ten bucks."

I sprung for the hour, and nervously took a seat at one of the flat black screens, with Annabelle and Darlene staring at me. Daryl's unseen command brought the screen to life. I clicked on the Internet Explorer icon, and was soon at the web site of the first firm I was planning to visit.

"Can I print something?" I asked.

"Twenty five cents," Daryl answered. I printed, scanned some more, looked at the other sites, printed more, and in 45 minutes I was finished. I checked my email and was disappointed to find no new messages. While I had been on the computer, Darlene had gone and returned, and now Annabelle was gone. Darlene came over to see what I was doing.

"Want to see our web site," she asked. I nodded.

"It's www.darleneandannabelle.com. Go ahead, it won't hurt."

I typed in the address and hit enter. Full-screen images of Darlene and Annabelle exploded into view. Each was wearing nothing more than pasties, the tiniest g-string, and a sultry look. My mouth dropped.

"Scroll down," Darlene said.

The text was like nothing I had ever seen. It sounded like an attorney had written it.

"We are Independent Escorts and in no way connected to an agency. We are available for outcall most anytime in New York. We are also available for travel. Sexy, Intelligent, Classy and sometimes Naughty is the best way to describe us. We prefer contact through e-mail initially until we are confident we have made a connection. Serious gentlemen only."

At the bottom of the page was a declaration. "Services offered on this site are legal adult escort services. Donations are for our time and companionship ONLY! Anything that may happen during that time is a matter of personal choice and consent between two adults and is not negotiated for nor compensated for in any manner. THIS IS NOT AN OFFER OF PROSTITUTION."

I closed the site and the computer, and approached the bar to settle my $4.25 printing bill.

"Are there any other services you'll be requiring this evening," Darlene asked, and her choice of words, along with the unexpected refinement of her diction, reminded me of the elegant hotel experience I had originally expected.

"No," I said, and then, not wanting to be impolite, added "No, thank you."

My eyes, completely on their own accord, slipped from her face to the hard ridges of her nipples bursting against the fabric of her orange top. Darlene smiled, and pulled her shoulders back just a bit more. Under the heavy makeup, she was pretty. I turned and ran up the stairs.

I changed into boxer shorts and a t-shirt, and set my travel alarm. Car horns, alarms, sirens, and violent shouts soon lulled me to sleep.

I woke before the alarm, showered without reference to any diagrams, and dressed quickly. While dressing, I looked at myself in the cracked mirror, and, egotistical as it sounds, I liked what I saw. I practiced my smile, which would be on display repeatedly today. Okay!

The stairs were cool and quiet; all of the occupants either sleeping or dead, and the morning air was brisk. I bought a bagel with butter and coffee at a deli on Eighth Avenue, and felt like a real New Yorker standing on the street with my breakfast, watching the early morning traffic.

The day passed quickly and just before 3:00 pm, I approached my fourth and last prospect, on Sixth Avenue in the fifties, an impressive high rise. Two of the previous three firms had indicated they probably had "go-fer" positions. They would get back to me in a few days. I left my cell number and email address with each.

Passing through the post 9-11 security procedures, my name on a list provided by Morgan, Heffer, and Stone, I rode the elevator to the 44th floor and walked across an elegant lobby to a reception desk.

"My name is Joshua Blake. I have an appointment with Ms. Barbara Coleman."

"I'll let her know you're here. Would you like to take a seat?"

I sank into a deep leather armchair. On the coffee table in front of me were the New York Times, Wall Street Journal, the Economist, and Fortune. It seems all law firms have the same newspapers and magazines in their waiting rooms. Maybe it's required by the Bar Association.

"You must be Josh," a pleasant middle aged woman sang out as she crossed the room toward me. I nodded and stood.

"Follow me," she said, turning before I could say a word. We walked down a long hallway. The lawyer's offices on either side were small and each was filled with files precariously perched on every available surface. The secretarial alcoves were far neater.

"Come in. Sit down." she said, taking her chair behind the desk. "Josh, I have your letter here," she began. "You're looking for a summer job?"

"Yes, until school starts at the end of August."

"Hmm, top 10% of your class at UMBC. NYU Law in September?"

"Yes."

"Good school," she said. "Many of our attorneys graduated from NYU. Is this your first time in New York?"

"I've been here to see Yankee games and to visit NYU, but this is the first time I'm actually living here and getting to see the city."

"Well, let's see," she said, "you're looking for an entry level job?"

"Anything, really. I just want to be inside a law firm, so I can learn something about the actual practice of law before I start classes."

"You say here you have good computer skills, and you worked on developing several web sites at college. We're in the middle of revising our web site, and we have a summer opening for another person on that project. That job would give you a pretty good idea what our firm is all about. How does it sound?"

"It sounds perfect," I said.

"It doesn't pay much, only $400 per week, no benefits."

Four hundred dollars a week was more than I had ever earned in my life. I gulped and said, "That would be fine."

"I just need to make sure the position is still open," she said, reaching for the phone. She left a message with someone.

"Where can I reach you?"

I gave her my cell number and email address.

"You have email here already?"

"There's an Internet Café in my hotel." Images of my new associates Darlene, Annabelle and Daryl flashed through my mind, but I chose not to share these with Ms. Coleman.

"Good," she said, rising. "I'll call you tomorrow. I think this'll work out nicely. We like to form relationships with law students early. It helps later when we're recruiting."

Ms. Coleman escorted me back to the elevator. I was jumping for joy at the prospect of useful employment and unexpected riches. Emerging at street level, I bounced into a sunny afternoon, and decided to walk to the hotel.

New York City on a beautiful May afternoon was breathtaking. My eyes were drawn to high rise buildings of glass and steel, and to older buildings with distinctive water towers on their roofs. Even the dirt was exciting.

When I reached 38th Street, I found my earlier concerns about the Broadway Big Apple had receded. The hotel still wasn't boutique, but it wasn't scary either. I nodded pleasantly to Daryl, who, surprisingly, smiled back. It was way too early for Darlene and Annabelle to have made their appearance.

I changed my clothes, walked over to the AMC, and ate two hot dogs while I watched a movie. Darlene was at the bar when I returned and she insisted on a full report of my day's activities. Actually, we had a fairly normal conversation, to the extent I could focus on anything but her magnificent breasts. She again asked if I had an interest, and I again declined, but, I have to admit, less strongly than the night before.

In the morning, I took the subway to Washington Square Park and the Law School's Office of Residential Life. A bulletin board was chock full of notices for summer sublets, including three that seemed to fit my needs. The first was a sun-filled apartment on LaGuardia Place near West 3rd Street, a third floor walkup with one bedroom, a small living room, and a view of a tiny corner of the park. I ran two blocks back to Residential Life, wrote a check for two months rent in advance, and made arrangements to move in the next day.

I walked back to the hotel, heading up Broadway as it passes diagonally through midtown Manhattan. My cell rang as I was looking sadly over the remnants of 9-11 memorials at Union Square. It was Ms. Coleman.

"You start Monday at 8:30 am."

In only two days, I had achieved my objectives. I had a more interesting summer job than I had dared to expect and a really nice furnished apartment for the summer. The sun was shining and life was great.

I packed my belongings, spent several hours wandering in the Times Square area, and returned to the hotel around seven o'clock.

Darlene was in the bar. She beckoned to me and I sat next to her. As before, she wanted to know everything about my day, and I found it perfectly normal and actually quite pleasant to have someone to tell.

"Don't you want to know about me?" she asked when I was done.

"Well, yes, I guess so," I stammered. "I am curious. You seem so intelligent and nice."

"So how did I get into this line of work?" she asked for me, and then answered her own question. "I started while I was still in high school, in West Orange, New Jersey. Mom lost her job, Dad was long gone, and I needed some extra money. It was easy. Lots of girls did it. Mostly businessmen, in their BMWs and Mercedes, cruising near the school on their way back to fancy homes in Livingston and Mendham. In the beginning we did it right there on Conforti Avenue, right in their cars, but that was way too risky, so we started making dates. They paid for motel rooms. Sometimes we even went to their homes, when the wife was away.

"I wanted to go to college, but we couldn't afford much, and I didn't get a scholarship, so I decided to keep on 'the life' until I had enough to pay tuition. I had a few different jobs, still hooking on the side, and then I moved to New York. I met Annabelle, and we decided to work together. It's much safer that way. We look out for each other. We started the web site the day after Christmas in 2001, and business has been great ever since."

I was flooded with questions but totally tongue-tied. No matter. Darlene just kept on going.

16   Lewis M. Weinstein

"Pimps and drugs. Two things to avoid. We do not do drugs. And we are not managed by any low-life pimp slimes. With the web site, we can be independent. We even have our own support group. It's called PONY, Prostitutes of New York. PONY provides legal and health referrals to sex workers, and advocates for the decriminalization of prostitution.

"You can avoid the pimps?" I asked. "They just let you say no?"

"Actually, the mayor's crackdown on crime has made the pimps less aggressive than they might have been before. I think they're afraid. So it's been good for us."

I didn't quite understand, and was going to ask more when Annabelle returned. A few minutes later, Darlene had to go and we said goodbye. It was absolutely surreal to be saying goodbye to these prostitutes who had become my first friends in New York, not counting Michael Kay on the side of the bus. But there I was, talking to Darlene and Annabelle like they were den mothers. The funny thing was they had become people to me, despite their appearance and profession.

"Now that you know our web address," Darlene said, "do promise to keep in touch." She leaned forward to give me a kiss, which, after a slight hesitation, involved her tongue.

On Thursday morning, I retrieved the rest of my luggage from Penn Station and spent the day setting up my apartment and exploring the neighborhood around Washington Square Park. I called my friend Tom Kaplan in Baltimore to tell him I was coming down, and could I stay with him and Barb for the weekend.

They were storing some of my clothes and other things in their house. Since I didn't start work until Monday, I would have time to retrieve more clothes and bring them back to the City. I took my first shower in my new apartment, put on my new white polo shirt, and went out to celebrate.

The best pizza in New York, a city justifiably proud of its outstanding pizza, can be had at John's Pizza on the Upper West Side. I had eaten there with my UMBC friends after a trip to New York to see a Yankee game in April, and I had a clear memory of the pizza, which was great, and the bartender, whose name was Bonnie.

I popped a tape in the VCR to catch the parts of the Yankee game I would miss while I was out, chose the cream colored Yankee cap I had bought outside the Stadium and set out from my summer apartment to the Mecca of New York City pizza.

Do you know how sometimes there's a little extra swagger in your walk, a little cool? Your heels click the sidewalk, even if you're wearing running shoes and can't hear the sound. That's how I felt when I emerged from the subway at Columbus Circle and stared at the huge silver globe next to one of Donald Trump's many towers. I had a New York City job, I was going to law school, and I was on my way to check out Bonnie the bartender.

Just past Sixty-second on Broadway is one of New York's movie houses that specializes in "art" films. I was attracted by a little courtyard behind the movie entrance. I had already learned to expect surprises in the big city, and here was another one. A pocket park, small waterfall, benches and chairs, old people sitting, kids running, two large borzois on leashes, and a lingerie shop displaying a poster of a spectacular woman wearing a thong.

Back to Broadway. Lincoln Center and the Metropolitan Opera were across the street to my left, and I thought how ridiculous one of those large opera singers would look in a thong. I think I laughed out loud.

John's Pizza is on 65th Street, but I remembered a Disney Store a block ahead, and decided to get a present for my God-daughter Katie, Barb and Tom's daughter. At the corner of Sixty-sixth and Columbus, I waited for a red light.

The light changed and I started across. An elderly woman also started forward from the opposite side of the street, but she slipped off the curb and fell forward. I rushed over.

"Are you hurt?" I asked, reaching down to steady her as she knelt in the street.

She seemed a little dazed, but answered, "I think I'm all right."

She was small and very thin, but stronger than she appeared. When I helped her up, she grabbed my shirt on both sides and pulled herself to her feet. I retrieved her pocketbook and gave it to her. She was flustered and a little embarrassed. Her knee was skinned and her hands were scraped, but otherwise she didn't seem too badly damaged. I smiled at her and she smiled back.

"You're a nice young man," she said. "Thank you."

The light changed again, and I watched her cross the street to make sure she was all right. There was a newsstand on the corner, and I bought some mints, preparation in case I got close enough to Bonnie.

The elderly guy in the newsstand had seen me help the old woman, and he said, with a big smile and a heavy Spanish accent, "That was nice. What you did." I thanked him, paid for the mints, and entered the Disney Store.

I found a great Eeyore doll for Tom and Barb's daughter Katie. The clerk said Eeyore was her favorite, I said mine too, and told her how pleased I thought my God-daughter would be. I paid with my Visa card and hustled back to John's.

Lewis M. Weinstein

Luck was with me. Bonnie was working, so I went to the bar, hoping for a conversation.

"What can I get you?" Bonnie asked.

"What's on tap?"

"Guinness, Bass, Bud Light ..."

"Bud."

She served the beer and went off. So much for my big conversation. I had done better with Darlene and Annabelle, but of course that was their doing, not mine. I sipped the Bud Light, and tried to think of something else to say. Bonnie came to my rescue, tossing a smile over her shoulder while serving a beer to another customer.

"Are you new here?" she said. "I don't think I've seen you before."

"I was here in April, after a Yankee game." Pause. Take the plunge. "I sure noticed you."

"You noticed, huh?" she said in her great New York accent, and my heart jumped. Was she flirting? Another dazzling smile. "Are you a big Yankee fan?" she asked, taking in my cap.

"I've always rooted for the Yankees. Even though I'm from Baltimore."

"Has that been a problem for you?"

"Sometimes."

"They play tonight."

"I know. I set my VCR. Don't want to miss anything."

"I'll put the game on in a few minutes. Would you like a table where you can watch?"

"That would be great."

"What's your name?"

"Josh."

"I'm Bonnie."

"I know," I said, and was rewarded with another spectacular smile. She went to the end of the bar and whispered something to the hostess, and I was soon seated, watching the Yankees on TV and Bonnie behind the bar.

The Yanks were playing the Tigers in Detroit. In the top of the first, Derek Jeter bounced one up the middle and Jason Giambi hit a line drive over the fence in right center field. Andy Pettitte retired the A's in order in the bottom of the first, finishing the inning by striking out Dmitri Young on a wicked slider.

My pizza arrived and no more runs scored while I ate. The pizza was as great as I remembered. After three innings, it was still Yankees two, Tigers nothing. I got one more great smile from Bonnie as I was leaving.

Before going to the subway, I walked a block the other way on Columbus to get a magazine for my trip to Baltimore.

"How much for *Sports Illustrated*?"

"$3.95."

When I paid for the magazine, the newsstand guy recognized me. "Hey, you're the guy who helped the old lady ... but it's still $3.95."

He laughed and gave me my change. He said something else, but his words were drowned out by the scream of sirens from an ambulance and two police cars flying around the corner.

I walked back to Columbus Circle, jumped on a waiting downtown subway, and twenty minutes later I was back in my apartment. I put on the TV, switched off the VCR, and watched the Yankees complete what became a relatively easy victory. I set the alarm for 6:00 am, and went to sleep.

It turned out to be the only night I ever slept in that apartment.

"Help me."

Kim Scott heard the weak voice as she neared Central Park West at 63rd Street, having completed a brisk six-mile run around the outer loop of the park. She stopped, but saw no one.

"Help," she heard again, and this time she realized the voice was coming from the bottom of an embankment to the left of the footpath. She leaned over and looked down.

"Oh my God," she said when she saw the old woman crumpled on the ground. She scrambled down and knelt next to the woman, recoiling at the blood streaming from her head.

"I'll get help," Kim said, but the woman's bony hand grabbed her arm in a fierce grip and held on tight.

"... nice young man ... helped me ... robbed me."

"Who?" Kim said. "Do you know who did this?"

"... white baseball cap," she said. She mumbled a few more words, and then her hand released its grip and slid away to the ground.

Kim climbed up the slope to call for help, but she knew it was too late.

TWO

I don't think I was ever more happy than the one morning I woke up in Greenwich Village. The sun was streaming in and a crisp breeze came through the open window. My life was fresh and full of promise. I dressed quickly and went out to explore my new neighborhood.

Washington Square Park early in the morning was a delight. Even at such an early hour, students and professors were rapidly crossing the park. There are about a dozen stone chess tables in a corner of the park. A few players were already out, and one of them tried to drag me into a game, but they play for money and I'm not very good, so I declined.

I found a small bodega, bought a bagel and a cup of coffee, and went back to the park to enjoy my breakfast outdoors. Then it was back to Penn Station. I purchased a roundtrip Amtrak ticket to Baltimore on a self-service ticket machine. At the top of the escalator heading down to the train, an elderly woman struggled with her large rolling bag. I carried it down for her, thinking me and old ladies were getting to be a habit.

New York to Baltimore takes about two and a half hours. I read my *Sports Illustrated* and then *Moneyball* by Michael Lewis, and the time passed quickly.

Every local channel made it the lead story on the Thursday night late news. Dozens of people walking along Central Park West and throughout the Lincoln Center neighborhood were stopped for on-the-street interviews. All expressed outrage and fear.

After years of well-publicized declining crime rates, this was the third murder in less than a month in areas that were the heart of the City's tourist trade.

On Friday morning, New York Daily News reporter Teri Scanlon watched Mayor Raymond Gardino as he waded into a hurriedly scheduled 8:00 am press conference at City Hall. He was flanked by Police Commissioner William Troncone and the commanding officer of the Central Park Precinct. For Scanlon, born in Florida and only recently relocated to New York after a decade working for several small papers in her home state, this was a big story, one of her first since being assigned the Manhattan crime beat.

"This murder is a terrible thing," the mayor said, "but we should remember ... crime is still way down, especially violent crime. The victim's name is Sarah Cooke. We believe her assailant

ran onto a subway at Columbus Circle and went to Brooklyn. An intensive manhunt is underway."

"So he got away?" came a brave voice from deep in the crowd of reporters.

The question was not put forward as a taunt. Nobody who valued their access to New York City's prime news source would dare taunt the often explosive mayor. But it lay there nevertheless, the challenge unmistakable.

Scanlon watched Mayor Gardino unsuccessfully try to smother his anger. He turned to the Police Commissioner, who pointed out someone standing in the crowd behind them.

"Detective Robert Watson from Central Park Precinct," said Mayor Gardino, "is in charge of the manhunt." Watson gave a brief outline of the steps underway to catch the murderer.

Storming back to his office a few minutes later, the mayor glared at the Commissioner and Captain who walked two strides behind him. "I want reports every three hours," he fumed. "We need an arrest. Soon."

Barb Kaplan and Katie were waiting for me at the venerable Charles Street train station in downtown Baltimore. Katie jumped up into my arms, and Barb gave me a hug and kiss.

"Tom's working," she said. "He's got to take every day he can."

I knew Tom and Barb were having a tough time. It had been difficult for them since Barb got pregnant during our freshman year at UMBC. First she, then Tom, had dropped out of college, and they had been struggling to make ends meet ever since.

I was the best man at their wedding, and it was a bittersweet night. Tom had been my best friend since grade school. We had played varsity baseball and basketball together since junior high school, and had both made the UMBC baseball team, but I knew he would not be playing any more. Tom was working construction, but he didn't work every day.

We walked to the parking area, and Barb handed me the keys to my old Toyota, which I had given to them to use while I was in New York. Barb had installed a car seat for Katie in the back, and as soon as she was settled, I pulled Eeyore from my duffel and gave it to her. She squealed with delight.

It had only been a week, but already it felt strange to drive. We soon arrived at the small house Tom and Barb had rented when they began living together. Katie, unleashed from her car seat, scrambled up the steps and waited for Barb to open the door. Their house was tiny but neat, or as least as neat as any home with a three year old could be.

Lewis M. Weinstein

Tony Marone watched the re-run of mayor's press conference on the afternoon news. Shit, he exclaimed quietly to himself, I didn't mean to kill her. And they know I came to Brooklyn. A sharp pain probed his gut. I can't let Mom see the blood on my jeans.

I went to Tom and Barb's small basement, where I had left a small bureau and a couple of suitcases. Seeing my possessions, even in someone else's home, brought back memories. My thoughts kept straying to summers past. I found my favorite picture of my parents. It was the Fourth of July, I was six years old, and Dad let me use his camera. It was the first photo I ever took, and it was one of the few treasures I packed to take to New York.

I finished packing, and went upstairs. Katie was down for her nap. Barb opened two beers and we sat at the small kitchen table and talked while I went through my mail, all junk, which had been forwarded to Madeira Street for the past week.

"Do you like New York? I mean, so far?" she asked.

"I love it. It's big, and so exciting."

"I think New York would scare me."

"Maybe at first," I agreed. "When I arrived, I couldn't find my hotel and it was a little scary. But then I made friends with two hookers in the hotel."

"You did what?" Barb screamed, laughing out loud. "Wait 'til Tom hears!"

"Did I hear my name?" came Tom's voice from the front of the house. He burst into the room, gave Barb a big kiss and then hugged me. Three more Buds were popped.

"Josh met hookers in New York, and now they're his friends," Barb said between loud laughs.

Tom smirked.

"It's true," I said. "And they have their own web site. Wait 'til you get a look at them."

There was a pause, as each of us considered the implications of this New York experience, big smiles on all three faces hiding private thoughts.

"What else have you been up to?" Tom asked.

"I got a job and an apartment."

"Big week," Barb said.

"I start Monday at a firm called Morgan, Heffer & Stone. I'm going to help them revise their web site."

"No doubt you'll get some ideas from your new friends' site," Barb managed to spit out between laughs.

"Maybe," I answered. "We can check them out later, after dinner. Can I take you out? Katie too, of course."

Sounds from Katie on the second floor sent Barb scurrying. Tom and I talked sports while she was gone. When Barb and Katie returned, I offered to take Katie for a walk while they got ready for an early dinner.

Detective Robert Watson sat at his cramped desk in the squad room of the Central Park Precinct and reviewed what NYPD had done in the last twenty four hours to find the killer of Mrs. Sarah Cooke.

An eyewitness had seen a man run from Central Park at about 8:00 pm, carrying a ladies' pocketbook. The man was thought to have entered the subway station at Columbus Circle, and the NYPD alerted all station attendants throughout the five boroughs.

Subway attendant Concolita Jones, in a commendable performance that would later win her an "employee of the month" award from the MTA, observed a man come off the train at the Fort Hamilton Parkway subway station in Brooklyn and throw what looked like a pocketbook into a trash container. She guarded the scene until a detective arrived.

Mrs. Cooke's pocketbook and Concolita Jones arrived at the Central Park Precinct in the same patrol car just before ten o'clock on Thursday night. A police artist guided Concolita as she made choices from a lengthy book of facial types and a composite emerged.

Brooklyn detectives and uniformed patrol officers fanned out, asked questions, and came up with nothing. They were at it again the next morning, but the day passed with no results.

Other detectives reviewed tapes from video cameras located outside the Mayflower Hotel and Trump International Pavilion. These tapes showed a man carrying a pocketbook running along Central Park West in the direction of the Columbus Circle subway station at 59th Street, but did not disclose any facial details.

A computer dump of all Metro cards used at the station within the twenty minute period from 7:50 pm to 8:10 pm produced a listing of one hundred thirty seven Metro cards, forty six of which had an accompanying credit card number. Detectives began the tedious process of identifying and contacting the known Metro card holders.

Central Park is different from all other NYPD precincts. There are no permanent residents and a large proportion of the people in or near the park at any given moment are tourists, who will not return. The Manhattan detectives, although anxiously aware that rapid preliminary statements were critical, knew their best chance wouldn't come until Friday evening, when the store clerks and people on the street more closely matched those who might have seen the perpetrator the night before. A large team of officers was assembled from neighboring precincts to perform a massive canvass.

With copies of the sketch based on Concolita Jones' description, the NYPD proceeded methodically, stopping people on the street and canvassing every store and restaurant within ten blocks of the crime scene.

When officers came to John's Pizza, Bonnie had not yet arrived and the hostess on duty had not worked the night before.

At 6:33 pm, Officer Peter Mackeneny entered the Disney Store on Columbus Avenue.

"This guy looks familiar," the clerk said, staring intently at the sketch. Several seconds later she said, "Got it. There was a guy here, maybe six feet tall, white polo, light-colored Yankee's cap. Cute guy. About 6:30 last night. He bought an Eeyore doll for his God-daughter."

"How did he pay?"

"Visa."

Tom Kaplan and some mutual friends were going to the Orioles game on Saturday night, and he tried to convince me to stay, but I decided to go back to New York. As close as I felt to Tom and Barb, our lives were heading in such opposite directions. Life in New York and law courses at NYU were so far from Tom and Barb's reach it seemed inconsiderate, even cruel, to talk about it, like I was showing off. Maybe I was rationalizing because I was so eager to begin my new life.

Barb made a great breakfast, and they took me to the station. We stopped along the way to see Mrs. O'Neil, a great friend of my mother before Mom died. I was back in Greenwich Village before noon.

THREE

Detective Robert Watson answered the phone in the cramped Central Park Precinct squad room he shared with three other detectives. As the "catching" detective, the one who had taken the call on Thursday night, Watson coordinated everyone working the case. The Crime Scene Unit, Medical Examiner, Forensics, other detectives, all would report to him and when they made an arrest, he would be the one to interact with the Manhattan District Attorney's Office.

It was late Saturday morning, and Watson was not happy. City Hall and One Police Plaza wanted results and, so far, he had little to give them. On the phone was Detective Frank Grabowsky from the Latent Prints Unit located downtown at One Police Plaza.

"Seventeen latents of interest from the pocketbook," Grabowsky said. "Eight belong to the deceased. The rest are from two different individuals. They're on the network now."

In another hour, Grabowsky called again. "Bob, we have a hit. Four of the latents belong to a 22 year old Caucasian male named Joshua Blake."

"Bingo," said Watson. "Same name as the Visa receipt from the guy at the Disney Store. Address in Baltimore."

Grabowsky continued, "Blake was printed three years ago, part of a group of college kids who busted up a bar. The charges were eventually dropped, but the prints stayed on file. No New York address. The Baltimore address is a college dorm."

"We have a billing address from the Visa receipt," Watson said. "BPD is already looking for him. The other prints?"

"No match."

"Have you completed elimination prints on family and friends?"

"We're working on it."

An hour later, Detective Joseph Graziano arrived with an update. "The Visa address is a friend of Blake's in Baltimore where his mail is being forwarded. Baltimore cops were there a few minutes ago. Blake was there last night, but he left earlier this morning to come back to New York. The friend gave an address in the Village."

"Go talk to him," ordered Watson. "Tell him we need his help on the case."

Watson leaned backed in his chair, pleased they were closing in on a suspect. Even so, something bothered him. Why would a kid from Baltimore commit a robbery in Central Park, ditch the stolen pocketbook in Brooklyn, go to Baltimore, and then come right back to the city the next day? Something didn't add up.

Nevertheless, he reported the latest developments to his Precinct Commander, initiating a flurry of telephone exchanges that within minutes reached the anxious ears of the Police Commissioner and the Mayor.

I unpacked the hanging clothes, put the photo of my parents in a place of honor on the night table, and was out of the apartment almost as soon as I got there. My first stop was the NYU book store on LaGuardia Place, just down the street, where I spent a pleasant hour looking at law books.

Wandering west, across Sixth Avenue, I became totally lost in the delightful winding streets of the West Village - Bleecker, Cornelia, Barrow, Bedford. I passed another John's Pizza, watched old men relax in a small park, teenage kids compete ferociously on a fenced-in basketball court, and skaters play street hockey. At Engine Company 24 there was a memorial to 11 men who had died at the World Trade Center.

"No farewell words were spoken, no time to say goodbye, you were gone before we knew it, and only God knows why." I thought about my dad going to work and never coming back.

Brick and brownstone buildings, tree lined streets with dappled sunshine, fire escapes, bicycles chained to posts, outdoor fruit and vegetable stands, motorcycles roaring three abreast, dogs of every size and description. A haunting photo of a young Sophia Lauren in a lace dress, deep within a dark and almost empty bar, one man sipping a beer, his back to beauty.

My last memories of freedom.

The light was blinking on the answering machine.

"Hi, Josh, this is Tom." His voice sounded troubled. "I hope this is your phone. It's not your message. Anyway, the police just came here looking for you. They wouldn't say what it was about. I gave them ..."

A loud banging on the door distracted me from Tom's message, and to this day, I've never heard the end of it. I cracked the door and peeked out.

"Joshua Blake?" a man asked.

I nodded. He showed me a badge.

"NYPD. We want to ask you some questions. Can we come in?"

I looked at the badge and it seemed legitimate, so I said, "Sure."

Two men, neither in uniform, filled the living room, which suddenly seemed tiny. Their identification said they were from the Central Park Precinct – Detectives Joseph Graziano and John Mackey. Of course I was nervous, but I knew I hadn't done anything wrong. Whoever was in trouble, it couldn't be me.

"Can we ask you some questions?"

"Sure," I said. "What's it about?"

I invited them to sit. Graziano sat on the sofa with me, but Mackey remained standing by the window.

"Were you near Columbus Circle on Thursday night?" Graziano asked. He took out a spiral notepad and began writing.

"Yes, I was. I went to John's Pizza for dinner."

"What time did you get there?"

"Maybe a little before seven. Why? What's this about?"

Mackey answered, "There was a woman killed near Columbus Circle on Thursday night and we're asking anyone who was in the neighborhood to help us."

"How do you know I was in the neighborhood?"

"We went to all the stores," said Graziano. "You made a purchase at the Disney Store. We traced the Visa."

"To Baltimore? Is that why my friend Tom left a message the police were looking for me?"

"Exactly."

The detectives exchanged glances and Graziano stood. "Can I use your bathroom?"

"Sure."

"Do you know this woman?" Mackey asked, coming over to the sofa and handing me a photo.

"Don't think so. Is this the one who was killed?"

"Yes."

Detective Graziano appeared with my polo shirt hooked onto the end of his pen.

"When did you wear this shirt?" he asked.

"It would have been Thursday night, I guess."

"Mind if I take it?"

At that precise moment, Detective Mackey stood between us and said, "You know what, we should go to the precinct and have you look at photos, see if you can spot anything we may have missed. Even some little detail may be useful. It would be good if you come with us. The detective in charge of the case will ask you some questions, and we'll bring you back when he's done. Okay?"

"Okay," I said, answering Detective Mackey.

Lewis M. Weinstein

Many months later, Detective Graziano would testify that when he asked for the shirt, I said "okay" to him.

We left, Mackey in front, Graziano behind, single file down the stairs. An unmarked car was parked at the curb. Mackey directed me into the back seat and closed the door. Have you ever been in the back seat of a police car with no handles and a metal gate separating your claustrophobic space from the front of the car? I felt like an animal in a cage. If we have an accident, I thought, I'll be stuck in here and I'll burn up.

We drove quietly, without sirens or flashing lights. The detectives were silent in the front seat. If I had any idea what was going to happen in the next several hours, I would have been terrified. Instead, in my still blissful ignorance, I was entranced with the beauty and boldness of New York at night. I gawked at the street life of Greenwich Village, and the large spot-lit office buildings along Sixth Avenue. I remember fountains sparkling in the light, beautiful round balls of water. We drove past the building where Morgan, Heffer & Stone has its offices, and I anticipated how exciting it would be when I started my new job on Monday morning.

We drove north around Columbus Circle onto Central Park West, and somewhere in the eighties, made a right turn into the darkness. In the middle of the park, we pulled into a small, dimly lit parking lot.

Central Park Precinct is over 100 years old and looks it. It may once have had character and even a touch of elegance, although it started life as a stable, but by the time I saw it, it was just cramped and run down.

"We can wait in the squad room. Detective Watson will be here soon," said one of the detectives. I was directed into a small room with four desks and four chairs filling almost every square inch. Without windows or air conditioning, it was stifling. Graziano left, but Mackey stayed, joined by a uniformed officer who did not introduce himself. We watched each other sweat. The guy in uniform had "CPP" pins on the collars of his shirt. One of the pins was upside down.

Graziano returned with a fit-looking man about my height, dressed casually in tan slacks and a dark green Ralph Lauren polo, just like the one in my unpacked suitcase. Mackey and the uniformed officer left. Graziano leaned against one of the desks and opened a notebook. The new man sat down opposite me.

"I'm Detective Robert Martin Watson," he said. "I want to ask you some questions." He paused, I nodded. "A woman was killed in Central Park on Thursday night. We're hoping you can help us with our investigation. Just get to the City?"

A Good Conviction   29

"Monday."

"Why?"

"I'm going to NYU Law School in September. I came here for the summer to learn about the City, work for a law firm."

"Which firm?"

"Morgan, Heffer & Stone. I just got a job."

Other questions followed. Where are you from? Where did you go to college? What did you study?

"Why do you need to know all this?" I finally asked. "What does this have to do with your investigation?"

He waited, and when the silence got oppressive, I answered. He saw the look of frustration on my face and there was just the hint of a smile at the corners of his mouth. I hated him.

"History. U.S. history."

"Family?"

"My parents are dead. No brothers or sisters."

"After you got to New York on Monday, what did you do?"

"I got a room at the Broadway Big Apple Hotel. On Tuesday, I met with law firms looking for a job. On Wednesday, I found a furnished apartment. On Thursday, I moved. On Friday, I went to Baltimore to see my friends and get some more clothes. I came back this morning. I walked around Greenwich Village, and went back to my apartment. Then you guys brought me here."

"What about Thursday night?"

"I went out to eat, at John's Pizza."

"Which one?"

"On 65th Street. I didn't know there was more than one until this afternoon."

"There's actually four. 65th Street is quite a distance from Greenwich Village. Why so far?"

"I had been there before, and the pizza's good." I didn't mention Bonnie.

"Do you recognize this woman?" Watson showed me the same photograph Detective Mackey had shown me in my apartment.

"Don't know her."

"Never saw her?"

"No."

"You're sure?"

"I never saw that woman."

I was confused by the line of questioning. They had brought me to the station, so they said, to ask about other people I might have seen, but instead they were asking about me. Of course in hindsight

I should have asked for a lawyer right then, but I hadn't done anything wrong, so I didn't. Big mistake. I learned later this is a mistake the police expect and count on.

Detective Mackey came in and whispered in Watson's ear. "Something just came up," Watson said, standing. "I'll be back in a minute."

Watson's minute became thirty minutes. When he returned, he asked more questions about Thursday night. Same questions. Same answers. Now it passed from confusing to irritating. We went over the same stuff two or three times more. Finally, Mackey came back, handed Watson a single sheet of paper.

"What's your blood type?" Watson asked.

"Uh ... B positive. Why?"

Watson paused for a long time and then he spoke slowly and distinctly. "Son, I've got bad news for you. You're under arrest for the murder of Sarah Cooke Thursday night in Central Park." He took a card from his pocket and read to me, "You have the right to remain silent. Anything you say can and will be used against you. You have the right to be represented by an attorney. If you cannot afford an attorney, the State of New York will provide an attorney for you. Do you want an attorney?"

If you've never been arrested, you can't begin to understand the fear that pulses through you when a cop says those words to you. Believe me, a Miranda warning read to you personally is not the same as hearing it on TV. My throat was so dry and constricted I could hardly breathe. I kept looking around for someone to help me, but there was no one there. I was flat out terrified. How does this happen in America?

"Yes, I want an attorney," I finally managed to say.

"Do you have an attorney you'd like to call?"

"No."

"Can you afford an attorney?"

"I don't know. I have some money set aside for law school. How much does it cost?"

I had visions of all the money I had saved for law school disappearing. All my plans destroyed. Destitute in New York City. Just this morning, I had been feeling my new life was so different from Tom's. Soon I would be as broke as he was. But I hadn't done anything wrong. Innocent people don't get charged with murder. How much I had to learn.

"Can you call someone at the firm you're working for?"

"I didn't even start work. I don't know any lawyers there, and besides, there's no one there now. What time is it?"

"It's 11:30. You can call someone at your firm in the morning. If you can't make arrangements before your arraignment, the judge will decide if you're eligible for a public defender."

"In the morning? Sunday morning?" I repeated. My situation was beginning to sink in. "I can't go home now?"

"No, you can't go home. Until further notice, you're a guest of the City."

"I need to go to work on Monday. It's my first day on my new job."

"Bummer," said Watson. "You can make a phone call now if you'd like, let someone know you're here."

The uniformed officer returned. "Stand up. Remove your belt and your shoelaces. Empty your pockets."

I came close to shitting my pants. This was incredible. My hands were shaking. I did as he said.

"I'll search you again now. Stand against the wall and spread your legs."

I felt, and was, totally powerless. The police make it very clear you have no options. You cannot object. You have no views anyone cares about. Your only choice is to obey.

"Hands out," Uniform ordered. When I complied, I was in handcuffs.

I remained standing, afraid to move, unable to think. Gradually, some small portion of my mind began to function.

"How do I make a long distance call?" I asked.

"You got a credit card?" said Uniform.

"It's in my wallet."

Uniform took the wallet from the table, removed the Visa card, and held it out to me. I raised my cuffed hands and took it. He led me from the squad room to a pay phone on the wall just inside the front door. I stood there, my mind a complete blank. Finally, I remembered Tom's number. Uniform stood nearby, watching.

"Hello," Tom answered in a groggy voice.

"Tom, thank God you're home" I gulped several times, trying to control my breathing enough to speak. My hand was shaking and the phone was banging into the wall. I was in a cold sweat. I don't know what I was trying to say, but I'm sure it made no sense.

"Try to calm down and tell me what's going on," Tom said.

I clenched my fists and took several deep breaths. "I'm charged with murder," I said. "I don't know what to do."

"What murder? You didn't murder anyone."

"Of course I didn't. But the police think I did and I'm under arrest. I can't leave. I'm going to spend the night in jail."

"Do you have a lawyer?"

"No. Who can I call? I don't know any lawyers in New York. I'm going to try to call my new firm in the morning. But I haven't even gone to work yet, and it'll be Sunday morning."

"Josh, where can I call to check on you?"

"I'm at the Central Park Precinct. Wait." I asked Uniform where I was going to be and could someone call me there.

"Have him call here. We'll let him know where you are."

He pointed to a number on the wall by the phone. I relayed this information to Tom, and we said goodbye. I felt as if my only lifeline, frail as it was, had just fallen away.

Uniform took me down the hall to a small cell. He removed the handcuffs and pushed me in. The metallic clang of a cell door closing terrifies me to this day, although by now I've heard it thousands of times. Nevertheless, whenever that awful sound assaults my ears, and despite the obvious differences, I also hear the soft final thump of the coffin lid sealing my mother to her eternal fate.

FOUR

Sing Sing Correctional Facility
Thursday, January 22, 2004

"Before I fell asleep last night, I saw the face again, the one in the murky water. I know who it is."

Spider laughs derisively from below, and growls, "It's only been a month, and you're startin' to lose it. Get a grip, man."

"I saw the face," I insist. "It was a police officer, but not in uniform."

"A detective?"

"I guess. He's looking at me, and there's a funny expression in his eyes."

"Why are you buggin' me with this shit?" Spider asks.

"Because I'm innocent," I say, unable to suppress a smile.

He says, as he has many times before, "There's not a guilty mother-fucker in this whole fuckin' place."

"He knew something," I insist.

"Sure, the detective knew something," Spider repeats mockingly.

"Something that would prove me innocent."

"Right."

"Well, humor me," I plead. "Suppose I really am innocent, and this detective is the only one who can prove it. How can I find him?"

"Find him?" Spider roars. I'm really entertaining him now. "Why should he give a fuck about you? He's on their side."

"Okay, you're right, but suppose I want to find him anyway. What do I do?"

"You are one dumb fuck," he says, and I silently acknowledge the truth of his conclusion. A Corrections Officer comes by on his pre-breakfast round and unlocks the deadlock on our cell. The brake, which controls all the cells on our gallery, is still on, awaiting the breakfast call.

"Write to your lawyer," Spider says when the CO has gone. "He'll know who worked on the case. While you're at it, ask him to send you a copy of the transcript."

"I don't remember my lawyer's address."

"You are fuckin' hopeless, man. Absolutely fuckin' hopeless." He stands next to his bunk and his bulk fills all the empty space in the cell. He looks at me with a bemused smile and shakes his huge shiny head. "Go read your prison file. It's all there."

I sat alone in the cell at Central Park Precinct for what seemed like four or five hours. Detective Watson appeared, freshly showered and shaved, wearing a coat and tie. He cuffed my hands behind my back, hustled me out of the station through the ladies locker room, and deposited me into the back of an unmarked car. Watson settled into the passenger seat and Detective Graziano drove. We were not noticed by any of the reporters standing near the front door of the station house.

Broadway, as dawn broke on Sunday morning, was virtually empty. We drove through Times Square, midtown, and into the maze of lower Manhattan - Chinatown, Canal Street, Little Italy. Graziano parked on an undistinguished side street amidst a group of police cars and vans. Sliding boards and jungle gyms in a small park across the street provided a single touch of color in an otherwise depressing gray landscape.

It's hard to get out of a car with your hands cuffed behind you and I felt a wrenching twist in my shoulders. There were several other cops and prisoners milling about. One of the cops banged on a large gate and it rolled up, revealing a passageway big enough for a van. We walked through, each group of cops and prisoners spaced far enough apart to avoid interaction. The cops paused to check their weapons and ammunition at a small booth just inside the gate.

We were at Manhattan Central Booking, also known as the Tombs, for the legendary jail which is part of the same complex. The building is actually 100 Centre Street. I learned later it contains police facilities, cells, courtrooms, and the offices of the Manhattan District Attorney. Watson leading, Graziano close behind, we went down a short set of stairs into a bleak institutional hallway. Other prisoners were lined up along the wall, handcuffed together. We went to the head of the line.

"Wait your turn, mother-fucker. Who the fuck you think you are?"

The hallway smelled from puke and sweat. Part of the smell was me, dirty and unshaven, with no change of clothes since I had dressed in Baltimore twenty four hours before. Watson showed some paperwork to the officer at the desk. "Fax back from Albany?" he asked.

"Yeah, but we need an 18b."

"DA affidavit?"

"ADA wants to talk with you first. Go upstairs when you get a chance."

"Which one?"

"Claiborne."

"He's here now?"

"Apparently."

Watson led me to another room, where I was fingerprinted. A ten print, they called it. Then we went somewhere else. I was totally lost.

Another officer gave orders. "Shoes off. Stand facing the wall. Hands on the wall. Date of birth?"

"March 30, 1982."

Another pat down, someone else's hands violating my body.

"Pass through the metal detector."

I went through without incident while my shoes were x-rayed.

"Put your shoes on."

More stairs. Up, down, no sense of place or direction. With my hands again cuffed behind my back, I stumbled. Watson reacted quickly and stopped my fall.

"Thanks."

"Be careful."

There were signs on the wall, in Spanish, empty corridors and other prisoners waiting. Watson led me to the head of every line. Papers changed hands.

"Date of birth?"

"March 30, 1982."

"Stand behind the table. Look at the camera." The cuffs were removed for the photo session. "Got to take a good one for the papers," said the cop working the camera. "They're out there clamoring already. Don't look at me. Look at the camera up there. Turn your head to the side. The other side."

I posed. This whole thing was incomprehensible. What was I doing in a police station at six o'clock in the morning, having my picture taken? Things like this weren't supposed to happen to people like me. "Move in front of the table." Full length shot, I guessed.

Papers appeared from the printer. "Not bad," Watson said, adding to his growing package. My mug shot and 10-print would soon be accessible to every police department in America. Another hallway, more cells, gates opened, gates closed. Signs on the wall proclaiming Halal food available and Stop TB. A room marked EMT.

"Date of birth?"

"March 30, 1982."

"Do you have any medical problems? Do you need to see a doctor?"

"No."

In a brightly lit cell crammed full of prisoners, I was the only white person, and very likely the only person who was there for the first time. Sullen looks were cast my way and I tried to avoid eye contact. These were not people I ever wanted to know and I was sure some of them would not hesitate to kill me. A few were stretched out on metal benches, snoring. One guy, wearing glasses and a tie, was huddled in a corner, his terrified eyes darting without focus. The noise was overwhelming and I couldn't think straight in the din. Thank God no one talked to me. There were no cops in sight. If someone picked a fight, it could get very ugly before help arrived.

One voice was louder than the rest, talking fast, talking rap. Everyone listened and laughed. The guy was a standup comic with a literally captive audience. I didn't understand a word he said. Terrified every second, my mind dysfunctional, I lost track of time. Somewhere along the way, the police had taken my watch. For safe keeping, they said. Five names were called. Cuffed behind the back, attached to a long chain, they were marched off together. Where? Why? No explanations offered. I waited, trying to be invisible.

My name was called. I answered, "Here," and felt stupid, like I was in elementary school. I maneuvered myself past other prisoners, trying not to touch anyone, head down.

"The rest of you, back away." The gate opened. "Blake, out."

Handcuffs, again behind the back. Into a small room, a woman in civilian clothes behind a desk.

"Sit down. This is going to be what we call an 18b interview, to determine if you need legal aide or not. I need to ask you some questions before you go up for arraignment." She stopped, as if needing my permission to continue. I stood silent, frozen, uncomprehending. "Sit down," she repeated. She was irritated. I sat.

"Name?"

"Joshua Blake."

"Date of birth?"

"March 30, 1982."

She asked about my family and current address. "How long have you lived at that address?"

"Three days."

"Will anyone be with you at the arraignment?"

"No one knows where I am."

"So that's a no. Are you employed?"

"I'm supposed to start tomorrow."

"What is your take home pay?"

"I don't know." She looked at me funny. Maybe she thought I was trying to be a wise guy, although Lord knows it wasn't the case.

"Any other source of financial support?"

"I have savings set aside for law school."

"Are you in law school?"

"I start in September."

"Are you currently in any treatment programs?"

"No."

"Arrested before?"

"Once."

"When?"

"A couple of years ago. There was a fight in a bar near my college. Charges were dropped."

Interview completed, more hallways, up and down more stairs, absolutely no idea where I was, where I was going, or why. No explanations. Cuffs removed, pushed into a small dark cell. Six or seven other sets of eyes, barely visible, peering at me as I entered their cramped space. Incredibly, in such a tiny space, someone was peeing, loudly, three feet away, into a metal urinal. The room reeked with the strong smell of urine.

One corner of the small cell had an even smaller space walled off. A prisoner was crammed in there, talking with someone outside the cell. His lawyer? I didn't have a lawyer. Nobody who cared about me had any idea where I was. I thought about our *bon voyage* party, a week ago, with Tom and Barb, and many of my college and high school friends. Another universe, one where what I said and thought actually mattered. I stifled a moan, and sat silently. No conversation here, no rap, everyone apprehensive. Time passed slowly. What happens next?

"Rodriquez, Hampton, Blake, Perez."

The gate opened. I was cuffed, but the others were not, and I wondered why, but I was too afraid to ask. A short walk, through a small doorway, and we emerged into a large, well lit, scruffy looking courtroom. "Over there," someone said, pointing to two adjoining benches. I sat down, hard, on a bolt which was protruding from the bench. I guess it was to attach handcuffs, but mine were not attached. The room had a high ceiling, with tall windows on each side, the judge on a raised platform, defendants and lawyers below, facing the judge.

This was my first appearance in a New York City court. I had often imagined myself in just such a setting, as a lawyer arguing a case. Probably not wearing handcuffs.

Roger Claiborne had been an Assistant District Attorney in the Manhattan Office of the New York County Prosecutor for sixteen years. Detective Watson had worked with Claiborne on several unremarkable cases, all of which had the usual result, straightforward, plea-bargained convictions. Watson was a little surprised Claiborne was going to handle a Sunday morning arraignment, which usually went to a far more junior ADA.

Claiborne sat in his small office on the sixth floor of 80 Centre Street, behind a plain, government-order, gray-green metal desk. He was surprisingly well dressed, wearing a summer weight tan suit, light blue shirt with pointed collars, and a brown and yellow striped tie. Must be a press conference planned, Watson thought. He looks nervous.

"Tell me what you've got, Bob. Give me the whole picture."

"At 8:00 pm on Thursday night, a runner named Kim Scott was exiting Central Park near 63rd Street. She heard someone calling for help and located the victim, an elderly woman later identified as Sarah Cooke, lying in a little gully next to the walking path. The victim was still conscious, but she died soon thereafter, apparently from wounds acquired when her head hit a rock.

"A few minutes earlier, a man named Adam Gordon had seen a young Caucasian man running from the park at 63rd Street. About six feet tall, athletic, white polo shirt, jeans, light-colored Yankees cap. The man ran toward Columbus Circle. We have him on video from the hotel and station cameras, but the cap hid his face.

"The runner, Kim Scott, got someone to call 9-1-1 on their cell phone. At 8:18, we notified all subway attendants in all five boroughs. At 8:34, a toll taker named Concolita Jones at the Fort Hamilton Parkway Station in Brooklyn saw a man wearing a light-colored Yankees cap and a white polo come off a Manhattan train, throw a ladies pocketbook into a trash barrel, and run from the station. No video there.

"The pocketbook contained identification of the victim and an ATM receipt, stamped at 6:15 pm. No money. By Friday noon, we had three latents of interest on the bag, one of which matched the victim. A police artist worked with the toll taker to develop a sketch, which we circulated. On Friday night, we got an ID at the Disney Store at Sixty-sixth and Columbus. The clerk provided a Visa charge slip with the name Joshua Blake, address in Baltimore. Saturday morning, we got a match on one set of latents. Same name."

"He has a record?" Claiborne asked.

"Arrested once in college. A fight in a bar. Nothing much to it. The charges were dropped."

"The unidentified latents?" Claiborne asked.

"Looks like just one more individual, but no match so far."

"How did you find Blake?"

"On Saturday, Baltimore police went to the Visa mailing address, which turned out to be a friend who said Blake had come to Baltimore on Friday and returned to New York Saturday morning. Gave us an address in the Village. When Blake showed up, we asked him to come to CPP to help in an investigation. We also retrieved a white polo shirt from his apartment, which Blake said he had worn on Thursday night. The shirt had blood on it which matched the blood type of the victim but not Blake's. We're doing the DNA, but it'll take a while."

"Legal search?" Claiborne asked.

"Detective Graziano says Blake gave permission. I think it'll pass."

"Great work, Bob," Claiborne said, standing. "We're good to go here. DCPI will notify the press and we'll talk with them after the arraignment." Claiborne was referring to the NYPD Deputy Commissioner for Public Information. "The mayor will be here. You should be available. And keep working. Get anything more we need to make sure we nail this guy. This is not a case we can afford to blow."

I stared blankly at the buzz of activity in the courtroom on what had to be the worst Sunday morning of my life. I made no sense of what was happening. Lawyers, judges, and police officers moved across my vision in a random parade. At one level, the important one, my mind was in such a panic it virtually ceased functioning. Yet, at the same time, I was acutely aware of insignificant little details.

Prisoners came and went as a young police officer called one case after another. Attorneys rose, spoke briefly, sat down, including one sharp-dressing Johnny Cochrane wannabe. Many of the prisoners were represented by a kindly looking man in his early fifties, no jacket, yellow button-down shirt with sleeves rolled up, khaki pants. When he came to the prisoner bench and politely introduced himself to the man sitting next to me, I learned he was a Legal Aide attorney.

Some prisoners pleaded guilty, accepting the sentence the judge had offered. Others pleaded not guilty and bail was set. A young female defense attorney with long brown unruly hair, wearing a black pants suit, successfully negotiated a lesser sentence, to which her client pleaded guilty. Another female attorney, a tall black woman, young and attractive, also wearing a black pants suit, stood behind a table to the left of the defendant table and spoke softly from time to time. She was apparently the prosecutor for all of the cases that morning, but I could never hear a word she said.

Each case took no more than two or three minutes, after which the prisoner was taken back to the holding cell area behind the courtroom. Every prisoner except me was black or Hispanic, young, tough-looking, and sullen. Almost all of them held baseball caps behind their backs when they stood before the judge, which reminded me that sometime during the night, the police had taken my Yankees cap. The public seating area in the large courtroom remained virtually empty.

A policewoman, her navy blue uniform shirt unbuttoned almost to the waist to reveal substantial breasts barely contained by a tight white t-shirt, walked with attitude from the public area past the defendant table and out the door to the holding area, enjoying the effect she produced on other officers, attorneys, prisoners and even the judge. A heavyset woman arrived, carrying a spray bottle, paper towels and a roll of toilet paper. She carefully cleaned a keyboard, table and chair, then sat down and sorted through what looked like old newspapers, placing some in plastic bags.

"Joshua Blake." I looked up and a police officer was motioning me to come forward. I walked to the table where the other prisoners had stood. There were two signs taped to the table. I stood where it said "Defendant stand here." The space behind the sign "Defense Attorney stand here" was empty.

"Do you have an attorney, Mr. Blake?" the judge asked.

"No sir," I answered. The judge looked at several attorneys standing nearby, all of whom quickly looked away.

"Mr. Mullin," said the judge, "if you're through talking with Ms. Reilly, would you please assist the court and represent Mr. Blake?"

This was apparently a request Mr. Mullin could not refuse. Ms. Reilly gave him a crooked smile, apparently happy the judge had not chosen her, and Mullin left the group of attorneys to stand next to me.

"Mr. Blake," the judge said, "I'm going to assign Mr. Mullin to be your attorney, for now. Your 18b interview suggests you're probably capable of paying a private attorney such as Mr. Mullin. You may choose to retain his services, or you may choose another attorney." Looking to Mullin, the judge continued, "Mr. Mullin, will you please talk with your client and let me know when you're ready to proceed."

"Yes, thank you, your honor," Mullin replied, taking a sheaf of papers from the officer. He motioned me back to the prisoner bench. A few minutes later, he came over.

"Joshua Blake?"

"Yes."

"I'm Larry Mullin." The short, stocky, prematurely balding, somewhat disheveled man in a dull brown rumpled suit and a Pink Panther tie did not give me confidence.

"I'm your attorney, for now" Mullin said. "Judge Cartegna assigned me."

"I heard. Can you tell me what's going on here?"

"Let's go into the consultation room. You go in this side," he said, pointing, "and I'll go in the other side."

I had seen other prisoners and their attorneys use the small cubicles next to the prisoner benches, and took my place as directed. When Mullin tried to squeeze through to sit opposite me, he crashed loudly into the narrow door and everyone turned to look. There was a glass panel between us, with an opening at the bottom through which we could talk.

"Here's what I know," Mullin said. "A woman named Sarah Cooke was killed Thursday night in Central Park. Apparently in connection with a robbery. It's been all over TV and the papers. You didn't hear about it?"

"No. I went to Baltimore first thing Friday morning."

"Well, the police think you did it. You're about to be formally charged. This is an arraignment hearing."

"Why ...?"

"I don't know yet. An assistant DA will present the charge. You'll get a chance to plead. Not guilty, I presume?"

"How can they charge me? I didn't kill anyone. My God, why is this happening?"

"I don't know what evidence they have. Later today, if you retain me, I'll get the police reports."

"They don't have to tell me anything? They can just arrest me and they don't have to tell me anything?"

"Eventually they have to tell us everything they know."

"When? Meanwhile I'm in jail!" My voice had risen, and Mullin cautioned me. I looked around, breathing heavily, struggling to maintain a coherent thought. This condition - not fully functioning, on the edge of panic - would be the way I was for months.

"We'll learn something soon," Mullin said in a low voice. "A little bit now in court, and then the mayor is having a press conference."

"The press is going to know before I do?"

"I'll do the best I can. But now we've got to get back before the judge."

"Can you get them to take these cuffs off?"

"I asked already," said Mullin. "They won't do it. This is a show. They think they've solved a very high profile crime in three days, and they want the world to know you're a dangerous guy. They're going to milk it."

"They didn't solve anything. They got the wrong guy."

Mullin asked a few more questions. He then left the cubicle and signaled the judge, who motioned for me. I walked the few steps from the cubicle to the table. This time, Mullin stood next to me.

"Ready?" asked the judge.

"Yes, your honor."

I looked behind me. The courtroom, which had been empty all morning, was now packed, and every set of eyes was staring straight at me.

"Look at the judge," Mullin whispered. "Stand up straight."

The wall behind Judge Cartegna proclaimed "In God we Trust." I'm not a religious person, but I had no one else in whom to place my trust, so I said a silent prayer. My eyes dropped to the judge, whose face was buried in the papers before him. There was a bustle of noise behind me. The judge raised his head and the room suddenly got very quiet.

A tall, thin, well dressed, sandy haired, almost patrician looking man, carrying a thin leather folder, came down the center aisle and strode to the table off to my left. He sat down, blocked from view behind a large computer screen. The young police officer stood before the judge and read aloud. "The People charge Joshua Blake with murder in the second degree, in connection with felony in the first degree."

"Mr. Blake, how do you plead?" the judge asked.

I looked at Mullin, who nodded, and I said, "Not guilty."

"Your honor, bail is requested," Mullin said.

The tall man shot up from behind the computer screen, and walked as close as he could to the judge, making himself visible to the crowded courtroom.

"Roger Claiborne representing the People, your honor," he said. "We oppose bail in this matter."

"State your reasons," said the judge.

"This is a crime of violence, the defendant is clearly dangerous, he has no ties to the community, and he's a flight risk."

Mullin jumped in. "Your honor, this man has no prior criminal record. He's a student, just graduated from college and soon to begin NYU law school. Far from being a flight risk, he has in fact just returned to the City from Baltimore."

His honor was not swayed. "Bail is denied."

My first thought was intense disappointment I would miss work on Monday. My great new job at Morgan, Heffer & Stone, gone before it even started. Then it dawned on me I was being sent to jail and had no idea when I would get out. I shivered uncontrollably and a feeling of weakness spread through my body. I had to grab the table to avoid collapsing. My eyes closed and I shook my head back and forth. Slowly the fog lifted and I could stand straight. I stared at the judge without seeing. I couldn't describe him on a dare.

There were a few more formalities and then two large police officers came to either side of me, took my elbows, and directed me back past the prisoner's benches and through the door to the holding cell area. Behind me, I heard a buzz of voices and the judge's gavel. I didn't see Mullin. I was completely, terrifyingly, alone.

Teri Scanlon, the *Daily News* reporter, stood at the back of the courtroom and watched as Roger Claiborne took long strides down the center aisle. She followed him into the large and rather dismal atrium, a corner of which bristled with TV lights and microphones. Dozens of reporters hollered questions as they ran to keep up. Claiborne ignored the questions and joined Police Commissioner William Troncone, NYPD Deputy Commissioner for Public Information Thomas Absinthe, several uniformed officers, and a man wearing a blue blazer and grey slacks, who Scanlon recognized as the detective who had spoken at the previous press conference.

"We'll wait for the mayor," the DCPI said, stilling the crowd. They didn't have long to wait, as a cluster of aides and security personnel soon preceded the arrival of New York City Mayor Raymond Gardino. He looked handsome as always, a short man in a dark blue suit, topped by carefully groomed white hair. He was a career New York City politician, long a member of the City Council, elected to succeed Rudy Giuliani in the aftermath of 9-11. The TV lights went on and the show began.

"The NYPD and the DA's office have done a fantastic job," Gardino said. "New Yorkers can be proud of their law enforcement team. Less than three days to make an arrest!" He turned to the phalanx of officers behind him. "Great job, guys!"

Twenty hands shot up. Gardino pointed to a reporter known to oblige with questions the mayor wanted to answer.

Lewis M. Weinstein

"Mayor," the reporter asked, "it's a little unusual to see you in court on a Sunday morning. Why are you here?" Unbelievable soft pitch, thought Scanlon. He should be ashamed.

"This was a terrible crime," Gardino answered, "taking the life of a lovely older woman who was enjoying her senior years with her family. I told the Commissioner and the other police officers I wanted a non-stop effort on this case, so the citizens of New York would not have to endure any longer than necessary the prospect of the perpetrator of this vicious crime remaining free."

Cut the speech, Mayor, Scanlon thought. Give us some facts.

"The police have done a terrific job – I got reports every three hours – and I wanted to be here to express my appreciation and the appreciation, I'm sure, of all the law-abiding citizens of our great city." The mayor consulted an index card he was holding and said, "I want to introduce Assistant District Attorney Roger Claiborne, who's going to prosecute this case."

Roger Claiborne stepped to the cluster of microphones and shook hands with the mayor. Scanlon thought they were meeting for the first time. Claiborne, however, did not seem uncomfortable. He spoke clearly and with confidence. "As most of you observed a few minutes ago in Part AR-1, Judge Cartegna presiding, a young man named Joshua Blake has been arrested and charged with the murder of Sarah Cooke. I have reviewed the evidence and it appears we have a solid case."

"Can you tell us about the evidence?" Scanlon asked.

"We have eyewitness and physical evidence linking this defendant to the crime."

Another reporter hollered out, "How did the police make this arrest so quickly?"

Claiborne looked perturbed to be moved off center stage so quickly, but he introduced the detective in the blue blazer and relinquished the microphone. Detective Watson seemed a little out of place in such august company, but he nevertheless gave a short professional description of how an extensive canvass, a police sketch, coordination with Baltimore police, and the stakeout of a Greenwich Village apartment had led to the arrest. It sounded to Scanlon like very competent police work.

A Good Conviction   45

I was with ten or twelve guys in a holding cell, the only one handcuffed, very much at the mercy of people who I imagined had no mercy. Everyone else seemed to know what was going to happen next, but I didn't have a clue, and not knowing made me extremely anxious. I struggled to keep from losing myself to total panic.

I remembered a time when I had driven into a deep fog on Interstate 95. With zero visibility, I was in constant fear of collisions from ahead or behind, but stopping was more dangerous than going on. My life had entered an unimaginable fog zone for which I was totally unprepared, but I kept telling myself I had to go on. Still unable to comprehend the bigger picture, I made myself focus on the minute details.

Guards appeared and handcuffed the other prisoners. I breathed a sigh of relief. They were no longer free to attack me. More time went by, and then we were each attached to a central chain, in groups of six. We stood for another ten minutes, and were marched out of the building into a closed courtyard and onto a waiting bus with a huge "DOC" on its side. Smaller print said "Department of Corrections." Despite the warmth of the day, chills cascaded through my body as I mounted the stairs, trying hard not to jostle the prisoners in front of and behind me. We were unhooked from the central chain as we entered the bus. I took the next open seat on the right side of the bus, uncomfortable with my hands still cuffed behind my back.

I could see out through heavily tinted windows but I don't think people outside could see in. The metal gate rose slowly as the bus inched forward, and the colorful playground across the street evoked an intense nostalgia for simpler, safer days. After a few turns, I saw signs for the Manhattan Bridge and we crossed the East River into a jumble of Brooklyn neighborhoods, where there were a lot of people on the streets. The bus left the city streets and entered a major highway, from which the control towers and parking structures of LaGuardia Airport were soon visible. Planes were landing and taking off. How I ached to be on one of those planes.

The DOC bus slowed to cross a narrow guarded bridge. It pulled in next to a low, ugly building. The sign said Rikers Island. "One at a time," a guard hollered. As we came down the steps of the bus, we were again chained in groups of six.

We were led to a large open room, which had been empty until we arrived, and were left standing there, still chained together. Every time there was stress on the chain, my body stiffened, terrified something would anger the other men on my chain, prompting who knew what violence. A large, unfriendly looking guard came in, unhooked us from the chain, and removed our handcuffs. Men milled around, and conversations began, mostly in Spanish. I was not part of it. I stood with my back against a wall and waited for someone to hit me.

Several times men were taken from the room, one at a time. When it was my turn, I was cuffed again and marched down a long hall to a large room. The sign said reception area. I was positioned in front of a small wooden table, and my cuffs were removed.

"Strip," said an overweight guard behind the table, without looking up. Stunned, I didn't move.

"Take your fuckin' clothes off! Now!"

My muscles froze, but I knew I had no choice. I pulled my blue polo over my head, remembered putting it on in Baltimore the previous morning, with Katie calling excitedly at my door that breakfast was ready. I was now in a different world, and the smell of pancakes had been replaced by the odors of my own filth. I realized how hungry I was.

"Put the fucking shirt on the table! Get a move on!"

Shoes, socks, jeans and underwear quickly followed, and I stood completely naked. Out of the corner of my eye, I saw other disrobing and naked men standing at other tables. I felt dirty and cold and, most of all, humiliated. I have since learned humiliation is one of the most important means by which prison guards control inmates.

The guard rustled through the clothes I had removed, still not looking up. I was clearly beneath his notice. Not that he had such a great job either, spending all day looking through prisoners' dirty underwear. I'm feeling sorry for this guy? He goes home at the end of his shift. When will I go home? Memories of me as a kid sorting clothes for the laundry on Saturday morning.

"Turn around. Bend over. Spread 'em." I did as I was told. "Okay, get dressed now. Fast."

My clothes were damp and dirty when I put them back on. The idea of taking a shower terrified me. There would be other guys in the shower room who would hurt me. Maybe I wouldn't be here long enough to take a shower. Where was Larry Mullin and what was he doing? Was he a good lawyer? Did good lawyers wear Pink Panther ties? Did Mullin give a shit about me?

Cuffs back in place, I was led to another room, where I recognized several men who had been with me in court and on the bus. The cuffs were again removed. I was surprised there was no door. Two men came in and handed out rolled blankets and sheets from a large cart.

"I want that one, white boy," snarled a voice behind me as soon as I got my blanket.

"Is it different?" I blurted, turning to face a lean, strong looking Hispanic man, several inches shorter than me. He wore a tank top and his muscular shoulders were enormous. Oh shit, I thought, what did I do? Now I'm going to die.

"You sayin' no to me?"

This was my first confrontation within prison walls, and although I was afraid like I had never been in my life, I instinctively knew I could not allow myself to be meek.

"This is my blanket," I said, embarrassed by the waver in my voice, but determined not to back off. "You have yours."

Four more Hispanics closed a circle around the two of us. Did any of them have a knife? No, I thought, we had all just been strip searched. I was bigger than any of them, but it was five to one, and I was no street fighter.

"You willin' to fight for a ratty old blanket?"

I gathered every bit of resolve I had, and answered, "I'd rather not, but I will if you make me."

There was a long terrifying pause, the circle closed tighter around me, and then a big smile crossed the leader's face. "Well, what do you know. White boy got guts." Extending his hand, he said, "Welcome to Rikers. My name is Alejandro Perez."

This was insane, and totally unexpected. Why had he backed off? Was it a trick? If I shook his hand, would he pull me down with some kind of move and stomp on me? I made my first prison decision.

"I'm Josh Blake," I said, reaching my hand out. "Nice to meet you."

Before our hands met, sirens blared and chaos erupted.

Despite significant reductions in the level of violence in the years since new NYPD accountability measures were implemented on Rikers, there are still one hundred violent incidents a month. Guards regularly employ a rapid, overwhelming response to prevent incidents from turning into riots.

Alejandro took my elbow, speaking softly. "Stand absolutely still. Don't say a word. If you move or speak, they'll club you. Do whatever you're told. Do it quickly. Don't ask any questions."

A column of guards ran at half speed down the hallway, boots stamping in unison, black helmets glistening, black batons held high. Hut! Hut! Hut! Hut! Angry shouts, some of pain. Prisoners were being hit. No one came into our room, and nobody ventured out through the open doorway. One prisoner, small and thin, cringed against a back wall, squeezing his eyes shut. Alarms blared from every direction. Then, as suddenly as it had started, it was over.

"Wasn't that fun?" Alejandro asked with a laugh.

"What was it all about?" I asked.

"Who the fuck knows? They don't even know. Maybe they needed exercise."

"What happens now?"

"Somebody'll be along to take us to our cells."

"There's no door."

"Don't you be leavin' now. The helmets are still out there, lookin' for more battin' practice."

I wanted to ask more questions, many questions, but I didn't know what was proper. Better to be quiet for now.

"Blake. Perez. Follow me." We were the first two called.

"Well, we're going to be roomies," Alejandro said, and I walked behind him out the door. Following Alejandro, I somehow felt better than if he had been a total stranger. I had known him for about fifteen minutes, beginning when he threatened to fight me for my blanket. This was my friend? Yet I thought he was.

We were led through several halls, better lit and more modern than those at Manhattan Central Booking. I was becoming an expert in prison décor. We passed into what seemed like a separate wing. The sign said George Motchan Detention Center, which I later learned was one of ten separate jails on Rikers. It is named after a Corrections Officer who was fatally shot in the line of duty. Originally used for women prisoners, it had been converted to a male detention center in 1988.

Our cell was eight feet by ten feet. Metal bunk beds took up one wall, a toilet with no seat and a small sink the other. There was a small barred window, and I was stunned by an improbable view of the skyscrapers of lower Manhattan, just a few miles away. I stared sadly at the empty space where the two tall towers had stood. Turning, I was amazed to see the cell door still open.

"View's worth four hundred a day," said Alejandro.

"I guess. It's magnificent."

"You'll hate it soon. You're here. No way you can go there."

"I won't be here long," I said.

"You plannin' to escape?"

"No, not that. I didn't do it. They'll figure it out and let me go."

"You fuckin' dreamin'? You're famous! They got you for a big one and they ain't lettin' you go."

"Famous? You know who I am?"

"Sure as shit. You're all over TV. You're the one killed the old lady."

"I didn't kill anybody."

"Right. Nobody here killed anybody."

My plans for this beautiful Sunday afternoon had been to wander around Greenwich Village and get myself psyched to be an assistant web designer at Morgan, Heffer & Stone. Instead, I was in a cell on Rikers Island and no one who cared about me had any idea where I was.

"How do you make a phone call in this place?" I asked Alejandro.

"Well, let's see. You ain't black and you ain't 'spic, so you are shit outa luck."

"What are you talking about?"

"Phones are power, man. Who controls the phones controls everything. So the deal is there's black phones and 'spic phones. Ain't no white phones."

This was lesson number one in a course I came to think of as Rikers 101. "I need to make a call," I said. "Won't the guards help me?" Lesson two followed.

"Guards don't give a shit about you. Besides, you start asking guards for help, you lookin' for nothin' but trouble."

"I don't understand."

"You see, you went to college but you don't know nothin'. Let me explain. You talk to a guard, somebody thinks you're snitching. Somethin' happens to somebody later, you get blamed." He paused and smiled. "Then somethin' happens to you."

"So what do I do? I need to call my friend."

"You're in luck."

"I thought you said I was out of luck."

"I'm going to make you an honorary 'spic. Come with me."

Alejandro led me out of the cell and down a corridor into a large common room where hundreds of inmates were wandering about. This was unbelievable to me. No handcuffs. Only a few guards. It bothered me even more when I noticed the guards didn't have guns. Everything I saw was new and strange and frightening. I had a permanent tight ball in the pit of my stomach.

There was a cluster of blacks in one corner of the room and a cluster of Hispanics in another. I walked next to Alejandro toward the Hispanics.

"Who you bringin' over here, Alejandro?" came a disembodied voice from the group.

"He's good," Alejandro said with a smile and a confident air. "He needs to make a phone call."

Like a parting of the waters, the crowd opened and I could see a phone on the wall. Alejandro was obviously someone of importance. He motioned me forward and I became number three in line. When my turn came, I dialed Tom's number and reversed the charges.

"Barb, this is Josh."

"Oh, Josh, we've been so worried. How are you?"

"Not good. I'm in jail on Rikers Island. I don't know what to do."

"Tom's on his way to New York. His train left an hour ago."

"How ..."

"He called the Central Park Precinct. They checked on the computer and told him where you'd be. He'll take a cab from the train station."

"It's expensive, Barb. He ..."

"You're arrested for murder and Tom is just going to wait in Baltimore and let you stew alone in jail?"

"Thanks, Barb. I really need someone."

"We know. We'll do whatever we can."

I hung up the phone and stood there, wondering what to do next. I felt totally isolated and alone. I wanted to be at the table at Mom's house surrounded by my friends. Not here, where even one phone call was so difficult.

Alejandro came over. "You look lost."

"I am. All these people are too much for me. Can we go back to the cell?"

"Sure. You can go."

"I'll never find it."

"I'll take you."

I paid more attention on the way back. The route between the cell and the big room wasn't complicated, but the thought of walking by myself amid a population of criminals was terrifying. Everything I had ever read about prisons came flooding back in a wave of incoherent images. Rape, beatings, slashings, razor blades, shanks. How could I survive in such a place? I remember saying to myself, over and over, "Get a grip. If you panic, you're lost. Use your brain." Good advice, not so easy to follow.

"Would you really have fought for an old ratty blanket? Five against one?"

We were back in the cell. I was standing by the window. Alejandro was sitting on the lower bunk.

"I guess. What choice did I have? But why did you pick a fight? Is my blanket better than yours? If it is, you can have it. Here, take it."

"I don't want your blanket. I just wanted to see what you would do."

"Why?"

"Not many white guys in here. Checkin' you out."

"I thought you were going to kill me."

"Maybe I would have. Maybe the Red Alert saved you," Alejandro said, laughing.

I surprised myself by actually smiling. "Look," I said, "you don't have to stay with me. I'm dog tired and I'm going to sleep."

As soon as Alejandro left, I realized how alone I was. The cell door was open. Anyone could come in and kill me. How could I sleep? But I was exhausted so I climbed into the upper bunk and did fall asleep. When I woke, the sun was setting behind the New York skyline. It was a beautiful sight.

I sensed a presence and turned my head. Standing at the cell door staring at me was the most frightening human being I had ever seen. He looked about fifty years old, maybe six feet four inches tall, two hundred sixty pounds at least. He had a shaved head and very dark shiny black skin. His belly extended over beat up, loose fitting blue jeans. A three day beard covered a badly scarred face and his arms were covered with faded tattoos. He wore dusty black sneakers, but his feet were so huge he couldn't pull the laces tight. He didn't move.

After several minutes of this mutual staring, the huge man's face contorted in an evil smile which frightened me even more. "You the college kid who killed the old lady?" he asked, in a deep, powerful voice.

I sat up and cracked my head on the ceiling. "I didn't kill anybody."

"But you did go to college?"

I didn't answer.

"Good. Now I know where you are." He turned, quite nimbly, given his immense bulk, and disappeared from view.

Who was this guy? What did he want? What did it mean he wanted to know where I was? I had no answers. The simple truth was I was in a horrible place, surrounded by horrible people, and I didn't know what to do. I crawled down from the bunk, afraid to go out, afraid to stay. I have no idea how long I stood frozen to one spot on the floor. When Alejandro returned, I asked him about my visitor.

"Not good," he said. "That was Abraham Smith, muscle for the Bloods. They must be confused by you using our phone, you know what I mean. So they want to know who you are. How you change things."

"I change things?"

"That's what they don't know. Everything on Rikers is in a sort of balance. But guys come and go every day, so the balance shifts."

Absurdly, I blurted out, "Like the balance of power in Europe before World War I?"

"Huh? I don't know nothin' about Europe. You know about shit like that?"

"I took several courses on European history."

"I wanted to go to college."

There was an awkward pause. Alejandro had just revealed something important about himself. Maybe this was why he had sought me out, why he was helping me. He knew who I was and he knew I had gone to college.

"It's not too late," I said.

"Fuck you know about it," Alejandro snapped.

There must have been dinner, but I remember nothing about it. I must have shuffled along with Alejandro in something close to an unconscious stupor. After dinner, they locked all the cells for the night. I climbed into the upper bunk and unrolled my blanket. To my surprise, it contained a small toiletries bag, with toothbrush, toothpaste, soap, and a plastic cup.

"What kind of toothbrush is this?" I asked, holding up the three inch brush made of very soft plastic.

"One you can't make into a shank," Alejandro answered.

I absorbed the import of this information and then asked, "When my friend Tom gets here, how will they notify me and get us together?"

"What fuckin' planet are you on?" said Alejandro from below.

"No, I'm serious. Tom is coming up by train from Baltimore. I want to give him the key to my apartment, and ask him to bring some of my clothes tomorrow." As I spoke, my voice trailed away. "None of that's going to happen, is it?"

"Not a chance."

"So he wasted his trip. And his money."

"You can see him tomorrow."

A Good Conviction

"Can I call him, or his wife, to let them know?"

"Sure. Just go to the concierge desk."

The lights went out. The upper bunk felt claustrophobic with the pitch dark ceiling only a few inches above my head, and I panicked. I felt buried alive. The knot in my stomach grew larger and tighter until it seemed like it must explode. I had never known a feeling like this, and I actually thought I might die. It would have been a blessing to pass out. Anything to make my panic go away.

Gradually, my eyes adjusted and the darkness resolved into shadows. Prisoners in other cells were talking, laughing, arguing. The sounds were maddening. I needed quiet. I needed to think. I turned over and buried my head in the pillow. Anything to avoid looking at the coffin lid above me. I gave myself another lecture. You've got to hold on. Don't let yourself become a basket case. You're not a coward. This feeling will end. Soon I got angry. What did I do to deserve this? When I was angry, I was less afraid.

I had to pee. No way, I told myself, terrified to leave the bunk. I resisted as long as I could and then slid over the edge, forgetting there was a ladder. I stepped hard on Alejandro's arm. As if he had expected me, he silently grabbed my foot and directed it to the edge of the lower bunk. My other foot reached the floor, and I stood there, in the tiny cell, with no idea where to go. I felt my way around the clammy wall until I reached the toilet. Not trusting myself to pee in the hole, I sat down. When I was done, the flushing sounded like a waterfall. I thought I was the only one, bothering everyone, but no one hollered out. I felt my way back to the bunk, climbed up the ladder, and pulled the blanket over my head.

The intense claustrophobia returned. How could I possibly last until dawn? For the first time in my life I understood how death could be preferable to living. I heard the muted voices of other prisoners, and mixed among their conversations, I detected at least two men who were crying. Knowing I was not the only one helped me settle down.

I forced myself to think about other things, like every detail in my sublet apartment - the color of the drapes, the chair, the television, the VCR. I felt bad for Tom, who had come all the way from Baltimore and was left adrift in a city he so disliked and feared. Where was he? Did he find a place to sleep? Would he stay?

My thoughts drifted to the coming morning. It would have been such an important day, starting a new job, meeting new people, working on the firm's web site. I would probably lose the job now, even if things got straightened out and I was released. How would I let them know what had happened? Maybe they already knew. If Alejandro had seen me on television, maybe Ms. Coleman or someone else at the firm had too. Guess what, she would tell everyone, our new employee was arrested for murder.

Lewis M. Weinstein

I must have slept, because when I woke, it was light.
And I was still alive.

SIX

After breakfast, I was taken to a small room without windows. Larry Mullin was slumped in a chair, a scowl on his face, shuffling papers. He smiled and pointed for me to sit down. He was still wearing the same rumpled brown suit. I sat across from him and drummed my fingers on the metal table, waiting.

"Here's what they've got," Mullin finally said, "at least what they're telling me so far. One, you were in the general vicinity when the murder was committed."

"There must have been a million people there."

"Two, you fit the description the victim gave before she died. Nice young man wearing a white baseball cap."

"What kind of description is that? It could be anybody."

"It could be a lot of people," Mullin agreed. "But there is something else. Your fingerprints were on the victim's pocketbook."

My heart skipped and I actually started to shake. I felt lightheaded, like I was going to pass out. "I didn't kill anybody," I managed to whisper.

"They think you did. Detective Watson wants to question you again. This time I'll be with you. But first, I need to go over everything that happened last Thursday. Let's trace every step you took Thursday night, minute by minute. You talk. Go."

I took a deep breath and began. "I came out of my apartment and ... I don't know! I can't remember!"

"You've got to remember," said Mullin. "It's the only chance you have. What time was it when you left your apartment?"

I closed my eyes and tried to visualize each step, concentrating as hard as I could. I mumbled things to Mullin and he listened without comment, making notes. I said which subway I had taken, and where I got off. I traced my path along Broadway. I even mentioned the thongs and the opera. When I got to Broadway and 66th Street, it hit me.

"That's it," I said. "An old lady fell off the curb. I helped her up. I picked up her pocketbook and gave it to her."

"Was she the one who was killed?"

"Must be, but I don't know for sure."

"You didn't recognize her photo?"

"No. I didn't look at it very carefully. And I didn't much look at the lady either. The whole thing took a few seconds."

"Did anyone see you help this lady?"

"Probably lots of people. The street was crowded. But how would we ever find them?" I tried to recreate the moment. "Wait! There was a guy at the newsstand."

"What newsstand?"

"On the corner. After I helped the lady, I bought some mints. The guy had seen the whole thing." Now my words came gushing out. "He said how nice it was. What I did. He saw the whole thing."

"Do you know his name?"

"Yeah, sure. When I bought the mints he gave me his business card."

"Josh," Mullin said, looking a little exasperated, "I want you to cut out the sarcasm. This is very serious business. You've been accused of murder. The police don't really like wise remarks, and right now, you don't want to antagonize the police. Understand?"

I nodded, and Mullin continued asking questions, taking me through my purchase at the Disney Store and to John's Pizza.

"After you left John's Pizza," Mullin asked, "where did you go?"

"First, I went back to the newsstand. I bought a *Sports Illustrated* to take with me on the train the next morning. Then I went to the subway ..."

"Which subway?"

"Columbus Circle. I took a downtown C-train back to Washington Square. Then I went home. I watched the rest of the Yankee game and went to sleep."

"That's it? Nothing more?"

We went over the same story two more times, and I guess Mullin was satisfied. I still didn't have my watch, but I think we had talked for more than an hour.

"Okay," he said. "You'll tell your story to Detective Watson. Is there anything more I need to know before we sit down with him?"

"I can't think of anything."

Mullin stepped out of the room and returned in a second. "They'll be down soon. Have you read the papers?" He handed me several articles from the *New York Daily News*. "There's also an Attorney Fee Agreement," he added. "When you get a chance."

"Can you help me with something?" I asked. Mullin nodded. "My friend Tom came to New York yesterday, but he couldn't see me. Would you call him and help arrange a visit? I don't know how to do it."

"What's the number?"

"One more thing," I said, feeling I was pushing it. "I was supposed to begin a job with Morgan, Heffer & Stone this morning. Could you call them and tell them why I'm not there?"

Mullin's face was a mixture of sadness and frustration. "Who should I call?" he said.

"Barbara Coleman."

Mullin said he would make the calls, and I started to look at the clippings, but just then the door opened. Even though I had just said there was nothing more to discuss, I felt I wasn't ready. Events were moving too fast, and everything was out of control.

Detective Robert Watson was accompanied by another non-uniformed officer who placed a vintage tape recorder on the table and plugged it into a wall socket. "Let's begin," said Watson, nodding to Mullin as he punched the record button and gave the date and time.

"We're here in the matter of *People v. Blake*," he stated matter-of-factly, but the words tore into my gut. The People versus me. Watson spoke the names of everyone present and asked his first question.

"Do you still insist you never saw the Cooke woman?" Watson asked, his face expressionless.

"I don't know anything about a Mrs. Cooke," I said.

"You're going to have to do better than that," said Watson, with just a flicker of a smile. "You know your fingerprints are all over her pocketbook."

"There's an explanation," Mullin said quickly. He nodded to me to begin.

"I helped an old lady who fell in the street," I said. "Maybe it was the same woman who was murdered."

"Tell me," Watson said, and I related the story of how I helped the old lady. I watched the tape spinning as I spoke.

"That must be how Josh's fingerprints came to be on the pocketbook," Mullin added when I was done.

Watson looked angry. "That's it? That's your story?"

"It's what happened," I said.

Watson laughed out loud. "You expect me to believe that bullshit. All of a sudden, after you talk with your attorney, you conveniently remember this whole story you never told us before."

"He has a witness," Mullin said quietly. "Tell him, Josh."

Back in my cell, but encouraged by the progress we had made, I read the newspaper clippings Mullin had given me.

The first was from Friday's *Daily News*:

Lewis M. Weinstein

**No arrests so far
in Central Park murder**

By Teri Scanlon

An elderly woman was killed shortly after dark last night, just inside Central Park, near 63rd Street and Central Park West. Robbery was the apparent motive. The woman, not yet identified, died from head injuries sustained when she was pushed down an embankment and crashed into a rock.

A young Caucasian male, wearing a light colored shirt and a white baseball cap, was seen fleeing the scene. He is thought to have entered the subway station at Columbus Circle. A subway attendant at the Fort Hamilton Parkway station in Brooklyn reported seeing a similarly dressed individual throw a pocketbook belonging to the victim into a trash container. Police are circulating an artist's sketch in an effort to identify the killer.

Mayor Raymond Gardino has pledged an all out effort to catch the killer, but New Yorkers are reeling from the third killing in the last month in one of the City's more pricey neighborhoods. This outbreak of high profile murders follows a long period in which the City's murder rate has fallen precipitously. Mayor Gardino, like Mayor Giuliani before him, has gained enormous political capital by taking credit for the improvement.

By Saturday, it was clear how high the stakes had become, for the police and also for the mayor:

**Mayor says
"We'll get this guy!"**

By Teri Scanlon

Mayor Raymond Gardino promised quick police action to arrest the man who killed an elderly woman Thursday night in Central Park. Gardino, obviously upset when pressed about a lack of leads, said, "Don't worry. We'll get this guy, and we'll get him soon."

A Good Conviction   59

Pressure on the police to solve the case is intense. This is the third high profile Manhattan murder in the last month. No arrests have been made in any of the cases, and the police often say murders are solved within a few days or not at all.

The NYPD is out in full force. Along the Upper West Side and in Brooklyn, over 100 officers are frantically searching for the killer. The woman, identified by a police spokesman as Sarah Cooke, aged 83, lived near the park and had just made an ATM cash withdrawal. The money has not been recovered, but her pocketbook was found in a trash receptacle in the Fort Hamilton Parkway subway station in Brooklyn.

Monday's paper reported how they had gloated after the arraignment:

Arrest made in
Central Park Murder

By Teri Scanlon

At a press conference at 100 Centre Street on Sunday morning, New York City Mayor Raymond Gardino announced the arrest Saturday night of Joshua Blake, of Baltimore, in the murder of Sarah Cooke in Central Park last Thursday night. Assistant District Attorney Roger Claiborne provided the details, "Blake was identified running from the scene of the crime and again when he disposed of the victim's pocketbook at the Fort Hamilton Parkway subway station in Brooklyn. There is physical evidence linking the arrested man to the victim."

Blake graduated just two weeks ago from the University of Maryland Baltimore County. He was planning to begin classes at NYU Law School this fall. He has no known friends or associates in the city. Attorney Lawrence P. Mullin, appointed to represent Blake at his arraignment hearing on Sunday morning, said, "My client is innocent. The police have the wrong guy, and I'm sure the facts will ultimately bear this out." Mullin offered no specifics on what those facts might be.

"What are you reading?" Alejandro asked as he walked into the cell. I gave him the clippings.

Lewis M. Weinstein

"I have good news," I said.

When he had finished reading, Alejandro said, "This is good news?"

"No. Not that. I told the cops about the newsstand guy. They'll find him and they'll know about the fingerprints, and they'll let me go."

"Fingerprints?"

"My prints were on the old lady's pocketbook."

"I repeat. This is good news?"

"When they know how they got there. She fell off a curb and I helped her up. I picked up her pocketbook. The guy at the newsstand saw it all. The cops will talk to him."

"I hate to tell you, but this just ain't goin' to happen. The cops won't find the guy, and if they do, he won't remember shit, and if he does remember, he won't tell them. And they don't want to know. They got a big important murder, and they got you. Case closed. You're stayin' right here."

At his home in the Flatbush section of Brooklyn, Tony Marone also read about the arrest in the Daily News. Oh, man, he almost said aloud before he caught himself, they got somebody else.

"What's so interesting in the paper, Tony?" his mother asked. "Since when do you read the paper every morning?" Tony looked up but didn't answer. He put the paper down and left the house. Mrs. Marone looked to see what had attracted her son's attention.

On West 38th Street, at the Broadway Big Apple Hotel, Darlene Brantley read the same paper.

"Shit," she exclaimed. "No way!"

"No way what?" her friend Annabelle asked.

"You remember the murder in Central Park last week? The old lady? Look here. They arrested Joshua. Here's his picture."

"Our Joshua? That cute kid who stayed here? The one you couldn't get to fuck you?"

"That one."

"Oh my God," Annabelle whispered.

"They must have it wrong," said Darlene. "That kid was nice. He was sensitive. Big and strong, sure, but he wouldn't hurt anyone."

"You remember him pretty good," Annabelle said.

I read and signed the Fee Arrangement retaining Larry Mullin as my counsel. If we went to trial, it would take a big portion of the money I had set aside for law school, but what choice did I have? I was still confident it would be just another few hours, or maybe at worst a few days. I refused to allow myself to believe Alejandro could be right. I had been in the wrong place at the wrong time, and I must have resembled the person who actually killed the old woman. But it wasn't me. Surely the police would learn the truth and I would be released.

When I try to recall those first days at Rikers, I make no sense of it at all. It was a constantly churning, incoherent, never-ending insanity. I was repeatedly faced with some new and often violent threat. I would look up and faces I didn't recognize were sneering at me. If they saw me looking, they would snarl or holler. Weapons were flashed. Where did they come from? Same place as the cockroaches, maybe. Or the disgusting smells. The place was awful, and it was unrelenting.

"Dead man. Dead man in the cell." The scream was actually more frightening than the message, since it was not the horrified cry one might expect but rather a cry of joy. Rikers had served up some afternoon entertainment.

The whole cell block picked up the chant. "Dead man. Dead man." The noise was deafening.

"What happened?" I asked an inmate running past my cell.

"Hanged hisself. Stupid jerkoff hanged hisself."

"Why?" I asked, but of course there's no answer to such a question. Lockdown followed within seconds, and I cringed alone until a guard brought Alejandro to the cell.

"Wasn't no suicide," Alejandro said as soon as the guard was out of hearing. "Rueben was murdered. It was the Bloods. Now we retaliate."

Who was Rueben? Who are the Bloods? Why did they kill him, if in fact they did? Who is the "we" that would now retaliate? What form will this retaliation take? And most crucial, what does this all mean to me? I was too frightened to ask any of those rational questions, so out of place in my suddenly irrational world.

Amazingly, nothing happened, not when the lockdown ended, not at lunch or through the early afternoon. Whether suicide or murder, for the moment at least it was just the way things were on Rikers. Alejandro said nothing more about retaliation. We were returned to our cells and locked down for the count before dinner.

Then, the loudspeakers blared and the Emergency Response Unit took the field. "Listen up. We are searching this cell block. When your gate opens, you will strip down for the officer. You will not shake your clothes. You will not speak during this search. If you

Lewis M. Weinstein

have a problem with this search, you will be escorted out of your cell and an infraction will be written against you. Officers are trained to defend themselves. If you resist in any way, necessary force will be used."

My first thought, I swear to you, was I was very sure nothing this exciting was happening at Morgan, Heffer & Stone at 4:30 pm on Monday afternoon. Thoughts of what my first day at work might have been like were driven from my mind when our cell door was abruptly opened. Four helmeted officers, dressed in black, carrying large shiny shields, stood in the corridor.

"Strip."

We did, each of us placing our clothes on our own bunk.

"Open your mouth," an officer said to me. I did as he said.

"Pull it wider with your fingers. Show me the bottom gums."

"Step out into the hall, hands against the wall."

Another officer gave Alejandro the same sequence of commands and he was soon next to me. A third officer rummaged through our cupboards. Mine, of course, was empty, but Alejandro's produced candy, other food, cigarettes, books, clothes, baseball caps, papers. Where did it all come from, since he came into the cell at the same time I did?

They had us drag our mattresses into the hall and ordered us back into the cell. Alejandro's mattress was placed on a table they had brought into the corridor and carefully searched. Nothing was found, and he was told to take it back. When they searched mine, I was terrified. I hadn't hidden anything, but suppose someone else had put something in my mattress.

"This one's okay," a guard said. I breathed a sigh of relief, retrieved my mattress, and lifted it back to the top bunk.

"Blake, out of the cell." I caught myself just before I asked why.

"Follow me," the guard said, and, still naked, I followed him down the hall.

"Introducing the new guy to the boss?" another guard asked as we walked by. At the end of the corridor was something that looked like an electric chair.

"Sit there." It was cold on my naked ass. Somebody threw a switch and I felt an electric hum, but I didn't die.

"Stand up. Back to your cell. Get dressed." Alejandro, already dressed, was not taken to the chair. The inspection worked its way down the corridor, and there were shouts from the guards whenever they found something.

"Looks like one. Oh yeah. Pull it out"

"Put a handle on that thing, it's fuckin' lethal."

Then the Darth Vadars were gone, and we could talk.

"How did you like the chair?" Alejandro asked.

"What was it?"

"The body orifice chair. BO.S.S. The letters stand for something, I don't know what."

"What's it for?"

"Must be like an x-ray or somethin'. They can tell if you have somethin' stuck up your ass. Like a razor blade."

"People stick razor blades up their asses?"

"Best place to hide 'em. Wrap it in toilet paper, put it into the finger of a rubber glove, tie a string to it, grease your asshole and shove it in. When you need it, pull the string."

Prison is not boring. With the perspective of time, I can see how interesting it was to learn all these fascinating little tidbits.

"What was the search all about?"

"Reuben got killed. They know somethin's goin' to happen, so they want to pick up as many weapons as possible."

"What were those shields the guards were carrying?"

"Stun shields. Fifty thousand volts. And do they love to use them.

"It's got to be hard to keep a lid on this place."

"The fuckers do a better job now than they used to. Before, they didn't care. Guys got cut, so what. Pricks deserve it, they said. Now, you get time. Slash somebody and get caught, you get serious time. Some sucker comes in for jumping a turnstile, ends up with twenty five years."

"Why would anybody do something so stupid?"

"Sometimes you don't have a choice. You'll find out. Guys are pickin' on you, wanting you to give 'em blow jobs and stuff. You have to earn your respect."

"Can't you explain what was goin' on?"

"Who the fuck cares? You slash, you go up."

"Up?"

"Attica, Coxsackie, Sing Sing. One of New York State's maximum security hotels.

"You've been here before?" This was the first personal question I had asked Alejandro since I told him it wasn't too late for him to go to college. I was afraid it would make him angry again, but it didn't.

"This is my third time on Rikers. All minor shit though, in and out in a few months. So far, I didn't get caught doin' nothin' here. But I'll be pushing my luck soon."

"Pushing your luck?"

"You don't want to know. Don't know, can't tell."

A guard came to our cell and handcuffed me.

"This way," he indicated.

"Where are we going?" I asked, but he ignored my question. He took me down several corridors to a large room filled with long tables. Inmates sat on one side of each table, civilians on the other. The cuffs were removed. The room was noisy, with a happy sort of noise different from anything else I had so far experienced at Rikers. The visitors were mostly women, many with children. It wasn't difficult to find Tom.

"Tom, It's so good to see you," I said as soon as I sat down across from him.

"This is so terrible, Josh. What happened?"

Tom was staring at me. I was dirty, because I wouldn't go to the shower room, and unshaven. I think I had already lost five pounds, and my unwashed clothes were hanging on me. Saddened by Tom's reflection of my appearance, I explained how I had helped the old lady, and how my fingerprints got onto her pocketbook.

"And then she was robbed and murdered?"

"Apparently."

"And they think you did it?"

"Yes. But there was someone who saw me help the old lady. The police will talk to him and then they'll realize they made a mistake and let me go."

Tom was looking off to the side, and I let my gaze follow his. A young woman was reaching under the table and giving a hand job to the inmate on the other side. As we watched, he spurted all over the floor and both of them sat up, trying to look innocent.

"This place is unbelievable," Tom said. "When do you think you'll get out?"

"I don't know. Soon, I hope. I have a lawyer."

"He called me. Larry Mullin. Told me how to arrange this visit. Listen, I brought some clothes and stuff. They made me leave it with them, but they promised you would get it later today."

"You got into my apartment?"

"No. The police still have it secured as a crime site. No entry."

"Then ..."

"I bought some stuff. No big deal."

"It is a big deal. This visit has cost you a fortune. I want to pay you back."

"No way. You have enough problems. And what would you pay me with anyway?"

"You're right. I don't have any money."

"Actually, you do. I deposited $100 in your account here. You can use it to buy things at the prison commissary."

"You know more about this place than I do."

"Mullin told me. He was very helpful."

"I'll pay you back when I get out."

"Okay," Tom said, and he had the decency not to ask when that might be.

"Tom, this place is a nightmare. Somebody committed suicide yesterday, only my cellmate says it was murder. Then the search team came, and we had to strip. They made me sit naked in an electric chair to see if I had any razor blades up my ass."

"Jesus!"

"I'm scared all the time. There's gangs here. There's a black gang called the Bloods and a Puerto Rican gang called the Latin Kings. There's going to be a war. I don't know what to do."

"Jesus!"

"My cellmate is named Alejandro Perez. He seems to be important. Maybe he's one of the gang leaders. He's taken an interest in me, and now I'm part of the Puerto Rican group. But this makes me an enemy of the blacks. Some huge ugly black guy came to my cell to check me out. Alejandro thinks they may want to kill me."

"Jesus!"

"And I've only been here for two days. It feels like a year. When I'm not terrified, I'm furious. How could this be? But I can't show it, or I'll get in even more trouble."

A buzzer went off, and a guard announced all visits would be over in two minutes.

"Call me," Tom said.

"I can only call collect."

"Do it anyway. You need someone to talk to."

"Thanks, Tom. I need something to keep me sane."

"It won't be long," Tom said. "You'll be out of here soon."

SEVEN

An intense feeling of loneliness came over me as I watched Tom Kaplan leave. I lined up with the other inmates to get cuffed for the return walk. The prisoner in front of me was not only handcuffed, but there was some kind of heavy bag, maybe burlap, placed over his hands and strapped tightly around his wrists.

Walking back to the cell, we passed a small group of inmates gathered around a tall man talking like a preacher. "Islam is the way," he said as I passed.

When we reached our corridor, I was overwhelmed by the stench of shit. A toilet had overflowed from one of the cells. It was not an accident. As we walked past, slop from the cell was thrown at the guard directly in front of me, hitting him flush in the face. The guard said nothing, pausing just long enough to note the cell. Ten minutes later, I heard batons banging, grunts of punches thrown and received, and an unconscious, bloody inmate was dragged past my cell. Other inmates on the corridor made an unholy racket.

Not much later, the cell doors opened and the inmates were free to go to the day room. I walked with Alejandro, in what soon became a large mass of Puerto Ricans and one white guy. This was different from the previous day, when there had been many small groups and quite a few inmates walking alone. Nobody was walking alone today.

We came up behind an equally large group of black inmates, and I recognized the hulk who had visited my cell the day before. Was it only yesterday? I was already losing all sense of time. The groups stayed apart, forming up in the far corners of the day room, but it was clear from the icy looks and body language a violent explosion was imminent. Ominously, there was no chatter.

"Blake." My name and several others were called out.

"Over here. Follow me." More corridors. In those early days on Rikers, I was lost much of the time.

"In here. Sit down." Four of us went into a small room with a television and a VCR. We took our seats and another guard announced, "There's a video. *Rikers Rules & Regulations.* Pay attention. It's stuff you need to know." He pushed the play button. When the twenty minute video was finished, the guard gave each of us a pamphlet, also titled *Rikers Rules & Regulations.* We were marched back to our cells. I was thrilled not to return to the day room.

I was well into my pamphlet, fascinated with the micro-managed, bureaucratic approach to every aspect of life, when

Alejandro returned. He was jubilant. "You missed it, brother," he said. "We had some shit!"

I waited. Alejandro dropped his pants and sat on the toilet, emitting a long fart.

"It was great," he said with a goofy grin. "Four guys slashed, and it went so quickly, the guards never knew who did it."

"How do people have weapons when they're watched so closely?" I asked, shaking my head in astonishment. "I thought you told me they really had a lid on weapons here."

"They do," Alejandro said, "but there's always a stash for special times."

"I don't understand. How did knives get to the day room?"

"Not knives. Razors."

"In people's asses?"

"In their mouths. Guys can carry two blades, one on each side of the mouth. The trick is to get them out before the other guy hits you in the mouth. You slash quickly, drop the blade, and get back to cover."

"It sounds like a military operation."

"And I'm the fuckin' four star general," Alejandro said with obvious pride. "We caused three casualties and only took one."

"Casualties?"

"The Bloods got three guys with 'buck fifties'."

"Buck fifties?"

"Slashes across the face take a hundred fifty stitches. If they live. Hey, we got the big motha was checkin' you out the other day. He won't be back."

It turned out Alejandro was wrong about Abraham Smith. The Latin Kings victory was only the first skirmish in a running battle. Rikers was in bloody turmoil for weeks.

On Wednesday morning, I met again with my attorney Larry Mullin.

"The cops found the newsstand guy," Mullin said. "His name is Angel Martinez."

"Did he remember me?" I asked, the tension unbearable.

"He says he saw someone help an old lady who had fallen."

My heart soared. Ever since Alejandro told me it wouldn't happen, I had been torturing myself. I relaxed for the first time in days, certain my nightmare was about to end.

Detective Watson came into the room.

"So now you know how my fingerprints got onto the pocketbook," I said to the detective. "How soon can I get out of here?" I switched back to Mullin and continued blabbering. "Did you talk to Barbara Coleman at the law firm? Do you think I can still have my job? I only missed three days."

Mullin stared at me. His face was gloomy, and my stomach contracted. Something was very wrong.

"You're a suspect in a murder, and this case is still under investigation," Watson said. "You're not going anywhere," and he added softly, "at least not yet."

"What do you mean?" I hollered. "You know what happened, why can't I leave? I need to get to work."

Mullin explained. "They're not going to release you, even if you did help the lady. They think you attacked her later, in the park."

I started to rise. Mullin grabbed my arm and held me down, but he couldn't stop my mouth. I screamed at the detective. "You know I didn't do it. But I'm the one you arrested and paraded around in chains. Now you won't admit you were wrong. How can you live with yourself?"

My head fell to the table. I pounded my fists weakly, sobbing uncontrollably.

When I looked up, Detective Watson was staring at me, a strange expression on his face. He looked like he was about to say something, but he got up and left the room without speaking.

Mullin sat patiently until I stopped sobbing.

"I'm sorry," he said. "Watson told me on the phone he wasn't going to release you. I should have prepared you better."

"What are we going to do? You know I'm going to die in here. I'm in the middle of a gang war."

"What?"

"I've been sort of adopted by one of the Puerto Rican gang leaders. I don't know why. But anyway, the blacks think I'm with the Puerto Ricans and they're going to kill me."

"Listen to me, Josh. You're better off part of some group than being a white college kid all alone."

"Now you tell me."

"I didn't want to scare you."

"Thanks. I couldn't possibly be more scared than I am. I can hardly breathe. The fear never stops. There's no way to get away from it."

"Let me tell you what's going to happen," Mullin said.

I stared at him, too distraught to say anything more.

"There's going to be a Grand Jury hearing, either tomorrow or Friday. You'll be charged and you'll be indicted. There's no chance you won't be indicted. I'll make another motion for bail, and I'll fight hard for it, but I expect to be turned down."

"Wait. Slow down. Can I testify at the Grand Jury? Can I tell them what really happened?"

"Yes, you can," Mullin said, but his expression conveyed how useless it would be.

"Isn't there any chance they'll believe me?"

"I'd like to say there is, but it would be a lie. There's no chance."

"Well, I'll try anyway."

"I don't think you should. The Grand Jury won't listen, but the prosecutor will. Anything you say can be brought up later, at trial. If you're inconsistent in any small detail, they'll use it against you later as proof you're lying."

"So I should just let them indict me for a crime I didn't commit?"

"You have nothing to gain and much to lose if you testify. I can't force you not to, but I strongly advise you don't."

"Is there any good news?"

"I wish there was," Mullin said. "After the indictment, a trial date will be set."

"When?"

"A few months. Maybe more. I'll prepare your defense. I'll be looking hard at whatever evidence the prosecutor has, and for any other evidence we can find. But I have to tell you their case looks very strong. In addition to the fingerprints, Mrs. Cooke's blood was on your shirt."

"Must be the same way," I said. "The old lady grabbed onto me when I helped her up."

"I'm sure you're right. But the prosecutor doesn't care, even if it's true."

I took a deep breath, exhaled, and asked, "Am I going to be convicted?"

"It's a tough case."

"Do you see how ironic this is?" I asked. "For years, my prime goal in life has been to become a lawyer. Now the law is coming down on me for something I didn't do."

I squeezed my eyes shut to keep from crying. Mullin rose and put his hand gently on my shoulder.

"I'll see you at the Grand Jury hearing if you decide to testify. I'm not allowed to speak, but I'll be there to learn as much as I can about the People's case."

The hopelessness of my situation was overwhelming and I think Mullin shared the feeling. "I'm sorry, Josh," he said. "I'll do everything I can."

Later in the day, I was handcuffed and transported back to 100 Centre Street, where I was put together with five other guys in a lineup. Mullin, who was there, told me later the subway station attendant from Brooklyn identified me as the one who threw Mrs. Cooke's pocketbook into a trash can at her subway station. There was also some guy who said he saw me run out of Central Park. Both of them picked me out of the lineup. Mullin said there would be another lineup for Angel Martinez.

"Roger," Watson called from across the hall.

Detective Watson approached ADA Claiborne in the ground floor atrium of 100 Centre Street, where several hallways converged into a large open space. "I was just at your office. I've been thinking about the Blake case," he said.

"What about it?" Claiborne asked. "I'm on my way to his grand jury hearing right now."

"I think there's problems with the case," Watson said. "Martinez says he saw Blake at 8:00 o'clock ..."

Claiborne turned and walked away. Watson stopped in mid-sentence. Then Claiborne came back. He spoke so low Watson could barely hear him, but his words were intense.

"I read Mackey's report," Claiborne said. "So what! Who's gonna believe an illegal alien who works at a newsstand? And it doesn't seem he was really certain anyway."

"Why did the kid come back from Baltimore? It doesn't add up," Watson said.

Claiborne took a deep breath. "Listen to me, detective. I don't know where you're going with this, but you need to stop right now. You arrested Blake, and you were part of a very big press conference to announce we had solved the crime." He spoke even more slowly, emphasizing each word. "I'm going to get this conviction. If you had anything to say, you should have said it before the arraignment, before the press conference. Nobody wants to hear this now."

Watson started to speak, but Claiborne waved him off. He raised his finger like a schoolmaster lecturing a student. "Don't you be the one to fuck up a good conviction."

Claiborne turned his back to Watson and walked quickly away.

EIGHT

Sing Sing Correctional Facility
Thursday, January 22, 2004

"R gallery on the chow," blares the PA system. The corrections officer pulls the brake, releasing the cell locks on the north end of the gallery, and then does the same for the south side, our side. The cell gates swing open, and sixty or so inmates swarm into the narrow corridor.

The CO has positioned himself to block the center passage, preventing inmates from crossing to the W gallery, which is back-to-back with R gallery on the same floor. We walk to the stairs at the end of the gallery, down one flight, then back along the full length of B-block on the first level, known as the "flats," into the long corridor leading to the mess hall. We jam up at the first locked gate, wait for the guard to release us, move to the next gate, jam up again, and eventually in this stop-and-go pattern, we reach the cafeteria.

The mess hall is a dangerous place. Angry inmates bump into each other, vie for seats, argue with COs, take extra food, throw food. It's unruly, noisy, and always on the edge of exploding. Breakfast is a daily gruel bearing no earthly resemblance to the maple & brown sugar instant oatmeal I used to enjoy almost every morning. The State of New York provides thin orange juice, watery eggs, cold toast, and weak coffee. I torture myself with a vision of my college dorm room, a newspaper on the table, Katie Couric and Matt Lauer chatting amiably on the TV in the background. My new reality dictates I take the next available seat at one of the large bolted down metal tables in a room with two hundred ugly, smelly, violent inmates. Huge exhaust fans roar overhead, everyone shouts, and since the hard surfaces absorb no sound, the din is overwhelming.

I've been here long enough to develop a convict's sixth sense, and I feel the spark running near me before anything actually happens. My lower back tenses. I brace for a smack to my head or a knife in my ribs. Each moment in prison is a new test, and it's inevitable something terrible will happen to me, as it does sooner or later to every inmate. Is today the day I'll die, or kill, perhaps because some hairy brute wants me to be his fuck boy?

The cavernous room, except for the roaring fans, has become eerily silent. I try to see what's going down without appearing to look. Spider's rule - avoid eye contact.

"Who you lookin' at?"

I spin my head, but thankfully the question is not directed at me. At the table behind me, a new prisoner, referred to as a fish, as in 'fish in a barrel,' is surrounded by hostile, evil, laughing faces. He's too young, too small, too pale. His long hair is greasy and unruly. His eyes are wide open, like saucers, unfocused. He doesn't have a chance.

"You interested in somethin'?" The voice belongs to Norman Hicks, a man scarred and hardened by many years in prison, so muscled as to appear inhuman. Spider told me about Hicks, convicted of three brutal murders, and warned me to avoid him.

The fish had apparently made the beginner's understandable mistake of staring at Hicks, his tattoos, his bulging muscles, the scar across his face. Hicks doesn't like this, and he has clamped his huge hand on the boy's thin shoulder. He squeezes, little effort on his part, but pain and fear distort his victim's face. I repeat my life-sustaining mantra. 'Don't even think of helping. Do not engage. It's not your business.'

The boy is saved, for the moment, when a fight breaks out in the serving line. Who? Why? The who varies every day, but the why never changes. Too many violent men are crammed together and constantly getting in each other's way. Any slight, real or imagined, brings a predictable and necessary response. Not to respond only invites further escalation.

The drama unfolds in plain sight. One of the men has a shank. Two quick slashes and blood spurts. Just as quickly, the shank hits the ground and is kicked away. Three guards run to the injured inmate. "Who did this?"

"Don't know," the victim answers loudly so nearby inmates can hear. To be a snitch, even after you've been stabbed, is not smart. Refusing to tell, on the other hand, will bring respect and may even help avoid some future horror.

The guards take the bloody prisoner away. Are his wounds serious? Will he live or die? No one knows and no one cares. The inmate who stabbed him has taken a seat, indistinguishable to the guards who seem never to know what has happened in front of their eyes, and surely don't have the remotest clue as to what is coming next. An inmate porter swabs the blood from the floor, and the other inmates, me among them, resume our breakfast, chatting as if nothing has happened, since indeed, nothing has. Norman Hicks seems to have forgotten about the skinny fish.

As I leave the cafeteria, a guard approaches me. "You playin' this afternoon? Can you beat The Bank?" he asks. I walk away quickly, trying to make it clear I have not answered.

A Good Conviction 73

I took Mullin's advice and did not testify at the Grand Jury. I was indicted for felony murder, which is murder in the commission of a felony crime, the felony being the robbery.

Mullin was also right about the bail. I went with him to the hearing and the judge turned us down flat. Assistant District Attorney Roger Claiborne argued I had no roots in New York, and was therefore a serious flight risk. He was right. After eleven days on Rikers, if I had a chance to run, I would've taken it.

There was more bad news. Mullin had tried to interview Angel Martinez several times, but kept missing him. Finally, he was told Angel didn't work at the newsstand anymore. Mullin got Angel's phone number from his employer, but when he called, the automated message said the phone had been disconnected.

Violence erupted again within minutes after I got back to Rikers. It was mainly between the Bloods, which was the worst of the black gangs, and the Latin Kings, the largest Hispanic gang, but many others used the occasion to settle their own scores.

I saw one inmate doing push-ups. Someone stood over him, pulled him up by his hair, and slashed his face with a razor blade. Another prisoner was slashed in the visiting room in full view of his wife and child.

Cuts to the face were the favorite targets. Alejandro explained. A scar across the face will forever mark the victim and provide irrefutable proof of the ferocity of the attacker and his gang. Gang members referred to slashings of their fellow prisoners as "putting in work," and each gang demanded more and more. Every new gang member had to "blood in" to prove his worth.

The Ninja Turtles, as the inmates called them, stormed the jail repeatedly, swaggering in their black uniforms, military boots, black gloves, black caps, pants tucked into boots. The prisoners fought back. One stabbed an officer with a pen, and in turn every bone in his face was broken, along with three batons. Another officer's face was slashed with a sharpened chicken bone. Three inmates were killed by other inmates. One bled to death after waiting over an hour for medical attention. Another, insane with fear, hung himself by stringing his bedclothes to a ventilation shaft. Nobody ever said this one wasn't a real suicide.

Ultimately, the unending supply of batons, pepper spray and 50,000 volt stun shields prevailed. Or maybe the gangs' energy just petered out, or so many inmates were forced to wear burlap mittens there was no one left to wield a razor. Dozens of the worst troublemakers were taken to the Central Punitive Segregation Unit, known for some never explained reason as the "Bing," where they

74   Lewis M. Weinstein

were held in solitary confinement with the expectation that many years would soon be added to their prison sentences.

Alejandro had been among the leaders of the chaos, but somehow he avoided the "Bing" and he was actually among those who negotiated the "Sixth of June Peace," as it came to be known. Life on Rikers was restored to normal, which meant slashings were reduced to three or four a week. Nobody committed suicide for over a month. Fights still broke out regularly – over food, telephones, what to watch on television – but these now resulted in smashed heads and broken bones rather than "buck-fifty" slashings.

I cowered in my cell as much as I could, going out only to eat, slouching along like an old man. I didn't shower or shave, hoping my beard, long wild hair and offensive body odor would make me seem as crazy as I felt. Maybe it helped, I don't know. I did have some close calls, but I was not attacked.

What did happen, however, was I lost all hope. Living in constant fear of being beaten and slashed, I ate virtually nothing, lost weight, always had a splitting headache, and felt weaker every day. My mind was a muddle, incapable of constructive or organized thought. When Mullin came to discuss something during those days, I didn't comprehend what he was talking about and surely made no contribution to the development of my defense.

I received at least one letter a week from Tom, but I read his attempts to keep up my spirits as evidence of his ignorance. In short, I gave up. I expected to be tried and convicted, and then I would go "up."

My life was over.

Detective Robert Watson, early to the courthouse for an appearance on a drug arrest he had made, slipped into a back row seat to wait. A witness was on the stand, about to be cross-examined. The defense attorney looked like a dangerous and beautiful cat ready to pounce. Watson sat back to enjoy the show.

"Could you please explain for the jury how you happen to be here testifying today?" the attorney asked, ever so politely.

"I guess the prosecutor thought I could be helpful," was the smart aleck answer. Big mistake, thought Watson.

"Just out of the blue, was it, the prosecutor thought you could be helpful." She offered the witness a pleasant smile. "Where did this happen?"

"What do you mean?" the witness asked.

"Where were you when the prosecutor had the idea you could be helpful?"

"Uh, I was in prison."

"Which prison?"

"Attica."

"Why were you there?"

"Objection," said the prosecutor, a young man who looked like he was still in high school. "The witness's criminal record is not relevant here."

"Your honor, the witness's reasons for testifying are the most relevant aspect of his testimony," the defense attorney insisted.

"Overruled," said the judge, visibly amused by the little drama unfolding in front of him. "You may answer the question."

"I was convicted of a crime," said the witness, losing some of his arrogance. Watson expected the attorney to be sarcastic – of course you were convicted of a crime – but she just asked her next question straight up.

"What crime?"

"Robbery."

"With a weapon?"

"Yes."

"What kind of weapon?"

"A gun."

"What's your sentence?"

"Ten to fifteen."

"How much left to go?"

"I've been in for two years."

"You like it there, in Attica?"

"Are you nuts?" the witness exclaimed. The judge started to say something, but didn't.

"I'll take that for a no," said the attorney, her face void of expression. "How did the prosecutor come to know you had information about this case?"

"Some detectives came to visit me in prison. They asked if I knew anything."

"About what?"

"About my new cellmate, and whether he had said anything about a murder they were investigating."

"And had he? Said anything?"

The witness did not answer. The defense attorney moved a little closer to him. She spoke very softly. "Had he said anything to you before the detectives visited?"

Still there was no answer. Even the witness, dumb as he was, now understood what was happening. The judge intervened, "Answer the question."

"No."

"Your new cellmate hadn't said a single word about any murder?"

"No."

"But later he did?"

"Yes, later."

"How long had you been cellmates when the detectives visited you?

"Six days."

Watson suspected the prosecutor had better have some powerful other evidence, because when this defense attorney was done with this witness, his testimony would be useless.

On his way out to get a cup of coffee, he checked the court calendar and learned the attorney's name was Maureen Reilly. Later, he asked around the department and learned that Reilly's skills at cross-examination had been recognized. The word was "don't stretch the truth, or she'll skin you alive."

Kathleen Hennessey came to America in 1960, shortly after the death of her husband and an ocean passage which took all of her meager savings. With her nine year old daughter, she moved in with relatives in the Sunset Park section of Brooklyn. Daniel Reilly made his emigration eight years later. Taking a room down the street from the Henneseys on 47th Street, he noticed the now seventeen year old Dolores Hennessey on his very first night in the new world. Their courtship was discouraged by Kathleen, who wanted her daughter to go to college, unheard of for Irish girls at the time, but Kathleen was powerless against the youthful urges. Daniel and Dolores were soon married.

Maureen Reilly was born exactly nine months later, and she grew up going to the same Catholic elementary and high schools as her mother. Even as a little girl, Maureen wanted to do things her way, and this independent nature grew as she got older, putting her in constant conflict at the all-girl Sister Mary Margaret Academy. As the years went on, it was grandmother Kathleen, who Maureen called Nana, who often had the responsibility of trying to make peace.

For Maureen Reilly, who had spent many hours in Sunset Park staring at the Manhattan skyline and imagining what kind of life might be lived there, being at Marymount College in Manhattan was an exhilarating change from the insularity of her Brooklyn Irish neighborhood. Every day, emerging from the subway, she felt the thrust and throb of the great metropolis, and she vowed to explore it and make it hers.

Maureen gained two new passions during her college years. The first was running. That a pretty Irish girl would put on short pants and run in public was completely alien to her parents' thinking, so Maureen never told them. Nana, on the other hand, supported her from the start.

Her other new passion was politics. The young governor from Arkansas who was mounting a run for the Presidency lit a fire in her she found surprising. William Jefferson Clinton came to Manhattan in the spring of 1990, when Maureen was a college sophomore. When Clinton worked a rope line and shook hands with Maureen, he looked her in the eyes like she was the only person on earth. She was smitten, and immediately signed up to work on his campaign.

Soon after, Maureen decided she wanted to be a criminal defense attorney. Nana especially encouraged her to follow her dream. Maureen was accepted to both Fordham and NYU, and chose NYU. The summer of 1992, before she started law school, was devoted to the presidential campaign. By the time Clinton's stirring victory in November finally gave her the time to concentrate on her law courses, she was horribly behind, and almost flunked out. Six months of near round-the-clock effort brought her back into good academic standing.

There was no better place to learn the ins and outs of criminal defense than the Manhattan DA's office run by the legendary Howard Markman. Maureen applied in the spring of 1995, one of sixteen hundred applicants for forty openings. Like the others who survived the early screening process, she was interviewed by Markman himself. She was impressed, and apparently so was he. She got the job.

Suzanne Dixon, one of Maureen's new friends in the DA's office, invited her to become the fourth occupant of a fourth floor walkup apartment only fifteen minutes walk from the DA's office. She loved living "with the girls" and being downtown gave her a chance to explore aspects of Manhattan she might not otherwise have found.

She went to all the museums, checking them off her list, and then invited Nana to come with her on return visits to the ones she came to love, especially the Metropolitan Museum of Art on Fifth Avenue. She took Nana to Broadway shows, late afternoon meals in Greenwich Village, shopping in Soho, to Rockefeller Center at Christmas time, to mass at St. Patrick's, and for walks in Central Park. She had a few boy friends, but only one lover, and that ended rather abruptly when the young man suddenly became engaged to a wealthy socialite.

As the new century was about to dawn, Maureen decided to end her apprenticeship as a prosecutor and begin her chosen career as a criminal defense attorney. The problem was she couldn't afford to take the risk entailed in opening her own office. Nana, as always, encouraged her to go for it. "Follow your heart," she said. "There will be a way."

And there was. Maureen knew an established criminal attorney named Salvatore DiCerbo, who had an office near the Manhattan courthouse and was looking to sublet space while sharing his secretarial and other services on an as-needed basis. She gave notice personally to DA Markman, thanking him for an unsurpassable experience. Markman said he was sorry to see her go but wished her well.

Her first clients were little guys in the drug scene, cases which came into DiCerbo's office and were handed off to her. Maureen achieved a string of lighter than expected sentences, and even a few acquittals, and word began to spread. She moved up the food chain to defend mid-level drug dealers, initially together with DiCerbo and then by herself. She took on assault and several manslaughter cases. She attracted clients of her own and learned the first law of criminal defense - get paid a lot, get it in cash, and get it all up front.

Maureen also became an active participant in the Innocence Project at the Benjamin N. Cardozo School of Law at Yeshiva University, founded by Barry Scheck and Peter Neufeld in 1992. This pro bono work gave her first hand knowledge of how badly the criminal justice system could sometimes function, and made her a dedicated proponent of reforms to prevent wrongful convictions and the death penalty.

Maureen Reilly's reputation had grown considerably by the time Detective Bob Watson first saw her in action.

"Josh, is that you?"

I stared at the beautiful young woman facing me across the visitor's table. She wore an elegant white jacket, skin tight jeans, a black sweater with a multi-colored scarf, and a black, little boy floppy cap. I had no idea who she was, but in the presence of her beauty, I became acutely conscious of the fact I had not showered or shaved in weeks. My beard and scraggly hair, and the smell I had gotten used to, suddenly became offensive and embarrassing.

"Josh, it's Darlene," she said.

I looked at her but still registered nothing. A tear formed in her eye, and her sadness destroyed the façade I had constructed around myself. Without exactly knowing why, I felt like crying along with her.

"You are one fuckin' mess," she said, and, suddenly we were both laughing.

"Thank you," I said. "Do I know you?"

"The Broadway Big Apple. Your first night in New York."

Recognition and confusion flooded through me. Two hookers, the internet café. "I remember now," I said. "What are you doing here?"

"I came to see you. The question is what you're doing here."

"I'm accused of murder. I'm being held without bail for trial."

"I read it in the paper. But that's not what I meant. How come you're accused? You didn't do it."

"You think I didn't do it?"

"Of course you didn't. You couldn't do anything like what they said. You know," she went on, "people in my business are good judges of character. We've got to be to survive. You're no killer. There's no way you could've done anything to hurt a frail old lady."

"Thank you," I said.

I hadn't thought about Darlene in the three weeks since I was arrested. Before that, at the hotel and when I was telling Tom and Barb about her, she was just a hooker. Now I looked at her with different eyes. She had taken the trouble to come all the way out to Rikers, to visit someone she barely knew. I wasn't sure what to think, except I was overwhelmed with gratitude.

"What can I do to help?" Darlene asked. The question had been asked in a serious, almost somber manner. Then she started to laugh, first a small laugh, but it grew into a loud uncontrollable guffaw.

"What's so funny?" I asked.

"It's not funny. I'm sorry. But I was just thinking you don't much look like a serious law student. You ever goin' to shave again? A shower wouldn't be a bad idea either. Maybe next time I visit, you can clean up a little for a girl?"

"You're going to come back?" I asked, hanging onto the incredible concept she was really going to be my friend. Somewhere, deep in the recesses of my mind, I was also reacting to being identified as a law student.

"So, are you goin' to shave?" Darlene asked with a lascivious smile.

One night we were treated to a TV special about Rikers. I heard loud hooting around the television and joined the crowd. One of the Rikers' many Chiefs was describing the use of electronic stun shields.

"The officer has the ability to burst the trigger that sends off 50,000 volts of electricity for six seconds, which stuns the inmate."

A captain flicked a switch, and bright blue sparks of electricity shot across the quarter-inch-thick piece of plastic, accompanied by a loud crackling sound. The chief explained, "We use it for cell extractions. The device incapacitates the inmate for 30 seconds. It gives the officers the ability to go in, put the handcuffs on the inmate, and take him out. The inmate is not injured."

"Fuck we're not!"

"Let the pig stick that thing on his balls and say he's not injured."

"We've purchased ninety shields at a cost of $545 each. It's been an extremely productive investment. As you know, Corrections Officers at Rikers do not carry guns, so the shields sort of evens the playing field."

The perky announcer asked, "You recently went through a period of considerable violence on Rikers. How do things stand now?"

"We had a bad time, but order has been restored, and we've given a pretty clear message we're not going to tolerate criminal activity inside our facility, just like you don't tolerate it on the outside."

The television screen displayed a graphic. *And this get-tough policy appears to be working. Last year there were just 70 inmate slashings and stabbings - a dramatic drop compared to the more than 1,000 such incidents a decade ago.*

Imagine, I thought, doing the calculation, how proud they are at having slightly less than one and a half slashings a week.

"I can't believe how different you are in just a few weeks."

Tom Kaplan was back on Rikers. I knew how difficult it was for him to get there, how much it cost. He probably lost work, too. But whenever I started to express my appreciation, Tom would say it was nothing, that I would do the same for him, and what are friends for. Besides, he proudly told me, I figured out the trains, and I can get here and back to Baltimore in the same day.

"I'm different?"

"You look jumpy. You've lost weight."

"I'm terrified here. There's violence, all around, all the time. Guys get hit or slashed walking down a hall, having breakfast, in the shower. I'm always watching my back, ready to defend myself. You can't trust anybody."

"Not even your cellmate?"

"Alejandro's all right, I guess. But he's one of the most violent and dangerous people here. That's good for me, unless some day he turns on me, which could certainly happen."

"The guys want you to know they're all rooting for you. M.J. and Sean and I had dinner the other night." He stopped abruptly. "I'm sorry. I wasn't going to tell you we were out to eat, since it's so out of the question for you here."

"That's funny, Tom. Remember when I was in Baltimore, and I didn't stay on Saturday."

"We were all disappointed."

"I was feeling so excited about New York and everything, and you and Barb were ... well, I didn't want to seem like I was bragging about something you couldn't do. Things sure have changed since then."

The pain on Tom's face reflected my own.

"I don't know if I'm going to make it," I said. "I feel as if I could get killed any day. I know I didn't do anything wrong and I don't belong here. I want to lash out and hurt people. But if I give in to those feelings, it'll be much worse. I'll be a marked man, a target. It's better not to stand out in any way."

Suddenly, in the midst of this self-pitying diatribe, I smiled. Tom was confused, like what could possibly make me happy.

"I had a visitor on Monday," I said. "One of the hookers from the hotel."

"Which one?" Tom asked with no hesitation.

"You looked, didn't you?"

Tom hung his head, embarrassed to admit he had gone to their web site.

"It was Darlene."

"Oh yeah," Tom said, rolling his eyes.

"I didn't even recognize her at first. Then she made me laugh, and we had an almost normal conversation. She made me promise to shave before she comes back."

"She's coming back?"

"Next Monday, she said. It's really nice of her, don't you think?"

NINE

"Tell me about your life before you came to New York."

Teri Scanlon, the *Daily News* reporter, had approached Larry Mullin and sought his permission to interview me. Mullin initially refused, but he changed his mind after learning she had already interviewed Assistant DA Roger Claiborne. Perhaps, Mullin told me, we can learn something. I think his decision was a reflection of how desperate our situation really was.

Scanlon appeared to be in her mid-thirties, a little chubby, very earnest-looking, her face dominated by old fashioned horn rimmed glasses. She was wearing a loose-fitting sweater over a dark pleated skirt. Who could know what she would write or if we should trust her. But the decision had been made, so I told about my childhood in Baltimore, sports in high school, my friends, UMBC, my parents.

"When did you come to New York?"

"Just about a month ago," I said, still bewildered at how much my life had changed in such a short time. "I'm supposed to begin NYU Law School in the fall and I came up for the summer."

"Do you want to talk about the night Mrs. Cooke was attacked?"

Mullin nodded his permission, and I told her about going to John's Pizza and the elderly lady who slipped off the curb.

"Why do the police think you did it?"

"The police say my fingerprints were on her pocketbook, and some of her blood was on my shirt. It must have happened when I helped her up."

"The ADA believes you followed her and attacked her in the park. Can you prove differently?"

"It's always hard to prove something didn't happen, but we're going to try," Mullin said.

"Did you need the money?" Teri asked.

"No," I answered. "I had enough set aside for the three years of law school. My mother died earlier this year and I sold her house. There's also my father's life insurance. He died some years ago, but Mom would never spend a penny. She insisted it should be used for my schooling. And I also had a good summer job."

"So you're just the victim of being in the wrong place at the wrong time and looking like whoever the real killer is? That's your position?"

"It's not my position, it's the truth."

"The ADA says you were seen with the victim's pocketbook in a subway station in Brooklyn," Scanlon said.

"He's wrong," I said, raising my voice. "I've never been in Brooklyn in my life."

"But the subway attendant said she saw you."

"She saw somebody else," Mullin said. "Maybe somebody who looked like Josh, but not him."

"After I ate at John's, I went home. But I stopped first at a newsstand. The newsstand guy could say I was with him, at just the time the murder was committed, but he's disappeared."

"I've tried to find him, but he's gone," Mullin said.

"What's his name?" Scanlon asked. She wrote in her spiral notebook, and when she was done, she looked up. "Can you tell me what's going through your mind?" She asked in a gentle way, as if she really cared. She even put her pad down.

"The last week in May was a terrific time for me. I got a job. I got an apartment. I was living in Greenwich Village. How great is that." I smiled and she smiled back.

"I was looking forward to a whole summer of fun in New York, lots of Yankee games, then law school. I felt great. Then it all fell apart ..."

Scanlon waited while I gathered myself. "I wake up in the middle of the night and I don't know where I am. I'm afraid every minute. I'm surrounded by killers. Guys have knives and razors. People get slashed all the time. And raped. I can't even think about what goes on here in a rational way. I actually think I'm going crazy."

I had nothing more to say and Scanlon had no more questions. We looked at each other for a long moment, and soon after, she and Mullin stood to leave.

"I left some things for you," Mullin said. "They wouldn't let me bring anything in here, but they said you'll get everything later today. It's stuff from your apartment ... clothes ... a photo of your parents."

At 7:15 am, just minutes after he had arrived at his 80 Centre Street office, Roger Claiborne saw the *Daily News* article by Teri Scanlon his secretary had carefully laid out for him. The headline jumped right at him.

Did They Get the Right Guy?

Helen had highlighted the important parts in the middle of the article ...

> But there may be some holes in the prosecutor's case. For one thing, there's no apparent motive. Blake was planning to begin NYU Law School this fall and he had sufficient funds set aside to pay his school and living expenses for the entire three years. Why would anyone risk such a promising future to steal $100 from an elderly lady, especially in Central Park with so many potential witnesses around?
>
> There's also a missing witness. Blake says a newsstand guy named Angel Martinez can give him a solid alibi for the exact time of the murder, but Angel is nowhere to be found. Angel, if you're out there, give a call.

And then the final dagger ...

> Unless ADA Roger Claiborne can prove, beyond a reasonable doubt, that Blake is lying, he and the NYPD may end up with egg on their face. And, if they arrested the wrong guy, who is the right guy, and where is he now?

Claiborne angrily threw the newspaper across his cluttered desk, knocking a stack of papers to the floor. He grabbed his phone and rapidly punched in the number of his best friend in the Manhattan DA's office.

"That miserable bitch!" he began, as soon as George Henson picked up.

"Calm down," Henson said. "I'll be right over."

Helen returned with Roger's first cup of coffee.

"Is this a peace offering?" Claiborne growled.

"Don't kill the messenger," Helen said. "I thought you should see it before the calls start." She retrieved the fallen files, carefully recreating the precarious perch on the desk, and was already beating a second strategic retreat to the outer office when Henson arrived. Henson had joined the DA's Office in 1988, a year after Claiborne, and Roger had helped him get oriented. Henson's appearance had an immediate calming effect on Roger.

"Did you read ...," Claiborne asked.

"Of course," Henson said. "Everybody read it."

"Well, that makes me feel better."

"It's not as bad as you're making it. It was on page twenty-three, with a small headline. Something to wrap the fish in tomorrow, unless you do something stupid."

"Like call a press conference."

"That would be near the top of my stupid list."

"How do you think the Mayor will react?"

"Depends on what you do. If I were you, I'd get word to him as soon as possible. Before he calls Markman. Reassure him your case is solid. Tell him this'll be water off your back. Not a worry in the world. No need to respond. The story will die."

"Good advice."

"Your case *is* solid, isn't it? No surprises out there?"

"It's rock solid," Roger said, but he was thinking of Detective Watson's warning and feeling more than a twinge of guilt at his lie to Henson. I'm building a trap for myself, he thought, even as he added, "No surprises."

Henson left and Roger called his boss, Sam Monti, the Chief of Trial Bureau 20.

"Sam, this is about the Blake case and the article in the *Daily News* today."

"Is there a problem, Roger?" Monti asked. "You seemed quite confident at our last staff meeting."

"No problem," Claiborne said. "I'm just wondering if we should communicate to the DA and the Mayor." Monti patched in the Manhattan DA, Harold Markman, who agreed they should call Mayor Gardino. The fact that the mayor took the call immediately was disquieting to Claiborne.

"Okay, guys," said Mayor Gardino after Claiborne briefly overviewed his case against Joshua Blake. "I agree. No response. If you tell me you've got everything under control, that's good enough for me. That's what I'll say if I'm asked." The Mayor paused, and added softly, "Just don't blow it." Claiborne felt another spike of fear. He was in big trouble and he knew it.

The intercom rang as soon as Roger put the phone down. "It's your sister Gwendolyn."

"Hi, Rog," came the always bright and cheerful voice.

"How are you, Gwen? Read the paper?"

"I called to offer moral support. You okay?"

"Thanks, but the reporter is way out of line. This case is a lock. Blake did it, and I'm going to nail him."

"That's great to hear, Rog. You know we're here for you if you need us."

Claiborne placed the phone down with a feigned gentleness, fiercely willing himself not to slam it with all of his might. He knew what Gwendolyn's call was really all about. His sister was giving him the family's message. Don't embarrass us, Roger, like you've been doing all of your miserable life!

Roger Claiborne was a product of Connecticut's gold coast in the southwest corner of the state, where the mansions were close enough to New York to permit easy rail commuting. His family had lived in Westport for five generations, and their New England roots predated the revolution. They summered on Martha's Vineyard, where they were prominent at the Yacht Club, and traveled frequently to Europe. Roger had sailed since he received his first boat on his fifteenth birthday. He was a good sailor, but never quite good enough to make a serious challenge at the annual regatta sponsored by the Edgartown Yacht Club.

Roger's father Alexander was a prominent neurosurgeon, on the staff at the Yale-New Haven Medical Center and at New York Hospital. Older brother Nicholas had followed his father's footsteps to Harvard Medical School and then joined him on the staff of New York Hospital. Nicholas had married a prominent socialite and lived in a spectacular Park Avenue apartment in the 70s. His sister Gwendolyn did her part by marrying an obscenely wealthy bond trader and living in one of the great old mansions of nearby Greenwich, Connecticut. Roger's mother Victoria had recently been elected to the Board of MOMA, the Museum of Modern Art. All members of the family, except Roger, had been prominently featured in the society pages of the New York Times.

When Roger graduated from Columbia Law School in 1987, there had been no offers from white shoe law firms, and Roger had taken the job with the Manhattan DA to camouflage yet another major disappointment. Offers to go into private practice on the defense side never materialized, and after sixteen years, his career as an ADA was also going nowhere. NYPD detectives divided all cases into easy ones, which they called "grounders," and hard ones, which they called "mysteries." Roger was assigned only grounders. No one in the DA's office trusted him with anything difficult.

With a sizable trust fund to supplement his salary, Roger lived alone on the Upper East Side, in a doorman cooperative his family's connections had secured for him. His life was comfortable and boring. Every day, he rode the Lexington Avenue subway downtown to Centre Street. He went to concerts and the ballet at Lincoln Center, and to Thursday night mass at St. Bartholomew's Episcopal Church on Park Avenue. He was a staunch Republican, thoroughly repulsed by the liberal Democratic politics which dominated New York City. Never, in all his years in the City, had he ventured to Greenwich Village, Soho, or Yankee Stadium.

Claiborne had been married once, a convenience for both parties. When it ended in divorce after three years, there had not been enough passion on either side to fight over anything, and it had probably been one of the least contentious settlements in the history of Manhattan's stormy matrimonial jurisprudence. There were no children. After the divorce, he had dated only sporadically, almost never leading to sex. He sometimes wondered whether his sexual proclivities were ambiguous, and this contributed to his declining self-esteem.

With it all, however, Roger Claiborne still dreamed, and there were moments when he envisioned how dramatic his life would become if he could become a high profile crime-fighter. Rudy Giuliani had risen from prosecutor to political star and Claiborne thought, even if no one else could have imagined it, why not me? The Joshua Blake case was perhaps his last ticket to that life.

The lulling sounds of Andras Schiff playing Felix Mendelssohn's *Songs Without Words* were not working. The elegant pre-war apartment, high ceilings, picture windows, fireplace, and sixteenth floor terrace with a spectacular view of the East River, offered no relief from the nagging sensation he was on the verge of a huge disaster.

It was an incredible piece of luck he even got the Blake case. He knew he had not been Sam Monti's first choice. Backus had been on vacation, Mariano was tied up with a long trial, and Roger was the only senior ADA available for a Sunday morning arraignment. He suspected he had kept the case only because of his family's influence. It couldn't have been an accident when Sam Monti showed up at one of Gwendolyn's fancy parties.

Now he had told Monti, Markman, and the Mayor the case was a lock. But Roger knew differently, and so did Detective Watson.

Damn Watson. Soon after their conversation, the case had moved, as did all homicides, to one of the city's specialized homicide units, in this case, Manhattan North Homicide. Although Watson was still nominally the detective in charge, Claiborne wasn't asking for any more investigation, so there was no activity. Watson, he was sure, was on to other matters and would not be poking around in the case.

But this didn't change the fact the detective was right. There were holes in the case. Larry Mullin, Blake's attorney, might not be impressive to look at, but he was a good enough lawyer to make a decent reasonable doubt argument. I'm going to lose this case, Claiborne forced himself to admit, and Teri Scanlon will make sure the whole world knows how Roger Claiborne fucked up again.

He cringed when the next CD began and the morbid strains of Mozart's *Requiem Mass* filled the room.

TEN

Wandering without any destination consciously in mind, Tony Marone found himself outside the Holy Cross Catholic Church in Brooklyn where his mother had taken him as a little boy. It had been years since he had been in any church. He stared at the imposing structure for several minutes, wondering why he was there, and slowly climbed up the steps.

He sat in the next to last pew. After a long time alone with his thoughts, a heavy set priest walked down the aisle and sat next to him. Tony overcame his instinct to bolt. He knew he needed that priest.

"Can I help you?"

"What makes you think I need help?"

"People usually come here when they want help of some kind. Maybe just to talk." The priest sat quietly and Tony was calmed by his presence.

"I guess that's why I'm here," Tony said softly, looking down. "Suppose I was to tell you something could get me in big trouble. Would you keep it to yourself?" He looked up to gauge the priest's response.

"If that's how you want it? Do you want to confess?"

"Confess? Shit no. I don't want to tell nobody but you."

"I didn't mean tell anyone else. I meant for you to go into the confessional box and tell me your sins and ask God for forgiveness. Are you a Catholic?"

"I guess I'm Catholic. At least I used to be. But I don't want to confess. I just want to talk."

"Okay."

"Will you still keep it secret? Just between you and me?"

"If that's what you want."

Tony gathered his courage. He looked away from the priest, his voice barely a whisper. "You know about the guy who got arrested for killing the old lady? It was in the paper again yesterday."

"The young man who killed the woman in Central Park?"

"Yes."

It took all of Tony's will power, but he managed to look straight at the priest, right into his eyes. It was probably the finest moment of Anthony Marone's life. "That kid didn't do it," Tony whispered. "It was me." Then the words came in a rush. "When I grabbed for her bag, she fought me a little, and she fell. Maybe I

Lewis M. Weinstein

pushed her, but not on purpose. She must have hit her head or something. I didn't mean for her to die."

"You need to tell the police," the priest said.

"No way," Tony said. He jumped up and ran out the door.

The overweight priest tried to follow, but he was much too slow. He stood at the church door and watched the boy disappear around the corner. He came back to the pew and sat down, catching his breath and pondering what he should do.

It wasn't a confession, but he had promised to keep it secret, and this was a promise not taken lightly by the Catholic Church. He didn't know the young man's name, so what could he tell anyone anyway? He hoped the boy would come forward on his own, although he admitted to himself it was unlikely.

In the end, he did what priests are trained to do. He prayed.

"Who is this?" Maureen Reilly asked.

Bob Watson repeated his name.

"I heard your name," Reilly said. "But who are you? Do I know you?"

"I'm a detective at the Central Park Precinct. I saw you in court a week or so ago. I'd like to get to know you, and I wondered if you'd have a cup of coffee with me."

"Does this have to do with a case? Do I represent someone you arrested?"

"Not that I know. I just wanted to meet you."

"That's very nice, detective, but I don't date police officers."

"There's always a first time."

"Maybe so, but not this time."

By the time Bob Watson had graduated from Montclair High School in June of 1987, he had made a name for himself as an athlete, and unlike most of his classmates, he had also made a career decision. Bob Watson wanted to be a cop. And not just any cop. He wanted to be a homicide detective in New York City. He practically inhaled everything written about the NYPD. In Montclair, cops were friends; across the river, they were heroes.

Al Pacino's stirring portrayal of Frank Serpico was a major influence on Watson's career choice. Many NYPD officers regarded Serpico as a troublemaker who had caused more harm than good, but for others, and for Watson two decades later, Serpico was the honest cop who had struggled against all odds and whose efforts had led to more productive reform than probably anyone else in the history of the NYPD. Serpico's story evoked in Watson an almost messianic desire to help a great institution achieve its noble potential. He felt about the NYPD the way many of his Irish friends felt about Notre Dame football.

Watson's parents were pleased with his commitment to doing good in the world but not so pleased at the venue in which he chose to do it. "You're one person, Bob," his father had said. "What can one person do to change the biggest police department in the world?"

"Then why did you name me after Bobby Kennedy and Martin Luther King?" Robert Martin Watson asked.

At John Jay College, Watson received a B.S. in Criminal Justice. He discovered nearby Central Park and ran two or three times per week, usually after classes and before taking the train back to Montclair. He also discovered opera. Serpico had loved the opera, so Watson tried it. He was thrilled by Puccini's *La Boheme*. The Met was only a few blocks from John Jay, so he could go over at the last minute, get standing room tickets, and eventually find a seat. He went several times each season.

Watson scored high on the civil service test and in the summer of 1991, he joined several hundred other recruits at the New York Police Academy on 20th Street in Manhattan. He graduated high in his class and his first assignment was Brooklyn's Seventy-fifth Precinct, one of the City's major "action" precincts. For eleven years, the six square miles of bodegas, take-out restaurants, burned out buildings, and record-breaking homicide, felony and drug arrests of the 7-5 was Watson's domain.

He dated widely and had two serious relationships, but both had ended short of marriage. Police work required a very special sort of companion, and from the examples of his fellow officers, not many had found a satisfying situation. Watson had chosen to stay single rather than settle, but he was feeling the pressure of that decision with each passing year.

Watson's goal was always to become a detective. He took every criminal investigation course the department offered and volunteered to work undercover whenever the opportunity arose. In July 1998, he was rewarded with his gold shield, and the next four years as a detective in the 7-5 were everything he had ever wanted. He built a solid reputation as a quality detective.

Then came an unexplained and disturbing transfer, and the worst period of Watson's police career. Watson was suddenly and with no explanation ripped away from his friends and from the intense police work he loved, and assigned to the "white glove" Central Park Precinct. He was devastated and furious. What had he done to deserve this? He saw himself thwarted in a no-action precinct, working beneath his potential, unchallenged, his career goals blocked. Paranoia and conspiracy theories, always in plentiful supply in the NYPD, plagued him.

Watson sulked in the CPP. The rumor spread he had been transferred because he was a screw-up, and his attitude and performance did nothing to contradict that conclusion. He didn't like his new commander, and he made no friends on the squad. His partner barely spoke to him.

"Who the fuck do you think you are?"

This was not the greeting Watson craved or expected from his former colleagues at the Seventy-fifth Precinct. He had been looking forward to the 7-5's Fourth of July barbeque, held each year in Prospect Park in Brooklyn.

Christine Parker, a detective he had worked with for years, did not let up. "You think this whole department exists to make you happy? So you got a bad transfer. It happens all the time. You got lemons? Make lemonade."

"It's nice to see you too, Christine," Watson said.

Several other officers joined them, and they all kept up the refrain. Obviously the 7-5 had received derogatory feedback from the Central Park Precinct.

"You're making us look bad."

"They think you're a loser who got dumped on them."

After another few minutes of everyone beating on him, a different perspective emerged.

"Did you ever think your transfer might be a test?" said Parker.

"What do you mean?" Watson asked.

"The word is Kerrigan was interested in you, and that he was behind your transfer." Lieutenant Brian Kerrigan was the head of the Manhattan North Homicide squad. Watson had met him several times, but had never had any deep interaction. MNH, of course, had been his career goal since he entered the department, but he had no inkling Kerrigan had his eyes on him.

"Where ... ?" Watson started to ask.

"Never mind where," said Parker. "But think about it. It would take real juice to get you out of the 7-5 and out of Brooklyn. You used to be a pretty good cop. You think the 7-5 lets the A-team go so easy?"

"Kerrigan," Watson said, awestruck. "A test?"

"And one you're failing royally," said Parker. "You better get your shit together before it's too late."

For the rest of the afternoon, it was softball, hot dogs, beer and police chatter, but nothing more about Central Park Precinct or Kerrigan. Watson enjoyed being with his friends, but as the afternoon blended into evening, he was unusually quiet and thoughtful.

When Detective Watson returned to work the next day, it didn't take long for the Central Park Precinct to know it finally had the detective they had expected seven months before.

Alejandro approached me in the weight room. Two weeks of lifting every day had already added noticeable bulk. My thinking was, the stronger I became, the better I could defend myself. And, I wanted to look good for Darlene.

"Do you know about Island Academy?" Alejandro asked.

"I've seen the posters."

"Some of our guys signed up, you know, to learn how to read better."

"Good."

"But they're havin' trouble. Could you help them?"

"Be a tutor?"

"Yeah, like that."

"Sure."

"Good. Let's go."

"Now?" I asked.

"This is Rikers, man. People come and go every day. People die here. You got to strike when the iron is hot."

I followed Alejandro to a corner of the big day room where four young men looked up expectantly.

"Listen up, guys," Alejandro announced. "Josh here is a college grad, and he's goin' to help you with your reading." He introduced me to Hector, Luis, Tonio, and Esteban.

"Tell me about your class," I said.

"What about it?" asked Hector, who looked to be the oldest.

"Where is it? When is it? How many students? Who's the teacher?"

"You goin' to teach us, or you goin' to ask a lot a questions?" came from Esteban, a skinny guy standing behind the others.

Alejandro smiled, waiting to see how I would handle the challenge.

"I'm here to help you," I said, also smiling. "Do you want me to help you?"

Nobody said anything, so I waited, perhaps taking a lesson from the way Detective Watson had questioned me at the Central Park Precinct station. Eventually, Hector got the point and answered. "We meet every Tuesday and Thursday morning. There's a classroom in the Kross Center, right next to the methadone detox unit. There's about twelve guys, but everybody doesn't come every day. The teacher's name's Teresa."

"Do you have books?"

"No. We have papers," said Tonio. He handed me several rumpled sheets.

"Better," Darlene said. "Oh, yes, much better!" She looked me over carefully, eyeing my clean shaven face and recently showered body.

"I have incentive. It's not every day I get a visit from a hot lady."

"You never said anything like that when we didn't have this table between us." She sighed dramatically. "Lord knows I tried."

"Maybe I should have," I answered with a nod and raised eyebrows. It's hard to convey how much this conversation meant to me, or how much I suddenly regarded flirting with a hooker as the most normal part of my life.

"Have things improved at all?" she asked.

"Actually, I'm getting along. I have a new job. I'm teaching a class two days each week."

"Nuclear physics?"

"Reading. Alejandro set it up."

"Tell me."

"It's a challenge. These guys have had a tougher life than I could ever have imagined. They've been shot and stabbed. Luis was tied up and thrown out of a window. Esteban saw his friend's family murdered. Their mothers were addicts. Never knew their fathers. Learning to read was never a priority."

"It's hard to rise above such a beginning. Why do they want to read now?"

"They want to make a real life, after they get out of prison. If they can't read, they can't get a job. I think it would also be good if they could write about their experiences. They have a lot of buried emotion always getting in their way. Writing about it could let them understand it and deal with it. Anyway, that's my idea."

"Josh, it's great you're helping these guys. It's so hard for them to ever get a decent job, make a decent life for themselves." A big smile came over her face. "Speaking of which, I'm now a college girl."

"Wow! Where?"

"I'm taking a couple of courses at City College of New York, and if I do well, I'm hoping to enroll as a fulltime student at Baruch College."

"What courses?"

"Modern American Novels and Introduction to Politics."

"Fantastic! Baruch ... interesting. You're already a good businesswoman."

"I'll put it on my resume," she said. "Hooker with a degree. Where will that go on the web site?"

I didn't want to think about her web site, or the clients it attracted, so I changed the topic. "Alejandro told me once he wanted to go to college, but he hasn't mentioned it again."

"Maybe you could bring it up. Encourage him."

"I think he's sort of afraid to even discuss it."

"Sounds too huge for him?" Darlene asked. "Sets up disappointment if he talks about something he doesn't think he can do?"

"Maybe," I said, impressed at Darlene's insights.

Darlene thought for a moment. "You could let him know it's okay to dream, even in here."

"I'll try to find a way to bring it up," I said, but actually I was leery about raising the topic again, given Alejandro's previous reaction.

"Are you, uh ..., still working?" I asked.

"Got to pay the bills. And now, tuition."

"Be careful."

"Thank you," Darlene said, a big smile lighting up her face. "Nobody much says things like that to me."

"You've learned to take care of yourself and plan a future. People here don't believe it's possible. One kid told me the other day he suffers from a terminal disorder called social stupidity. But he's not stupid. Far from it. He just doesn't see a way."

"They don't think they deserve success," Darlene said.

"Exactly. It's tragic."

"How's your case going? I saw the article in the paper. It looks like someone believes you."

"Teri Scanlon wrote a nice article. But nothing changed."

"Don't give up. Something good will happen."

I didn't say anything for awhile. Actually, I was thinking probably nothing good was going to happen, and that talking with Darlene across a table was about as good as it was going to get.

Lewis M. Weinstein

"Do you want to tell me what it's like here?" Darlene asked.

"That'll cheer me up?"

"You're not going to get cheered up until you get out of here. But maybe talking about life here will help you deal with it."

"There's not much to talk about."

"You expect me to believe that? You could write a book about what goes on here."

"There's an idea. Do you think anybody would be interested in how to get an extra two minutes of hot water when you take a shower, or about the ecology of the roaches and rats who live with us, or maybe about the terrific work opportunities. My job is washing towels."

"Sounds fascinating."

"Actually, there's a lot more going on in the laundry than you would think. Like everything else here, it's a racket."

Darlene did look interested so I continued, "Nobody cares about towels. That's why I got the job. But the guys who do the clothes have a whole thing going. They steal things, set them aside, and then sell them. Sometimes back to the original owner. You could end up buying your own shirt for a pack of cigarettes."

"You're kidding me. The guards let this go on?"

"The guards don't care. Maybe they're in on it, I don't know."

"See. There's a story there somewhere."

"Religion," I said.

"Religion?"

"More chapters of the story. It's comes at you from everywhere. Islam, especially. There's a very serious effort going on to convert black prisoners to Islam. It's a very organized recruiting drive."

"Al Qaeda?"

"I don't know ... could be."

"Do they get a lot of converts?"

"I think they do."

Darlene was suddenly serious again. "Are you in danger here?" she asked.

"All the time. Being with Alejandro is a help. He's a real power here. But even so ..."

"Is there sexual pressure? Rape?"

"All the time. Strong guys force weak guys to be their sex slaves. Then they rent their slaves to others."

Darlene shuddered. "You ...?"

"I'm strong, and I'm with the Hispanics. So far, I'm okay."

The look of distress on Darlene's face was interrupted by the buzzer signaling the end of the visiting hour. We stood, she leaned across for the one quick kiss permitted, and she was gone. I'm not sure discussing my life on Rikers had made me feel any better, but I was looking forward to Darlene's next visit with a feeling I found quite surprising.

Larry Mullin was trying to convince the court that evidence of Mrs. Cooke's blood found on my shirt should not be allowed to be introduced at trial since the shirt was obtained improperly by the police. A hearing on his suppression motion had been scheduled and Mullin came out to Rikers to discuss it with me. I reviewed what had happened that day in my apartment, and he prepared me for the questions he would ask and what he thought ADA Claiborne would ask on cross-examination. Mullin also updated me on what else was happening with my case.

"I still haven't been able to find Angel Martinez," he said. "He doesn't work at the newsstand anymore, and nobody seems to know where he is. His phone was disconnected and there's no new listing anywhere."

"The police don't know where to find him?"

"They say not," Mullin said. "I got Angel's address from somebody at Manhattan Homicide and went there. Nobody knew him, or if they did, they weren't talking. That reminds me to ask again for the detective's report. We should have all the discovery by now, but we don't."

"What's discovery?"

"The prosecutor is required by law to give us all the evidence and reports obtained or prepared by the police or anyone else during the course of the investigation. That's called discovery. We have some of it, but some key reports are missing, I don't know why. Claiborne keeps saying he'll send it, but it never comes. I'll keep after him." Mullin paused. "Actually," he said, "it's been long enough. I'm going to bring a motion to compel delivery."

"Detective Graziano, were you in Joshua Blake's apartment on the night of May 31, 2003?"

We were in court for the suppression hearing. The trial had been assigned to a judge named Phyllis Berman, and she would also handle any preliminary motions and hearings. Larry Mullin was representing me and Assistant District Attorney Roger Claiborne represented the People. It was a public hearing, and I noticed Teri Scanlon in the spectator section. She gave a little wave.

"Yes, sir," Graziano replied.

"Can you tell us why you were there?" Mullin asked.

98   Lewis M. Weinstein

"We were hoping to gain information regarding the attack on Mrs. Sarah Cooke in Central Park." Graziano had a clipped way of speaking that many cops have, overly precise and a little pompous.

"You're referring to the attack on Thursday, May 29, 2003, two days earlier?"

"Yes."

"What led you to go to Mr. Blake's apartment?" Mullin asked.

"We thought he might have information about the attack."

"Why?"

"He was in the area on Thursday night."

"How did you know he was there?"

Detective Graziano explained how the police had organized a canvass of the neighborhood and learned about my purchase at the Disney Store.

"Did you go to the homes of everyone who made a purchase in the neighborhood on Thursday night? Or did something else lead you to Mr. Blake?"

"Mr. Blake's fingerprints were on the victim's pocketbook."

"So Mr. Blake was a suspect?"

"He was a person of interest."

"Meaning?"

"He would become a suspect if more evidence led us in that direction."

"Did you tell Mr. Blake he was a potential suspect?"

"No."

"What *did* you tell him?"

"We said we wanted his help in solving the crime."

"So you lied to him?"

"It wasn't a lie. We did want his help."

"You wanted his help to implicate himself. And so you tricked him."

"Objection," said Assistant District Attorney Roger Claiborne, rising from his chair. "Mr. Mullin is testifying."

I recognized Claiborne from the arraignment hearing, tall and thin, with what seemed to me like a fake aristocratic accent.

"This is a hearing, not a trial," said the judge. "I think I can sort it out, Mr. Claiborne. You may continue, Mr. Mullin."

It was the first time I paid any attention to Judge Berman. She seemed to be in her fifties. Her face was kindly, although she did not smile. I liked it when she put ADA Claiborne in his place.

A Good Conviction   99

Mullin continued. "Did you have an arrest warrant when you were at Mr. Blake's apartment?"

"No," Graziano answered.

"A search warrant?"

"No," Graziano repeated, his attitude conveying how demeaning he felt it was to answer such stupid questions.

"Was Mr. Blake wearing the shirt with the blood on it?"

"No."

"Where was the shirt?"

"It was laying on a chair, in plain view," the detective responded, careful to state the 'plain view' criteria Mullin had explained was required to make it a legal search.

"You saw it while you were talking to Mr. Blake in his living room? After he invited you into his apartment and you hadn't told him he was a potential suspect?"

Claiborne started to object but looked at Judge Berman and thought better of it.

"It was in his bedroom."

"You could see the shirt in his bedroom when you were in his living room?"

"No." Graziano was now visibly annoyed. "I had to go to the bathroom. I asked if I could use the bathroom, and he said okay."

"Is the bathroom in the bedroom?"

"No."

"So you had permission to use the bathroom but you entered the bedroom without permission."

"The door was open, and I could see the shirt."

"You could see blood on the shirt from the bedroom door?"

"I could see the shirt was stained."

"How far from the door was the shirt?"

"Maybe ten feet."

"Was there a lot of stain on the shirt?"

"Enough."

Mullin walked back and forth, his body language showing his exasperation with Graziano's evasive answers. His voice, however, remained polite. "Could you be a little more specific, Detective Graziano. How much stain?"

"A smear."

"Please be specific. How big a smear?"

"A small smear."

At this point, Mullin went to a nearby table and retrieved the shirt. He showed it to Graziano. "Would you tell us the size of the smear you saw from ten feet away?"

Graziano looked at the shirt. There were actually two smears, one on each side at roughly hip level where Mrs. Cooke had grabbed me when I helped her up. Graziano looked at both, as if he was trying to determine which one would be more plausible to have seen from a distance. From where I was at the defense table, I could barely see either one.

"Maybe a half inch," Graziano finally said.

"Is the stain dark and bright?"

Graziano looked up at Mullin, anger replacing annoyance. "No it's not," he said, faced with the obvious truth in his hand.

"So it's your testimony you saw the shirt, with this half inch stain on it, from the open door of the bedroom, ten feet away." Mullin took the shirt back from Graziano and positioned himself ten feet from Judge Berman.

"This is what the officer says he saw from the bedroom door," Mullin said, holding up the shirt.

"That would be the bedroom you did not have permission to go into," Mullin said, walking back to the witness. "What did you do next, Detective."

"I inspected the shirt."

"From the door?"

"I went into the room. I saw a piece of evidence in plain view and I inspected it. It looked like blood to me."

"Did you leave the shirt where it was and obtain a search warrant?

"No."

"What did you do?"

"I picked it up."

"In your hands?"

"No. I used a pen."

"Then what?"

"I took the shirt back into the living room, and I asked Mr. Blake if it was okay to take the shirt back to the precinct."

"You came into the living room carrying his shirt on your pen, and you showed it to Mr. Blake, who, let's remember, had not been told he was a potential suspect, and you asked his permission to take the shirt?"

"Objection," said Claiborne. "Already testified."

"Sustained," said Judge Berman, and I liked her a little less.

"Did Mr. Blake answer you?"

"Yes."

"What did he say?"

"He said okay."

"He said okay, you can take my shirt?"

"He said okay."

"So you took the shirt?"

"Yes. I placed the shirt in a plastic bag and took it with us to the precinct."

"So you placed Mr. Blake under arrest?"

"No. We didn't place Mr. Blake under arrest."

"Why did he come with you, then?"

"We asked him to come to look at photos, to see if he could identify the perpetrator."

"You still didn't tell him he was a suspect?"

"No."

"But you took his shirt?"

"Yes. With his permission."

Mullin paused, and Judge Berman started to excuse Graziano, but Mullin interrupted, "One more question, Detective. Did the police actually show Mr. Blake any photos of suspects after you brought him to the Central Park Precinct?"

"I don't know."

"Let me re-phrase my question. Did you personally show any photos to Mr. Blake?"

"No."

"Did you use the bathroom?"

"What?" asked Graziano.

"You asked permission to use Mr. Blake's bathroom. Did you use it?"

"No."

Claiborne had no questions and Graziano was excused. Now it was my turn to testify. This was the first time I had been on the stand, and I was nervous.

"Did Detective Graziano ask permission to take your shirt?"

"Yes, I think he did."

"Did you give him permission?"

"No, I did not."

"Did you know he took the shirt? I mean at the time, when you left the apartment, did you know he had the shirt?"

"No."

"How was it he took the shirt and you didn't notice?"

"When Detective Graziano came back into the living room with my shirt, the other detective stood up and asked if I would go with them to the precinct. He stood between me and the other guy."

"Detective Mackey stood between you and Detective Graziano?"

"Yes."

"So you couldn't see Detective Graziano standing there holding your shirt?"

"Once the other detective stood up, I didn't see the shirt again."

"So you didn't know he took it?"

"No."

"But you agreed to go to the precinct with them?"

"Yes. When I said 'okay,' it was in response to Detective Mackey's question. He asked me if I would go to the station and I said okay."

"You never answered Detective Graziano when he asked if he could take the shirt?"

"No."

"You didn't know you were a suspect, or a potential suspect?"

"No."

"You were tricked?"

"Yes."

Mullin summarized his arguments for the judge, repeating that the detectives had no search warrant, that I had not given permission, and that they had no right to the shirt or any evidence subsequently obtained from it. He said something about "fruits of an illegal search."

When it was ADA Claiborne's turn, he simply and quickly stated the police had followed proper procedure, and I had given permission. He also mentioned the police had later obtained a search warrant, after I was arrested, and went back and made a comprehensive search of the apartment, so they would have found the shirt anyway.

Mullin said the subsequent warrant search was irrelevant, but Claiborne acted as if there was no chance he would lose the argument, and he was right. The next time Mullin came to Rikers, he told me Judge Berman had decided against us. The shirt and the blood evidence would be introduced by the prosecution at my trial.

ELEVEN

Hector began our eighth week of classes by reading aloud a searing story describing the death of his little brother. His story had even greater impact because it was so unexpected. I think he had written it several weeks before, but it took him a long time to overcome the fear of being ridiculed for showing anything other than macho emotion.

> *"Pacho was three years old when he died. He was playing along the curb, in front of our house. I was on the step, and Mama was in the house. It was just before dark, a summer night. There was no warning. One moment it was peaceful, beautiful really. Two cars came flying around the corner, guns blazing. We didn't see him get hit, but when the cars were gone, Pacho was laying in the street. He was bleeding a lot. Mama came out and screamed. Pacho died before the medics got there. We never knew who was in those cars, or why they were shooting. I was eight when this happened, and I was supposed to be watching Pacho. What could I do?"*

"Did your Mama blame you?" asked Luis.

"She never said," Hector answered, "but I think she did."

"Hector, your story is very powerful," I said. "Very well written."

"But what's the point?" he answered. "Pacho's still dead. Mama's dead now too." Hector might have added, "and I might as well be dead." I think that's what he was feeling.

"Is there a point?" I asked the others. "Why write things that make us sad?"

"Get it out, man, you know what I mean?" said Esteban.

"What good does it do?" asked Tonio, and my small group looked at each other, pondering Tonio's question. They turned to me and although I felt totally inadequate, I had to say something. I surprised myself when the words seemed to flow.

"Maybe if other people know your stories, it will lead to change," I said. "It's hard for those of us who have not grown up with violence to understand how this affects those who do. Living on Rikers, I

Lewis M. Weinstein

know what it means to always have to watch your back. You can never relax. This changes your sense of the future. When you're constantly aware of how quickly your life might end, maybe you can't afford the luxury of thinking about what your life might be."

"Nice speech," said Hector, "but you fuckin' don't know nothin'. White people don't give a shit what happens in our world."

"Some do," I said, and I took out a book called *Inside Rikers*. "My friend sent this to me. Any of you ever hear of this book?"

"What friend?" asked Tonio. "That hot blond woman who visits you every Monday?"

"Yes," I said, surprised, wondering what else they knew about me. "Darlene saw it in her college bookstore and thought you might like it. This book was written by a woman named Jennifer Wynn, who spent a lot of time here. She knows how hard it is on Rikers, and how hard it is when you leave. She thinks learning to write, and to communicate what you know and feel, like Hector just did, can lead to something better. Anybody want to read this?"

"What fuckin' good can it do?" asked Tonio.

"If you know about other people, it makes you less alone," said Esteban.

"Anybody in that book actually make it when they got out?" Tonio asked.

"Several," I said. Then nobody said anything for a long time. Maybe they were thinking about whether there was any chance they could make it, somehow, against all the odds.

"Okay. I'll read it," Tonio said, adding with a cynical laugh, "Will I understand the big words?"

"Maybe not," I said, "but you can bring the book here and we'll figure them out together."

Excited by what had just happened in class, I rushed off to tell Alejandro how well his idea was working out. But he wasn't there. He had gone to court in the morning, and didn't return. Was he released? Was he transferred to some other prison? I never found out. Two days later, I had a new cellmate. That's the way it is in prison.

"The rest of the discovery finally arrived," Mullin said as I entered the small interview room. "I still don't know what took Claiborne so long, but I guess Judge Berman's order finally pushed him along." He handed me a large box. "Read through this," he said, "and then we'll discuss it the next time I come up." We had already been through the first box he sent out almost two months before.

"What's in it?"

"There's a lot of stuff. What's important are the written reports from cops at the scene in Central Park and the subway stop in Brooklyn where they found Mrs. Cooke's pocketbook. Also ..."

"I've never been in Brooklyn," I interrupted with the by now rote statement I made every time someone mentioned Brooklyn. "I have no idea how to get there."

"There's also the fingerprint report," Mullin said, ignoring my comment, "and Detective Mackey's report of his interview of Angel Martinez. He backed up your story completely, just like Watson said."

"Did Martinez remember the second visit?"

"There's nothing in Mackey's report about a second visit, and I still can't find Angel to ask him about it. I went again to the address in Mackey's report, but he doesn't live there anymore, if he ever did. Nobody would say where he was, if they know."

"I just can't get a break," I mumbled. "It's September. I should be in law school now."

"I have a date in court next week to set a trial date," Mullin said. "I'll try to delay it as long as I can."

"No," I said. "What's the point of delay. Let's get it over with."

That was the exact moment I finally lost hope. Blood, fingerprints, eyewitnesses, the State had everything they needed to convict me, and we had nothing. I didn't kill Mrs. Cooke, but it sure was going to look as if I did. I was experiencing the fury and powerlessness I had seen in others here on Rikers. It's easy to see why people don't care about their futures when they think they have no future. I was also beginning to understand why people decide to kill themselves.

Mullin looked frustrated, but he couldn't have been nearly as upset and afraid as I was. Before he left, he drove one more nail into my coffin.

"There's a copy of the police blood report on your shirt. The DNA matches Mrs. Cooke."

"This is Larry Mullin. I got your number from Joshua Blake"

"I remember you," Tom Kaplan said. "Thanks again for your help when I came up to Rikers the first time."

"Now I need your help," Mullin said. "Or Josh does. I'm getting organized for the trial, and we need what are called character witnesses, people who will come and say what a good guy Josh is."

"That won't be hard," Tom said. "Josh has lots of friends. Everybody'll want to testify for him."

"Will you help me organize the witnesses?"

"Of course. How many?"

"Maybe four or five. Josh suggested some guys he played baseball with - Sean Chadwick, Steve Lewin, M.J. Martini. Those are the ones he hung out with."

"I'll call them. When will the trial be?"

"Probably November."

"I have an idea," Tom said. "Josh is accused of attacking an old lady. What if one of the witnesses was an older woman, who could say how kind Josh was to her."

"That would be very helpful," Mullin said. "Who do you have in mind?"

"You know Josh's mother died this spring?"

"Yes."

"There's an elderly lady named Mrs. O'Neil. Josh's mother used to take care of her. When Mrs. Blake died, Mrs. O'Neil was devastated, but Josh just picked up where his mother had left off. Went to see her practically every day, made sure she had food, fixed things in her house. When Josh moved to New York, he asked me to stop over to see her. I go about once a week. She always asks about Josh."

"Could Mrs. O'Neil make a trip to New York?"

"She's pretty frail, but her mind is good. I think she would come up if I bring her. Would you like me to ask?"

Darlene Brantley caused a stir each time she visited. It began in the visiting room, where her stunning appearance elicited sex-starved looks, whispers, and even some audible comments. Other inmate's wives and girlfriends must have hated her. But it didn't end there. After each visit, and she was there almost every Monday, I was besieged with questions. Did you used to fuck her? Does she do good blow jobs? Did you get a hand job today? I never told any of this to Darlene, although I suspect she would have been more amused than offended.

It's no easy matter to get to Rikers by public transportation – Darlene took two subways and a bus. Once there, she was subjected to the humiliation of pat downs and searches. I was too embarrassed to ask if they did body cavity searches. She never complained, but other inmates told me it happened regularly to their women.

We often talked about her college courses. She had just started a new semester, and she was dressed like a coed, with jeans and a light blue sweater. I told her about Hector's story and how my students were reading the Jennifer Wynn book she had sent.

"Is there anything more I can do to help?"

"There is something else. I want them to read a novel called *The Outsiders*. Did you ever hear of it?"

"Sure. Read it in high school. Who didn't?'

"My students didn't. Could you get me four copies?"

"Coming right up from amazon.com."

This discussion hadn't fooled Darlene for a second. "Something's wrong," she said. "What happened?"

"I met with my lawyer last week." I paused, not wanting to say what came next. "We're going to lose," I said finally, hanging my head, "and I'm going to be locked up for the rest of my life."

Darlene reached across the table, a clear violation of the rules, and took my hand in hers. The look on her face just melted me. I didn't believe I was capable of having the feelings that surged through me.

"You can't know that," she said. "Something good will happen."

"Something good already has," I said, and I think she understood. She squeezed my hand.

"I get so angry," I said. "I wanted to be a lawyer. Now look what the law's doing to me, and there's nothing I can do about it." I held onto her hand until a guard started to move toward us. "Thank you, Darlene."

Then I remembered something I wanted to show her, and slid a picture of Katie across the table.

"She's adorable. Who is she?"

"My god-daughter. My best friend Tom Kaplan's daughter. Her name is Katie."

"And Eeyore?"

"I bought that Eeyore for her, just after I helped the old lady. You know, if I wasn't going to the Disney Store, I would have turned off Columbus at Sixty-fifth, and I would never have met Mrs. Cooke. I would be in class now, at NYU Law School."

As soon as she got back to the City, Darlene called Tom Kaplan.

"I'm a friend of Joshua Blake's," she said, introducing herself.

"Josh told me you visit him. He said he met you at the hotel when he first came to New York."

"You've seen my web site?"

"... yes, I have."

"There's more to me than what you saw there," Darlene said.

"Josh cares a great deal about you," Tom said.

"And I about him."

There was a pause on the line while Josh's two best friends considered what they had just said.

"Josh is getting more and more depressed," Darlene said, breaking the silence. "He tries hard when I visit, but I can see he's going downhill."

"It's almost to be expected," Tom said. "What's happened to him is so unreal."

"And unfair," Darlene said. "He's a good guy, and he's been beat up bad. He showed me a picture of your daughter with Eeyore. He really loves her."

"I'll keep sending him things from Katie. She's drawing pictures now, you know, with crayons."

"Josh would like that."

"Is there any hope he'll win his trial?" Tom asked.

"He doesn't think so," Darlene said. "He never had much hope, but I think he has even less now."

"It's such an unfair world sometimes," Tom said. "The best guys get the worst."

It was a stupid little candy store holdup. Two young robbers netted about fifty dollars and were caught by a passing cop as they ran out of the store. They were taken to the Seventy-fifth Precinct Station, where they were booked and printed. Two guys named Anthony Marone and Marco Picollo. A minor crime, no weapons used, they were arraigned and quickly released on five thousand dollars bail pending trial.

Whenever I was alone, I slipped into anger and despair. Night brought out all the demons and sleep was almost impossible. But if I kept busy, I could avoid thinking about my horrible life, so I threw myself into the classes. I talked to Teresa, the Island Academy teacher, and we worked out a team approach where I would amplify aspects of her weekly lessons. I added writing assignments, challenging my students to express aspects of their lives they had never dealt with before. The copies of The Outsiders arrived and were assigned for future discussion. I tried not to think that my student's lives, and my efforts to help them, were probably equally futile. I tried especially to avoid thinking my own life was likely to be just as useless.

Sometime in October, I had a visit from Abraham Smith, the huge black man who had come to my cell after I had used the Hispanic telephone. His "buck-fifty" scar had healed, but as Alejandro had predicted, it was awful to look at, stretching across his face from the right side of his throat across his lips and nose, ending near his left ear. I was terrified to see him standing at my open cell door, especially since Alejandro had been gone for weeks and I felt very much unprotected.

"You're still here," he said.

"You too I see."

"My name is Abraham. People call me Abe."

"I know." I hesitated, unsure what to say next. "I'm Joshua Blake. People call me Josh."

"I know," Abe said. He smiled, and his scar was even uglier.

"Did you come here to kill me?" I asked with as much bravado as I could muster.

"If I did, you'd be dead by now," was the deadpan answer.

"You might as well come in." Abe had remained outside the cell, and his conformance to the unwritten rule you never entered another inmate's cell without permission had given me the courage to speak as I did. Now he shuffled inside the doorway, but remained standing.

"You been helpin' some 'spic kids with how to read and write," he said.

"Yes."

"Would you teach me, and some other black guys?"

So now I had the Hispanic guys on Tuesdays and Thursdays, and the black guys on Wednesdays and Fridays, and Darlene on Mondays. A regular full balanced life. As the days until my trial continued to dwindle, and I anticipated the prospect of being found guilty and going to prison forever, this is what kept me going.

I slowly came to understand that my students were likely to be known for the worst thing they did in their lives. Sadly, many of them had probably not yet committed that deed. Most of them had been on Rikers more than once, and they fully expected to return again. It just never occurred to them they could lead normal lives, have a legitimate job, a wife they cared about, and children they would actually see and raise.

Most of them had not been charged with violent crimes, although they were all prone to violence. They were drug addicts and drug dealers, smalltime mostly. Many had been or were now homeless. Every single member of both of my classes came from one of New York's dead zones - Central Brooklyn, Southeast Queens, Spanish Harlem, the Lower East Side, the South Bronx. None had more than a tenth grade education, and according to Teresa, none read at much more than an elementary school level.

But here they were, and I enjoyed being with them. I found mystery stories with minority heroes, all black despite my search for

Hispanics, and we had intense discussions about Detective Louis Kincaid in the P.J. Parrish novels, the Abe Glitsky character created by John Lescroart, and, best of all, Walter Mosely's Easy Rawlins. They did love Easy, especially Abraham Smith.

My students all had a keen understanding of human nature when it involved being angry and getting even, but, understandably, very little empathy for people reaching out to love someone. There was an occasional poignant moment when I could sense those kinds of feelings just below the surface. Someone would say something incredibly tender, and then, embarrassed, he would quickly cover it over with something crude. Even after Hector's story about his brother, they rarely allowed themselves to write anything less than totally macho, their emotions having been sealed by their devastating lives. They knew they were sorry losers in the land of the free and the rich, and it made them furious and frustrated.

Larry Mullin came to Rikers on the last Wednesday in October. This was our final meeting before the trial. He had accepted my decision and a surprised Judge Berman and ADA Claiborne had concurred, and the trial was set to begin in early November. Now we were almost there. We had discussed it all several times, but we went over everything again, spending the better part of a day discussing the evidence Mullin expected Claiborne to present, and what he expected to present in the defense case. We talked a lot about my testimony, what he would ask on direct examination, what Claiborne would ask on cross-examination, and how I should answer.

"You need to tell the truth, of course, but the manner in which you answer makes a big difference. Sometimes you want to answer just the question asked, as quickly as possible. Other times you can use the question to go further, to say something we want said."

We talked more about when to volunteer more and when not to. Then there were the etiquette lessons. "Always be polite. Don't ever be a wise-ass. Look at the jury every once in a while. Don't slouch. Most important," Mullin concluded, "don't get angry. At least don't show it if you do."

"But I am angry. I'm furious at this whole thing."

"You can't let the jury know. They won't like it."

"Are they so stupid they don't know how I feel?"

"Josh, Josh, Josh," Mullin said softly, shaking his head. "Please."

"I'll try," I said, but we both knew our case was pitiful, and I at least felt we had no chance. Mullin didn't say so, but I think he had the same opinion. The ADA, reflecting his confidence, had never offered a plea bargain, and Mullin didn't think he would. I was going to be convicted of a crime I had not committed and I was going to spend the rest of my life in prison.

There was nothing more to say or prepare. Larry reminded me he would see me on Friday, when we would begin jury selection.

Tom Kaplan brought my best suit, all three of my dress shirts, and three ties. He also brought news. Sean Chadwick, Steve Lewin, and M.J. Martini would be coming up to testify for me. But the big surprise was Mrs. O'Neil.

"Will she be able to stand the trip?"

"She cares a great deal for you, Josh. If she's alive, she'll be there."

"You know, as bad as things are, I'm still very lucky. I mean to have friends like you and the guys, and Mrs. O'Neil. But also here. It was good luck that Alejandro sort of took me under his protection. And teaching the other guys, which I sort of fell into. That's good for me as well as them. They've become friends."

"I'm glad to hear you talk like that. Darlene and I are very concerned about you. It's understandable, of course, but you seemed to be slipping into a rather deep depression."

"You talk to Darlene now?" I said, surprised. "What does Barb think about that?"

"I don't think she's comfortable with it, but she accepts that Darlene is your friend."

"She is, Tom. More than any other girl I've ever known. She's a very special woman."

"I have something for you," Tom said.

"Security let you bring it in?"

"Yes, they did," he said. Tom dug in his pocket and pulled out a handful of papers. He unfolded them on the table between us. Katie's drawings, a mélange of bright colors, scribbles, and incoherent shapes.

"They're beautiful," I said, shaking my head. "I told you I was a lucky guy."

"Why the fuck should I care about some dumb white kids named Ponyboy and Sodapop who live in Oklahoma?"

"Where is Oklahoma anyway? Is it near Brooklyn?"

I waited, hoping one of them would attempt to see the connections between themselves and alienated kids everywhere. It was a blessing for me to be with my students. Focused on them, I could briefly forget the trial.

112   Lewis M. Weinstein

"Those kids had money," Hector said. "They had opportunity. Nothin' like us."

"Rich kids," said Esteban. "Fuck we care about them."

"No," Hector said. "I'm talkin' about the poor kids."

"The greasers?" Esteban asked.

"Even the greasers had more than we do," Hector said. "This story don't mean nothin' to us."

"Let me ask you something, Hector," I said, opening the book. "Here it is. Ponyboy says 'It ain't fair! It ain't fair we have all the rough breaks.'"

The guys were quiet. I wondered if Hector, or any of them, had read as far as page forty-three, or if they had, what they remembered. This was our first discussion of S. E. Hinton's classic story *The Outsiders*. They had been asked to read the first three chapters.

"Hector, you think the greasers didn't have it so bad. So why does Ponyboy think they had all the rough breaks? If he has it as good as you think he does, why does he think it's not fair?"

"Cause it's worse than the other guys," Tonio said.

"Even if you got some good things," said Esteban, "if some other guys got more, then it ain't fair."

I was thrilled. They had read it, every single one of them, and from the ensuing discussion, it was clear they had already talked about it among themselves. They focused on violent and uncaring parents, getting saved by your gang, dropping out of school, sticking up for your buddies.

"Could you write a story like *The Outsiders*?" I asked.

"No way," said Luis. "You need to go to college to be smart. Like you, white boy." I ignored the 'white boy' which I knew was not meant to be insulting or threatening.

"Would you be surprised," I asked, "to learn *The Outsiders* was written by a girl who was still in high school?"

"A girl? No way."

"Susan Eloise Hinton. Seventeen years old. She wrote about something important to her." I let that sink in. "Each of you have stories to tell. I'll bet you could write them, too. Hector's story about his little brother was every bit as good as this book."

"It was just a few sentences," Hector mumbled.

"That's how you start. Then you think about what must have come before and what must come next. After your brother was killed, what happened next? Let part be real and part be made up.

Let the characters help you. Before you know it, you have ten pages. S. E. Hinton started with just one sentence."

Hector had a look on his face that encouraged me to think he might try. He was waiting trial on a manslaughter charge, and he expected to go up, so he would likely have plenty of time. Crazy way of thinking you get when they lock you in a cell.

"Let's all read chapter four for Tuesday's class. Somebody gets killed." I ignored their cheers.

"Johnny Cade kills a guy. He says he had to do it, he had no other choice. I want you to think about whether he really did have to do it. Think about situations you've been in, when you thought you had to do something, and you did it. After it was over, and there were bad consequences, did you ever think, if you could do it over, you might do something else?"

It was a great discussion, and the best thing was I never thought about my trial.

TWELVE

"All rise."

Judge Phyllis Berman walked briskly onto her small stage and looked down imperiously on everyone assembled in her eleventh floor courtroom. The Supreme Court of the State of New York was, despite its name, the primary trial court, whereas the highest court in the state, the court of last resort for most cases, was called simply the Court of Appeals.

The courtroom assigned to the First Judicial District, Criminal Term, was a step up from the Arraignment Court on the first floor, but hardly the sumptuous mahogany image portrayed in the movies. The tile floor was far from spotless, the beige walls had not been painted in decades, and the high windows along one side of the courtroom were covered with a thin layer of dirt. The Great Seal of the State of New York on the wall behind Judge Berman had seen better days, as had the wooden chairs with slatted backs lining the defense and prosecution tables. The American flag standing behind the judge's chair, however, looked pristine.

Larry Mullin had filled me in on Judge Berman's background. She was a graduate of Columbia College and Columbia Law School, and had gone into private practice in 1982. Her first public service was as a member of the local Community Board in her Upper East Side neighborhood, a favored point of entry for many aspiring New York politicians. Appointed by the mayor to a judicial vacancy in 1985, and subsequently elected to the Criminal Court, she was known as an experienced jurist who did not get rattled. But she was also known to be, like most other judges, generally sympathetic to the prosecution and police.

"Good afternoon, ladies and gentlemen," said Judge Berman, addressing the jury. "As you know, we are here in the matter of the People of the State of New York against Joshua Blake. The jury has been chosen and we're now ready to begin the actual trial. The prosecution is represented by Assistant District Attorney Roger M. Claiborne." Claiborne stood, smiled at the jury, and sat down. "The defense is represented by Mr. Lawrence P. Mullin." Mullin stood, smiled, sat. Puppets on strings.

"The defendant is Joshua Blake." Mullin put his hand on my shoulder. Trembling, I rose. "Look straight at the jury," Mullin whispered. I can imagine how frightened I must have appeared as I glanced in the jury's direction, afraid to make eye contact. I scanned the crowd and saw Darlene Brantley and Tom Kaplan sitting together. Teri Scanlon was there too. "Sit," whispered Mullin.

Jury selection had taken several days. I had tried to pay attention, but it wasn't possible. All I could think was how my life was being destroyed, one slow step after another, all very legal and proper of course, and utterly horrifying. I sat ramrod straight as Mullin had instructed, trying not to look angry. But I was angry, as well as scared, and I'm sure it showed. When the trial was over, I fully expected to be separated forever from all the dreams and plans that had energized the first twenty-two years of my life.

"Are the People ready with their opening statement?" Judge Berman asked.

Roger Claiborne was tall, elegant, and supremely confidant. He wore a well tailored blue suit, with tiny pinstripes, a white shirt with pointed collars, and a red tie. Gold cufflinks flashed when he moved his arms. There were two other men with him at the prosecution table, each in a blue suit, white shirt and red tie. This must be the official prosecutor's uniform for when you are about to destroy someone. Very patriotic.

Claiborne walked to the front of the room and stood next to an easel on which was displayed a poster-sized photo of Mrs. Cooke, her daughter, and her three young grandsons. Mrs. Cooke seemed like she had been a kindly old lady, although I did not recognize her face. The one brief time I had seen her, she had been more frail than she was in the photo. Nobody could look at that picture, certainly I couldn't, without feeling profoundly sad at her tragic fate.

Claiborne spoke in a clear voice, deep and unhurried, with a slightly patrician accent. He reminded me of George Plimpton, which is probably an insult to Mr. Plimpton.

"Ladies and gentlemen of the jury, my job at this juncture is to explain what this case is about, and to give you a preview of the evidence the People's witnesses will later present in detail. The defendant is charged with the related crimes of robbery in the first degree and murder in the second degree, both stemming from his vicious attack on Mrs. Sarah Cooke in Central Park just before 8:00 pm on the night of May 29, 2003."

As much as Larry Mullin had attempted to prepare me, listening to Claiborne speak, I panicked. My heart raced and I could hardly breathe.

Claiborne walked deliberately to the front of the jury box, drawing each juror's attention. He spoke softly and with evident caring. "Sarah Cooke, a woman who was enjoying her senior years in close contact with her loving family, was suddenly and brutally taken from them. Without any warning, Monica Edwards lost her mother and Brian, Harry, and Christopher Edwards lost their grandmother."

Claiborne stared at the family photo, forcing everyone else in the courtroom to do the same. It looked like it had been taken in a park. Central Park? Maybe just a short distance from where Mrs. Cooke had been killed? It was heartbreaking.

I heard a sob and saw Mrs. Cooke's daughter Monica, sitting in the first row behind the prosecutors' table, dabbing her eyes with a tissue. Claiborne waited, letting the jury absorb the feeling. When he spoke again, he was understated, serious, and utterly convincing.

"The People will prove the defendant Joshua Blake killed Sarah Cooke during the commission of the crime of robbery."

I wanted to disappear. I was humiliated as well as terrified. I wanted to scream I didn't do it. Instead, I continued to follow Mullin's instructions, sat straight, and kept my face clear of all expression, even as my stomach burned and my chest felt like it would explode. I felt so bad I wondered if I would even live through the trial. Claiborne's opening statement was brief and to the point. His final sentences were daggers straight to my heart.

"The defendant's fingerprints were found on Mrs. Cooke's pocketbook.

"Mrs. Cooke's blood was found on the defendant's shirt.

"A total of five eyewitnesses will link this defendant to these crimes.

"This evidence ... fingerprints ... blood ... eyewitnesses ... will prove beyond a reasonable doubt the defendant Joshua Blake did indeed cause the death of Mrs. Sarah Cooke."

"The defense cannot and will not prove Joshua Blake is innocent." Mullin's opening line clearly stunned the jury. I could see the surprise in their eyes.

"Oh, Josh never attacked Mrs. Cooke and the prosecutor's evidence will not prove he did," Mullin continued, "but proving the other side, that something didn't happen, can often be very difficult, maybe even impossible.

"Think about things in your own life you didn't do, and ask yourself whether you could prove you didn't do them. For example, could you prove you didn't have coffee this morning? Could you prove you didn't speak with anyone when you entered the courthouse this morning? You might have a very difficult time proving you didn't do those things.

"Fortunately, the American system of law does not require a defendant to prove he didn't commit the crime. Joshua Blake, like all defendants in America, is presumed innocent unless he is proven guilty. The burden is on the State of New York to prove Joshua Blake is guilty beyond a reasonable doubt. If the State doesn't prove guilt beyond a reasonable doubt, and they won't be able to because it is not true, then you must find Joshua Blake not guilty.

"You will learn during the course of this trial that Josh did indeed meet Mrs. Cooke on the night of May 29, 2003. In fact, he saw her fall in the street and he immediately rushed over to help her. That's when Mrs. Cooke's blood got on Josh's shirt. That's when Josh's fingerprints got onto her pocketbook.

"And that was the only time Joshua Blake ever saw Mrs. Sarah Cooke.

"Someone, later the same evening, attacked Mrs. Cooke and caused her death, but that person was not Joshua Blake. The person who attacked Mrs. Cooke has not been arrested. He's still out there."

Mullin became more conversational. "Let's talk about motive," he said. "It's the most important part of this case and the DA isn't going to mention it ... because there isn't any. As you listen to the testimony in this case, I'd like you to think about motive, and to consider the following facts, all of which will be presented in evidence.

"You will learn how terrific Joshua Blake was feeling on the night of Thursday May 29, 2003. It had been probably the best four days of his life. He was planning to attend NYU Law School in the fall. He had come to New York just a few days before to look for summer employment, and he had just been offered a great job with a prominent New York law firm.

"Josh's whole life was in front of him. He wasn't wealthy, but he had sufficient funds to pay for all three years of law school, and now he had a summer job with a higher salary than he had ever earned before.

"It makes no sense to think Josh would risk all he had going for him to commit any crime, let alone to mug an elderly lady so he could steal a few dollars which he didn't need. Joshua Blake had no reason to commit this crime, and he didn't commit it.

"The simple fact is Joshua Blake was at the wrong place at the wrong time. He helped Mrs. Cooke, and his fingerprints got on her pocketbook and her blood got on his shirt.

"The murder of Mrs. Cooke in Central Park was a very high profile crime. The NYPD and the Manhattan DA's office were under intense pressure, from the mayor, the press, and the public. They were desperate to arrest and convict someone for this terrible crime. So they looked at the fingerprints and the blood and chose to ignore how they really got there, which by the way, they knew. They pounced on Joshua Blake and never, in any investigation done by the NYPD or the DA, did anyone ever look for the real perpetrator.

"The NYPD and the DA's office have made a terrible mistake.

"It's not easy to admit a mistake when you've been so public about claiming credit for brilliant police work and a rapid arrest. We don't expect the police or the prosecutor to admit their mistake.

"But we're here to correct it for them.

"Joshua Blake helped Mrs. Cooke when she fell down. He was in the wrong place at the wrong time. Nothing more. Not guilty of any crime."

Mullin stared quietly at the jury for a few seconds, then came over and took his seat next to me. Judge Berman announced that testimony would begin the next morning. She admonished the jury not to discuss the case with each other or with anyone else, and not to read press accounts or watch television reports about the case.

"You did a great job," I said to Mullin, "but this is a real uphill battle, isn't it?"

On that same afternoon, Maureen Reilly finally agreed to have a cup of coffee with Detective Robert Watson. He had asked several times, and his persistence finally prevailed. Watson was in court to testify in the Blake case, and Reilly had a hearing in another matter.

"You know, I was there at the arraignment," Reilly said.

"Blake's arraignment?"

"It was a Sunday morning. He didn't have an attorney and Judge Cartegna chose Larry Mullin. We were standing next to each other. He might as easily have picked me."

Watson silently thanked Judge Cartegna for not choosing Reilly, which would have made it impossible for him to be staring at her at this very moment. Her long brown hair was parted in the middle, and hung loosely on either side of her freckled face. She was thin, but with outstandingly rounded hips and full breasts. Watson realized a second too late he was staring and quickly asked a question.

"So, what do you like to do when you're not in court?" Watson asked.

"One thing I don't do is date cops," Reilly said, but she smiled and Watson remained hopeful.

"Okay. When you're not in court and you're not dating cops, what do you do?"

"I walk around the City. I go to museums. The Met, especially."

"Ever go to the opera?" Watson asked, as he had long planned.

"No."

"Would you like to?'

"A cop who likes opera. Intriguing." Reilly smiled without opening her lips, an inscrutable, mysterious smile.

"Can I take that for a yes?" Watson said, almost unable to contain the excitement welling up in him. "I have two tickets to Madame Butterfly on the Tuesday before Thanksgiving."

"How did it go today?" Hector asked. Our class was meeting to discuss the ending of *The Outsiders*.

"Not well," I said. "I didn't hurt that old lady, but the evidence says I did. The ADA has an easy case. I think I'm going to be found guilty."

"Now you know what it's like to be us," Tonio said.

"What do you mean?" I asked.

"Always guilty," said Tonio.

"Born guilty," said Esteban. "Don't matter what the truth is."

We looked at each other with a level of understanding and profound sadness I would never have thought possible. These students of mine had become friends, and they were sharing my grief as I had come to share theirs.

"At least Ponyboy got acquitted," I said. "What did you think about the ending? Did you cry?"

"Cry!" said Hector. "You don't cry about some story."

"I cried," said Luis.

"Why?" I asked.

"I was happy for him," Luis said. "He got his life together."

"He got a second chance," said Tonio.

Hector put his hand on my shoulder and said quietly, "Josh, don't give up. It looks bad, but don't quit. Ponyboy didn't quit."

"Almost," said Luis.

"But he didn't," Hector insisted.

"Have you thought any more about writing your own stories?" I asked.

"I could write a better story," Hector answered.

"Better than The Outsiders?" said Tonio. "It says on the back of the book The Outsiders is the best selling young adult novel of all time. Hector, you fuckin' nuts."

"I don't think Hector is nuts," I said. "He can write very well. And he has a lot more experiences to write about than S. E. Hinton had when she wrote The Outsiders. So do you, Tonio. All of you have important stories to tell."

My class was unusually quiet. This was a new concept for them. I don't know if they believed me, but at least they were thinking about it.

The portly bailiff could not have seemed more bored as he announced the thirty-second case of the morning, "People against Anthony Marone and Marco Picollo."

The defense attorney who planned to represent both defendants stood to respond. "Your honor, Mr. Picollo is here and ready to proceed, but Mr. Marone has not appeared. I don't know where he is."

The judge didn't miss a beat. "Issue a warrant for Mr. Marone. Notify his bail bondsman."

THIRTEEN

In court the next day, Larry Mullin gave me a copy of the *Daily News*, pointing to a brief article by Teri Scanlon. The headline read "Good Samaritan or Murderer?" Scanlon contrasted the two theories of the case presented the day before by ADA Claiborne and Mullin. "Was Joshua Blake simply in the wrong place at the wrong time," she wrote, "as his attorney contends, or did he commit a terrible crime, as the prosecutor would have it? Perhaps the answer will become more clear today as the prosecution's witnesses testify."

Every morning, Trial Bureau 20 Chief Sam Monti met with DA Harold Markman to update him on the three or four cases in which he was then taking a special interest. These morning coffee meetings had been going on for years. The Blake case had been on the list for several weeks.

"How did Roger do yesterday, Sam?" Markman asked, pointing to the article in the *Daily News*.

"He was solid. The opening was good. Nothing spectacular, but the case hangs together."

"That's eighty percent of it, you know," Markman said for the untold thousandth time. "Most jurors make up their minds on the opening statements."

"I think he's going to be fine," Monti said. "We've been rehearsing for weeks."

"Keep me advised," said the DA. "At the first hint of a problem, give me all the details. This is Roger's first big case ... in how long?"

"Ever," Monti said.

"Your honor, the prosecution calls Kim Scott."

I watched an attractive woman, blond hair, very fit looking, perhaps in her early fifties, walk demurely to the stand. She took the oath and sat down. Assistant District Attorney Roger Claiborne, elegant as always in a gray pin-striped suit and a white shirt with gold cufflinks, moved confidently toward his witness.

"Your full name?"

"Catherine Amanda Scott. People call me Kim."

"Ms. Scott, can you tell us where you were on the night of May 29, 2003?"

"I was in Central Park, completing a short run."

"How long was this run?"

"Six miles." I heard a flutter from the galleries as people considered whether they thought six miles was a short run.

"Would you tell the jury how you first saw the victim?"

"As I was leaving the park after my run, I heard a woman's voice calling weakly for help. I looked into the shadows behind a low stone wall, but I didn't see her. I stepped across, and then I saw her, crumpled against the side of the wall. There was blood all over her face."

"Did Mrs. Cooke say anything?" Claiborne asked.

Kim Scott closed her eyes, as if she were visualizing that horrible moment. "Mrs. Cooke said, 'he seemed like a nice young man. He helped me and then he robbed me.'"

"Did she recognize her assailant?"

"It seemed that way to me."

"Objection. Speculation." I jumped when Mullin called out loudly beside me.

"Sustained," said Judge Berman. Addressing herself to Ms. Scott, the judge said, "The witness will limit herself to what she heard and saw, not to what she thinks the victim may have meant."

"Did she say anything else?" Claiborne asked.

"No." Scott, looking a little surprised to be chastised by the judge, caught her breath and appeared to sob silently. "Then she died."

"Thank you very much, Ms. Scott," Claiborne said.

"Your witness, Mr. Mullin," said the judge. Mullin took a few seconds to shuffle some papers on the table, but when he rose, he didn't take anything with him. His rumpled suit and shuffling manner did not compare well with the commanding presence of the prosecutor.

"Did Mrs. Cooke describe the appearance of the person who attacked her?"

"No."

"Did you see the person who attacked Mrs. Cooke?"

"No."

Mullin came back to the defense table, apparently through. He started to sit, then, still stooped over, looked up at the witness.

"One more question, Ms. Scott," he said. "Was Mrs. Cooke wearing glasses?"

"I didn't see any glasses."

Roger Claiborne went through his remaining witnesses with calm professional precision. There were no histrionics, just clear compelling testimony, quickly rendered. As each witness testified, I felt my life ebb further away.

The first officer on the scene, a young uniform cop named Hernandez, told what he had seen, including the nature of Mrs. Cooke's wounds. Claiborne held up her bloody dress for the jury to see. Mullin, on cross, asked if the officer had seen or recovered any eyeglasses. He hadn't.

The pretty young girl from The Disney Store came next. She had identified me from a police sketch and had produced the credit card receipt that enabled the police to track me down. "Do you see the man in court today who made the purchase in your store on the night of the murder?" She pointed at me.

Bonnie was next. I went all the way to John's Pizza because I wanted to get to know her. If I hadn't wanted to meet Bonnie, I would not have been there, and none of this would have happened. She testified I was there but could not remember precisely when I had left.

"So far, Claiborne's presented two witnesses who saw you in the neighborhood and two witnesses who saw Mrs. Cooke after she was attacked. This afternoon he'll try to establish links."

Mullin and I were having sandwiches in a small meeting room near the courtroom. A court officer stood guard outside the door. It's hard to convey how good a tuna fish sandwich, a diet Pepsi, and a bag of chips can taste after months of prison food.

"There are no links," I said, but with a lack of enthusiasm brought on by weariness and frustration that the truth didn't seem to matter.

"There are two eyewitnesses scheduled for this afternoon, Adam Gordon and Concolita Jones. We know eyewitness testimony is often mistaken, but juries tend to believe them anyway, if they seem like credible people. If there's any hole to go for, I'll try to break them down."

Two people, presumably honest and respectable individuals, are going to testify they saw me running from Central Park and in a subway station in Brooklyn. It wasn't me! I want to scream and holler and hit. It's so unfair. My head feels like it will explode, and I can feel the blood rushing through me. Maybe I'll just die and it will be over.

While the prosecutor drives nail after nail into my coffin, the defense case is almost non-existent.

"We need Angel Martinez," I said.

"But we don't have him. I was still looking last weekend. No trace."

"You were out looking for him again?" I asked.

"I went back to his last known neighborhood on Saturday, asked around."

"I really appreciate that, Larry," I said.

After the lunch break, Adam Gordon testified he had seen a man run from Central Park toward Columbus Circle.

"He was young, maybe six feet tall, athletic looking, wearing a white polo shirt, jeans, and a light colored baseball cap."

"Do you see that person in court here today?"

He pointed at me, setting off a buzz in the courtroom and Judge Berman's gavel.

"Was the man you saw running from the park carrying anything?"

"He had a woman's pocketbook in his hand."

"Was the man you saw covered with blood?"

"Not that I noticed."

Mullin's cross-examination was excellent. He saw an opening and went for it.

"Mr. Gordon," Mullin asked, "this all took what, three or four seconds from the time the man burst out of the park until he was past you and gone?"

"Yes," said Gordon.

Mullin soon got Gordon to admit he was startled when the man appeared suddenly in front of him. He was wearing non-prescription sun glasses at the time, but he wore prescription glasses to read and drive.

"So maybe you didn't get such a good look?" Mullin asked.

"I saw him good enough," Gordon insisted.

Was this enough to build an argument for reasonable doubt? I thought Gordon's testimony was actually fairly weak.

Not so with the next witness. Concolita Jones, the attendant at the Fort Hamilton Parkway subway station, marched to the witness stand and settled her heavy body into the chair. She was sworn in and Claiborne smiled and said good morning. She smiled in return. She seemed quite puffed up to be the center of attention. This was a big day in her life.

Claiborne asked questions about where she was born, how long she had worked for the MTA, and whether she wore glasses. Brooklyn, twelve years, no.

Then he produced a small spiral notebook which he gave to the witness, and asked Ms. Jones to read aloud the notes she had written when the police had called. "Young man, Caucasian, six feet, white polo shirt, jeans, light colored Yankees cap. Carrying a ladies handbag."

"Did you see someone who fit that description?"

"Yes. He was the last one off the train at 8:34 pm. He looked around, like he was afraid of being seen. Then he threw something into the trash barrel and ran out of the station."

"Did you get a good look at him?"

"I sure did. Straight on."

"Later that same night, Ms. Jones, did you meet with a police sketch artist?"

Claiborne showed Ms. Jones the sketch drawn from her description. Then he showed it to the jury.

"Look at the jurors," Mullin whispered to me. "Don't look away."

"Ms. Jones, do you see in court today the person who threw Mrs. Cooke's pocketbook into the trash barrel?"

"Yes. It's him," she said, pointing at me.

"Thank you," said Claiborne, "no further questions."

Larry Mullin took Claiborne's place. He first asked if Ms. Jones had seen the contents of Mrs. Cooke's pocketbook. She had not.

"Ms. Jones," Mullin then asked, "did you see any blood on the man's shirt?"

"No."

"Did you see any blood on the man's jeans?"

Concolita Jones' statement to the police had included her observation of dark stains on the man's knees. Since there was no blood on my jeans, this was a strong point for us, a point ADA Claiborne had ignored in his direct examination.

"Yes," the witness said, "There were dark stains on his knees."

"Ms. Jones, could those stains have been blood?"

Claiborne jumped up to object. "This witness is not an expert. How would she know if the stains were blood or not?"

Mullin countered, addressing Judge Berman. "We're not asking if the witness performed any tests, only what she saw."

Judge Berman thought for a moment. "I'm going to reserve my judgment on the objection. Mr. Mullin, why don't you see if you can qualify this witness, not as an expert, but as an experienced observer."

No attorney ever wants to ask a question to which he doesn't know the answer, but Larry Mullin had no choice. He did a masterful job. Or maybe he was just lucky.

"Ms. Jones, you've been a station attendant for how many years?"

"Twelve years."

"Have you ever seen anybody in your station with blood on their clothes?" If Mullin was as tense as I was, I don't know how he got the question out.

"Many times," Ms. Jones answered.

"Would you please elaborate?" Mullin asked with a palpable sigh of relief.

After Ms. Jones had talked for more than five minutes, describing one lurid incident after another, with no sign of stopping, Judge Berman interrupted. "The witness may answer the original question. Will the recorder please read the question."

"Ms. Jones, could those stains have been blood?"

"Could have been," she said, and I could have kissed her.

A clerk from Chase Bank testified Mrs. Cooke had made an ATM withdrawal of one hundred dollars at 6:25 pm on the night she was killed, and testimony from a police officer established the ATM receipt had been found in her pocketbook, but not the money.

Judge Berman then said court would recess for the day, but ADA Claiborne asked if he could present one more witness so he didn't have to bring one of New York's finest back another day. He said it wouldn't take long, and Judge Berman gave permission to proceed. Detective Robert Watson was sworn in.

Watson testified I was the one he had arrested. He briefly described the way the Visa receipt from the Disney Store had led the police to Baltimore and back to Greenwich Village. He was on the stand for less than five minutes, and there was nothing in Watson's testimony Mullin felt compelled to ask him about on cross-examination.

I had already said goodbye to Abe Smith and the rest of his group, and this would probably be the last time I met with Hector and his class. Once I was found guilty, which I fully expected would happen, I would be moved from Rikers to one of New York State's twelve maximum security facilities.

"So, what have we learned?" I asked. Nobody responded.

"You didn't learn anything?"

"We learned," said Hector. "We just don't want to talk about it tonight."

"What do you want to talk about?"

"We want to thank you, Josh," Tonio said. "You paid attention to us. You listened to our stories. You got us to tell our stories."

"We never had a better teacher," said Esteban.

"Whatever happens in your trial," said Hector, "don't give up. You still have a life."

At one of the lowest points in my life, I was suddenly and surprisingly flooded with positive emotions. We had formed a bond of friendship totally unpredictable when Alejandro got our little class started. That Alejandro was gone, and soon I would be too, spoke to the transient nature of life in prison, maybe life anywhere, but I knew I would always carry with me very special feelings for this group of men.

"I have a present for you," I said, forcing back the tears beginning to well in my eyes. "Darlene sent it."

I gave a small package to Hector, but before he unwrapped it, he handed it around, and each one touched it. I think they all wanted to rest their fingers where Darlene's had been. When it came back to Hector, he ripped off the paper, which the prison staff had already opened and resealed. He smiled broadly when he saw the DVD of the movie made from S. E. Hinton's book.

"Ponyboy come to life," he said.

Esteban read from the cover. "Tom Cruise is in this. Ralph Macchio is Johnny Cade."

"Hey, wasn't he the Karate Kid?"

"Emilio Estevez. Rob Lowe is Sodapop. From West Wing. Patrick Swayze is Darry."

"You watch *West Wing*?"

It was almost time for us to return to our cells for the night. "Anybody remember when Ponyboy and Cherry talked about sunsets?" I asked.

Luis answered, "They could see the same sunset from different parts of town."

Everyone turned toward the barred windows, and, jammed together, we stared at the New York City skyline. The sun had set hours before, but it didn't matter. We had all seen it set many times.

"I'll be gone soon," I said, struggling to keep my composure, "but some day, wherever I am, I'm going to be looking at a sunset ..." I wanted to add I would be thinking of them, and I would really miss them, and how important they had become to me, but I was choked up and the words would not come out. From the looks on their faces, however, the words were really not necessary.

FOURTEEN

I had spent another restless night, getting maybe an hour of sleep. Despite being freshly showered and shaved, and dressed in my best suit, I felt more haggard with every passing day.

The first witness was Detective Frank Grabowsky, Senior Fingerprint Analyst in the NYPD's Latent Prints Unit. He was almost bald, overweight, and, wearing an inexpensive suit, he seemed more like an accountant than a cop. Claiborne took him on a numbingly detailed journey through the mysteries of fingerprint matching.

"An automatic recognition of an individual based on his or her latent fingerprints requires matching the latent print against a large number of known exemplars in a database. If the computer finds a candidate, it indicates the basis for the potential match."

"Does a computer make the identification?" Claiborne asked.

"Not at all. The computer provides the candidate. Then an examiner compares the latents to the known exemplar."

"Could you tell the jurors what you mean by the expressions 'latents' and 'known exemplar'?"

"By latents I mean the prints which were lifted from a particular piece of evidence, in this instance from Mrs. Cooke's pocketbook. Typically, this would not include all ten fingers, and some of the prints might be smudged. The known exemplar is a set of fingerprints, all fingers and thumbs, which we refer to as a ten print, taken in controlled circumstances from a known person."

"The latent prints taken from Mrs. Cooke's pocketbook were compared with the FBI data file, correct?"

"Yes."

"And this computer comparison with the FBI file yielded Mr. Blake as a candidate match for the latent prints found on Mrs. Cooke's pocketbook?"

"Yes."

"The NYPD prepared a ten print for Mr. Blake?"

"Yes."

"And what did you do?"

"I compared the latents from Mrs. Cooke's pocketbook to Mr. Blake's ten print."

Claiborne's assistant brought forward several huge blowup charts and placed them on easels visible to the jurors. Claiborne had Grabowsky explain in the complicated language of whorls, loops and ridges how he had concluded the latent prints were indeed mine.

Detective Grabowsky's testimony about the actual fingerprints was professional and completely believable. Four of my fingerprints from the ten print were exact matches to latent prints lifted from Mrs. Cooke's pocketbook.

There was no disputing those damning facts, and Mullin, when it was time to cross-examine, took the only tack open to him. "As I stated in my opening remarks, Mr. Blake will testify he helped Mrs. Cooke when she fell, and he picked up her pocketbook which she had dropped and returned it her. Would I be correct in saying your testimony is in no way inconsistent with Josh's explanation of how his fingerprints got onto the pocketbook?"

"It doesn't prove his story," Grabowsky said.

"That wasn't my question, Detective, as I am sure you are well aware." Mullin was as angry as I ever saw him get in court. "Will your honor please ask the witness to answer the question."

"So ordered."

"No, it's not."

"It's not inconsistent. It could have happened exactly the way Josh will testify?"

"Objection," said Claiborne. "Asked and answered."

"Sustained," Judge Berman agreed, and that concluded Grabowsky's testimony.

Assistant Medical Examiner David Chou, a very precise looking man in a tan suit, testified Mrs. Cooke had died from head injuries sustained when her head hit a rock. Mullin's cross-examination was productive.

"Dr. Chou," Mullin asked, "did you have occasion to look at Mrs. Cooke's hands?"

"Yes I did."

"And what did you see?"

"Both hands were scraped, on the palms and on the fingers."

"Were the scrapes on Mrs. Cooke's hands consistent with falling into a street and stopping her fall with her hands?"

"Yes. There were small tar residues in the scrapes which would be consistent with falling in the street."

"Could those scrapes have occurred when Mrs. Cooke caught herself where she fell in Central Park?"

"No. The ground where she fell was soft. No tar."

"And she didn't catch herself on the rock?"

"No. Her head hit the rock directly. If she had caught herself on the rock with her hands, she would not have suffered the injuries which caused her death."

After a short break, Detective Joseph Graziano testified he had taken a polo shirt from my apartment. He said he had done so with my permission. Graziano's glib lie infuriated me, but Mullin had lost his earlier motion to suppress this evidence and was not permitted to bring those arguments up again, so the jury never heard how the shirt had actually been taken without permission. Cops lied, and the system protected their lies. I told the truth and nobody listened.

"After Mr. Blake was arrested, was a search warrant issued?"

"Yes. I conducted the search," Detective Graziano said.

"Did you find any jeans with blood on the knees," Claiborne asked. Knowing from the subway attendant's testimony what would have come on cross-examination, Claiborne preferred to have it come from him on direct.

"No," said the detective.

On cross, Mullin got Graziano to say there was a pair of jeans on the chair in the apartment, but no blood on the jeans.

"So you didn't see any stains on the knees of any of Josh's pants like those which Ms. Jones saw on the knees of the man who she saw throw Mrs. Cooke's pocketbook in the trash barrel at the Fort Hamilton parkway subway station?"

Claiborne objected and was overruled.

"No, I did not see any blood on the jeans," Detective Graziano said.

The final prosecution witness was a DNA expert who testified it was indeed Mrs. Cooke's blood on the shirt Detective Graziano had taken.

As he announced the prosecution rested, Claiborne looked supremely confident that he had made his case, and I couldn't disagree with him, except of course for knowing it wasn't true.

"How did it go this morning, Roger?"

Claiborne had returned to his office for lunch at his desk, and George Henson had popped in for an update. Henson, who had handled many murder cases in his years in the Manhattan DA's Office, knew this was Claiborne's first high profile trial, and he was rooting for his friend.

"Not bad," Claiborne responded with a smile. "We finished our witnesses. I think it's a strong case."

"Did Mullin do any damage on cross?"

"A little. There was blood on the pants of the guy in Brooklyn, but no blood on the defendant's pants. Not a problem. Blake must have thrown them away."

"Who will defense call?"

"No surprises there. A couple of character witnesses, an eye doctor, Detective Mackey, and then the defendant. Not a problem."

"Mackey?"

"There's a witness defense can't find. Mackey interviewed the witness, and they'll want him to say what the witness told him."

"That's hearsay," said Henson.

"That'll be my argument," Claiborne said, smiling confidently.

"Will the blood on the pants be important?" I asked, as Mullin and I again had our lunch together in the small room near the courtroom.

"It should be. The subway attendant saw blood, there was none on your pants, so it wasn't you the attendant saw. That's what we'd like the jury to think. Of course, Claiborne will say there was time to wash the pants or throw them away."

"Like you said in your opening statement, it's sometimes impossible to prove something didn't happen."

"Well, now it's our turn to try," Mullin said.

"What's the point?" I asked. "I'm dead meat."

Mullin sighed. I think he knew we had little chance of winning an acquittal. He wouldn't say so, but he knew. The problem was we had no alternate story to tell, no other possible killer to suggest to the jury. Nevertheless, he once again took me through the witnesses who would testify for the defense, the questions he would ask me when I took the stand, and what Claiborne might ask me on cross-examination.

"Don't lose your cool," he said, as if I had any cool left to lose.

After lunch, Ms. Barbara Coleman answered Larry Mullin's questions about the job I had been offered at Morgan, Heffer & Stone and how much I would have been paid. Silly as it sounds, when I saw Ms. Coleman in court, I was embarrassed I hadn't shown up for work. I felt I had let her down after she had been so nice to me.

Tom Kaplan looked terrible on the witness stand. I had never seen him so upset, even when he visited me on Rikers. He had gained some weight, although on his six foot two inch frame he could handle a few pounds, and nothing about him looked right. His clothes didn't fit well, and he kept squirming. Maybe he was just frightened to be testifying. Or frightened for me.

After Tom told about the two of us in Baltimore, high school and college, Mullin asked, "Did Josh give you his car?"

"When he decided to go to New York, he said he wouldn't need the car, and he gave it to me and Barb. He said we could use it until he needed it again, but we both knew that day would never come."

"How much was the car worth?"

"Three thousand, maybe a little more."

"So if Josh needed money, he could have sold the car?"

"Yes."

Tom told about my visit to Baltimore, how I didn't appear upset when I was there, how I was anxious to get back to New York. "Josh was excited about his new life, and he wanted to start right away. He wouldn't even stay for an Orioles game."

Roger Claiborne, in his cross examination, had Tom repeat he was my friend. Although he couldn't actually say so, he wanted to leave the impression Tom would lie to protect me.

His last question, exactly as Mullin had predicted, was whether I had discarded any bloody jeans in Baltimore. Tom of course said no, but the question raised the possibility in the juror's minds.

Mullin had found someone to testify that over one million Yankee caps had been sold in the New York metropolitan area in 2002, and at least 25,000 of these were gray or white or some other light color. The things you learn.

The next witness was Dr. Renee Greco, Mrs. Cooke's optometrist, an attractive woman in her early forty's. After a recitation of her education and experience, Mullin asked, "When did you last examine Mrs. Sarah Cooke?"

"April 7, 2003."

"And, based on your examination, what can you tell us about Mrs. Cooke's vision when she wasn't wearing her glasses?"

"Her right eye," said Dr. Greco, "has compound hyperopic astigmatism with presbyopia, and her left eye is corrected for simple hyperopia with presbyopia."

"Could you explain Mrs. Cooke's condition in lay terms?"

"Without glasses," Dr. Greco said, "Mrs. Cooke's vision was blurred at close distances, less so at far distances."

"She could see well enough to walk around without her glasses, even outside?"

"I wouldn't recommend it, but she could do it."

"Why wouldn't you recommend it?"

"She would have trouble with the closer details."

"For example, if she wasn't wearing her glasses, might she be prone to falling off a curb?"

"Objection," called Claiborne. "Requires speculation."

"The witness is an expert," said Mullin. "The speculation is within her expertise."

"Objection overruled. The witness may answer."

"Without her glasses," Dr. Greco said, "the curb would appear blurry to Mrs. Cooke and she might well trip."

"If she tripped, and someone helped her up, and she wasn't wearing her glasses, would her vision of the person who helped her also be blurred?"

"Absolutely. She would have a general sense of the person, but the finer details, of the person's face, for example, would not be clear."

"Defense calls Detective John Mackey," Mullin said after Dr. Greco had left the stand. The detective took his seat, a large man, straining against his blue blazer, politely waiting to be questioned.

"Detective Mackey," Mullin asked, "did you interview an Angel Martinez in connection with this case?"

"Yes."

"Is this a copy of your report?" Mullin asked, walking toward the detective with a paper in his hand.

"Objection, your honor," said Claiborne. "This will be hearsay evidence, and the People will have no chance to cross-examine a witness who is not here."

Mullin quickly responded, "The People had an obligation to produce the witness and they have not done so. The People should not benefit from their own failure."

"Approach," Judge Berman said, and both Claiborne and Mullin stood at the bench, having an animated conversation I could not hear. They soon adjourned to the judge's chambers.

"Your honor, I would like this conversation to be on the record," Mullin said.

Judge Berman raised her eyebrows and looked to Claiborne, who hesitated but did not object. She sent for the court reporter and everybody waited while the reporter set up her equipment.

"Okay," said the judge, "now what is this all about?"

Mullin spoke first. "There is a witness, or potential witness, named Angel Martinez. Detective Mackey interviewed him shortly after Mr. Blake was arrested. According to Mackey's report, Martinez did see Mrs. Cooke fall and Josh help her up, which confirms Josh's account and provides a perfectly reasonable explanation for his fingerprints and her blood."

"Mackey's testimony is hearsay," Claiborne interrupted. "Without Martinez to testify, we can't cross-examine him. Martinez has never, for instance, identified Mr. Blake."

"If you had found him like you should have, he'd be here and he would identify my client," Mullin said, his anger obvious. "The People are responsible for producing him, and if they can't, then the detective's testimony should be heard as the best available substitute."

"Comment, Mr. Claiborne?" Judge Berman asked.

"We've done our best. Martinez is gone," Claiborne said.

"Your honor," said Mullin. "Martinez also provides an alibi for Josh at the time of the attack. Josh went back to Martinez' newsstand after he ate dinner, and he was there at 8:00 pm, exactly the time Mrs. Cooke was attacked. If Josh was with Martinez, it would be impossible for him to be the one who attacked Mrs. Cooke in Central Park."

"Mr. Claiborne?"

"There's no evidence Martinez knew anything about where Blake was at the time of the attack," Claiborne said.

Judge Berman asked for Mackey's report, and Mullin gave her the copy he had been about to give to Detective Mackey. She read it, then asked Claiborne, "Do the People know anything about Martinez' whereabouts?"

"No, your honor," Claiborne said.

"What have you done to look for him?"

"Detectives have gone out several times," Claiborne said. "They've asked in his neighborhood, checked with his employer, tried to track telephone and credit card records. Nothing."

"Have you also looked for him, Mr. Mullin?" the judge asked.

"Yes."

"And you haven't found him either?"

"No."

Turning back to Claiborne, the judge asked, "Does Detective Mackey have anything more to say than what's in this report?"

"No, your honor," Claiborne said.

Judge Berman made her decision. "It's a shame for your client Mr. Martinez is not available," she said to Mullin, "but since he's not, I'm not going to allow the detective's testimony, at least about this interview. Do you have any other questions for Detective Mackey?"

"No, your honor," Mullin said.

"All right, then, let's get back to court."

Back in the courtroom, Judge Berman explained to the jury, "It is a fundamental principle of a fair trial that witnesses must be available to be cross-examined. The detective will not be allowed to testify as to what he was told by a person who is not available to be cross-examined. You are not to speculate on what his testimony might have been. As far as you're concerned, it doesn't exist."

"The witness is excused," the judge said, and Detective Mackey left the stand.

If Angel had been there, he might've testified it was me who helped the lady, and he might've remembered the second time we met. Might've, could've, didn't.

Mullin finished our case, except for my own testimony, with my friends who had driven up from Baltimore to testify what a good guy I was, and with Mrs. O'Neil. Sean Chadwick, M.J. Martini, and Steve Lewin said wonderful things about me, bringing back memories of different times, which seemed a century or more ago. Mrs. O'Neil was an incredible witness.

She walked slowly and painfully to the stand, and the comparison between this frail old lady and the one who had been murdered was obvious to everyone.

"Mrs. O'Neil, how long have you known Joshua Blake?"

"I would say for at least ten years. He was just a little boy then."

"How did you meet?"

"It was through his mother. Mrs. Blake was a saint, you know. When I got to where I couldn't move so well, she used to come around every single day, see if I was all right, bring some food. Some days she sent Josh."

"What did Josh do when he visited?"

"He would read to me. He did some shopping. But mostly we would talk. Oh, it was so wonderful to talk to him. Even when he was little, he knew lots of things. But mostly, he had the patience to listen to an old lady talk. Most boys wouldn't do that."

"This went on for several years?"

"Oh, yes. Years. Then, when Mrs. Blake passed away, it changed.

"How did it change?"

"Well then Josh came more often. He took over for what his mother had done. And he would call at night, too, to make sure I was okay."

"What happened when Josh graduated from college and moved to New York?"

"Several weeks before he left, he made arrangements for a visiting nurse service to check on me, paid for by Medicare. I understood. That was the best he could do."

"Did you see him again?"

"Oh, yes. When he came down to Baltimore to get his stuff, he came over to visit with me for a little while. That was Saturday morning, on his way to the train station."

ADA Claiborne had no interest in hassling Mrs. O'Neil, and she was excused. The court clerk helped her down from the witness stand. Then she did something that was so nice I still get chills thinking about it. As she was walking towards the spectator section, she strayed from her path and came over to me. She bent down and gave me a big hug. Now, we all know no one is supposed to touch a prisoner in court, but nobody was heartless enough to stop her.

Tom Kaplan, Josh's other friends, and Mrs. O'Neil were on their way to lunch at a deli near the courthouse, walking very slowly, when Darlene Brantley caught up with them.

"Can I join you?" she asked.

Darlene was conservatively dressed, for her, in a dark pants suit, but her beauty was still astonishing. M.J., Sean and Steve all gawked.

"Some city, New York," said M.J.

"Let me introduce Josh's friend Darlene," said Tom, turning first to Mrs. O'Neil.

"Your testimony was wonderful, Mrs. O'Neil," Darlene said.

"Thank you, dear," said Mrs. O'Neil, as confused as the others.

When they were seated in the deli, Darlene sat quietly and listened to everybody discuss their morning's experience. It was the first time any of them had testified. They were all obviously distraught at what was happening to Josh, and hoped that they had done some good by their presence.

Finally, Mrs. O'Neil turned to Darlene. "Have you known Josh long?"

"I met him in May, the first night he was in New York," Darlene said. "He was so excited then, just a big kid in the big city. Everything looked so good for him." Darlene looked down. "Then it all fell apart."

"Darlene visits Josh on Rikers," Tom said. "Every week?"

"Almost," Darlene said.

"What do you do in New York, dear," Mrs. O'Neil asked.

"I go to college," Darlene answered without any hesitation. She looked at Tom, who signaled with his eyes her answer was good enough for him.

"How's Josh doing?" Sean asked. "It must be horrible there."

"It is," Darlene said. "He's coping, but some days he's so depressed, not knowing if he'll ever get out, afraid he'll be killed while he's inside."

"Do you think he has a chance?" asked Steve.

"I'm no lawyer, but I've been here every day but one. The case against him is very strong. Even though he didn't do it."

"Anybody who knows him would know he didn't do it," Mrs. O'Neil said.

By then, lunch was over, and they made their way back to the courthouse to be there when Josh testified.

Suddenly I was in the witness chair. Despite the hours of intense preparation, I didn't feel prepared.

"Do you swear to tell the truth, the whole truth, and nothing but the truth, so help you God?"

As I answered, I thought how little difference my truthful statements were going to make. Following Larry Mullin's direction, I tried to hide my fury and frustration, sat up straight, and looked at the jury as pleasantly as I could.

Mullin walked near the witness chair. He smiled and nodded to me, silently trying to say 'it's okay.'

"Would you tell the jury your name?"

"Joshua Blake."

"Where were you born?"

Mullin had explained he would ask these kind of questions to help me settle down. It would also paint a picture for the jury. "I want the jury to know you're a good guy," Mullin had said. "Just let your personality come out."

There were more questions about my parents, college, my plans for NYU Law School, and my week in New York. Then Mullin took a long pause and I tried to stay calm as we reached the most crucial minutes of the trial. I would tell my story and maybe there was a chance the jury would actually believe me.

"I wonder if you can tell the jurors what you were doing the week before you came to New York."

I told about graduating from college, saying goodbye to my college friends, and also finishing some details related to the sale of my mother's house.

"Your mother had recently passed away?"

"Yes, in March of this year."

"You were close?"

"Yes. My Dad died when I was fifteen. Mom and I were very close."

"Josh, it's important for the jury to understand your financial situation when they think about whether you would possibly have robbed someone for a hundred dollars."

"Objection," Claiborne said.

"Stick to questions, Mr. Mullin," Judge Berman said.

"Josh, how much did you receive from the sale of your mother's home? The net amount, after paying off the mortgage, real estate commissions and any other costs."

"There wasn't much mortgage left. Mom had owned the house for twenty-one years. I ended up with $137,000."

"Did you receive any other monies when your mother died?"

"Yes. There were some insurance policies, and there was still the money from my Dad's insurance. Mom had never spent it, except to use some for college tuition. All together, there was another $75,000."

"If my arithmetic is accurate, you had $212,000 in the bank when you came to New York last May. Is that accurate?"

"Yes."

"You had enough for your law school costs and living expenses for three years?

"That's how I figured."

"So you didn't need another $100?"

"Objection."

"Withdrawn. Let's move to another topic. Have you ever had any problems with the law?"

I was of course expecting this question. Although it was probable Claiborne would not be able to ask that question on cross, Mullin wanted to ask it on direct. His thinking was the jury already knew a check of the FBI file had revealed my fingerprints, and they would be likely to speculate on how my prints got onto the FBI database. Better for us to tell them than for them to guess something much worse.

"Yes," I said. "It was in my sophomore year at college. A group of us went out after a baseball game, to a bar. A couple of the guys got into a fight with some other customers, and some chairs got broken. I wasn't involved in the fight, but when the police came, they arrested everybody. We all spent several hours at the station house, during which we were fingerprinted, and then the bar owner came down and said he wasn't going to press any charges, so we were all released. The guys on our team who had been there, including me, chipped in to pay for the broken chairs. Two hundred dollars, I think it was."

"Any other times you were arrested?"

"No, sir."

"Let's talk about your week in New York," Mullin said, and he led me through a description of my summer job search and the sublet apartment.

"I have never been more excited in all of my life," I said. "I loved New York, I was ready to start a new job, and law school in the fall. Everything was just perfect, until ..."

Mullin gave me a moment to gather myself, then said, "Josh, it's time to talk about the night Mrs. Cooke was attacked."

I told how I was going to John's Pizza and how, at 66th Street, a woman slipped off the curb and I helped her up, gave her the pocketbook she had dropped.

"What happened next?"

"The lady walked away."

"Did you know her? Had you ever seen her before?"

"No to both questions."

"Did you get a good look at her?"

"No. It all happened in a few seconds."

"Did anyone else see this happen?"

"Lot's of people, I suppose. There were a lot of people on the corner."

"Did anyone say anything to you about helping the lady?"

"Yes. I stopped at a newsstand and bought some mints. The man at the newsstand said how nice it was I had helped the lady."

"Objection," said Claiborne. "Hearsay."

"Sustained," the judge said quickly. "The witness may not testify regarding what another person said."

Mullin had tried, and failed. He asked, "Did you ever see the lady again?"

"No. Never."

Mullin walked to the defense table to let the jury absorb the testimony. Then he resumed.

"Josh, you said the lady fell at 66th Street, but John's is at 65th Street. Why did you walk past 65th?"

"I was going to the Disney Store to get a present for my god-daughter Katie, for when I saw her in Baltimore the next day."

"Did you buy a present for Katie?

"Yes. I bought her an Eeyore doll."

"So after you helped Mrs. Cooke, you went to the Disney Store?

"Yes."

"... and then to John's Pizza?"

"Yes."

"And after you finished eating, what did you do then?"

"I went home."

"Do you know what time it was when you left John's?"

"It was just about 8:00 o'clock. I left after the Tigers batted in the bottom of the third inning."

In response to Mullin's questions, I told about stopping at the newsstand again on my way home. I knew from our prior discussions Mullin really wanted to have me say Angel Martinez recognized me, but he didn't dare ask.

"Did anything unusual happen when you were at the newsstand?"

"An ambulance came by and police cars. I remember the sirens made it hard for me to hear what the guy was saying."

"And then?"

"I took the subway and went home."

"You didn't go to Brooklyn?"

"I've never been in Brooklyn in my life."

"After you left John's, did you go to Central Park?"

"No, sir. I walked in the other direction, to Columbus."

"Did you rob Mrs. Cooke and cause her death?"

"No, sir."

"Did you throw Mrs. Cooke's pocketbook in a trash can in Brooklyn?"

"No, sir."

"You went to your apartment in Greenwich Village and went to sleep?"

"I watched the end of the Yankee's game. Then I went to sleep."

"What time did you get home?"

"About 8:30."

Mullin asked about blood on my jeans. I said there was no blood.

"Was there a washing machine in your apartment?"

"No."

"A laundromat nearby?"

"There probably is, but I hadn't found it yet."

"Did you wash your jeans?"

"No. I threw them on the chair, with the shirt."

"You threw them on the chair. You didn't throw them away?"

"No, sir. They were still there when the police came on Saturday night."

Mullin sat down, and ADA Roger Claiborne jumped up to take his place. There was almost no time for me to re-group before the most important part of the trial was upon me. Fortunately, Claiborne began with a question we had anticipated.

"Mr. Blake, when the police came to your apartment and showed you a photo of Mrs. Cooke, did you tell the police you had helped a woman who had fallen and it might be Mrs. Cooke?"

"No, sir, I did not." I tried very hard to keep any angry edge out of my voice.

"And when you were taken to Central Park Precinct and subsequently arrested for the murder of Mrs. Cooke, did you remember then you helped a woman who might be Mrs. Cooke?"

"No ... no, sir."

"When did you remember ... this convenient memory you claim explains your fingerprints on Mrs. Cooke's pocketbook and her blood on your shirt?"

"When I was meeting with my attorney and we re-traced each step I took."

"This was when?"

"Monday morning."

"So all of Saturday night, and all of Sunday, you didn't have anything to say about helping any woman who had fallen?"

"No," I said. "But ..."

Claiborne interrupted, quickly moving on to his next question. "You said you took a subway home after you ate?"

"Objection, your honor," Mullin said loudly over Claiborne's question. "Mr. Blake has not finished his answer."

"I'm satisfied with the answer," said Claiborne.

A flash of anger crossed Judge Berman's face and was quickly controlled. "The witness may complete his answer," she said, her tone totally flat and emotionless.

I explained that the photo the police showed me was small and several years old, and I had seen it for only a few seconds, that I had only been with the lady at 66th Street for a few seconds, and I was busy helping her up, and I never really got a good look at her. I finished by saying "I can't really be sure even now it was the same lady. But it must have been, because of my fingerprints and all."

"Did you throw away the jeans with the bloody knees?"

I gritted my teeth. "No, sir, I did not. My jeans had no blood on the knees, and I left them on my chair.

"No further questions, your honor," Claiborne said. Larry Mullin rose, as we had planned.

"Re-direct, your honor?" he asked, and was given permission to proceed.

"Josh," Mullin said quietly, "The DA has implied you're telling a lie to explain the fingerprints and blood. He wants the jury to believe if it really happened the way you say, you would have known it was Mrs. Cooke you had helped from the picture the police showed you in your apartment."

"Objection. Counsel is making a speech."

"I'm ready to ask my question, your honor," Mullin said before Judge Berman could respond. She nodded and Mullin walked to the evidence table.

"Is this the photograph Detective Mackey showed you in your apartment?"

I said yes, and Mullin, with Judge Berman's permission, showed the photograph to the jury. "I'd like each of you to look at this photograph, and then look at the likeness of Mrs. Cooke on the poster there, and decide for yourself if you could be absolutely certain the two photos are of the same woman. Take all the time you need." The jurors, each in turn, did as Mullin had asked. When they finished, Mullin came back to the witness chair.

"Josh," Mullin asked, "how long were you with Mrs. Cooke when you helped her up?"

"Not long. Maybe ten seconds at most."

"And, while you were with Mrs. Cooke for maybe ten seconds at most, did you stare at her face and memorize her facial details?"

"Objection. The witness has already testified about this," Claiborne said.

"Overruled," Judge Berman said. "You may answer."

"I hardly looked at her face at all. I ran over, I was bending down, helping her up, picking up the pocketbook, giving it to her."

"Now let's go back to the time in your apartment when Detective Mackey showed you this photo. This was when?

"Saturday night."

"And you had seen Mrs. Cooke when?"

"Thursday night."

"How long did you look at the photo Detective Mackey showed you?"

"A few seconds."

"And on Saturday night, looking at the photo for a few seconds, you didn't recognize the woman you had seen for a few seconds on Thursday night?"

"No."

"On Monday morning, you and I met on Rikers. Correct?"

"Yes."

"What happened then?"

"You asked me to tell you everything I had done on Thursday night, minute by minute. When I re-traced all of my steps, I remembered helping the lady and picking up her pocketbook."

"So then you knew it was Mrs. Cooke you helped?"

"No, I still didn't know for certain. My recollection of what she looked like isn't clear. But I thought it must have been her. The fingerprints must have come from then."

"So that's when you told Detective Watson about helping the lady?"

"Yes."

"Thank you, Josh," Mullin said.

"Anything, Mr. Claiborne?"

"No, your honor." It was the first time I had seen him look a little less confident. Mullin had done a good job turning things around.

"The witness is excused," Judge Berman said, and when I was back in my seat, she addressed the jury. "It's almost three o'clock. We're going to adjourn for the weekend. On Monday, we'll have closing arguments from both attorneys, after which I'll give you instructions on the law. I want to urge you again not to discuss the case among yourselves or with anyone else, and not to watch TV reports or read the newspapers about this case. Do you all understand?"

A Good Conviction   145

Judge Berman watched carefully while each juror shook his or her head, then said, "Court is adjourned."

By the time I came down from the witness chair, Tom and my other friends were gone, on their way back to Baltimore with Mrs. O'Neil. Mullin told me he would see me on Sunday at Rikers, and I was hand-cuffed for the now familiar trip on the DOC bus.

As I was taken away, I saw Darlene still standing, alone, in the back of the courtroom. She gave a tentative little wave, and I responded with what must have been a very wan smile.

The headline over Teri Scanlon's article in the *Daily News* got right to the point.

Where's the motive?

By Teri Scanlon

All the witnesses have testified, and the attorneys will present their closing arguments on Monday. There seems to be no question that the defendant Joshua Blake had some contact with the victim Mrs. Sarah Cooke. His fingerprints on her pocketbook and her blood on his shirt attest to that contact. But, did Mr. Blake, as the prosecutor contends, attack and kill Mrs. Cooke? And, if he did, why?

ADA Roger Claiborne has brought a strong case with one glaring omission. The prosecutor has not said a word about any possible motive. Why would a young man who was far from destitute and with everything to look forward to, throw it all away on a senseless attack on an elderly lady? It seems likely the case will go to the

jury next week with that
question unanswered.

Unanswered, and making no difference whatever, I thought as I read the article.

Sing Sing Correctional Facility
Thursday, January 22, 2004

Because I'm athletic and strong, and also because I'm here for murder, the most respected of crimes, my first month at Sing Sing has not been as bad as it otherwise might be. I was asked to join a basketball team with four other guys named Stump, Knuckles, Frankie, and Cream. No reserves. Break a leg, keep playing. We're all in for murder, so the team is called Death. The court is almost regulation size, with stands holding 200 spectators, and it's full and noisy. "Hey, mother-fuckers, you better win! I got three packs on you today."

We play two twenty minute halves, no time-outs. Two inmates referee. Once, long ago, guards were refs, but one guard foolishly called a foul at a crucial moment, and was slammed so hard when play resumed he broke his hip. Now they use inmates. Which means no fouls are called.

Death is matched against The Bank, a team comprised of five bank robbers. It's the third game for each team, and both are undefeated. On the opening tip, a sharp elbow is driven into my ribs before I even move. I stick out my foot, push hard as the guy who hit me turns, and down he goes. Undefended, I receive a pass at the left of the foul lane, rise up, drill it.

The game is ragged, fast, and brutal. At half time, The Bank holds a four point lead, but Death comes back, ties the game, and wins on a last second shot by Cream. I score twelve points and don't break any bones. It was a good afternoon in Sing Sing.

FIFTEEN

Larry Mullin was intense and focused. No rumpled brown suit today. He wore a well-fitting conservative dark blue suit with a light blue shirt and a blue and red striped tie. He stood at the defense table, facing the jury.

"Ladies and gentlemen of the jury, as I said in my opening statement, it is not the defendant's task to prove his innocence. In fact, the defense is not required to prove anything. In our system of law, it's up to the People to prove guilt beyond a reasonable doubt." Mullin paused, then spoke with emphasis. "It's clear the People have not met their burden. The People have failed to prove guilt beyond a reasonable doubt. Let me explain why."

Mullin shuffled through some papers on the table, then, without taking anything with him, walked over to stand near the jury box. He smiled, a man at ease.

"Let's start with what's not in dispute." Another pointed pause. "First, we obviously don't disagree a small amount of Mrs. Cooke's blood was on Joshua Blake's shirt and his fingerprints were on her pocketbook. If those things weren't true, Josh would never have been arrested and we wouldn't be here today.

"Josh has told you he saw Mrs. Cooke fall down, he rushed over to help her, and she grabbed his shirt. That's where the blood came from. You heard testimony from the Assistant Medical Examiner that Mrs. Cooke's hands were scraped in a way consistent with falling in the street ... and not consistent with falling on soft ground in the park.

"After Mrs. Cooke fell in the street, and after Josh helped her to her feet, he picked up her pocketbook, and gave it to her. That's where the fingerprints came from."

This of course was the point in the story when we needed Angel Martinez' testimony, or at least Detective Mackey's. Without either, Mullin went on as best he could.

"The prosecutor would have you believe the blood and the fingerprints could *only* have happened when Mrs. Cooke was attacked in Central Park. But with Josh's testimony, and the testimony of the Assistant Medical Examiner about Mrs. Cooke's scraped hands, we know the prosecutor's theory is not correct. Josh's shirt had a small amount of blood, consistent with the fall on the street. The knees of Josh's pants had no blood. I'll come back to those pants in a minute."

Mullin, who had been standing near the jury, walked back to the defense table, then turned to face the jury from there.

"The evidence in this case," Mullin said, "leads not to certainty but only to doubt. And reasonable doubt leads to a not guilty verdict." Mullin moved closer to the jury and spoke in a conversational tone.

"Let's consider the story the prosecutor would have you believe and see if it makes sense. The prosecutor's theory is Josh knew that Mrs. Cooke had money in her pocketbook, and he followed her to Central Park, robbed her and caused her death.

"But think about it ... We know Josh saw Mrs. Cooke on Columbus Avenue, but what happened then? Mrs. Cooke left, and we don't know where she was until an hour and a half later, when she was attacked in the park. But we do know where Josh was.

"Did he follow Mrs. Cooke and lurk about, waiting for an opportunity to rob her?

"Of course he didn't. Josh went to the Disney Store to get an Eeyore doll for his god-daughter, and then to John's Pizza, where he ate pizza and watched the Yankees on television until about 8 o'clock. He did not follow Mrs. Cooke and could not possibly have known where she had gone or where she would be when he finished eating. There's a whole lot of reasonable doubt in those facts, which are undisputed by the prosecution."

"We have testimony from her optometrist. Mrs. Cooke's eyesight without glasses was poor at close distances, and she could not distinguish details such as a person's face. We know she was not wearing her glasses. She saw one person who helped her up, and she saw another person in Central Park. There's no way her vision was good enough to know if it was the same person or not. More reasonable doubt."

Mullin paused for several long seconds, staring at the jurors. He brought his hand to his chin and then dropped it to the rail in front of the jury box. He tapped nervously several times.

"This case is about two terrible tragedies.

"Mrs. Sarah Cooke was robbed and killed."

Mullin paused, as if contemplating what could possibly be as terrible as Mrs. Cooke's murder.

"The second terrible tragedy is that Joshua Blake ... who did nothing wrong ... nothing at all except help Mrs. Cooke when she fell ... has been arrested for a crime he did not commit."

Mullin went to the evidence table, found Josh's shirt, and took it close to the jurors.

"Let's talk about the blood," he said. "You can see a small smear of blood on each side of the shirt." He held up the shirt so the jurors could see. "The blood is on both sides of the shirttails, just where

Mrs. Cooke grabbed the shirt when Josh reached over to help her up."

Mullin went back to the evidence table and came back with several crime scene photos.

"Now let's look at the crime scene, and I apologize to Mrs. Cooke's family, and to all of you really, but I have to point this out. There's blood all over the place. Kim Scott testified to the amount of blood. So did Officer Hernandez. Whoever it was who pushed Mrs. Cooke down and took her pocketbook would have to be covered with far more blood than the tiny little bit found on Josh's shirt.

"Concolita Jones, the subway attendant who saw the killer - the real killer, not Joshua Blake - said the man she saw had stains on the knees of his pants. Just the kind of stains someone would get on his pants if he knelt down to take Mrs. Cooke's pocketbook.

"Detective Graziano has testified he didn't see any stains on the knees of Joshua Blake's pants. You can be certain, if there had been any blood stains on Josh's pants, the NYPD would have found them and Mr. Claiborne would have made sure you knew all about them. That's reasonable doubt. In fact, it's more than reasonable doubt. Concolita Jones saw stains on the pants. There were no stains on Josh's pants, so it couldn't have been Joshua Blake who Ms. Jones saw at her subway station in Brooklyn."

Mullin looked down, composed himself, and continued.

"The person who did commit this terrible crime is still out there, probably still wearing one of the thousands of light colored Yankee caps sold in New York each year and maybe even walking around in Brooklyn wearing pants with blood-stained knees. Joshua Blake has never been to Brooklyn in his life and his pants had no bloodstains on the knees.

"After helping Mrs. Cooke, Josh bought a present for his god-daughter Katie and ate at John's Pizza. He went to his apartment in Greenwich Village and went to sleep. The next morning he traveled calmly to Baltimore and spent a pleasant day and evening with his friends Tom and Barb Kaplan and their daughter Katie. On Saturday morning, Josh took a train back to New York, and he spent all day walking around Greenwich Village.

"This is not the behavior of a guilty person. Far from it. When Josh got home on Thursday night, he threw his shirt and pants on the chair, where they remained until the police arrived on Saturday night.

"Joshua Blake's testimony makes sense, and it sounds like the truth ... because it is the truth. The prosecutor, for all his promises, has not proven any different, and in the United States of America, the burden of proof is always on the prosecutor, not the defendant.

"The most difficult testimony for me, and perhaps for you, is the testimony of Concolita Jones, the subway attendant at the Fort Hamilton Parkway station. She saw the killer, the real killer, and she described what she saw. But what she saw was a strong young man, six feet tall, wearing a light colored Yankees cap, a white polo shirt, and jeans, the exact description she wrote down when the police called her and asked her to be on the lookout. It was the general appearance and the clothes she described, not the actual person, and surely not the facial details."

Mullin went to the evidence table, found the police sketch prepared from Concolita Jones' description, and showed it to the jury.

"Look at this sketch and then look at Josh sitting over there. This sketch could be hundreds of people. Thousands. It was the clothes and the Yankee cap the Disney Store clerk remembered, not the face in this sketch. It is Joshua's bad luck the real killer was someone who looked at least a little like him, wearing similar clothes and a light colored Yankees hat.

"There is certainly good reason to doubt that the person Ms. Jones saw was Joshua Blake.

"You will hear the prosecutor claim the People have proven their case beyond a reasonable doubt. With all due respect, the prosecutor's opinion doesn't count."

Mullin walked closer to the jury. "Neither, for that matter, does mine," he said. "Not even Judge Berman's opinion matters.

"The only opinions which count are yours. You members of the jury are the sole judges of what to believe and what not to believe. It's an awesome responsibility. And no matter what the prosecutor claims he's proven, if you're not convinced beyond a reasonable doubt, then you must vote not guilty.

"I want to finish with something I raised in my opening remarks. It's actually the most important part of this case, something the prosecutor never mentioned. Not once.

"Joshua Blake had no reason to attack Mrs. Cooke. The prosecutor didn't even try to guess at a motive, because it would have been ludicrous to do so. Josh was going to begin law school in a few months, and he had all the money he would need, $212,000 in the bank, plus a great summer job.

"It makes no sense for Joshua Blake to risk throwing away his wonderful future to rob an elderly woman of a few dollars. The prosecutor, who must prove his case beyond a reasonable doubt, has not presented a single shred of evidence or even speculation to indicate any conceivable motive why Joshua Blake might commit such a crime. Without motive, there must be reasonable doubt, and with reasonable doubt, you must vote not guilty.

"Joshua Blake is not a murderer. He's a caring person. He rushed to help Mrs. Cooke when she fell down, and he never saw her again.

"Please let this terrible mistake end. Let Joshua Blake's nightmare finally be over. Find Joshua Blake 'not guilty' and let him get on with his life."

When Mullin came back to the defense table, I whispered "terrific job," not that I thought it would make any difference.

One of ADA Claiborne's assistants placed the large photograph of Mrs. Cooke and her family where the jury could not avoid seeing it, while Claiborne himself stood quietly near the jury box.

"Ladies and gentlemen of the jury, you've heard the evidence and you must soon decide whether this evidence proves beyond a reasonable doubt the defendant Joshua Blake robbed and caused the death of Mrs. Sarah Cooke."

Claiborne spoke slowly in an unemotional conversational manner. "This case really comes down to three simple questions. One, do you have any reason to doubt Joshua Blake's fingerprints were on Mrs. Cooke's pocketbook? Two, do you have any reason to doubt Mrs. Cooke's blood was on Joshua Blake's shirt? Three, do you have any reason to doubt that the person subway attendant Concolita Jones saw was Joshua Blake?"

Then he paused, drew himself up to his considerable height, his posture reminding me more of a professor teaching the law than a prosecutor arguing a case.

"There's no doubt about the defendant's fingerprints on Mrs. Cooke's pocketbook. There's no doubt about Mrs. Cooke's blood on Mr. Blake's shirt. And you saw Concolita Jones look directly at Joshua Blake and say he was the one she saw. So there's no doubt at all about any of the crucial elements of proof in this case.

"But there is doubt about some of the testimony in this case, and I'll tell you whose testimony creates doubt. It's Joshua Blake's concocted story of helping Mrs. Cooke when she fell. Mr. Mullin did the best he could to have the defendant explain why it took three days for him to remember his convenient little story, but does that make sense to you? Do you have reasonable doubts about Joshua Blake's convenient little story, for which there is absolutely no corroborating evidence?

"It's the defense attorney's job to present everything in the best possible light for his client. Mr. Mullin is a fine attorney and he's worked hard and well in this case. But he didn't have much to work with, and he has done nothing to create any reasonable doubt about the central facts that prove the defendant's guilt. Let me repeat them once more.

"Mrs. Cooke's blood was found on the defendant's shirt.

"The defendant's fingerprints were found on Mrs. Cooke's pocketbook.

"One eyewitness saw the defendant running from Central Park immediately after the attack on Mrs. Cooke, carrying Mrs. Cooke's pocketbook.

"Another eyewitness saw the defendant, in the Fort Hamilton Parkway subway station, throw Mrs. Cooke's pocketbook into a trash barrel.

"That evidence is sufficient for a fair and impartial jury to be convinced beyond a reasonable doubt the defendant is 'guilty' as charged."

I listened to Claiborne and knew I was a goner. Larry Mullin had done his best, better than I thought he would do, but it wasn't going to be enough. I knew I was innocent, but I couldn't fault the jury if they convicted me, based on the evidence they had before them.

Perhaps there's a moment just before you drown when you know you're going to die, you know there's nothing to be done about it, and you just let yourself drift away. That's how I felt when Assistant District Attorney Roger Claiborne finished his closing argument.

Just as the witnesses and attorneys each had their moment, now the spotlight switched to Judge Berman. She would have the last word, explaining the applicable law. She spoke slowly and clearly, and was obviously learned and erudite, but I think her task was impossible. She went on for thirty-five minutes, and it was simply unrealistic to expect the jurors to absorb so much law. I remember nothing of what she said. Probably the jury didn't either. But she tried valiantly. Suddenly she was concluding.

"This case is now in your hands. I'm certain you will take your civic responsibilities seriously and make a fair and impartial decision based solely on the evidence before you."

The jury was led away. The wait had begun, but it didn't take long.

The jury's deliberations took only a few hours, during which I was kept in a cell at the Tombs, adjoining the courthouse. I was brought back to the courtroom and stood next to Larry Mullin to hear the verdict.

"As to the charge of robbery in the first degree, how do you find the defendant, guilty or not guilty?"

"Guilty."

"The jury has unanimously reached this verdict?"

"Yes."

"As to the charge of murder in the second degree, how do you find the defendant, guilty or not guilty?"

"Guilty."

After again ascertaining the verdict was unanimous, Judge Berman thanked the jury and announced she would set a date for sentencing. I would be taken back to Rikers to wait.

I suppose you might think I was devastated by the verdict, broke down, got angry, cried, anything. Actually, it was none of the above. I had long since expected to be found guilty.

Larry Mullin actually seemed more distraught than I was. He said he would look for some basis to appeal. I didn't have the energy or enthusiasm to even respond.

Teri Scanlon sat in her office, struggling unusually long with what should have been a simple story. Ever since she had interviewed Joshua Blake on Rikers, she felt something was wrong with this case, but she was unable to put her finger on it, and it bothered her. She was already late for a dinner date, but the words would not flow. She typed one word at a time, wondering if her editor would let her express the opinion she was formulating.

It was a very predictable verdict. Fingerprints, blood, eyewitnesses, the jury was given powerful evidence to convict Joshua Blake of the murder of Mrs. Sarah Cooke last May in Central Park. Deliberations took only a few hours, and the decision, as in every criminal case, was unanimous.

Yet something lingers that just doesn't sit right. Why would a young man with everything to live for destroy his life with such a stupid

Lewis M. Weinstein

inexplicable act of violence?
This case, like so much else in
our times, makes no sense.

Scanlon went on to describe the crime, the evidence, and the courtroom scene in the traditional way of such articles. She quoted ADA Claiborne praising the NYPD, and Mayor Gardino praising Claiborne. She noted that defense attorney Mullin was planning to appeal, and concluded that "Mr. Blake can surely expect to spend a long time in one of New York State's maximum security prisons." Her editor allowed it all except the comment on our times, which he said was too broad a thought for a courtroom report.

Assistant District Attorney Roger Claiborne stayed in his office in order not to miss a single congratulatory call. George Henson sat with him, sharing the first major victory of his friend's previously mediocre career.

"Thank you, Mr. Mayor," Claiborne said. "Yes, it is good for New York. Makes the voters feel safe. Glad I could be helpful."

"Yes, Gwendolyn, it is a great victory. A party Saturday night? In Newport? I think I can make it. Someone you want me to meet? Okay, I won't bring a date."

ADA colleagues who had ignored him for years jammed into his office. When he went to lunch, several joined him, and he was clapped on the back when he walked down the hall. The elevator operator, who had never before so much as acknowledged his presence, gave him a thumbs up. Lunch at Forlini's on Baxter Street, a block from the courthouse, was interrupted by a constant stream of well wishers, many of whom he did not recognize. Attorneys, cops, even judges.

A new life beckoned.

Lincoln Center was magnificent on a perfect November evening. Outside, the cool air embraced elegant people and the glistening fountain. Inside, the magic of the Met's chandeliers rising as the lights dimmed. From the first almost imperceptible movement of his baton, the Metropolitan Opera Orchestra responded as if wired to every nuance of conductor James Levine's direction.

Madame Butterfly is a great first opera, and Maureen Reilly was entranced. She was also pleasantly surprised by the very knowledgeable NYPD detective who provided history and perspective to the tragic love story unfolding on the stage. Bob Watson had made a brilliant choice for his first date.

I was returned to Rikers, but to a different wing of the jail, and I didn't see anyone from either of my classes. I actually made myself drift into a stupor, since anything else would have brought more pain than I could handle.

There was a blizzard of legal activity – pre-sentence reports, comments from both attorneys, memoranda filed, and a hearing – after which Judge Berman sentenced me to life in prison, eligible for parole after twenty years. I was marched out of her courtroom for the last time, and the next day I was sent "up the river" to the Sing Sing Correctional Facility in Ossining, New York.

SIXTEEN

Sing Sing Correctional Facility
Thursday, January 22, 2004

I've been at Sing Sing for a little more than a month, and there's no such thing as a typical day, but this one, starting last night with the face in the murky water, the stabbing at breakfast and the basketball game in the afternoon, has been even more chaotic and tense than usual. I'm hoping for a peaceful hour or two watching television. There are two TVs in the rec room, at the opposite end from the basketball court. The choice tonight is between a re-run of *The Survivors* and an old Bogart movie. With lights out at 10:00 pm, I won't see the end of the movie, but I already know how it ends.

I choose a metal seat as far from any other inmates as I can manage. Just as I lose myself in the film, I hear a raspy voice. "I could suck you dry."

I catch my breath and concentrate on my mantra. Do not engage. Behind and to my left, the whispered voice repeats, "I could suck you dry. I could do it tonight."

A chill passes over me. I shake my head to dispel the sudden dizziness. There is no way to be alone in Sing Sing. Hundreds of violent, disturbed people, including the guards, constantly surround you, insuring a total lack of privacy. Reluctantly, I turn to the voice and recognize the pale, sickly smile of an inmate named Rudolph. Naturally, everyone calls him Reindeer.

Reindeer is Barney Coyle's punk, his prison wife. Barney is going to be getting out soon, so Rudolph needs a new husband. "No, thank you," I say politely, forcing a smile. What I want to say is "Let me alone, you sick bastard. Keep your filthy mouth to yourself, or I'll bash your face against the bars until even your mother won't recognize you." But, in my short time in Sing Sing, I've learned certain things. If I insult this pathetic scum, I'll also be insulting his protector, and Barney Coyle will be obliged to take up for his wife. Then I'll have to fight, or be stabbed. So I plead silently for Reindeer to just go away and leave me alone, knowing Coyle is lurking somewhere in the room, watching to see if his punk is dissed.

Hogie Carmichael plays the piano and Lauren Bacall sings. She was so beautiful when this movie was made, eighteen years old. I saw her picture in a magazine last year, and she's still beautiful in her eighties. Will I ever feel a woman's softness again? Bacall finishes her song and Reindeer has gone, searching for a more accommodating protector.

After his buddies at the 7-5 read him the riot act at the Fourth of July party, Detective Robert Watson's attitude changed, as did his performance. By June, he was hearing rumors. Lieutenant Brian Kerrigan of Manhattan North Homicide was indeed interested in him. In October, he was invited to Homicide headquarters at the 2-5 Precinct on East 119th Street in Spanish Harlem. Kerrigan wanted to chat.

Kerrigan told Watson the transfer to CPP had been his idea. He wanted to find out if Watson, as ingrained as he was in the ghetto cop mentality of the 7-5, could also display the patience and polish to deal with the upscale residents, politicians, and press in Manhattan. "For awhile," Kerrigan said, "I thought I had made a mistake. But you finally came around."

Watson was furious, and he let Kerrigan know it. "Why didn't you tell me?" he asked.

"It was part of the test," Kerrigan answered. Watson didn't buy Kerrigan's answer, and he harbored an uneasy feeling about whether he could completely trust such a Machiavellian boss. But Manhattan North Homicide was the goal of his professional existence, so he kept those thoughts to himself.

The Lieutenant made his decision quickly. In January 2004, Watson was re-assigned to Manhattan North Homicide, which, since its formation in the early 1970s, has handled murder investigations for all precincts from 59th Street to the northern tip of Manhattan. Watson became the most junior man in an elite department where experience meant everything. At the age of thirty five, he was an NYPD homicide detective, but he had no illusions he was anywhere near as capable as the brilliant, street-wise men around him.

"I need to get laid. What about those two hookers over there?"

"Are you kidding? A man as prominent as you've become, pickin' up a hooker in a bar. Not a good idea, Roger. Besides, they're not hookers."

Roger Claiborne and Frank Grabowsky had settled in for a quiet after work drink. Claiborne liked to be with cops, but, even after his triumph in the Blake case, most of the detectives he worked with showed little interest in spending time with him after the job. Grabowsky, however, was usually available, and they alternated between Merchants NY on First Avenue, where they were this evening, and the slightly fancier Manhattan Lounge, further uptown on Second Avenue.

Whenever Grabowsky testified in one of Claiborne's cases, the ADA made him feel important. Frank had dreamed of going to medical school, but he never got in, and settled for police forensics and an undistinguished career in the Latent Prints Unit of the NYPD. His moments on the stand, center stage, a respected professional whose opinion mattered, were the high spots of his otherwise dull life.

"It's been a long time," Claiborne said.

"I thought you said you had a hot date coming up," said Grabowsky.

"I do."

"A friend of your sister?"

"No. The friend's older sister," Claiborne said with an ironic smile.

"So you'll get laid."

"Maybe."

"So what's the problem?"

"It's been so long."

"Oh, I get it," Grabowsky said. "You think you need practice. No bad reports coming back to your sister."

"Something like that," Claiborne admitted.

"I know just the lady for you. Tell her I recommended you, then I'll get something special next time I see her."

"Frank, I'm shocked. You know a hooker?"

"I have needs. They're not all satisfied at home, if you know what I mean."

"Is she good?"

"You'll find out for yourself. But you can see what she looks like. She and her partner have a web site."

"Hookers have a web site?"

Grabowsky wrote the web address on a napkin and gave it to Claiborne. "Check out Darlene," he said with a leer.

Spider, my cellmate, is my main man in prison. He's the source of great wisdom, keeping me safe, keeping me alive. Although reticent at first, he has gradually told me quite a bit about himself. Some of it may even be true.

Spider's real name is Durwood Johnson. He says he's fifty-five years old, has been married twice, and has a daughter, but has no contact with any of his family. He was born in the Midwest, Michigan I think he said. His father was a drunk who couldn't hold a job, and his mother was a waitress, often working two or even three jobs. Not surprisingly, Spider revered his mother and hated his father. Both are apparently deceased.

Spider's first exposure to juvenile court occurred after an older boy bragged about fucking Spider's sister, who was fifteen at the time. Spider, then twelve, grabbed a two-foot piece of pipe and beat the guy into oblivion. The sister, whose name he never mentioned, died two years later in a car crash.

Spider was asked to leave high school in his junior year. He joined the army, hated it, but has retained powerful patriotic feelings to this day. After the army, he had a succession of construction, road labor, and other muscle jobs, always moving on. He says he's seen thirty-two states. He robbed people occasionally, sometimes with violence. "Always with my hands," he said, "never a gun. Didn't need one." He has yet to relate how or why he received the spider web tattoo which covers his entire back and buttocks, and I'm not anxious to ask. Did the tattoo come first, or the nickname?

Spider's been in prison several different times, in several states. As he tells it, the shining moment of his life led to his present incarceration. He had awakened after a long drunk, in a camp of vagrants outside a small rural town in upstate New York. He noticed a group of men in a circle, hootin' and hollerin'. "Some had their dicks out and were waving them in the air. It was disgusting." They had captured a young girl, stripped her naked, and were methodically raping her, one after another.

Spider says the girl reminded him of his sweet first wife. As with his sister many years before, he played the knight errant, waded in, busting heads. The girl escaped, and just as Spider finished choking one of the men to death, the police arrived. For his gallantry he was convicted of aggravated manslaughter and sentenced to 20 to life, same as me. He regards it as a just sentence, and does not regret what he did. The girl did not come to his trial and did not corroborate his story, but he never expected she would.

I take Spider's advice and look at my prison file. The brown manila folder is delivered without complications. I sit at a square metal table in the prison law library and stare at the label.

> #37654886
> JOSHUA BLAKE
> Arrived: December 16, 2003
> Sentence: Life Imprisonment
> Eligible for parole: December 16, 2023
> Home address: None
> Next of kin: None

I'm thankful for the quiet of the library, so unusual at Sing Sing, and I allow myself to daydream about my childhood in Baltimore, when I had a home address and next of kin. I think about summer days, baseball, studying history, falling in love, getting laid, graduating. I think about my one glorious week in New York City.

Other memories intrude like hurrying dark clouds across my sunny sky. A frail old lady is killed in Central Park Precinct, a rap singer performs at the Tombs, I'm chained in a DOC transport bus, a disgusting person named Reindeer hisses at me.

With a start, I realize my half hour has almost passed and I haven't even opened the file. I thumb through the pages until I find Lawrence P. Mullin's Manhattan address. Manhattan, focus of my dreams, place of my destruction.

The first time Tom Kaplan visits me at Sing Sing, he brings sad news. Mrs. O'Neil passed away two weeks after the trial.

"Was the trip too much for her," I ask, terrified that she had died because of me.

"No," Tom says, "it wasn't the trip."

"I lost a great friend," I say.

"She was your friend, and she did love you. All the way back to Baltimore, she told stories about you. You were one of the best parts of her life. Of course, the guys couldn't stop talking about Darlene."

"What?"

"She joined us for lunch. I thought all three of them were going to explode. She is some good looking woman."

"Did ..."

"She said she was in college. That's all."

"Thanks, Tom."

Tom brings me up to date on what was going on with him and Barb, and gives me more drawings from Katie.

"How is it here?" he finally asks. "I have to say, I never thought I would see the inside of Sing Sing."

"Me either, and it's worse than Rikers. Except, I've been lucky again in a cellmate. At least I think I'm lucky some of the time." I tell Tom all about Spider, which leads into the face in the murky water and the transcript I'm expecting soon.

"It's making me crazy," I say. "There's got to be some way to get out of this place. I hope I can find something in the transcript. It's odd, though, looking into this now. All the time before and during the trial, I felt I had no chance, and now, I have this idea maybe there is a chance. I keep seeing that look on the detective's face. Why didn't I see it before?"

"Maybe you were too scared to think," Tom says. "I would have been. I wish I could be more help."

"Tom, just you being here is so important for me. And the guys, and poor Mrs. O'Neil."

"Has Darlene been up yet?"

"Not yet. She's been real busy with college. But she writes all the time."

"That woman is something," Tom said, "and she really cares about you."

"Blake. There's a package for you. Go to the package room and pick it up."

"Thank you, CO."

This is the transcript, I hope, and I wonder how long it's been there. Corrections Officers are arbitrary, unknowable beings. For reasons you'll never understand and can never predict, they can be civil or belligerent. They can toss your cell looking for contraband drugs in the middle of the night, or they can act like normal people and even seem helpful. But they can never be relied on, and they are never your friends.

The package is four inches thick, and heavy. Of course it's been opened and searched. There are five volumes of transcript and a short letter from Larry Mullin. Mullin's letter mentions an enclosed list of the police officers who worked on my case, but there's no list. I ask the inmate working behind the counter and receive a blank stare in return.

Mullin also says he filed a one page notice of appeal with the Appellate Division for the First Judicial Department a few days after sentencing. This preserves our right to file a "perfected" appeal which is due by May 15. The question, of course, is what could be the basis for such an appeal. Right now, Mullin doesn't seem to have any basis that he thinks might succeed.

My plan is to find something in the transcript to explain the look I think some detective gave me, which may or may not have actually happened. I'll write to this detective and ask for his help. It's more desperate hope than a plan, but what else can I do? Not having the list is a problem. Who will I write to if I find something worth writing? I begin with the transcript for November 5, 2003, day one of *The People of the State of New York against Joshua Blake*.

I've never read a transcript, and doing so makes me feel like the lawyer I had expected to become. At first I try to memorize every word. That doesn't work, of course, so I stop making any conscious effort to remember and allow myself to absorb the flow of the trial. The prosecutor's case is strong, and a queasy feeling in the pit of my stomach tells me I'm on a hopeless quest.

In bits and snatches, I read through the entire transcript three times. This takes about a month, and I'm very conscious of the running clock. I make a list of the prosecution witnesses: (1) Kim Scott, the runner who found Mrs. Cooke's body, (2) the first police officer on the scene, (3) the clerk at the Disney Store, (4) Bonnie from John's Pizza, (5) Adam Gordon who said he saw me running from Central Park, (6) the subway attendant Concolita Jones, (7) a Chase Bank clerk, (8) Detective Robert Watson, (9) a fingerprint detective named Frank Grabowsky, (10) an Assistant Medical Examiner, (11) Detective Graziano who took my shirt from my apartment, and (12) a DNA expert who said it was Mrs. Cooke's blood on my shirt.

When I read Detective Watson's brief testimony, I realize it's his face I've been seeing in the murky water. It was on Rikers, and he had just told me I wasn't getting out even though Angel Martinez had backed my story of helping the old lady. I screamed at him, and he gave me the look that's still haunting my nights.

I obsess over my list for another three days. I look at it when I'm eating, in the yard, even on the toilet. These were the people whose testimony convinced a jury I murdered Mrs. Cooke. Whatever it is I'm looking for, I haven't found it yet. I've had the transcripts for five weeks and I have nothing to tell Detective Watson.

From the fifth floor window in her new "working" apartment, Darlene Brantley watched the tall thin man walking along West 53rd Street. He looked vaguely familiar. When she heard his voice on the intercom, she knew she had heard it before, and when she opened the door to let him in, she was certain.

Her first reaction was panic. Then she was embarrassed. Then she began to think maybe this was an incredible opportunity to help her friend. All this in a split second, and all of it because the tall man was without doubt Assistant District Attorney Roger Claiborne.

Darlene didn't have much time to think about how this fortuitous meeting could be helpful to Josh, because there were no preliminaries. Claiborne was taking her clothes off within a minute of entering the apartment. Their lovemaking took less than three minutes. Darlene, wanting to learn more, sought to prolong Claiborne's stay.

"You paid for an hour," she said. "Would you like a drink?"

"I just don't seem to be able to ask," Claiborne said, making himself comfortable on Darlene's sofa, sipping the Dewar's on the rocks she had provided.

"What are you talking about?"

"With other women, I can't seem to bring up the subject of sex."

"You're not supposed to ask," Darlene said. "You just do it. Same as you just did."

"It seems different. I'm dating this woman, and it doesn't seem to be happening."

"How many dates so far?"

"Three."

"Three dates and no pussy. Not good."

"I'm sure my sister is embarrassed."

"Why would your sister know?"

"She set me up with this woman."

"You think your sister knows you haven't fucked her yet?"

"Gwendolyn knows everything."

Darlene watched Claiborne getting excited again. He, like most guys, got hard as soon as she said the magic words pussy or fuck. It was so easy.

"Maybe you should take a more direct approach. What's her name, this sister of a friend's sister?"

"Charlotte."

"So you say to her, 'Charlotte, I think it's time we fuck.'"

"She would be shocked."

"You think? She went on three dates with you. She's obviously interested. She's anxious, for crying out loud. If you just let her know what you want, you'll be in her hot sweaty pants in a flash."

Claiborne's breathing had quickened, and Darlene placed her hand on his arm, stroking gently. She slid her fingers along his leg. He was hard and ready. She grabbed a condom and they were under the sheets again. She was pleased because she wanted to make sure he came back.

"Blake, you have a visitor. Take off your clothes and hand them out."

Another strip search. I hate them. I think it's also humiliating for many of the COs, although some seem to enjoy the power it confers. It's a routine I'll never get used to, like sitting on the toilet in full view. Twenty years, say once a week, adds up to a thousand strip searches. This is an unbelievable way to live. I get dressed.

I'm handcuffed and led through a series of corridors, from one building to another, up and down crumbling paint-peeling stairwells, through four gates, each of which must be unlocked to allow me to pass, and finally, to the door marked "Visit Room." The cuffs are removed. "Your visitor is at table four."

There are large signs hanging from the ceiling over the tables. I see the number "4" and look for my visitor. Darlene waves and my heart jumps. We've exchanged letters, but I wasn't expecting her.

I have carefully read *Standards of Inmate Behavior*, distributed to all inmates by the New York State Department of Correctional Services, along with the specific rules which apply at Sing Sing, so I know a quick hug and kiss at the beginning of a visit is permitted. I wish I had brushed my teeth, but it's too late.

Darlene rises as I walk toward her. She leans across the table, and I can sense the response around me. She is flat out gorgeous, and the entire room sucks in a breath to watch. I put my hand on her shoulder and my erection is instantaneous. Darlene leans closer to me, and I feel her breasts against me as we hug. She kisses me on the cheek and pulls back. She knows the rules, too.

I sit down and try to control my breathing and pounding pulse. I look at her with a stupid smile on my face, afraid of what I can no longer keep from happening, and, incredibly, I explode into my pants. I shiver and cover my face with my hands. I don't dare look at Darlene. I don't know what to do. Does she know what just happened? Does the whole room? I peek through my fingers and Darlene is covering her face and giggling.

"Wow," she says. "Some reaction."

"I'm sorry. I'm so embarrassed."

"Don't apologize, baby. You must have needed that."

"I don't know what to say."

"Suppose we start with hello."

"Hello," I say. "It's been a while."

"Somehow I guessed," she says, smiling. "I'm sorry it took so long for me to get here. How are you?"

This is surreal, as I simply ignore my soaked pants and proceed to tell Darlene what has happened since I last wrote to her.

"I've been reading the transcript of my trial, looking for something."

"What?"

"I don't know." I tell her about the face in the murky water, now identified as Detective Robert Watson, and the look I think he gave me. "I'm looking for something to tell that face."

Darlene looked at me with a puzzled look on her face. "This is new, Josh. All the time you were at Rikers, you were depressed and sort of lethargic. Not that you didn't have reason to be. But now, you seem more motivated and energized. What happened?"

"Maybe there's only so far down you can go. Maybe I have to live up to all those nice things the guys and Mrs. O'Neil said about me. Maybe it's you."

"Whatever it is, it's good," she says, blushing just a little. Then she gets very serious. "Maybe I can help."

"How? That would be ... What are you thinking?"

"It's ah ... embarrassing. I hope you won't be angry."

"I won't be angry," I say.

"Well, you might be," she says. "I'm fucking your prosecutor."

I'm speechless.

"Roger Claiborne," she says. "He was your prosecutor, right?"

I nod, still unable to speak.

"A few weeks ago, this man called. When he showed up, I recognized him. He's been back several times. He's going to be a regular."

I take some time to absorb this astonishing information. Of course I know she's a hooker, and it's her job to screw guys. But I try not to think about the actual events, and now graphic visuals are flashing in my mind like slides in a Powerpoint presentation. Claiborne in court, Claiborne naked, Darlene naked, Claiborne and Darlene naked together. I'm searching for the "off" switch to make it stop.

Darlene can see I'm angry. But I'm being stupid. She's my friend. She didn't seek this guy out. She probably doesn't even like him. He's just a paycheck for her. Absurdly, I wonder if Social Security is deducted. I smile, an ironic smile, but a smile nevertheless.

"You find this amusing?" she asks, smiling back.

"You're my friend and you're fucking the guy who put me here. I find that amusing. Don't you?"

"Well, he's not much in the sack. He ..."

"Spare me the details."

Darlene reaches her hand out to cover mine. "No touching," says a guard, so quickly he must have been watching her. She pulls back, but the feeling had been wonderful and comforting, and this time, not arousing.

"I thought it might be useful for you," she says. "Somehow."

We talk for the rest of the hour. I ask about her courses and I remember to tell her about Mrs. O'Neil.

"She was a nice lady," Darlene says. "Did I tell you I had lunch with her?"

"You didn't, but Tom did. Apparently you made quite an impression on my friends. Tom says they couldn't stop talking about you."

We laugh together, and then the hour was up. Prisoners leave first. At the door, I looked back and waved, a cauldron of feelings bubbling chaotically within me.

The area around 13th Street, between Fifth and Sixth Avenues, is one of hundreds of self-sufficient Manhattan neighborhoods, with all needs satisfied in a three block radius. For Maureen Reilly, it was a huge step to take her own apartment on the fourteenth floor of a twenty story high rise. In her circle of friends, she had been the only one to leave the DA's Office for private practice, and now she was the first to move to her own apartment. It would mean a subway ride to the downtown courthouse and her shared office with attorney Salvatore DiCerbo, but it was past time to leave her ADA roommates and become an independent adult.

Reilly was pleased when Bob Watson offered to help her move. It was frighteningly domestic, but more than a little exciting, to have Watson's masculine presence in her apartment after so many years with the girls. When Moishe the Mover had finished carrying her few pieces of furniture and a dozen or so cartons of possessions into the apartment, and the two of them were alone, Watson took her in his arms, and they shared a kiss that stirred emotions and appetites.

"Let's have an early dinner in the neighborhood," Reilly said. "Then we'll come back here, to unpack and maybe hang some pictures."

"Good idea," Watson said, "I'm hungry." His smile told Reilly his hunger had nothing to do with food. But then, neither did hers.

Maurizio's Trattoria, down the street from Reilly's new apartment, offered a full range of Italian dinners and an excellent selection of red wines. They sat in the rear of the mostly empty restaurant, two hours before the Saturday night dinner crowd. The setting sun slanted through the street side windows, casting a soft glow on the frescoes depicting Italian village life.

The setting induced talk about travel, first to Italy, where neither had been and both would like to go, and then to Ireland. Reilly had visited her family in County Mayo several times and Watson, who had been to Ireland when he was a teenager, had been enchanted with the green hills and spectacular seascapes of the

Dingle Peninsula. Maybe, Reilly allowed herself to dream but didn't dare say aloud, we'll go together someday.

She was pleased with the way her unexpected relationship with this police detective was evolving. They had dated for nine weeks without going to bed, in part due to the constant presence of Reilly's roommates. It's time, Reilly thought, declining dessert, for me to see this man naked.

Alone in the elevator, she stood in front of him, both facing the door, and he pulled her back against him. She could feel his erection against her hip, feel herself respond, feel the change in his breathing and hers. She could not get the key in the door quickly enough, barely remembered to chain the door. They started undressing in the living room, leaving clothes in their wake until they reached the unmade bed.

"No sheets," she said in a husky voice.

"Doesn't matter," he responded. "Pills?"

"Yes."

The last rays of the setting sun bathed their bodies in a magic light. His touch was surprisingly delicate, his lovemaking anything but. She came before he did, a first in her experience, and then came again. Only then did he pour his heat into her, and she came again. Sometime in the night she found some sheets and a blanket, a brief interlude in their almost constant lovemaking.

"I never believed people could actually do this," she said sometime before dawn.

"I can't get enough of you," Watson said, kissing her legs and between her legs, then entering her again.

By the time they actually fell asleep, the sun was rising. Reilly put on a pot of coffee, and began frying bacon.

"The naked chef," Watson said, reaching around her from behind, and once again she felt him strong against her.

SEVENTEEN

Spider and I are no longer cellmates. Double bunking is used at Sing Sing only when there are too many new prisoners, and inmates are re-assigned to single cells as soon as they open up. Since we're both still in B-block, however, we share the same rec.

"How you doin' with your transcript?" Spider asks as we fight the blustery March wind.

"Not so good. I don't know what I'm looking for."

"Talk to me," he says.

The prisoners are in their normal groups, and Spider and I are the only ones who dare to invade spaces which "belong" to others. As we walk, we pass close to a large group of black inmates. Spider nods pleasantly, receives fierce glares in return.

"I keep reading and re-reading," I say as we move on. "Nothing comes to me."

"So you're fucked. Welcome to the team."

"There was one witness who didn't testify." Spider says nothing so I continue. "It was the newsstand guy, Angel Martinez. The prosecutor intended to call him, and he was on our witness list too, but nobody could find him."

"What did this guy know?"

"He saw me twice the night the woman was attacked. The first time, he saw me help the woman when she fell. He would have corroborated my explanation for the blood and fingerprints. He saw me again, at about eight o'clock, which is when the woman was attacked, so he would have been an alibi witness for me. We both heard sirens going to the park. If I was with Angel Martinez, I could not have been the one who was seen running out of the park with the lady's pocketbook."

"You told this to the cops?" Spider asks.

"I told Detective Watson."

"Watson?"

"The face in the murky water."

"How could I forget?"

"Watson sent another detective to interview the newsstand guy. Martinez remembered the woman falling down, but he didn't say anything about the second time he saw me. Maybe he didn't remember."

"Your lawyer interviewed Martinez?"

"He tried, but he couldn't find him. The guy had disappeared."

Spider stops in his tracks, at the very closest spot our path comes to the group of inmates he's tormenting, pointedly oblivious to the resulting agitation. A bemused look comes into his eyes, and suddenly I get it.

My first reaction is anger. "He knew! The god damned prosecutor knew!"

Spider licks his lips and nods his bald head up and down in triumph, so pleased to have once again demonstrated his superior intelligence.

"Martinez did remember. The prosecutor knew I was somewhere else when the murder was committed. He knew I wasn't the killer and he convicted me anyway. He lied to the jury!"

Then I understand the opportunity this presents. If I can prove I wasn't the killer, I'll be released. They wouldn't keep someone in prison if they knew he was innocent, would they?

But Spider knows different. He faces me straight on, puts one huge hand on each of my shoulders. "First thing you gotta realize," he says, "is knowing the truth doesn't change shit. Nobody cares. Nobody's goin' to listen. Your only chance is that detective. If he knows the truth, and if he wasn't the one who made the evidence disappear, maybe he'll help. Probably not, but it's the only chance you got."

My fingers tremble and I have great difficulty organizing my thoughts, all the time struggling to contain my fury at what has been done to me. My mind wanders. I'm distracted by Katie's drawings, which are taped all over my walls. I destroy half a pad of paper on a dozen drafts.

Finally, the letter is as good as I can make it.

Dear Detective Watson,

My name is Joshua Blake. In May 2003, you arrested me and charged me with the murder of Mrs. Sarah Cooke in Central Park. You questioned me once at the Central Park Precinct and twice more on Rikers, and you testified at my trial.

I told you I helped Mrs. Cooke when she fell, and there was a newsstand guy at Sixty-sixth and Columbus who saw it happen. I also told you this newsstand guy saw me a second time.

You sent someone to talk to this guy, and later you told me he remembered the lady falling down and me helping her. His name was Angel Martinez.

I thought this would lead to my release, since it shows how my fingerprints got onto Mrs. Cooke's bag. When you told me I wasn't going to be released, I hollered at you and called you names. I hope you will forgive me.

But then you looked at me in a strange way, and I felt there was something you weren't saying, as if you knew something important. Maybe you even thought I might be innocent. This look didn't last long, and maybe it was my imagination, but it's all I've got.

Of course I testified about helping the lady and being at the newsstand later, but without anyone to back up my story, I guess the jury didn't believe me. My lawyer wanted Martinez to testify, but he couldn't find him.

If Angel Martinez remembered our second meeting, wouldn't that prove I couldn't have been the one who attacked Mrs. Cooke?

Detective Watson, I don't have any place else to go for help. I'm going to die here for a crime I didn't commit. You're my only chance.

I know every convicted person says he's innocent. Maybe there wasn't any look. But if you really did know something, could you tell me what it was? Will you help me?

When the letter is completed, I experience a great sense of hope. I'm finally doing something constructive. But there is also dread and foreboding. Suppose I'm wrong about the detective's look, and even if there was a look, suppose he doesn't want to be bothered about someone he had barely met, and a case long over.

For over a decade, Roger Claiborne had dreaded the weekly meetings of the thirty or so prosecutors of Trial Bureau 20. His views were never sought, and he was reluctant to speak, since when he did he was usually contradicted, or worse, ignored. Over the years, many younger prosecutors had joined the bureau and rapidly surpassed him.

Claiborne's triumph in the Blake case had changed everything. The mayor called. He gave interviews to the press. He was invited to lunch by powerful people. Elevator operators knew his name. He began to receive heavier cases, challenging cases that had passed him by for years. Mysteries, not grounders. Surprisingly, he did well. With his newfound confidence, he took on complex cases and difficult defense attorneys, and he won case after case. His stomach stopped bothering him and he actually looked forward to difficult days in court as a challenge he knew he could meet. He was now on call for homicides, and when his silent beeper vibrated at Lincoln Center, he was thrilled to tell his date he had to leave Beethoven and head to a murder scene in the East Village.

His secretary Helen knew they were moving before he did. "New digs, Mr. Claiborne," she said one bright Monday morning, and before the week was out, Roger had a significantly larger office with a view of the park.

His social life had also become dazzling. He went to parties on the East Side, and was actually looking forward to the spring season in Newport. He rented a car and spent a long lazy weekend exploring the possibility of a summer rental in the Hamptons.

Wherever he went, people asked him about his role in fighting crime in the big city, and, given the kind of cases he now had, he always had something fascinating for his listeners, especially the young sexy ones. His brother Nicholas invited him to a party at the Park Avenue apartment, and Roger became the star of the evening when the mayor arrived and sought him out for a quiet private conversation. His Mother invited him to a black-tie party at the renovated MOMA, and it was Roger's picture, with his date *du jour*, in the Sunday Times.

Yet, underlying Claiborne's new social and professional status, there was still his basic insecurity. He hid it well, but sometimes it came out in conversations with his fellow ADA George Henson, who was still his only real friend in the Office.

"Are you enjoying all this?" Henson asked Claiborne one day at lunch.

"Only if it lasts," Claiborne responded.

"What do you mean? You're getting great cases, and you're getting convictions."

"That's true. And I'm thinking about a Hamptons rental this summer."

"So what's the problem?"

"I don't know."

"You worry too much," Henson insisted. "What could be bad? Let yourself enjoy."

"Eight twelve," she said, looking at her watch. "How're you doing?"

It had not taken Bob Watson very many strides to realize he couldn't keep up with Maureen Reilly for very long. He had managed the first eight minute mile, but that was about his limit. He took two huge gulps of air and tried to answer, but no words came out.

Reilly eased her stride, and a few minutes later, breathing more easily at what he guessed must be a ten minute pace, Watson could finally speak.

"Thanks," he said. "How long can you keep that pace?"

"I've done five miles at an eight minute pace. I don't think I'll be able to run that fast for a whole marathon. At least not yet."

"What's the longest distance you've run?"

"Ten miles."

They ran side by side in silence for the next several miles, appreciating the sights of Central Park on a glorious Saturday morning in the early spring. There were no leaves on the trees yet, but there was nature's tease, an almost imperceptible smell of what was coming. It was crisp, the sun was bright, and the park was alive with throngs of runners, bikers and skateboarders enjoying the New York weekend blessing of no cars on the park roads.

Reilly pulled a few steps ahead, and Watson enjoyed the view. Great ass. Strong, well shaped legs. This woman had it all. He had taken her to the opera in November, there were several more dates, and they had been lovers for the past six weeks. They were at a delicious high-tension stage in their relationship where each knew something special was happening, but there was still a tentative edge to every look and touch. He caught up, lightly brushing her shoulder as he drew even, and hoped she felt the same quickening thrill he did. She rewarded him with a glorious smile.

"Once around," she said. "Six miles. Enough for me. How about you?"

Thank God, Watson thought. "If you're ready to stop," he said, "it's okay with me."

They eased off and began to walk toward the footpath at 63rd Street. As they neared Central Park West, Watson suddenly felt uncomfortable. He stared at the sharp drop-off along the left side of the path and the rocks below. The old lady, he thought. This is where she died. What was the kid's name? Something bothered him.

"Will I see you tonight?" Reilly asked.

They were intimate, and growing closer all the time, but they were not yet constant companions, so it was not automatically assumed they would be together all weekend.

"I'm working this afternoon. Suppose I pick you up at eight. Dinner in Little Italy?"

"Brooklyn Heights?"

"You got it."

In the thirteen years since he graduated from John Jay College and moved into his own place, Sunday breakfast with his parents in Montclair had been a frequent treat. Watson tried to make it at least once a month. Mom served a huge meal - bacon and eggs, home fries, pancakes - enough cholesterol to offset weeks of careful eating. Sometimes his two younger brothers came too, but this time it was just him. Just as well, he thought. I've got lots to talk about.

Conversations with his Dad had been a central part of his life for as long as he could remember. His father had been his only real sounding board for the many questions, doubts, anger, and frustration which went with being a New York City police officer. They took their coffee and sat facing each other on the back yard swing that had been there since he was a little boy.

"I've been seeing someone," he began. The swing went gently back and forth several times before he added, "Her name is Maureen Reilly."

William Watson was a professor of European History at Seton Hall University, with a particular specialty in the impact of religion on affairs of state, such as in Northern Ireland.

"Irish?"

"Second generation, grandparents from Westport, County Mayo."

Bob and his father had engaged in numerous discussions about the ancient British takeover of Ireland, and the ongoing struggle to create peace after seven hundred years of betrayal and violence. Professor Watson thought the Brits and the Prods were pretty much wrong about everything, but the IRA's over-reactions were often just as terrible. The Watson family had been to Ireland once, an unforgettable summer week when all three boys were teenagers.

"Catholic," Bob said, anticipating his father's next question. "She's a lawyer, a defense attorney."

"Cops don't generally fall in love with defense attorneys."

"Who said anything about love?"

"You think I can't tell?" A slow smile creased the Professor's face.

"I saw her do a cross-examination and she made me squirm. I asked her for coffee and she said no."

Watson shrugged and held his lips together. "But I tried again. What I really like about her ..." Watson paused. "Well, among other things." He blushed, surprised he was being so open with his father. "I can talk to her about my work. She's not a cop and her views are different, but she's part of the system. She understands."

"Your mother and I have always had interesting and meaningful things to talk about. It's a blessing, I think. There are so many couples who don't." He smiled. "I hope this works for you."

"I'll keep you posted. Meanwhile, I'm also loving my job."

"After the bad time in Central Park, you find Manhattan Homicide more to your liking?"

"You know I hated CPP. So little to do, so many celebrities. But homicide is great. The pace is unreal. Crime happens so fast."

"I thought the murder rate was down in New York?"

"It is, but there's still enough. I'm working on eleven jobs as we speak, four where I caught the case and I'm in charge. I'm the junior guy, but I'm running those four jobs. With lots of help, of course. Lt. Kerrigan is actually working with me on two of them. Some commanding officers could care less what their guys do, but Kerrigan gets involved. It's so different." Watson knew he sounded like a naïve rookie but he didn't care. He was excited, and his father was the one person with whom he could always share his excitement. "The 7-5 was a terrific place, with motivated officers, also a great commander ... but there's a level of professionalism at Homicide that's just amazing. Every detective does his job so well, and there's always a plan, especially if there might be violence. Options, backups, everything is thought out first."

"It's great to hear you so excited, with the job as well as with the girl," Professor Watson said. "Let's go inside and tell your mother about this Irish lass."

EIGHTEEN

"You sure are one hot woman," Bob Watson whispered, tracing his finger along Maureen Reilly's thigh, around her hip, heading towards but never quite reaching what both knew was his target.

"Is that what you tell all your girls?"

"Only one girl for me."

Reilly curled herself back into Watson's lean powerful body, and he shivered with excitement. She was drifting off to sleep after a delicious love-making, luxuriating in the privacy of her new apartment, but Watson had other ideas. His hand continued to explore the possibility of a repeat performance and then, abruptly, he pulled away.

"I got a letter today."

Reilly rolled closer.

"It's from a kid who was convicted of killing an old lady in Central Park last summer. Joshua Blake. We actually ran by there last Saturday. Near Central Park West at Sixty-third."

"Sure I remember," Reilly mumbled sleepily. "It was all over the papers. The first time we had coffee, you were in court for the Blake case. Actually, I saw him at arraignment. Larry Mullin got the case, but Cartegna could have picked me."

"It was back when I was in Central Park Precinct. I managed the first few days of the investigation. I actually made the arrest, and I interviewed the kid two or three times."

"Why did he write to you?"

"He thinks I gave him a look once like maybe I thought he might be innocent."

"So he has a vivid imagination."

"No. He doesn't. I remember exactly what he's referring to. I did give him a look. And I almost said something, just like he thinks. The case wasn't that good."

"What?" asked Reilly, raising onto her elbows.

"I didn't think it was strong enough to take to trial, and I told Claiborne, but he insisted on going ahead."

"Claiborne? Roger Claiborne was the ADA? You told him the case was weak?" Reilly sat straight up, took her time bringing the sheet over her breasts.

"There was a guy named Angel Martinez who worked at a newsstand on Columbus Avenue. Blake said he helped the old woman when she fell off the curb, an hour or so before she was

176   Lewis M. Weinstein

killed. Angel saw it happen and corroborated Blake's story. Blake claimed his prints on her pocketbook and her blood on his shirt were from when he helped her. He said he never went to the park, never saw the woman again."

"What he did an hour before doesn't prove he didn't attack her later." Reilly said.

"I'm sure that's what Claiborne argued, and the jury must have agreed with him. But there was more. This Angel guy also said Blake came back to his newsstand a second time. If it's true, and the timing is right, then Blake was with Angel at the exact time somebody else was robbing the old lady."

"Sounds like a good alibi. The jury didn't believe Angel's testimony?"

"Apparently they never heard it."

"Why not?" Reilly asked.

"According to Blake's letter, Angel couldn't be found. Blake doesn't even seem to know Angel remembered the second time they met."

"Did he?"

"Yes. It was in the report."

"Mullin missed it?"

"I guess. Angel's recollection about Blake's second visit, and the extra fingerprints, seemed like enough for reasonable doubt, at least the way I saw it.

"Blake was screaming we should let him go. I was about to say something to Blake's lawyer when he saw the look on my face, but I didn't. I figured it wasn't my place, and he would get it anyway when he got discovery."

"Extra fingerprints?" Reilly asked, her eyes widening.

"Blake's latents were on the victim's handbag, along with the victim's. But there were other latent prints on the victim's handbag that were never identified," Watson said.

"Sounds like plenty of reasonable doubt for me," said Reilly. "Mullin's a good attorney. He should have been able to get an acquittal."

They rolled onto their backs and lay next to each other for a long time, holding hands, each deep in thought. Finally, Watson broke the silence. "I messed up too," he said. "I just let it go. Job done. Next job."

Watson stared at Reilly, took several deep breaths. He sat up, facing away from her, not looking at her as he spoke. "Ever since I got the letter today, I'm thinking I should have done more."

"But you did tell Claiborne."

"A few days after the arrest, I went to see Claiborne at 100 Centre. He was actually on his way to the Blake grand jury hearing. I told him I thought the case had holes in it."

"And?"

"He blew me away. Said a nobody like Angel Martinez wasn't credible. Didn't care about the other latents. Blake's prints are on the old lady's bag, he said, and that's what counts. We have a good case here, he said. Don't you be the one to fuck up a good conviction."

"And then?"

"A few days later, the case went to Manhattan North Homicide, and I never touched it again. I was nominally still in charge, but I just let it go."

Reilly massaged Watson's bare back. "So what are you going to do about Blake's letter, Mr. Detective Robert Martin Watson?"

"What can I do now? The case is long over."

"Maybe not," Reilly murmured.

New detectives in the Manhattan North Homicide squad have to prove themselves. Whatever they've done in previous assignments doesn't count. The only way to achieve the respect and loyalty of the other detectives is to be found worthy in the field, with them. Graduating from John Jay with honors, passing the detective tests with flying colors, all those years in the 7-5, being recruited and chosen by Lieutenant Kerrigan - none of that meant anything in the eyes of Detective Robert Watson's new peers.

When Watson caught the call at 6:30 am, he had no idea this would be the day he earned his spurs at Manhattan North Homicide. The call came near the end of his overnight shift. His partner Gary Lowrey had taken a vacation day, so Watson drove alone to West 183rd Street in Washington Heights, just north of the George Washington Bridge.

There was a dead body, and the first uniform patrol officer on the scene, a kid named Bernstein, had cordoned off the area. Several other patrol cars had arrived, but as yet, no brass and no other support units. As the "catching" detective, Watson would be in charge. Uniformed officers of all ranks, and even the more senior detectives, would look to him to lead, and watch how he did it.

A substantial crowd had gathered, and it was not a friendly group. Perhaps fifty people were milling about in small shifting groups, with more arriving. Several blue uniforms maintained the scene. It wasn't ugly or out of control yet, but the smell was in the air.

Watson instructed Officer Bernstein, who looked terrified and overwhelmed, to extend the cordon of yellow tape, pushing the crowd another twenty-five feet away. As he watched the crowd retreat, Watson wondered if the killer was among them, enjoying the spectacle he had created. He scanned the faces, looking not for a particular person but for the kind of movement that triggered suspicion. He thought he noticed a sudden tensing by a small man wearing a red sweatshirt, but he kept his gaze rotating, not wanting to frighten off his target before he had resources to deal with him.

Watson moved slowly to the far side of the scene so the dead body was between him and the man who had attracted his attention. He took out his pocket-sized digital camera. His first shots were focused tightly on the body, but his eyes remained on the crowd. He extended the telephoto lens and raised the camera angle slightly. Four quick shots captured the red sweatshirt target and those near him. Watson lowered the camera and took another ten shots of the body, but his eyes never left the crowd.

Police procedure dictated the next ten minute's work. Watson prayed he would remember everything he was supposed to do, and his target would stay put while he did it. He assigned one of the patrol officers as Recorder, telling him to keep an accurate record of every person who showed up, time of arrival, name, rank, badge number, why they were there, what they did. The Patrol Supervisor from the Thirty-fourth Precinct was the first to be so recorded, followed quickly by an Assistant Medical Examiner and a Crime Scene van. The ADA was late as usual. That was all normal.

What wasn't normal were the others. Watson counted eight in all, there might be more. Several walked around like detectives, others slid into the crowd. Something was going on. This was not a routine killing. None of the newcomers approached him to identify themselves or explain their presence.

"I asked you not to move the body yet," Watson said, addressing the Medical Examiner, who had laid out a body bag and was preparing to disobey Watson's direction.

"Yes, but ...," the M.E. said, looking in the direction of a portly detective standing on the other side of the body.

Watson's status as the detective-in-charge was being challenged. He looked around, but no help was in sight. The decision was his to make and the time was now. He walked over and introduced himself. For his trouble, he received a look of disdain and an unintelligible mumble.

"Could you say that again," Watson asked, struggling to stay polite. "I didn't get the name and unit."

"And who the fuck are you?"

"I'm the detective from Manhattan North Homicide in charge of this investigation," Watson responded, "and you, whoever you are, are not giving any orders to anyone, unless my chain of command tells me otherwise. Are we clear?"

"This investigation is way over your level, dickhead, and you would be well advised to step aside."

"When I am so ordered," Watson said, "by someone with authority to do so, I will be happy to step aside. Meanwhile, I give the orders here and that body stays where it is."

Before he actually saw him, Watson felt the presence of Lieutenant Brian Kerrigan at his side. He was no longer alone, but had he made the right decision? Who had he alienated? Would his boss stand by him? He turned toward Kerrigan, pointedly placing his back to the other detective. "The possible perp may be in the crowd," he said quietly. "Red sweatshirt. I have photos. The body should stay where it is so the crowd stays put long enough for us to approach the suspect. The fat detective over there has a different idea. I don't know who he is, or what jurisdiction he may have, but I told him I was in charge and the body was not to be moved." Watson held his breath waiting for Kerrigan's reply.

"I heard the last part," Kerrigan said quietly. "I'll back you. Hold the body. Fuck the fat boy."

Watson nodded to the M.E., who must have overheard since he was laughing into his hand. The M.E. stopped preparing the body bag. Hearing more familiar voices behind him, Watson turned to see two more detectives from the MNH squad.

"I'd like to find out what that nervous guy out there knows," Watson said. He asked one of the newly arrived MNH detectives to come with him.

"I'll manage the scene, including your new best friend," said Lieutenant Kerrigan, slipping easily into a role subordinate to the catching detective.

Watson and Banyon moved slowly away from the body toward the crowd. When they ducked under the tape, the tension level rose perceptively, people stirred, and the murmurs became more ugly. The guy in the red sweatshirt edged back. As soon as Watson took a purposeful step in his direction, he bolted.

The crowd blocked Watson and Banyon, and by the time they broke through, the red sweatshirt had a twenty five yard lead. But he was slow and Watson was not. The footrace lasted for less than two blocks and ended with a spectacular open field tackle at the corner of One Hundred Eighty Fifth and Broadway. Watson waited for the arrival of two uniform patrol vehicles and left Banyon to arrange transport of the suspect to MNH headquarters. He returned to the scene of the killing to find both the body and fat boy gone.

"We caught the guy," Watson reported to Kerrigan. "He's on his way to Homicide."

"Good," said Kerrigan. "I let the body go, and fat boy went with it. It seems our victim this morning may have been the subject of several ongoing investigations. Unfortunately, those conducting said multiple investigations had never seen fit to share said knowledge until this very day at this very place." Kerrigan laughed out loud. "Imagine that," he added.

"Did I screw up, boss?" Watson asked.

"Depends who you ask," Kerrigan said. "Not in my book, you didn't. Maybe fat boy from DEA feels differently, but we'll deal with him. You will have to share the guy you caught, though. Lots of people want to talk to him."

"Including me," said ADA Roger Claiborne, who had come up behind them.

"Nice of you to show up, Roger," said Kerrigan. Watson was surprised at the Lieu's sarcasm, even as he tried to sort out his own feelings. He had not seen Claiborne since the time in the courthouse, but those memories had recently been refreshed by Joshua Blake's letter and his emotional conversation with Maureen Reilly.

"This is higher profile than you know," Claiborne said.

"How do you know what I know?" Kerrigan growled. "You got something you want to say, spit it out."

Claiborne took a step back and seemed to notice Watson for the first time. He pointedly ignored Watson and spoke to Kerrigan. "This is a complicated case, Brian. DEA, FBI, lot's of people have an interest. I'll coordinate with you."

"No, I don't think so, Roger," Kerrigan said. He stared into Claiborne's eyes and offered no explanation.

"What do you mean?" Claiborne asked.

Kerrigan folded his arms across his chest and looked at Claiborne the way he might look at smelly fish. "Don't you know how things work in Homicide, now that you're such a famous homicide prosecutor and all? Let me explain it to you. Detective Watson caught this job, and you'll coordinate with him. Detective Watson will tell me whatever I need to know."

"Yesterday was my best day ever as a cop."

"What happened?" Professor Watson asked his son, who had come to New Jersey to share a late breakfast with his dad at the Tick Tock Diner near the Meadowlands sports complex.

"There was a murder in Washington Heights, and it was my catch. The scene was crawling with detectives. DEA, FBI, all kinds of brass, but I was in charge. The DEA guy wanted to give the orders, but I didn't let him, and my Lieutenant backed me up. I picked a suspect out of the crowd, and when we approached him, he ran. We caught him and brought him in."

"Any shots fired?"

"No. Just the one that killed the victim, before I got there. The suspect, if he was the shooter, had ditched the gun before he returned to the scene."

"How did you identify the suspect?"

"The guy was edgy. I had an intuition."

"Why did he hang around? Not smart."

"Not smart says it all. If I've learned anything on the Job, it's that most of them are pretty dumb."

"Sounds like an exciting day. Anything else going on? How's things with the defense attorney?"

"Good. She's taking me to a play tomorrow night. Off Broadway, way off, in the Village." Watson paused. His father, always patient, waited.

"There is something else, Dad. I got a letter the other day from a kid I arrested last year. He's in Sing Sing now."

"Why did he write?"

"He wants me to help him get out."

"It's usually your job to put them in, not get them out," said Professor Watson. When his son didn't answer, he asked, "Is the kid innocent?"

"Actually, I think he might be."

Again, Professor Watson waited patiently while his son took time to formulate his next thought.

"Since I got Blake's letter, I've been thinking I did a really lousy job investigating his case and maybe it's at least partly my fault he's in prison."

Watson looked to his father and received the unspoken encouragement that had always been part of their relationship. Good times or bad, his father was always supportive. "The case was weak. There was evidence which proved innocence."

"But the jury wasn't convinced?"

"The jury may never have seen it. It seems the inconvenient evidence never made it to the trial."

Watson saw the question in his father's eyes. "No, not me. But there were things I should have done. The investigation was second rate. When we found enough to convict Blake, we stopped looking. Everybody was frantic to have the case solved. The mayor was all over us, and the press.

Professor Watson's face showed how much he understood his son's anguish. But still he didn't speak, didn't criticize. He knows there's more, Watson thought.

"I was in a funk," Watson said. "You know I didn't want to be at CPP, and I let it affect my performance. Joshua Blake is in Sing Sing because I screwed up."

"I think you're being a little harsh on yourself, Bob," Professor Watson said. "Is there anything to be done now?"

"It may be too late."

The Exonerated is based on the stories of former death-row inmates who were subsequently found to be innocent and released. The program says the play is "for the exonerated and for those who are still waiting."

"You know, you defense attorneys think everyone who's convicted is innocent. Some of them really are guilty," Watson said to Reilly as they waited in the tiny theatre on Bleecker Street for the show to begin. Every seat was filled, perhaps attracted by a celebrity cast which included Gabriel Byrne and Susan Sarandon.

"Most of them are guilty," Reilly said. "Even many who are found not guilty. But that doesn't change the horror for those who are actually innocent. Especially if they're executed."

"Maybe it's worse to face a life in prison," Watson said.

"It's always better to be alive," said Reilly.

"I'm not sure," Watson said, as the lights lowered.

The stage was bare except for a line of armless chairs. An elderly man spoke. "This is not the place for thought that does not end in concreteness." Lights came up on a man and a woman. "I found my father's body ... my mother's too ... they had been hidden, and their throats were slashed ... they had me arrested."

Other characters appeared and left. Their stories were mesmerizing. "This girl, she got killed. And the cop came to my job the next morning." One case after another ... "they gotta find somebody ... you have been charged with first degree murder ... they have the power ... questioned without benefit of counsel."

After the play, Susan Sarandon introduced one of the people who had actually sat on death row and was later freed. She didn't say much, but her presence was searing. She, like the others, was trying to make what she could of the rest of her life. She mentioned the others who had died too soon, before they were exonerated.

"No time in this world to talk about dreams," Reilly said to Watson as they left the theatre. "That line haunts me."

A Good Conviction   183

"When Joshua Blake came to New York, he had a dream," Watson said. "Now he has a nightmare."

"What are you thinking about?" Reilly asked.

After the emotional wrenching of *The Exonerated*, going out to eat just didn't seem right, and they had gone instead to Watson's apartment on West 5th Street. They stood on his small terrace with a spectacular view of the Hudson River and New Jersey, silently sipping their wine. Reilly had been amazed Watson owned such an apartment, and he had explained how, after 9-11, property values had plummeted and he had purchased the apartment for a fraction of its value.

"Blake's letter," Watson said. "I keep hearing the sound of cell doors clanging shut." After a long pause, he added, barely above a whisper, "I think there's a good chance he didn't do it." Another pause. "I'm also thinking it wasn't a coincidence you took me to that play tonight."

Reilly weighed her words carefully. "It happens," she finally said, "more often than we want to know. There are lots of innocent people in prison. Sometimes it's just bad luck. Circumstantial evidence can pile up and it looks like you're guilty even if you're not."

Another long pause, wine glasses refilled, absorbing the beautiful night view. "But sometimes," Reilly continued, "it starts out as an honest mistake, and then somewhere along the line things change, and nobody's willing to admit they were wrong. Could be what happened to Blake. He was in the wrong place at the wrong time. Maybe it seemed like a good case in the beginning."

She raised her hand to still Watson's objection. "I know you thought it was weak. But there was surely enough evidence to make the arrest. Let's give Claiborne the benefit of the doubt for a moment. Let's say he really believed, in the beginning, that Blake was guilty. But the other evidence, inconvenient though it was, should have resulted in more questions being asked, other leads pursued. It didn't happen. Why?"

"Claiborne wanted the conviction too much," Watson said.

"Maybe," Reilly said. "But it couldn't have been just Claiborne. Maybe police officers were involved. What happened to the report you read, the one that mentioned Josh's return to the newsstand? If Mullin knew about the second meeting, Josh would have mentioned it in his letter. Why didn't they know? Did Mullin ever know about the unidentified latents? What else was known but not revealed? Who hid it? It might have been Claiborne, but it might have been others."

"A conspiracy against this kid? He wasn't that important." Watson re-considered what he had just said. "Maybe he was. A murder in Central Park is a major bad for this city, and there was heavy pressure to get a conviction. Same as those stories we saw tonight, isn't it? Somebody really needed a conviction, and any perp would do."

"Exactly," said Reilly, with a vehemence she made no effort to conceal.

"You're angry," said Watson.

"It's awful when people's lives are ruined," Reilly said, shaking her head, her eyes narrowed.

"It's too late now," Watson said.

"Maybe not," Reilly said softly. "Look, you have good instincts. You think something was wrong here, why not look into it?" She paused, deciding how hard to push, then went on, "There was an article last month in the New York Times. A Dominican kid got twenty years to life for a murder he didn't commit. Turns out the prosecutor failed to disclose the existence of a witness who could have helped the defense."

"I remember the case," Watson said. "We talked about it because the State paid this guy $300,000."

"It doesn't happen often, although there was a $5,000,000 settlement last year after a guy had served five years on a rape charge. The Bronx prosecutor had withheld evidence. Of course, nothing ever happens to the bastards like him. The Bronx DA said it wasn't intentional. My ass, it wasn't intentional! But proving it is another matter entirely. I have the article in my office. I'll make a copy for you."

Reilly could see Watson's mind working before he spoke. "You think the department likes it when you re-open a closed case?" he said. "You think they give merit citations?" Watson looked away, avoiding her eyes. "The department agrees with Claiborne," he continued. "Don't fuck up a good conviction. As far as the NYPD is concerned, this was a real good conviction. Why should I get involved?"

Reilly hesitated. She was acutely aware their own growing relationship could be threatened by the tension building between them over this case.

"Because it's bothering you," she finally said, "and because you're a good man."

Perhaps, she thought, this is how I'll get to know just how good a man he really is.

NINETEEN

Teri Scanlon was assigned to write a story on the re-surfacing of an old murder case. She was reading her final draft.

> Fourteen years ago, there was a notorious shooting at the Palladium nightclub in Manhattan. A year or so after the shooting, two men were convicted of the murder and sent to prison. End of case?
>
> Not quite.
>
> Something very strange is brewing in the Palladium case. It turns out that an unrelated federal narcotics investigation led to a witness who says the guys in prison had nothing to do with the murder, and he knows who did. Now that former federal prosecutor has gone into private practice, and his new law firm has taken the case of one of the Palladium defendants on a pro bono basis.
>
> Defense attorneys plan to file a motion to overturn the guilty verdict, based on what is called newly discovered evidence, and also on the failure of the prosecutor to turn over to the defense evidence which tends to prove innocence. It is expected that the motion will be filed before this year is out, so stay tuned. This could be interesting.

When Scanlon finished reading, her mind traveled to Joshua Blake, whose trial she had covered the previous November. She had always wondered about his conviction. The questions she raised in her articles about the Blake case had drawn the ire of the DA's office, communicated to her through her editor, which made her even more curious. Now here was this Palladium case, ancient history reborn. How many cases like this were out there? Missing evidence? Hidden evidence? Could Joshua Blake have been convicted because the jury didn't know everything the prosecutor knew? Now there was a troubling thought.

Scanlon, still a relative newcomer to the big city courtroom beat, went to the internet and did several Google searches, keying in 'withheld evidence', 'prosecutorial abuse', and 'overturned convictions.' It didn't take long to find a series of articles published in the Chicago Tribune in 1999. When she downloaded the articles and began to read, she was appalled.

The Trib reported on hundreds of cases where convictions had been overturned, many if not most because the prosecutor had hidden evidence tending to prove innocence. Scanlon soon found the seminal case, *Brady v. Maryland*, which established the absolute responsibility of the prosecutor to identify and give to the defense what is called exculpatory evidence, either tending to prove innocence or conflicting with the prosecutor's theory of the case. In other words, the prosecutor is obliged to help the defense. Yeah right, she thought, in whose lifetime?

The next day Scanlon went to see her editor and got permission to follow her nose, not only with respect to the Palladium and Blake cases, but also into the broader issue of prosecutorial abuse in New York City.

The day after I sent the letter to Detective Watson, I'm returning from the mess hall, jammed into the narrow corridor before a locked gate. Several inmates jump me and I fight back. I've been squelching my anger and avoiding confrontation for so long, I can't believe how good it feels to finally lash out and land a punch. The COs break it up quickly, and nobody uses a shank, but we all receive Inmate Misbehavior Reports. I'm placed in keeplock, which is the equivalent of solitary confinement, except you stay in your own cell. The SHU, Special Housing Unit, also known as the Box, is generally full and reserved for the worst cases.

A misbehavior report results in an automatic three or four days in keeplock, followed by a hearing before the Adjustment Committee, which listens to what you say and then finds you guilty as charged. The Committee sentences me to thirty days keeplock, less the four already served. Locked in my cell for twenty three hours every day, I have no law library, no mess hall, no regular rec, nothing. Worse, I'm now perceived as a troublemaker, so I can expect closer attention from the COs. With so many rules, I'm sure to break more.

When you're in keeplock, you don't get regular recreation time in the yard. Instead, you get what's called keeplock rec, with just the other guys who are also on keeplock. So of course the first guy I see when I enter the yard is one of the inmates who attacked me. He spots me, walks over, scowls, and says, "Fuckin' white brotherhood."

"What are you talking about?"

"Aryan Brotherhood, asshole," he says. "Don't play dumb with me. You and that big bald bastard."

So that's what this is all about. Spider was part of an Aryan Brotherhood gang at Attica. He was transferred to Sing Sing, he said, to break up the group at Attica. His taunting of the blacks in the yard had certainly been purposeful. Was he planning to form an AB gang here at Sing Sing? This black guy evidently thought so.

So now what? All I want is to be left alone, but it doesn't seem possible. Currents swirl around you in prison, sucking you in. With an inmate population sixty percent black and another thirty percent Hispanic, less than two hundred white inmates are disbursed in a sea of color. Neutrality is not an option. The whites have no choice but to band together. From what I know about the Aryan Brotherhood, I can't imagine myself as a member of that group. Spider hadn't tried to recruit me when we were cellmates, so maybe he doesn't see it either. But now the blacks have identified me as a friend of Spider's and thus their enemy. I'm going to need protection.

"You think jumping on me was smart?" It was lame, but it was the best response I could come up with at the moment. Afterwards, I realized how much it sounded like a threat, confirming my AB association.

"You sayin' I'm stupid?"

"I don't even know you. What's your name anyway?"

"Fuck you need to know my name for?"

"Look. We're going to see each other for another twenty five days of keeplock rec. Might as well know each other's names. I'm Josh. Josh Blake."

"I know who you are, mother-fucker."

We walk around the yard, side by side, silent. After two turns, we separate. Ten minutes later, the PA screams, "Keeplock rec is over. Line up to return to your cells."

I turn toward the gate. When the line jams up, as it always does, a low voice behind me says, "You can call me Cutter."

From then on, every time we're in keeplock rec, I make sure to know where Cutter is, and I keep my distance. There are no further interactions between us. Perhaps he's decided to wait until he can discuss things with his gang. Fine with me. As soon as I get out of keeplock, I need to discuss things with Spider.

"Enough already," Watson said. A week had passed since Reilly first suggested he re-investigate the case, and Watson was getting irritated by her relentless pressure. They were having dinner near the courthouse, before Reilly went back to her office and Watson off to the night shift. It was not a relaxing dinner.

"If you want to file an appeal, do it."

"There's not enough evidence," Reilly said. "Not even close."

Watson buried his head in the menu, not wanting to hear what she was going to say. She said it anyway, as he knew she would.

"You're the only one who can make this happen. Find Angel Martinez and see if he'll testify. Find out who the unidentified fingerprints belong to, and see if he's the real murderer."

"I think I'll have the veal scaloppini," Watson said. "You?"

Reilly stared at Watson with fire in her eyes.

"Okay, listen to me," Watson finally said. "What you're asking will take time, more time than I have, and other people would have to be involved. I'm not sure I can even get authorization to look at a closed case. Lots of folks won't like it if I start asking around."

Watson debated whether to say what was really on his mind, decided yes, knowing the risks. "It's one thing for you to sit in your office and write appeals. It's another thing to be out on the street, where the bad guys can be on you in seconds, and you need your buddies to back you up. Maybe they don't come, or they come too late, and you're wounded or dead."

Watson heard himself, but he didn't quite believe what he was hearing. He knew he had a lot of the responsibility for Blake being in Sing Sing. Was he just afraid to stand up? Was he a coward?

"You're right," Reilly said, but Watson believed she meant just the opposite and he was furious.

"It would probably be a waste of our time anyway," Reilly continued. "Nobody ever wants to take on a prosecutor. Roger Claiborne has become a New York City folk hero. The DA's office would certainly fight any effort to open the case again. Who knows whose dirty laundry would be dragged out? Maybe some guys at homicide even."

She lifted her eyes, pursed her lips, shrugged her hands. "So why bother?" she said. "So the kid stays in Sing Sing. Why should we care?"

Reilly clamped her lips closed and Watson could feel the explosion she really wanted to let loose. He waited for the next assault to begin, but Reilly was finished. Then Watson became afraid there would be no next round. Maybe Reilly was so disgusted with him she would drop the idea of re-opening the Blake case, and drop him too. He ordered the veal. Reilly ordered sea bass.

"Tell you what," Reilly said after the waiter had left, "don't do anything just yet. I'm going to visit a client in Sing Sing in a couple of days. I'll call Larry Mullin and arrange to see Blake while I'm there. Then we'll talk more."

Watson relaxed, glad for the opportunity to delay his decision.

"When was sentencing?" Reilly asked.

"I don't know. December. Why does it matter?"

"You get 150 days from the date of sentencing to file your appeal. So there's only another month or so."

This woman will not give up, Watson thought. Do I love that in her, or hate it?

"What am I going to do with him?" Reilly asked. "He thinks the kid is probably innocent, but he won't do anything about it."

Unable to concentrate at her office, Reilly had called her Nana. This happened often, and Nana was already aware of Bob Watson and the Blake case.

"Why?" Nana asked. This was exactly the question Reilly wanted, and it was typical of the way she and Nana had discussed things for years. Nana always seemed to know what Maureen wanted to talk about and how to draw it out.

"It's complicated. Nobody wants to go back and re-open what they all think was a good conviction. If Bob starts rooting around, turning up who knows what, people will be embarrassed, angry. It could hurt his career."

Reilly hesitated. She knew once she said what she was about to say, out loud to Nana, there was no going back. "But he's got to do what's right. I couldn't continue with him if he doesn't."

"Is he responsible for that young man being in prison? Did he make mistakes in the investigation?"

"I don't think he made mistakes, but he did leave some things undone. There are explanations for what he didn't do, but the bottom line is yes, he has some responsibility, and he knows it. But still he hesitates."

"Maybe the price is more than you can appreciate," Nana said. "But he didn't say no yet, did he?"

"No, he didn't," Reilly said. "Serves me right for getting involved with a cop, doesn't it? Cops are a strange breed. They don't like being wrong."

"Who does?" said Nana.

"But when they're wrong, an innocent person ..."

"You're sure this young man is innocent?"

"No, I'm not sure. I'm going to go see him."

"At Sing Sing? How exciting. But you be careful, Maureen."

About ten days into my keeplock sentence, I return to my cell after rec and something seems wrong, like someone had been there. Of course this is impossible. The cells are locked while we're gone. I look around and don't see anything unusual, so I lay down and begin to read my book, but the feeling won't leave me. I look under the blanket, under the mattress. Nothing. I tell myself to stop being paranoid.

Twenty minutes later, I'm on the toilet. Why I reach behind me I'll never know, but I find a small plastic package taped to the back of the toilet. I'm terrified, afraid to even touch it, with COs walking along the corridor. It's a small package, drugs of some kind I guess. Has it been there for months or just a few minutes?

I get back on my bunk and try to read. Then it comes to me. If someone planted those drugs while I was out, I can expect my cell to be tossed. Soon. I practically jump back to the toilet, reach behind me, pull the package from the seat, and dump the contents into the toilet. I tear the plastic wrapping into pieces and flush it all away.

"Stand. Remove your clothes."

I've made it by less than thirty seconds. The CO is someone I've never seen before. Sent to get me? By whom? Why? The CO searches my cell. He's smart enough not to go directly to the back of the toilet, but when he does, he seems disappointed.

The next day at keeplock rec, an inmate I don't know approaches me in the yard. I'm tense, expecting another attack. But he slows only enough to whisper, "Look under your mattress," and keeps on walking. Now I'm crazy to get back to my cell. What if it's searched again before I get there?

There's a four inch shank under the mattress, a heavy nail wrapped at one end with tape to make a handle. Is this another attempt to get me in trouble? Or was it put there by someone who knows I'm going to need it? Should I keep it or turn it in? It would be laughable to turn it in. Who would believe me? I'll throw it away. Where? Only outside my cell, which means not until tomorrow's rec. Now I have the damn thing overnight and if they search for contraband, I'm screwed. But meanwhile, I'm armed, and given all of my pent-up frustration and anger, I find the idea of engaging in mortal combat isn't all bad.

There's no search, and the next day I'm on my way to rec with the shank hidden in the sleeve of my jacket, trying to stay calm. Nothing happens on the way out, or in the yard, but, on a premonition, I change my mind and keep the shank.

Walking back to my cell, I turn a corner where I'm momentarily out of sight of the CO. With no warning, I'm surrounded and someone is slashing at me. I feel the rip through my jacket. My own weapon is out. The attacker, surprised, backs off for an instant and I bury the shank in his belly, jam it as hard as I can with the heel of my left hand, and keep walking. By the time he screams, I'm seven steps away. I hear the guards behind me, but I never stop walking until I'm sitting on my bunk.

Part of me is shaking, and part of me is thrilled. It's like I had a huge boil, and it finally burst. Sure it hurts, but there's also a considerable relief. I remind myself that what I've done will surely have consequences. I also think I'm no longer the same nice boy Mrs. O'Neil was talking about at my trial.

But at least I'm alive.

Fortunately, the two inch cut on my side is not deep. I have to hide it, because if the COs see fresh blood, they'll make me for the other guy in the fight and I'll be off to the Box. Solitary for months. For sure they'll add more time until I'm eligible for parole.

I'll be okay unless I'm strip-searched and I pray I won't have a visitor. I decide to skip rec for the rest of my keeplock time, which means fourteen consecutive days inside my six by nine cell. I've been told the first sign of prison madness is a sense the cell is collapsing in on you, and I've always had touches of claustrophobia. This is going to be a test.

The next day another guy I don't know looks into my cell. "Spider says he's glad he could help." He gives me a chocolate bar. He returns every day I remain in keeplock, each time with another chocolate bar. I do push ups and read my one book over and over. I use every power of my declining mind to force the walls to stay put.

But I have way too much time to think. I'm going to die in prison. Next time I'll be the one with the shank in my gut. I flinch with the imagined pain. Why hasn't the detective answered? It's unrealistic to think he will. Why should he care about me? These things don't happen to ordinary people, just living their lives, trying to make something of themselves. This is America, not some dictatorship where people are snatched off the street and sent to prison.

I've been afraid before. When I was a little kid, walking home in the dark, seeing shadows, imagining someone ready to jump out and grab me. But there's a big difference. I got home, and Mom had cookies, and it was warm and safe. Here, there's never any respite, no comfort zone. There is only endless, excruciating fear. Unless I die.

I see people who shiver in corners, bruised and bloody, passive receptacles for whatever anybody wants to do to them, including unspeakable sexual acts. They shuffle along, mindless vegetables, having lost whatever strength and resolution they once had. They can't fight back any more.

It's relentless, and it works on you until you just give up. Anger is good for me, so I think about my trial and the aristocratic prosecutor, who always seemed in charge, always knew what he was going to do next, always knew he would succeed. I picture him here, walking in a deserted hallway. I imagine sinking my shank into his gut, turning it, ripping back and forth until he has no functioning internal organs and I'm covered by his blood. This is my therapy, and I feel better.

"I was really surprised to get your call. How are you involved in the Blake case?

Maureen Reilly settled into the tiny windowless conference room Larry Mullin shared with several other single practitioners. Reilly had been surprised to find any lawyer's offices quite this far west on 23rd Street. It was almost New Jersey. She had worked with Mullin several times when she had been an ADA but had never been to his office.

"Remember Bob Watson?" she asked.

"He was the arresting officer. Josh wrote to him. Sent me a copy."

"Bob and I ..." Reilly paused, still not sure how to describe their relationship.

"I get it." Mullin said.

"Anyway, Bob told me about the letter, and about the case. He said he always thought it was a weak case."

"I really messed up, didn't I," Mullin said, and it wasn't a question.

"Maybe it wasn't your fault," she said.

A perplexed look came onto Mullin's face. Reilly was moved by his obvious concern for his client.

"Did you know Angel Martinez corroborated Josh's story about the second time he saw him?"

"No," said Mullin. "How do you know that?"

"It was in the police report," Reilly said. She watched a look of self-disgust spread over Mullin's face.

"How could I miss it?"

"Maybe it wasn't in the copy of the report you got."

"Oh, shit."

Mullin abruptly left the room. He returned with a large file box, which he placed on the conference table. He found the file marked "BLAKE DISCOVERY" and retrieved Detective Mackey's report of his interview with Angel Martinez. He read it, read it again, and threw it on the table.

"There's nothing here about a second visit," Mullin said. "Was there more? Do you have a more complete report?"

"Not yet, but Bob remembers reading it at the time."

"So Claiborne lied to Judge Berman."

"When?" Reilly asked.

"I had Mackey on the stand," Mullin said. "We didn't have Martinez, so I wanted to ask Mackey what Martinez had said to him. Claiborne objected on hearsay. We went into chambers. I said about the alibi, and Claiborne said there was no evidence of any alibi. But he knew different and he flat out lied."

"Too bad it wasn't in open court where there'd be a record."

"There is a record. I asked Berman to have the conference in chambers recorded."

"Score one for the good guys," Reilly said.

"I came so close," Mullin said. "I had Mackey on the stand."

Mullin bowed his head, and Reilly waited. When he looked up, she said, "There's more." Mullin stared at her.

"There were additional latents on the victim's pocketbook. Never identified. Did you know?"

"Of course not," Mullin groaned.

He opened the discovery file and located the fingerprint report. "Mrs. Cooke, Josh, that's it. There's no mention of unidentified latents. I had the fingerprint guy on the stand. He knew there were other latents and I never asked him?"

Mullin's eyes flashed at Reilly, showing anger. "Did Watson know there were more prints?"

"Yes, he knew," Reilly said. "But he didn't know that you didn't know. He didn't know that your discovery was incomplete."

"Incomplete, my ass," Mullin snarled. "It was altered. I can't believe they withheld exculpatory evidence."

"Watson told Claiborne early on he thought the case was weak," said Reilly

"And Claiborne ..."

"... I don't know. Somebody tanked the exculpatory evidence. Maybe it was him," said Reilly.

"Markman runs a straight up office," Mullin said, referring to the Manhattan District Attorney Harold Markman.

"I agree," said Reilly.

"I never dreamed they would do anything like this. I accepted what I got in discovery and didn't think to push for more." Mullin looked up at the ceiling. "You know, it took a longer time than usual to get the Blake discovery. I finally went to Judge Berman and got an order. This must be why. Claiborne was hanging on to the Mackey and Grabowsky reports until he had a chance to doctor them." Regaining eye contact with Reilly, he asked, " Do you know what was done to those reports and who did it?"

"Not yet."

"Can we get proof?" Mullin asked, hope written all over his face.

"Maybe," Reilly answered. "I gather you'd like to try."

"I sure would. I think about Joshua Blake a lot. I don't have so many clients I really think are innocent."

"Mind if I help?" Reilly asked.

"Will Watson help? We'll need him."

"Maybe," said Reilly, pleased that Mullin had gotten right to the crucial question. "It's a big risk for him. He's a good guy, and he's really upset by this case, but he hasn't decided yet."

Mullin gathered up the truncated discovery versions of the interview and fingerprint reports. "I'll make copies for you," he said, walking out of the room.

"When he returned, he asked, "Have you ever done a motion like this?"

"No," Reilly said. "Have you?"

"I've done several. It's a motion under Criminal Procedure Law section 440, based on newly discovered evidence not known at trial.

Mullin paused as if he didn't want to say what came next. "You know it's practically impossible. Even if we got proof we thought was solid, it's still a huge mountain to climb. No judge will want to overturn this conviction, no matter what we show him."

"I know," Reilly said.

"There's not much time left for a direct appeal," Mullin said, "but fortunately, there's no deadline for a CPL 440 motion. We have to find the evidence, identify willing witnesses, write a brief. You know they'll fight us. Claiborne will learn what we're doing. NYPD will put out every obstacle you can imagine."

"Don't fuck up a good conviction," Reilly said softly.

"What?"

"It's what Claiborne said when Watson told him there were holes in the case."

"Didn't care at all about Josh, or justice."

"I'd like to meet Josh, see if he's up for what has to be done. Actually, I saw him at the arraignment. Do you remember I was there?"

"You were in arraignment court? No, I don't remember you being there that day. But let's go see Josh. I'll go with you."

"I'm going to be in Sing Sing tomorrow, with a another client. I thought I'd try to see Josh while I'm there. Can you come?"

"Not tomorrow. But you go ahead, there's no time to waste. I'll call and set it up."

It was one of those slow days when no new cases came in, and nothing was developing in the old cases. Detective Robert Watson put in an unbroken day on his paperwork backlog. He reviewed notes from field investigations, generated reports on several active cases, and made plans to follow up additional leads. The work went well, and he found it calming.

But disquieting thoughts about Joshua Blake kept intruding. Images of Maureen Reilly with a new boyfriend, after she dumped him for someone she could be prouder of than the frightened, unprincipled excuse for a cop he had become.

"Who gives a fuck about me?" Serpico had said twenty years ago. "I don't have a friend in the department." Frank Serpico did the right thing, would not go along with the graft, bribes, and shakedowns by cops. He paid for it with a bullet in his face and a ruined career.

I'm sworn to uphold the law against everyone who breaks it. The Blake conviction was wrong. Somebody altered evidence. How will I live with myself if I just walk away? I did walk away once, but now I have another chance.

The pendulum swung. He thought about his career and what it would mean to lose it. Police work was hard enough when you were part of a team, respected and cared about. What if he suddenly became a pariah, if no one talked to him, if his cases became less important, if all avenues for advancement were cut off?

All his life, he had only one career goal, and at thirty-five, he was among the elite at Manhattan North Homicide. Some day he might achieve a precinct command. Chief of detectives? Even higher? He envisioned all such opportunities floating away, beyond the grasp of someone stupid enough to fuck up a good conviction. He remembered a line from *The Exonerated.* "No time in this world to talk about dreams."

Joshua Blake had dreams. He was supposed to go to law school. Did he have a girlfriend? Did he dream of getting married and having children? What does he dream about now, in his cell?

He knew in his heart what he should do, but a voice in his head continued to ruthlessly tabulate the consequences. I'll go through a door and, just like Serpico, nobody will be behind me. I'll call for backup and no one will respond. Of course they'll come, but they'll be just a few seconds late, and I'll be dead.

Some years ago, Watson had purchased a poster at the Kennedy Museum in Boston and it now hung in a place of honor in his apartment. John Kennedy was sailing alone, and the poster read "One man can make a difference, and every man should try." Did President Kennedy, or his brother Bobby, after whom Watson was named, always do the principled thing, or did they pick their battles and avoid tilting at windmills.

Compromise, after all, is the currency of politics. But I'm not a politician. I'm a cop, sworn to uphold the law. Naïve, he thought, to imagine police work without politics, to imagine life without compromise. Martin Luther King, who he was also named for, didn't compromise. He continued his fight against impossible odds. John Kennedy, Bobby Kennedy, Martin Luther King. All three were assassinated.

Finally, blessedly, somebody killed somebody on 137th Street, and Watson was released from his paperwork and his self-imposed mental torture.

TWENTY

Larry Mullin left a message another attorney was going to visit. I'm terrified about being strip searched, but it turns out okay. Many inmates have multiple knife wounds, and my trivial two inch cut draws no comment.

We meet in an attorney visitation room, a small windowless space with a metal table and two metal chairs, all bolted to the floor. Maureen Reilly introduces herself and explains that Detective Robert Watson had shown her my letter. She tells me she's a defense attorney who used to be a prosecutor in the same office as ADA Roger Claiborne. She says she was in court the day of my arraignment, and it was just the luck of the draw the judge chose Larry Mullin and not her to represent me.

Normal conversation, so unusual for me, helps me relax. I look at her long brown hair, done in ringlets, and her pretty Irish face. It turns out she really is pretty, but of course any woman looks good in prison. She's medium height, very fit, and I guess not much more than thirty years old. She exudes energy and determination, which is just what I want to see. She finishes by saying, "I think you got a raw deal. I want to help you," and my heart soars.

"Tell me about yourself," she says, and I give her the brief version, concluding with my week in Manhattan and the trip to Baltimore.

"And then?"

"On Saturday night, two detectives knocked on my apartment door. They said they had some questions to ask me, so I let them in."

"Did they say you were a suspect?"

"No. They said they were investigating a murder. They asked where I had been on Thursday night."

"What did you tell them?"

I repeat the details, although it's clear from her questions she already knows everything. When I finish my story, she asks, "When you got home, what did you do?"

"I watched the rest of the Yankee game and went to sleep."

Reilly purses her lips. She seems to be considering how she wants to say something that will be difficult for me to hear. "The police, and the prosecutor, knew Angel Martinez had seen you the second time," she says, and her eyes are fierce with anger. When I see her look, a chill runs through me. If anyone can help me, it is this woman.

"It was probably the police who chased him away," she says, quietly, matter of fact.

Lewis M. Weinstein

"That's what Spider said."

"Who's Spider?"

"He used to be my cellmate. He figured it out."

Reilly has confirmed Spider's intuition. ADA Roger Claiborne sent me to prison, knowing I was innocent. My mouth opens and closes several times as the speechless rage grows. Reilly waits patiently for several minutes while I get myself together.

"Did Detective Watson know?"

"He knew Angel Martinez had seen you the second time."

"Why didn't he say something?"

"He thought the information would be given to your attorney, as it should have been," Reilly says.

She pauses, and I know there's bad news coming. "Josh, you need to know Martinez' statement wouldn't have proven your innocence. Not by itself. It would have raised doubt, but the police and the prosecutor may still have thought you did it, and may still have convinced a jury."

"You said 'not by itself.' There's more?"

"Yes." There is pain and anger on Reilly's face, and it takes a while before she's ready to go on.

"There were more latent fingerprints on the victim's pocketbook, besides the victim's and yours. The police couldn't find a match."

"Why didn't my lawyer bring that up at the trial?"

"He didn't know."

"It was his job to know!"

"It was the prosecutor's responsibility to tell him, and he didn't," Reilly says, her voice rising. "Larry Mullin received an incomplete fingerprint report. At trial Claiborne asked the fingerprint witness about Mrs. Cooke's fingerprints and yours, and never mentioned the others. Mullin didn't know about the other latents so he didn't ask."

"That mother-fucker! Oh, excuse me, I'm sorry."

Reilly laughs. "No need to apologize, Josh. You said it exactly right. Roger Claiborne is a rotten mother-fucker."

I don't know how long we sit there, both of us seething. Finally, I shrug. "What now?"

"If you want me to, Josh, I'm going to try to find the truth and get you out of here."

I clench my fists and close my eyes, take a deep breath, so afraid I didn't hear her correctly. "You're going to help me?"

"I'm going to try. With Larry Mullin. We'll work together."

Reilly takes a long pause, and there's a pained look on her face. "I'm usually proud to say I'm a defense attorney, but some days I'm embarrassed to admit I'm an attorney at all. Our system is broken. Prosecutors, police, some of them, too many, too often, will cheat to win. They hide evidence, like they did in your case. Sometimes they make up evidence, or get a witness to lie. They put innocent people in jail. What they do is against the law, but they almost never get caught. And what's worse, if they do get caught, they never get punished. I mean never, not one time in the whole United States of America in the last fifty years."

While Reilly is telling me how innocent people get wrongly convicted, my mind is elsewhere. Of course I'm thrilled she believes I'm innocent. But would she still want to help if she knew I had recently stabbed a man with intent to kill? What if she knew how much I wanted to bury a shank in Roger Claiborne's belly, and that I really would do it if I had a chance?

"But maybe this time," she says, "it'll be different. I want to be straight with you. We don't have enough evidence yet to get a new trial, and we may never get it. The DA's office and the police will fight us every step of the way. But if it's okay with you, I'll talk to Larry Mullin, and I'll get back to you in a week or so."

I tell her it's okay with me and she gets up to leave. "By the way," she asks, "when you got home after the pizza at John's, did you turn your VCR off?"

"As soon as I got home. Why?"

"It establishes the time you got home."

They sat near the back of a cozy French bistro on Second Avenue in the fifties. There must be a thousand of these places in New York, Reilly thought, each more charming than the next, each with marvelous food. Restaurants don't survive in this city unless they're good, and this one had been around for decades.

The waiter announced the specials. Reilly, who knew the restaurant well, told Mullin everything on the menu was superb. They ordered, had a glass of wine, and shared small talk. Reilly was not impressed with Mullin's range of interests or his social skills. The food was delivered, the presentation surprisingly elegant compared with the simple surroundings, and they began to eat, still avoiding the topic which had brought them together.

"Do you think the sauce on Josh's meal tonight will match this?" Mullin asked, pointing his fork.

"Jesus, Larry, stop torturing yourself. It wasn't your fault," said Reilly, thinking maybe it wasn't going to be so pleasant working with Mullin.

"How's he holding up?" Mullin asked a few bites later.

"He's beaten down," Reilly said, glad to focus on Josh and not the disheartened man sitting across from her. "It tortures him that something so horribly unfair could have happened to him. He helped an old lady and his whole life spun out of control. He seems like a really nice kid who got a horrible break.

"I'm actually impressed he's still fighting," Reilly continued. "He has a powerful need to believe his life can be put together again. But it wouldn't take much to push him over the edge. All day long he sees and smells that awful place, railing inside at the unfairness of it all. Sooner or later he'll crack. He'll get killed or kill someone else. Either way, it'll be over. I think he knows this, and there may come a day when he prefers death to an endless, hopeless waiting."

"Did you tell him how difficult it would be?" Mullin asked.

"I told him it would be difficult," Reilly said, "but I didn't say impossible."

The French sauces held less interest with each passing moment, and both lawyers pushed food around their plates, lifting small, now tasteless, portions to their mouths, finally giving up completely, their faces set in lifeless stares.

"We have to help him hold himself together until we can get a new trial," Mullin said.

"If we can hold ourselves together." Reilly paused and took a deep breath. "What do you say we stop feeling so discouraged about everything and get to work. We need a plan, and a timeline."

The energy flowing from Reilly's challenge changed everything. Mullin produced a yellow pad from somewhere, and for the next two hours they talked law. Reilly was pleased to learn Mullin had done his homework, and done it well. He knew every possible basis for a motion to overturn a conviction based on newly discovered evidence and failure of the prosecutor to disclose evidence in his possession. As the discussion went on, Reilly began to see Mullin in a new light. It was obvious he was very capable, and cared a great deal.

It being a French restaurant in New York, nobody hurried them. They drank coffee, peed, drank more coffee. Mullin filled eighteen pages with tightly scribbled notes, and they had a plan.

"Why are we doing this?" Reilly asked with a wry smile when they were done. "It's likely we'll fail, we'll surely lose money, and we'll make enemies in powerful places."

Mullin pushed his chair back from the table and stretched his legs before he spoke. "When I went into the law," he said, his internal focus somewhere far beyond Reilly and the bistro, "this is the kind of case I dreamed about. Fighting against all the powerful forces the criminal justice system can throw at you. Nothing to gain, at least not money. But somehow, in my unspectacular little practice, it's what I've always wanted to do. Usually I work for guilty people. But this time ... this client ..."

"So it's the noble cause, is it," said Reilly. "You're a regular *Don Quixote*, tilting at windmills, dreaming the impossible dream?"

"Why not?" said Mullin. "Suppose we win. Wouldn't it be great?"

"I agree."

"I know. You wouldn't have taken the time to see Josh if you weren't already furious about what's been done to him. You wouldn't be sitting here for three hours if you didn't have an intense passion for justice."

Reilly looked at Mullin in a way she just knew not many women ever had. She let her look convey the respect and admiration she was feeling, and she could see the impact this was having on her new associate.

"It sure would feel good," she said, choking a little on the words and feeling a charge of electricity rip through her body.

She cooked sesame crusted salmon and scalloped potatoes ala Emeril, straight from a Food Network recipe, supplemented by salad bar from the local deli, with fresh fruit and cookies for dessert. Maureen Reilly was entertaining her friends at her first dinner party in her new apartment. It was a tight squeeze, but she had managed four folding chairs around the small table.

Suzanne Dixon was first to arrive, with a bottle of Chianti and a bag of home baked chocolate chip cookies.

"Joan and Elyse will be right along," Suzanne explained, "I had an errand to run."

The four women had been her roommates for almost a decade. The other three were all career Assistant District Attorneys, sharp lawyers working their way up in an organization that had long provided major opportunities for women. A woman was now head of the sex crimes unit, and they all took pride in the fact she was doing a terrific job. None of them had a serious relationship, so the lack of privacy in a shared apartment had been a payable price. Reilly had moved in part due to her own changed circumstance.

Maureen opened the wine and put her store bought cookies away. Sure enough, Joan Peterson and Elyse Letterman arrived soon after. There was the usual New York chatter about plays, movies, and celebrity sightings. There were lots of questions about Maureen's hot new boy friend.

"He testified in a case I had last week," said Elyse. "If he wasn't taken, I'd be jumping all over him."

"You keep your hands off," said Maureen. "I saw him first, although actually, he saw me first."

"And you resisted for how long?" asked Joan.

"Way longer than I should have," Maureen answered.

"Have you ...," asked Joan, and Maureen's blush provided the answer. "Good for you," Joan screamed.

"Very good," Maureen agreed.

Talk inevitably drifted to gossip from the DA's Office.

"How is Mr. Markman?" Maureen asked.

"Same as ever," said Suzanne.

"I don't think so. I think he's less involved than he used to be," Elyse said.

"Finally slowing down?" Maureen asked.

"Could be," said Joan. "I can hear the sound of his arteries hardening through his closed door."

Reilly laughed. You could always count on Joan to say something profound in a witty way. But she was nevertheless troubled. Did Markman know about the Blake case? There were only two possibilities. Either he didn't know what Claiborne had done or he was a party to it. She couldn't believe he would knowingly do anything so horrid, but it wasn't comforting to think he had missed something either.

Several bottles of wine later, the evening drew to a close. Maureen was thrilled, and they all vowed to make it a regular thing. After they left, Maureen called Watson.

"The coast is clear."

My cell is unlocked and I've survived my month of keeplock. I go to breakfast and then to regular recreation. I walk around the familiar yard, and can't believe I actually missed it. I find Spider.

"Thanks," I say, knowing it's not necessary to mention the shank or any other details.

"It's my fault you needed it. I should have warned you." Spider looks me over, seems pleased with what he sees. "You did good."

"Did he live?"

"Barely. He's in the Box for 60 days." Spider is referring to solitary confinement.

"Then he'll be back at me. Or his friends will."

"Maybe not," Spider says. "But you won't survive if you're alone. Us white guys are way outnumbered."

I've already reached the same conclusion, and it's also clear to me a major battle is looming. I wait for Spider to explain his plan. He always has a plan.

"You ever hear of the Aryan Brotherhood?" So Cutter was right.

"Nazis? White Supremacists? Disgusting people."

"Great bunch," Spider says, laughing. "There's a few of those guys here."

"I've noticed."

"It's an opportunity. There's a place for you."

I'm terrified by whatever Spider is about to tell me. In the back of my mind I'm thinking he's always had a place for me in his plan. He knew and I didn't. Pieces are about to click into place and I'm going to be drawn into something I want no parts of.

"The Nazi shit works for some guys, but it means nothing to me. As far as I'm concerned, it's just business. White men are at risk here and we need power to protect ourselves. We're going to get the power by taking control of the prison rackets. We'll make deals with the black and Hispanic gangs, divvy up the distribution channels, set rules we can all live with. We'll establish ways to deal with conflict so it doesn't escalate, and we'll share the profits. I've been preparing for this since I got here, and now it's time to put my plan in motion. You remember Cutter? From keeplock rec?"

"How do you know ..."

Spider just stares at me. Like how could I think he wouldn't know.

"Cutter is a Blood. We've made a deal. He's selling it to his guys."

"Who's we?"

"I'll get to that. There'll be more deals, with the other gangs. First, you need to know some history you probably didn't learn in college. You were a history major, right? You like history?"

I keep walking, enjoying the large space and the sky overhead. Spider keeps talking.

"The Aryan Brotherhood started in San Quentin in 1967. There's a tradition of hatred of blacks, Jews, Muslims, but now, like I said, it's more like a business. Drugs, protection, extortion ... telephone privileges, laundry, food distribution. It's all for the taking. The blacks and spics have it all here, but they're not doing much of a job with it. I'm going to take a piece, in the name of the AB. My plan is to make my share grow, because I'll set it up so everyone benefits. Internal discipline is key, and organization. Recruitment, training, security officers, foot soldiers, enforcers, investigators, treasurers, record keepers."

I'm shaking my head, and my jaw drops open. I was this guy's cellmate for a month, and I never heard a word of any of this. All of a sudden, he's Don Corleone with a long term strategic plan to build illegal market share in Sing Sing. I'm thinking he's totally insane. How can he pull off something so audacious? Spider just keeps going. In his head, it's all worked out.

"I was number two man in the AB at Attica. We had it organized pretty good there, but this will be better. I'm startin' from scratch here. No dead wood to clear out."

"The other guys, they're just going to let you move in?" I ask. "Let you take a piece of their action?"

"It's simple. You start outside."

It's not simple to me. What is he talking about?

"You get some guys to exercise leverage outside. Talk to families, you know, take pictures. When you show what you have to the guys in here, they're more willing to listen, and then I help them see the logic of doing business together. Expand markets. New lines. Nobody gets too greedy, everybody profits."

"You get guys outside to exercise leverage? What guys? Where do you learn this?"

"You pick things up. In prison, you have lot's of time to think. You make a plan." Spider, as he often does, switches the conversation away from himself. "Let's talk about you. First up, the guy you cut won't be any more trouble. Cutter talked to him. You're cool."

I'm not relieved. The price for this protection will be steep. Spider has sucked me in real good. First with figuring out my case and the letter to Detective Watson, and now with the shank in keeplock. A paranoid thought. Did he set me up for keeplock so he could add to my indebtedness? When did he actually make his deal with Cutter, before or after we spoke? I don't have long to ponder. The first installment on Spider's investment is due. One of the first rules of business in prison is rapid turnover. There is no *status quo*. Get your return quick or you may not get it at all.

"You know a lot of law, right?" Spider asks.

"Hardly. I didn't even start law school."

"But you got in. Close enough. We need a corporate charter and by-laws. I want you to write them."

"What?"

"We need rules, an organizational structure, a way to deal with our enemies and integrate new alliances.

"Who are you? Where did all of this come from? Did you used to run General Motors?"

"I've been in prison a long time and I've seen how it works. I've also read a lot. We need a strong central government, a banking system, a diplomatic corp."

"You sound like Alexander Hamilton."

"Thank you. He was a brilliant man. So what do you say? You want to be my Attorney General?"

"Sounds more like *consigliore* to me."

"That's good. I like it. *Consigliore* it is."

Recreation is over. There will be no more conversation with Spider until tomorrow. I haven't said yes, but can you imagine saying no?

That same afternoon, when Tom Kaplan comes to visit, I'm in the full macho throes of having just knifed a guy and become a prison mob under-boss.

"What's going on with you?" Tom asks, not five minutes into our conversation.

"What do you mean?"

"You're different. Before, you were nervous and depressed. Now you have a swagger. I was concerned about you being depressed, but I'm even more frightened by what I'm seeing now."

"It's all a façade," I say. "If I tell you some things, you have to promise you won't tell anyone. Not even Darlene."

Tom promises, and I tell him, speaking very quietly, about my recent experiences in keeplock, stabbing a guy, and Spider's role for me in his grandiose plans. He shakes his head in disbelief.

"Josh, this is not like you at all," Tom says.

"You're right, but I can't be the nice guy I was and survive in this place. I'm not happy about it, but I really have no choice." As I'm saying this, it occurs to me I sound just like Johnny Cade in *The Outsiders*. Was he wrong? Am I?

Our conversation passes to less anxiety fraught topics. When Tom leaves, I think more about what I said. I reject the idea that I have other options. You have to actually live in a place like this to understand what it's like. I'd rather be aggressive about my life here than cringe in a corner like some other prisoners do. If you cringe, you're a dead man.

"So the two of you drank wine all night and agreed I should risk my career and maybe my life. Nice."

"It was coffee."

"What?"

"We only had one glass of wine. Then it was coffee."

Reilly knew she was not going to have any sex, and this made her very unhappy. Watson was wearing a tight t-shirt and jeans, and he looked particularly lean and strong. There was a special edge about him, something in the sharpness and tension of his eyes. Maybe Elyse's lust had added to his allure. But as she told him about her visit with Josh and her discussion with Mullin, he got progressively more irritated. Not tonight, she sighed.

So far, Watson had not bought in, and without his investigative skills and the NYPD resources he could bring with him, the plan she and Mullin had evolved was doomed to fail. It's stupid to make this a test of our relationship, she thought. It's not fair. I really like this guy, and I'm risking everything for a kid I barely know.

"Why do you care so much about this kid?" Watson asked, as if he knew what she was thinking. "You said yourself even if we get the evidence, we probably won't win. Blake will stay in prison, but my life at NYPD will become a nightmare you can't begin to imagine. Why? And don't tell me anymore about that play *The Exonerated*."

So there it was. She could press on, implying he was a wimp, so afraid for his own safety and career he wouldn't do what was clearly the right thing, which would pretty much ruin everything between them. But she couldn't drop it either.

"It's wrong for Josh to be in prison," she said, retreating to safer ground.

"Of course it's wrong. There's lots of things wrong in this world."

"Maybe you should see Josh," Reilly said. "Talk with him face to face like I did ... before you make a decision."

Watson's face turned from angry to pensive to amused. "You called Larry Mullin a *Don Quixote*?" he asked. Reilly breathed a sigh of relief.

"He surprised me," she said. "There's more to him than you might think. He hasn't done much that most people care about. Not successful in the traditional ways. But he has a passion for justice, and he thinks this is the case to define his life, give it a meaning he's always wanted it to have. Larry is really upset about this case. He thinks it's worth taking a risk for."

"What risk does he take?" Watson snapped.

Reilly knew Watson didn't care if Mullin took a risk. He cared about his own risk, and he was not pleased with the pressure she was bringing on him. But she also believed Watson wanted to be a good cop, do the right thing like Frank Serpico he was always talking about, like the JFK poster in his apartment. This was one of the qualities that had attracted her to him.

Watson didn't storm out of Reilly's apartment. He was polite, oh so polite. But leave he did, with no sex, with barely a good night kiss, and without setting their next time to get together, which had become their habit. Reilly was heartbroken. She prayed for the patience and wisdom to see it through. Then she called Nana.

Watson drove north on the Henry Hudson Parkway. He was off duty, but still, he was pursuing a piece of police business he had no authorization to touch. He was risking everything he had worked so hard to get. Would Lieutenant Kerrigan support what he was doing, if he knew? If he decided to do more, should he tell Kerrigan or try to do it on the sly? How deep was this going to get?

So what do I hope to accomplish today? What is Blake going to tell me I don't already know? No, he thought, it's not what he tells me, it's him. Is he up for this? Will he be of use? Can I trust him? Is he worth it?

Am I worth it? Am I what I want to be? Some white knight I am, turning and running rather than take a risk to do what's right. I'm disappointing her and I'm disappointing myself. The whole thing is probably hopeless anyway. Risk so much for what?

He entered the historic town of Ossining, and was bearing west toward the river and the prison. He let his mind wander over what he knew about the infamous Sing Sing, and, as was true for many things, he knew quite a bit. The name came from an Indian phrase *sin sinck*, which means stone on stone. The prison had been constructed on an abandoned mining site in the 1830s, when the standard punishment was hard labor in total silence. The first electric chair, invented by Thomas Edison, came to Sing Sing 100 years ago, and the town was so embarrassed it changed its name from Sing Sing to Ossining. Julius and Ethel Rosenberg were electrocuted. Willie Sutton escaped. The Yankees used to play games against an inmate team, and Babe Ruth was said to have hit his longest home run on the prison field, right over the wall and out of the prison, a flight that mirrored many inmates' dreams.

The imposing prison walls came into view, rising above the train station. Sing Sing is the only prison in the world with a commuter railroad running through it. You can't really see the whole place from outside, just a portion of the twenty five foot wall, broken by guard towers. Incongruously, joggers were running next to the prison wall, along a grassy area overlooking the Hudson River.

I'm alone in a comfortable conference room, sitting at a decent wooden table, staring at a coffee pot and two cups. Windows look out to a larger office, and normal looking people walk around. Amazingly, I'm not handcuffed. I hadn't expected a visitor, and have no idea what's going on, but this is sure very different from the loud bustling visitors room, or the austere attorney visiting room where I had met Ms. Reilly. Somebody with power arranged this meeting.

Through the window, I see a familiar face watching me. It's the face from the murky water. "I got your letter," Detective Robert Watson says as he enters. He actually reaches out his hand, and we shake, firm and friendly. I hadn't seen him since the day I ranted at him on Rikers. He doesn't look angry. He's wearing khakis and a blue button down shirt, with a light jacket against the cool spring weather. He takes the jacket off and hangs it on the back of the chair. He's lean and strong, ruggedly good looking. It hits me he must be Reilly's boy friend. Why else would he have given her my letter. I look at him with new respect. Reilly wouldn't be with a loser.

"I know," I say. "Ms. Reilly was here."

Watson sits across from me and starts out as if he had rehearsed an opening line. "You were right when you hollered at me."

"You think I'm innocent?"

Watson pours two cups of coffee, pushes one across the table to me. My heart is in my throat as I wait for his answer. "I think you could be," he says. Then he adds, "You understand what I think means nothing. Unless it's proven, and a judge believes it, nothing will change."

"But you'll try?" Despite Watson's presence at Sing Sing, and despite what he had just said, I sense he hasn't yet made a commitment to actually help. I'm right.

"There's big risks," he says, "for anybody who touches this thing."

"What do you mean?"

"The case is closed and nobody wants it re-opened. The department has moved on. The DA's office got their conviction. The mayor held his press conference. Powerful people will stand in the way of anybody who wants to re-open the investigation. It would be embarrassing."

"So your career is at stake?" I ask, struggling, probably without much success, to hide my anger. Why did he come here if he's afraid to get involved?

"You're right. It is," Watson answers, and I'm surprised at his bluntness. This is not the direction I had wanted this conversation to take.

"But it's my life," I say. He opens his lips, sighs, his eyes bore into me, and then I understand.

"You want something from me," I say. "What is it?"

Another long sip. Watson refills his cup. Mine hasn't been touched.

"Can you handle this?" he asks.

"I don't understand."

"It may take years. Can you last it out? Can you stay out of trouble? Above all, don't say anything to anybody?"

"I talk to my former cellmate," I say.

"You'll have to stop."

"No I don't. It was Spider who figured out what the prosecutor did. I need to talk with him." I don't think it's necessary to mention I've already told Spider about Ms. Reilly's visit.

Watson waits, and I'm not sure what to say next. It occurs to me it's stupid to continue to talk with Spider about my case. Spider has agendas I can't begin to fathom, and he can no longer be trusted. Since I've become part of his AB gang, I think I'm actually more alone than I was before, and I know I'm not smart enough or experienced enough to carry it off. Watson will find out, and then he'll walk away.

"Well?" Watson asks, shaking me from my thoughts about Spider. I have to say something.

"I'll be there," I say, "all dressed up in my best suit, the day my new trial begins. Whatever it takes, I'll be there." Does this sound convincing or does it come off as melodramatic bluster? Once on the path of boldness, however, there's no turning back.

"Can I trust you?" I say, hardly believing what I've said when the words are out.

"Can *you* trust *me*?" Watson snaps. "What are you talking about?"

"I have a friend. She's a hooker. She has information that could be very helpful for me, but I don't want you to arrest her if she tells you."

"You're negotiating with me," Watson says, but there's a sly flicker at the corners of his lips and I like what I see in his eyes. He stands and faces the window for what seems like forever. When he turns back, he shows a big smile. I've passed his test.

"You got balls, kid," he says.

"It has to do with one of her clients."

"Talk to me," he says, curiosity bursting from every pore.

"His name is Roger Claiborne."

Maureen Reilly was nervous. Watson had left a message on her cell. "Meet me at Pomodoro at six. We'll have dinner and talk." She couldn't tell anything from his voice, but she was afraid he was going to break up with her. Why else a public place to talk?

Why was she doing this? Was Joshua Blake that important to her? No, it wasn't just Blake, she kept telling herself, but she found it difficult to put in words what her real motivation was. If I can't explain it to myself, she thought, how will I ever make Bob understand? She had arrived early and was sitting at the bar with a glass of wine when she spotted Watson through the front window. Her heart jumped. Please don't let this end tonight.

Watson gave her a peck on the cheek and the maitre'd led them to a small table toward the back. They looked at the menus, ate the complimentary *bruschetta* with olive oil, said nothing that mattered. A heavily accented Italian waiter listed the specials and they placed their orders. A cop who eats fish, she thought inanely. Another sip of wine. Finally there was nothing else to do but talk.

Watson had asked to meet, so he began. "I went to Sing Sing yesterday," he said. "Joshua Blake has been through a lot, but he's not beaten." Watson's face suddenly creased in a smile that communicated both amazement and admiration. "Can you believe that kid had the nerve to challenge me. He asked if he could trust me?"

As Watson spoke, his face had softened, and there came to Maureen Reilly the thrill she felt on those rare occasions when the entire world became perfectly aligned into a kind of spiritual oneness she could never explain but nevertheless knew was real.

"He's worth fighting for," Watson concluded. "He won't let us down."

"The fight could be costly," Reilly said. "We could let him down."

"I owe him this one," Watson said. "I didn't do my job the way I should have."

"Of course you did. It was Claiborne."

"It was Claiborne, but it was also me." Watson stopped, obviously uncomfortable, and Reilly was again fearful.

Watson took a deep breath. "When I was first at CPP, I hated it. I had been transferred from the 7-5, and I felt the whole Central Park thing was beneath me. It affected my work. I didn't care as much as I should have.

"Red flags were popping that maybe Blake wasn't the perp, and there were things I should have done to nail it down one way or the other. But nobody wanted to hear it, and I didn't push like I should've. Maybe if I had still been at the 7-5, and surely if I was at MNH, I would've gone to my bosses. But when I was at Central Park, at least then, I didn't have any connection, and I wasn't comfortable.

I should have gone anyway. I let Claiborne get away with his 'good conviction' bullshit when I could have stopped it right there."

Watson's head dropped, his eyes avoiding contact. "I've been wanting to tell you ever since I got Blake's letter. I guess I was afraid you would think less of me."

Reilly covered Watson's hand with her own. He looked up.

"Nobody's perfect, Bob, and even the good guys don't have a good day every day. You're a good cop, and a good man. You couldn't have convinced Claiborne anyway."

"I should have made sure Mullin got the evidence."

"There's no way you could have imagined he wouldn't get it."

Watson lowered his head to their intertwined hands, kissed her fingers gently.

"It's not too late," she said. "We can still make it right, you and me. And Mullin. We're going to get Josh out." A tear came to her eye.

"Don't go soft on me now," Watson said.

Reilly felt the tear run down her cheek and didn't care. "I was so afraid. Bob. I didn't want you to go away. I love you."

Watson's smile melted her. "I'm not going anywhere, Maureen," he said. "I love you too, more than I can say." He took a deep breath. "Thank you."

Their platters came, and everything tasted marvelously better than it ever had before. They talked quickly as they ate, discussing the evidence they would need. Suddenly, Watson looked like a little boy with a secret. He fiddled with his water glass, took his time gazing around the restaurant, delaying the moment. Reilly knew he was about to spring something great on her.

"I have some news," he said.

"I can tell," she said.

"Roger Claiborne is fucking a prostitute who just happens to be a friend of your new client."

"Oh, my, my, my."

TWENTY-ONE

At the end of his shift the next day, Watson extracted the three inch thick expandable folder containing the Blake file from one of the ugly gray-green file cabinets lining the   squad room walls. He found the usual folders with autopsy, blood and fingerprint reports, detective interviews, property vouchers, and, amazingly, in an unsealed and unmarked manila envelope, the videotape Reilly had told him to look for.

Watson slid the tape into the side pocket of his sport jacket and decided to push his luck. He carried the folder to his desk, and began thumbing through the thick sheaf of DD5s, the supplementary reports which detectives and officers write for every single item of information pertinent to a case.

"Grab a cold one before heading home?"

Gary Lowrey, Watson's partner, was standing in the doorway of the squad room. How long had he been there? Had he seen the videotape?

"Thanks, but I've got a date with Maureen." Watson raised his eyebrows and grinned lasciviously. "As soon as I finish here."

"What's all this?" asked Lowrey directing his eyes at the files spread on Watson's desk.

"An old case of mine, from CPP."

"Cold case?" A cold case, although not active, is also one which has not been solved.

"No, it's closed. But I had something I wanted to check."

Lowrey looked at him for a long second, nodded pleasantly, said "See you in the morning," and left. Watson, thankful Lowrey had not asked one more question, was pretty sure his partner knew there was more to the story. This was exactly the way a wedge was driven into the trust so essential when two detectives worked together. Sooner or later, his evasion would be exposed. Lowrey might never mention it to Watson, but he would know, and he would be alert for the next time. I'll talk to Kerrigan tomorrow, Watson thought, and then I'll explain to Gary. He was not fifteen minutes into the Blake case, and already he was paying a price.

Watson went back to the file, refreshing his memory of the investigation. He pulled out Detective John Mackey's report of his interview with Angel Martinez and held his breath. Something ... or nothing? Mackey had written in an abbreviated Q&A format:

Q: corner of 66/Col last Thurs night?

A: yes.

Q: see the person in this photograph? (Blake)

A: don't know. See lots of people.

Q: recall woman slipping off a curb?

A: remember that. this the guy who helped her? let me see that again.

Q: recognize now?

A: could be. not sure.

There was no mention of Josh coming back to the newsstand a second time, but Watson knew it had been there when he first read the report. So what had happened to the rest of Mackey's report? And who scared Angel Martinez away?

Watson closed his eyes and tried to picture Joshua Blake in his cell at Sing Sing. His thoughts shifted to Roger Claiborne, enjoying the benefits of what Watson was now sure was Blake's tainted conviction. You knew, you bastard. I told you there were holes in the case, and you blew me away. You better be ready now, because I'm coming after you.

Watson ate the sub he had purchased on the way home - light on the oil, lots of hot peppers - and settled in to watch Blake's videotape. He fast-forwarded through the pre-game show and several innings of the game, slowing the tape to regular speed only to watch Jason Giambi's screaming line drive home run.

When the screen went blank, he rewound to the beginning of the game, wrote down the position of the tape counter and the time, and played the tape at regular speed. He watched carefully until the tape showed the big Yankee scoreboard, from which he took the clock time. He correlated the clock time with the tape position, continued running the tape until the end, and again noted the time. He did a quick calculation and dialed Reilly's number.

"I watched the tape."

"And ...?" Reilly asked.

"It was the Yankee game, just like he said. Josh shut the tape off at 8:28."

"So ..."

"... the perp was in Brooklyn at 8:34. Blake wasn't. Blake isn't the perp."

"Did Claiborne know?" Reilly asked.

"Maybe. There's no report with the tape, so it doesn't look like anybody ever bothered to play it. It doesn't make me feel very good about NYPD. Or Homicide. Or me. I was still in charge of the case when we picked up this tape."

"Can you make a copy?"

"Already did," Watson said. "I'll return the original in the morning."

"If you add this tape to Angel Martinez' testimony and the other latent fingerprints, you have a very persuasive reasonable doubt argument," said Reilly. "If that evidence had been presented to the jury, Josh would never have been convicted. If it had been known to Sam Monti, they would probably have dropped the charges."

"At least now he can get a second trial," Watson said.

"I doubt it," said Reilly. "I'll see what Mullin thinks, but I think probably not."

"How can that be?" Watson said.

"We don't have enough hard evidence to prove what we think we know. They all close ranks, even when they know they're wrong. Granting a new trial means admitting the system made a serious mistake. They'll need hard provable facts, not conjecture."

Watson was quiet, and finally Reilly asked, "Are you all right?"

"No. I feel terrible. I was in a position to do the right thing and I didn't do it."

"It wasn't you who hid the evidence," Reilly said.

"Lieu, I have a problem," Watson said, after knocking at Lieutenant Brian Kerrigan's office and receiving permission to enter. The office was like hundreds of other NYPD cubicles throughout the city - dirty green cinderblock walls, a locker, two filing cabinets, and the *Patrol Guide*, *Penal Law*, and *Criminal Procedure Law* in a glass-doored bookcase. Kerrigan's desk was standard NYPD green metal with a gray formica top covered with glass. A photo of his wife and three kids was the only personal touch.

"There're things about the Blake case that aren't right."

"The Blake case?" Kerrigan asked. "I didn't know we were working on a Blake case."

"We're not. Joshua Blake was arrested for killing a woman in Central Park in May 2003. He was convicted last November."

"Your case at CPP?" Kerrigan asked.

"For a few days. Then it came here, to John Banyon."

"Why are you looking at it now?"

"New information has come to light," Watson said, sounding far more pompous than he had intended.

"What information?"

"Three pieces of exculpatory evidence were known to the prosecutor but not turned over to the defense. At least one report was changed to delete what was inconvenient for the prosecution's case."

"You think we altered evidence?" Kerrigan asked, his face flushing.

"No. I don't think so," said Watson, adding "I think it was the prosecutor, Roger Claiborne."

"Claiborne?" Kerrigan raised his eyes, his face expressing something far more complex than the single word question. "But you're not sure, are you?" Kerrigan asked, not expecting an answer. "What evidence?"

"First was an interview with a witness who alibis the defendant at a time and place which would make it impossible for him to have committed the attack. Second was a set of unidentified latents on the victim's bag, probably the actual perp. Third was a videotape from the defendant's apartment proving he could not have dumped the victim's bag in Brooklyn. The videotape may have been an honest mistake."

"But not the alibi and the latents?"

Watson took a deep breath before he answered. "No," he said softly. One word, but it was a bell, once rung, which could never be un-rung. Prove the charge, and people will be upset with you. Fail to prove it, and it will be even worse. Watson's NYPD future was now firmly set on the axis of the Joshua Blake case.

"Does Banyon know you're looking at his case?"

"No."

"He'll find out soon. Why are you doing this?"

Watson had expected this question, but what he had planned to say no longer seemed suitable. Hesitating, his eyes settled on the photo of Kerrigan's family and he took a new tack. "You have a son," he said.

"He's a junior in high school."

"Suppose he was arrested, convicted, and sent to prison for a crime he didn't do? How would you feel? What would you do?"

"Blake's not your son."

"I'm just trying to make the point. It's horrible what happened to him. Somebody's got to stand up for what's right."

"You understand some people are not going to like this," Kerrigan said.

"I know," Watson said, looking straight at Kerrigan. This was the crucial moment. Kerrigan would help, or he would blow him away. If the latter, his NYPD career would be down the tubes from here on out. He wondered how Maureen Reilly would like life with an over-qualified security guard.

"What do you want to do?" Kerrigan asked.

Watson exhaled, and his still lingering resentment at how Kerrigan had tricked him with the CPP transfer evaporated. "I want to find Angel Martinez," Watson said. "He's the guy who gives the alibi for the time of the attack. Check videotapes from the security cameras. Compare the clothes the perp was wearing with stuff we took from Blake's apartment. Check Blake's Metro card to determine exactly when he entered the subway."

"None of that was done?"

"I don't know. I didn't do any of it."

"You'll need help," Kerrigan said. "Do you trust Banyon?"

"I don't have any reason not to," Watson said, although in truth he wasn't really sure. "Best bet it was just Claiborne, not anyone here."

"Aren't you still working with Claiborne on the DEA thing?"

"Yeah, I am."

"Oh, this is going to be interesting," Kerrigan said, smiling broadly. Watson again had the feeling there was something he was missing.

"I'm going to re-assign you to be Banyon's partner. We'll just do a switch. Lowrey will pair up with Banyon's current partner. Tell John everything you know and start looking for Angel Martinez. Keep me informed and let me know if you need anything."

Kerrigan came around the desk and put his hand on Watson's shoulder. "The word from the 7-5 was you weren't afraid to do what you thought was right, no matter the consequences. That's one of the reasons you're here. This thing took real courage and I'm glad you came to me. No talk outside the squad until I say so."

I am, in a strange way, engaged in the practice of law. My license comes not from the State of New York, but from one Durwood Johnson, aka Spider. My first legal assignment is to prepare a corporate charter for the Sing Sing chapter of the Aryan Brotherhood, or at least what my imagination tells me such a document might be. Each day I give handwritten pages to Spider, and the following day I receive back an updated typed version. How does he do these things?

Other things appear. Sandwiches, sodas and muffins are delivered to my cell. Paper, pens, books, the *New York Times*. Terrified with all this contraband, I find I am not to worry. My cell is no longer searched. Ever. Other cells are tossed, but the guards simply nod to me as they pass by. Peripheral benefits of working for the devil.

Spider may or may not be the devil, but it's for sure I don't know how to measure him anymore, if I ever did. He's a complex man, intelligent, driven, ruthless, and very capable. His prison enterprises have grown like a well funded corporate monolith. He has acquired functioning operating divisions. He has created new business ventures with entrepreneurial flair. Spider's fingers are in every pie. Money, forbidden in Sing Sing, is flowing in waves. Where does he keep it?

I meet with him in his cell, and I can't believe what I see. He's got a real mattress, colored blankets, and a throw pillow. A small oriental carpet on the floor. A television tuned to the Discovery Channel. Prominent on his small desk are recent copies of *Aryan Sentinel*, *Supreme White Brotherhood*, and *Secrets from the Bunker*. On the wall is a photo of Muhammad Ali in his prime.

Since Spider's takeover, life on the galleries is less frenzied, although two inmates are killed, one black, the other white. I suspect the recently deceased were reluctant recruits into the new order, and their deaths send a clear message to the rest of B-block. Spider says one day, seemingly out of nowhere, "A man tolerates no disrespect. A stand-up man seeks out disrespect and destroys it."

In the yard, there are dramatic changes. Cliques that had long ignored each other first nod acknowledgement, then speak, and soon work together. The Aryan Brotherhood, still a feared symbol of racial hatred, has surprisingly emerged as an agent for peaceful collaboration. Black and white divisions of related enterprises hold staff meetings, all of which I attend. Cutter, serving a long sentence for armed robbery and assault with a deadly weapon, is a regional manager. Spider, of course, is CEO.

What Spider has accomplished is awesome. The prison laundry has been transformed from an inefficient operation which regularly lost and destroyed clothes into a slick customer-friendly, highly profitable business. Inmates now pay for this formerly free service. So do a growing number of guards. It's easy to pick out those who don't or can't pay the freight, since they walk around in filthy tatters. There are less of them each week. Soon, the business will expand beyond B-block, first to Tappan, and then to A-block. Everything is laid out in a multi-month strategic schedule.

The prison bakery has new products and regular delivery routes. Additional product development is under way. Phone calls, which had always been a harrowing experience, can now be scheduled in advance, and when your time comes, the phone is always available. There is a fee for this service, of course, and if you don't pay, you don't make any calls. Inmates thus pay Spider for the privilege of making collect calls. If we had a balance sheet, the prison phones would be listed as a corporate asset.

The increased profits are shared and, so far, everyone who matters seems happy. Violence has fallen to a trickle, and what does occur has the look of discipline and enforcement instead of random anger and retaliation.

The biggest challenge, however, is still ahead. Spider's strategic vision is to build his organizational strength before taking on the most lucrative market sector, the prison drug trade, where he will face his first significant competitive opposition from the Columbians who have controlled the drug trade in Sing Sing for years. I think he may be biting off more than even he can chew, but I don't share this opinion with him.

I should feel ashamed. I do feel ashamed, and I'm terrified Watson and Reilly will find out what I'm doing. But at the same time it's intoxicating. I actually feel productive and useful. So far, however, I'm resisting Spider's suggestion to get an AB tattoo.

"I want you to talk to Fernando Franco. He's on R gallery, where we used to be. Ask him what he thinks he can bring to the company." This from Spider when he pulls me aside at the conclusion of a B-block staff meeting at afternoon rec. He glances at a cluster of Hispanics across the yard, catches the eye of someone waiting for a signal, and links his gaze to me. Diplomatic credentials have been exchanged. Your office or mine? With no further direction, Spider knows I will explain to Franco how the Hispanics, who have so far been outside looking in, can share in the new wealth.

This is my life now. I'm Spider's *consigliore*. Today is the first anniversary of the day I arrived at Penn Station, so full of very different expectations. I remember trying to find the Broadway Big Apple hotel, seeing Yankee announcer Michael Kay's picture on the side of the bus, meeting Annabelle and Daryl. And Darlene.

Fernando Franco, who is not housed on my gallery, nevertheless magically appears next to me in the mess hall line. We agree to meet in my cell after dinner, where I tell him his initial exclusive franchise will be to market laundry and telephone services to Hispanics in B-block.

Pricing structure and management fees are quickly settled. All Hispanic assets will be inventoried, turned over, and re-issued in accordance with the new organizational regime. Here's the charter. Any problems? I thought not. You'll start out with these defined objectives. If you do well, additional glories may be yours. Failure is not an option. Here's who you report to and when. You discuss nothing with anyone else. Is everything perfectly clear? Good. We have a deal.

It's too easy, and it makes me sick. But I'm in, and I can't imagine a way out.

"You knew a friend of mine when you were on Rikers," Fernando says, when the business is done, and this causes me to look at him, for the first time, as a person. He's old enough to have significant gray hair, and his deep voice projects a serious, even solemn demeanor. What was his crime? How did he become a leader of the Hispanics? None of my business unless he chooses to tell me. He also has a charming smile, which is now displayed.

"My friend's name is Hector Rodriquez. He's over in A-block. He told me to tell you he's still writing. He speaks very well of you."

Memory can be such a faithless lover. Rikers is already a distant memory, Hector and his friends long forgotten. Images of Ponyboy and Sodapop flash in my head. Sunsets I did not watch.

"Tell Hector I said hello. I'd like to read what he's written."

"There are men in this prison who also need such help," Fernando says, his formal way of speaking calling to mind a movie portrayal of Spanish nobility. "To learn to read, to write letters, maybe even to write stories."

It's time for him to return to his own cell.

"Will you help?" Fernando asks, and I see a path for me to a place independent of Spider, doing something I can be proud of.

"Yes, *Senor* Franco," I reply, adopting his dignified manner. "It would be my pleasure to be helpful."

Reilly, Mullin and Watson met for dinner at Buona Notte on Mulberry Street in Little Italy. As soon as they ordered their drinks, Reilly began. "Let's recap. What do we know? What do we suspect? How are we going to get the proof we need to get some very reluctant judge to give Josh a new trial?"

Watson and Mullin ignored her. They had their own business.

"I should have cross examined you," Mullin said to Watson.

"And I should have made sure you had all the evidence," Watson responded.

"That was Claiborne's job, not yours," Mullin said.

"Okay, guys," Reilly said, "glad you got that out of the way, but looking back is not going to accomplish anything. Where do we go from here?"

Mullin continued to address Watson, "I'll file the direct appeal in a few days, based on technical errors in the trial, such as evidence that should have been excluded, objections that the judge improperly overruled, improper jury instructions. We'll file that appeal, because you never know, but we expect to lose it. There really weren't any serious technical violations during the trial."

Mullin looked to Reilly, who signaled him to continue. "What we need is new evidence *not* presented to the jury at trial. And, even if we find and present such evidence, we'll still have the high burden of convincing the court that this new evidence would have led a jury to a different verdict."

Reilly watched Watson to see how he would react. She had told Watson everything Mullin just said, and the way Mullin was presenting it could be considered condescending. But Watson was fine, no cop macho in evidence, and she was relieved.

"Even with new evidence, do we have a chance?" Watson asked.

"There's always a chance," said Mullin.

Watson sipped his beer. "Why is it going to be so hard?," he asked. "If the judge believes Angel Martinez and the video tape, then Josh could not have been at the scene of the crime, and he could not have gone to Brooklyn after the crime. He's got a perfect alibi."

"Not perfect," Reilly answered. "The trial jury didn't believe Josh, and we don't have Martinez to testify. A jury might not believe Martinez, even if he were there. The tape is new, but it's not nearly enough."

"Since we're being skeptics," Watson mused, "I guess the tape could have been programmed to go off. Josh might have set the timer before he left."

"That makes no sense?" argued Reilly. "He set the tape so he wouldn't miss any of the game."

"It's not likely," said Watson. "I'm just saying it's not absolute proof."

"So we need Angel Martinez," said Mullin.

"I'll find him," Watson said. "I spoke with Kerrigan yesterday and he authorized me to look for him. I'll be working with John Banyon, who handled the case when it first came to Homicide."

"Do you trust him?" Mullin asked. "Maybe he helped Claiborne keep evidence away from me."

"I don't know," said Watson, and the table became very quiet. "Anyway, Kerrigan told me to work with him."

"Kerrigan's your boss?" asked Mullin.

"He's the Commander of Manhattan North Homicide," Watson said. "And a really good guy. He could have told me to forget about Blake, but he didn't. It's not going to be a piece of cake for him either. By the way, he seems to have a thing with Claiborne. Any idea what?"

"No, but I'll ask around," said Reilly. "Meanwhile, you've got to do it Kerrigan's way. But maybe we should also try to find out who really did attack Mrs. Cooke."

"The unidentified latents?" Mullin asked.

"Yes," said Reilly.

"I'll have to ask Kerrigan," Watson said to Mullin. "To check the prints means going to Grabowsky, and Kerrigan was clear there was to be no contact outside the squad without his approval. And remember, there was no match."

"That was then," Reilly said.

Watson caught up with Detective John Banyon in the squad room at MNH early the next morning.

"Well, here's my new partner," Banyon said. "What the hell's going on, Bob?"

"Lieu made a decision," Watson said. "Not for us to reason why."

"I have a feeling you can do better."

"Let's go have a quiet cup of coffee," Watson said.

"Sure. We got nothin' else to do but catch bad guys, and they're not going anywhere."

Both men were silent as Banyon drove. Watson used the time to run through the little he knew about Banyon. Nineteen years on the force, much of it in narcotics, came to homicide three years before. Married, not known as a party guy, lives in Queens. No complaints about his work.

"I didn't know you like soul food," Watson said as they pulled up to the M&G Diner on West 125th Street.

"You can get regular food too," said Banyon, and Watson got the point. Banyon had driven far enough from Manhattan North headquarters that they were unlikely to meet other detectives from the squad, just in case their conversation got out of hand. They found a quiet corner booth with good sight lines.

"I'll have an omelet with everything. Bacon on the side, crisp. Home fries and rye toast, no grits," Banyon said. "My friend here is paying."

Watson ordered an English muffin. "This has to do with the Joshua Blake case," he said. "Do you remember it?"

"Vaguely. The kid attacked an old lady in the park and she banged her head and died. He's up state now. Why ..."

"I don't think he did it," Watson said quietly.

"Really?" Banyon said, hostility lying just beneath the surface. "As much as I remember, the case was a lock. Actually, now that I think about it, we didn't have much to do with it. The case was pretty much made before it got here, and the ADA never asked for any additional followup." Banyon paused, searching his memory. "Hey, wait a minute. That was your case at CPP, wasn't it? Why did you change your mind?"

"It was never a lock," Watson said. "I told the ADA right from the get-go there were things didn't add up. But he wasn't buying. He was locked into Blake and he went for the conviction, no other theories to confuse things, thank you."

"What was wrong with the case?"

"Blake had a solid alibi, and there was another person involved who was never identified."

"What are you talking about?" Banyon asked, his face reddening and his voice rising. "I don't remember any alibis, or any other suspects. Are you saying I fucked up?"

"Not you. Me, maybe, but not you. I saw the evidence at the precinct before the case was assigned to Homicide. My guess is it was altered before you got the file."

Watson waited while Banyon settled down and processed what he had said. They were quiet a little longer as their food was served.

"Go on," Banyon said as he buttered his toast. "You have my attention."

Watson took a deep breath. He got it all out without stopping once. "Blake was placed three blocks from the scene at the time of the attack. Testimony from a newsstand guy named Angel Martinez I'll bet you never knew about. A VCR tape, taken from Blake's apartment in Greenwich Village, puts him in the apartment at the exact time the perp was seen in Brooklyn. There were unidentified latents on the victim's pocketbook, probably the guy who ditched it in Brooklyn."

"Who was Blake's lawyer? All that reasonable doubt and he couldn't get his guy off."

"It wasn't the attorney's fault. He never got the exculpatory evidence. The interview report with the newsstand guy was altered – no second visit. The fingerprint report was also altered – no mention of the unidentified latents. And the video – as far as I know, nobody ever looked at it."

Banyon stared at Watson, his forkful of eggs suspended in mid air.

"Something else is bothering me," Watson said. "The way the case just disappeared. I worked with you guys several other times when I was at CPP, and with Brooklyn Homicide all the time when I was in the 7-5, and I never remember another case where the catching detective didn't stay involved."

"I don't think you were purposely excluded, Bob, but we just didn't have anything to do, so there was no reason to talk."

While the waitress poured more coffee, Watson thought about Banyon's explanation. It could be true. The more he thought about it, a purposeful exclusion of him from the case would have needed somebody with a lot more juice than Claiborne. Probably it was as Banyon had just said.

"Why are we having this conversation?" Banyon asked when the waitress left. "This case is long over. What got you started again?"

"Blake wrote to me, asking for my help. I discussed it with Maureen Reilly, and then I went to see Blake at Sing Sing. He's up for life with twenty before the possibility of parole, and I don't think he did it. For sure he didn't get a fair trial."

"Reilly?"

"We've been dating for several months."

"I didn't know that. She's a tiger in court," Banyon said, "and I've got scars to prove it." Banyon put both hands on the table, smiled slightly, and asked, "What do you want from me?"

Watson knew Banyon wouldn't be happy he had talked to Kerrigan first, but there was no way around it. "I talked to Lieu yesterday," he said, again speaking quickly. "He wants us to work the case together, look for the newsstand guy." Watson repeated the steps he had discussed with Kerrigan.

"The trail is almost a year old," Banyon muttered. "You know the odds on coming up with anything now. How long did Lieu give you?"

"Us. Give *us* you mean." Watson smiled.

"Okay, us. How long?"

"He didn't say."

"You have an address on this Angel character?"

"He's probably not there anymore, but it'll be a start."

"Well, what are you sitting there for?" Banyon asked. "Pay for my breakfast while I get the car. I'll talk to Lieu this afternoon about the fingerprints. Who did the workup?"

"Guy named Frank Grabowsky."

Watson and Banyon went to the address Detective Mackey had recorded almost a year before, in a poor but lively Washington Heights neighborhood populated mainly by Dominicans. Nobody at the address knew Angel Martinez, although one or two remembered a lawyer looking for him.

"This is pointless," Banyon said after an hour of trudging door to door. "It's been too long."

"Let's try the prostitutes," said Watson.

"At ten o'clock in the morning?"

"No. Tonight. I'll meet you at the station at ten tonight."

On the way back to Homicide, Banyon received a call from Lieutenant Kerrigan. When he hung up, he said, "Lieu says it's all right to contact Grabowsky."

They were out again that night, and spent hours with prostitutes and street informers, but their efforts were fruitless. Two more days and nights and Watson was convinced Martinez was long gone. If anyone did know where he was, they were not about to tell the NYPD. Over the next several weeks, he checked again with Angel's employer, searched tax records and credit card usage, and came up blank. Angel Martinez had disappeared without a trace.

Detective Frank Grabowsky was an experienced and respected fingerprint technician. Watson arrived at his office at One Police Plaza first thing Monday morning. After the initial chit-chat, with Watson doing most of the talking, Grabowsky asked why he was there.

"I'm looking for some information," said Watson.

"Name it."

"Do you remember the Blake case?" Watson asked.

There was dead silence and a sharp uptake of breath, and Watson knew it was about to get ugly.

"What's the matter, Frank?"

"Don't bullshit me, Bob. You wouldn't be here if you didn't know."

"I know five latents on the lady's bag were never identified," Watson said, struggling to contain the anger in his voice. Grabowsky offered nothing. Watson continued, "Did you finish the elimination prints? Were the unidentified latents a family member? A friend?"

"We didn't finish," Grabowsky said in a whisper. "We stopped right after Blake was arrested. You know how it is, busy on other things."

"Frank, what I know is you never mentioned those additional latents at trial and the wrong guy is in Sing Sing."

"You don't want to do this," Grabowsky said.

"Yes, I do," said Watson. "You know what Sing Sing is like? Can you imagine being there, life with twenty, when you didn't do a thing but help an old lady who fell down?"

"I can't help you," Grabowsky said in a hoarse whisper, his fingers beginning to tremble.

"I'm getting the idea real quick," Watson answered. "You know this one stinks."

"I got nothin' more to say."

TWENTY-TWO

Watson returned to Manhattan North Homicide and fifteen minutes later, his phone rang.

"Don't go there, Bob," said a voice he did not recognize.

"And where would that be?" Watson asked.

"You know fucking right well what I'm talking about. Let it be, Bob. It's over. Don't fuck up a good conviction."

"Is this a threat?"

The voice took on a patently phony tone the caller didn't even try to conceal. "Of course not, Bob. It's just good advice you should take. You and your girl friend have too much to lose."

The phone clicked before Watson could say anything more. He was furious, but he told himself to stay calm. He imagined how Kerrigan would react. And Reilly? She'll go ballistic. He dialed her number.

"I had a phone call a few minutes ago," Watson said, trying hard to keep his tone less ominous than he felt. "After I spoke to Grabowsky."

"Who was it?" Reilly asked.

"I didn't recognize the voice, but it was a very clear message. 'The Blake case is over. Don't fuck up a good conviction.' Do they ever get tired of saying that? And he mentioned you."

"Me?"

"The warning was for both of us."

"Why do people do this for that prick?" Reilly said. "What does he have on them?"

"They're in it together," Watson said.

"Who's they?"

"Whoever Claiborne needed to keep the evidence hidden."

"Who knew about your meeting with Grabowsky?"

"Kerrigan knew I was going, so did Banyon. Plus whoever Grabowsky told after we left."

"Claiborne?"

"Maybe. It wasn't him on the phone. This is bigger than just Claiborne. Bad crime, quick arrest, successful trial, a good conviction all around. The brass was happy. The mayor was happy. It's long over, and everybody's forgotten."

"Joshua Blake hasn't forgotten."

"I tried that line of argument," Watson said. "Grabowsky wasn't buying."

"So what now?" Reilly asked. "The clock is ticking. I'm going to Sing Sing later this week and I'm not looking forward to telling Josh how little we've accomplished."

"The answer is out there. I'll keep looking for Angel Martinez," Watson's confident words could not suppress the feeling, inexorably growing in the pit of his stomach. It was just too late and the cards were stacked too high against Joshua Blake.

I'm in the yard, trying to stay away from Spider, who has started to give me headaches with his unrelenting focus on business questions, when I see the smiling face of a former friend. Hector Rodriquez shakes my hand, and then surrounds me with an unexpected hug. Across the yard, I catch Spider's bemused look.

"*Amigo*," Hector says, "it is very good to see you, although I wish it was not here."

"How've you been?" I ask.

"Not bad. But I have not risen as you have, *senor consigliore*. How did you become such an important person? Or maybe I should not ask."

"It's okay. Spider was my cellmate when I first got here. He's been my friend."

"Such a friend," Hector says, and I sense multiple layers of meaning. Fodder for future discussions, perhaps. Then again, perhaps not.

I ask about the others from Rikers. Luis was released when his short term was up. Tonio and Esteban were still there when Hector's trial concluded and he was transferred to Sing Sing.

"Ten years," he says. "It's a long time." He seems embarrassed. "But perhaps not so long as you. I'm sorry, my friend. I know that you, unlike me, are innocent."

"Fernando told me you're still writing."

"Yes, indeed. My little story about Pacho was published in the magazine at Rikers."

"You're a published author!" I say, and Hector beams.

"I have written another story," he says. "It is longer, more complex."

"I'd love to read it."

"It happens I have it with me," he says with a smile, reaching into his back pocket and withdrawing a carefully folded sheaf of papers. "I owe you much, *Senor* Josh."

I look quickly at the tiny, single spaced writing. "May I take this with me?"

"I would be honored."

"I'll treat it as the treasure it is."

"I have watched many sunsets and thought of our little class. You gave us confidence to write."

Hector's reference to sunsets makes me feel guilty. Although I had been the one to suggest that we, like Ponyboy in *The Outsiders*, could use the sunsets as a way of remembering our friendship and our accomplishments, I have not done so very often myself.

"There are several others here who wish to form a new class with you. I have told them what we did on Rikers. Are you willing?"

I agree instantly. Suddenly, I can't wait to lose myself in thoughts and lives outside my own new world of criminal enterprise. Two days later, Hector appears with two other inmates and we have our first class. Spider, of course, asks all about it, but he seems okay with it and never mentions it again. He has more than enough to keep his mind fully occupied.

Central Park on a Saturday morning in May is about as good as it gets in New York City, but Bob Watson was not enjoying the day. He pulled into the precinct lot and parked next to Detective John Mackey's car. He had not been back to Central Park Precinct since his transfer five months before.

"Hey, here's the big time homicide detective, come to visit us lowly precinct types."

Watson smiled at the greeting from the desk sergeant. "Hi, Sarge. Anybody working today?"

"Bob Watson?" John Mackey's voice boomed from the adjoining squad room, and the detective emerged, hand outstretched. "What brings you here on this fine spring morning? Not a social call, I imagine."

"No, it's not," Watson said, his tone serious enough to wipe the smile from Mackey's face. They went into the squad room and Watson sat at his old desk, facing Mackey as he had so many times before.

"You remember Joshua Blake?" Watson asked.

"Sure. The kid who killed the old lady."

"Actually," Watson paused for several counts, "I don't think he did."

Mackey leaned over and flicked the door closed. "What are you up to, Bob?" he asked. "You don't have enough to do at Homicide, you need to open closed cases?"

"You interviewed a guy named Angel Martinez," Watson said. "I'd like to see your interview report."

"You checking up on me? Who do you think you are?"

Watson sighed, looked down, and folded his head in his hands. "It was me who fucked up, John, not you. I helped send an innocent kid to Sing Sing, and now I can't get it out of my mind."

"Kerrigan know you're here?"

"He knows."

"Tell me what's going on?"

"Will you hold it close for now?"

"You're not in a position to ask, Bob," Mackey said. "But I'm not your enemy. Try me."

"Okay. The thing is your report was altered. The copy at Homicide is different from what I remember reading here. There was exculpatory evidence that never went to the defense."

"Oh shit."

"Exactly."

Mackey wheeled his chair toward the cabinets lining the wall behind him. He found his DD5 report and handed it to Watson, who read silently.

Q: corner of 66/Col last thurs night?

A: yes.

Q: see the person in this photograph? (Blake)

A: don't know. see lots of people.

Q: recall woman slipping off a curb?

A: remember that. this the guy who helped her? let me see that   again.

Q: recognize now?

A: could be. not sure.

Watson turned to the second page.

Q: anything else?

A: no. maybe.

Q: what maybe?

A: maybe the guy came back

Q: when?

A: later

Q: same night?

A: I think so

Q: how much later?

A: maybe an hour

Q: hear anything unusual the second time?

A: sirens. lots of sirens.

Q: was he carrying anything?

A: not that I noticed.

"You did a good job, John. Asked exactly the right questions. You understood what it meant?"

"Sure," Mackey said. "It wasn't a perfect alibi, but it could've become one. If Martinez met Blake and made a positive ID, it would have been powerful."

"Why didn't we do that, John?"

"The case went away. There was an arrest. Nobody was asking any more questions. But defense counsel should have raised it."

Watson reached into his jacket pocket. He gave Mackey a copy of the report from the MNH file. "This is what defense got," he said.

Mackey compared the report Watson had given him to the one he had written. "Who did this?" he asked, his anger obvious.

"I think it was the ADA," Watson said. "Others might have been involved."

"Where is this going?" Mackey said.

"I don't know. Not any place good."

"There's more?" Mackey asked.

"You always ask the right questions, John. Yes, there's more."

The two detectives looked at each other and the sadness passing between them was palpable. They both loved the NYPD, and had devoted their professional lives to it. They both understood the implications of the papers now lying side by side on Mackey's desk.

"I'll make a copy for you," Mackey said, rising.

When he returned, he handed Watson the copy of his report, returned the original to the folder, and the folder to the file cabinet.

"I'll testify if you need me," Mackey said.

Watson had viewed the police copies of the videotapes from the surveillance cameras mounted on the hotels along Central Park West. They showed the presumed perpetrator running south toward Columbus Circle, carrying what looked like a handbag, but they weren't clear enough to distinguish the clothing detail Watson hoped to be able to compare with Joshua Blake's clothes. Maybe the original tapes were better.

After leaving Mackey at CPP, Watson drove to the Mayflower Hotel at 62nd Street and Central Park West. The hotel was closed and boarded up, soon to be demolished in favor of luxury condominiums. The news at the Trump International Hotel in the next block was equally depressing.

"I'm sorry, but our tapes are re-used after thirty days," the on-duty manager said.

Back at his office at Manhattan North Homicide, Watson went to the Blake file and extracted the list of Metro Cards obtained from the Metropolitan Transportation Authority. The list included all Metro Card numbers used at the Columbus Circle station between 7:50 and 8:10 pm on the night of May 29, 2003.

If a Metro Card had been paid for by a credit card, the credit card number was also indicated on the list. There were one hundred thirty seven Metro Cards on the list, of which forty six had been purchased by credit card. Watson remembered directing detectives to identify each credit card holder and contact them, either as suspects or witnesses. Of the forty six, only twenty names had been identified and only eight of those had been contacted. Then the work had stopped, presumably when Blake was arrested.

Watson retrieved Blake's wallet and Metro Card from property. On the back of the card was the date purchased, May 27, 2003, and an ID number. Blake's ID number did not appear on the MTA list, which meant Blake took the subway before 7:50 pm or after 8:10 pm, or not at all. And since there was videotape of the perpetrator running on Central Park West at roughly 8:00 pm, and the perpetrator showed up in Brooklyn at 8:34 with the lady's handbag, the perp must have entered the subway between, say, 8:01 pm and 8:05 pm. More proof the man on the videotape was not Blake. Perhaps Blake had paid by cash even though he had a Metro Card, but it wasn't likely.

If Watson could find Blake's card used outside the 7:50 to 8:10 time range, it would be powerful new evidence. He called the MTA. It took forty five minutes working through the MTA bureaucracy on a Saturday afternoon to find a Transit detective who could help. "Sorry, detective. We keep those records for six months, then they're automatically erased."

Watson hung up and laid his head on the desk. He didn't stir for a full ten minutes, reflecting on Joshua Blake's incredible bad luck and his own incompetence. Then, not ready to face Reilly or anyone else, he took the MTA list and spent the next five hours sitting at his desk calling credit card companies until he had completed the task of identifying everyone who had used a Metro Card purchased by a credit card at the Columbus Circle station between 7:50 pm and 8:10 pm on the night of May 29, 2003. What possible good this will do, he had no idea. He returned the list to the file and picked up the phone to call Maureen.

She knew from his first words he was beyond consolation. She listened quietly and then invited him over. He was even more forlorn than she had expected. She asked him to open a chilled bottle of French white, and they sipped the wine while she cooked an omelet. They ate at the small table near the open window, and the sounds of the city drifting up from 13th Street allowed them to remain silent without the silence being oppressive.

"Let's walk," she said when the dishes had been cleared and rinsed, and they descended to the street. They held hands as they walked around the block, past the Cardoza Law School and the First Presbyterian Church, proclaimed by its sign to house the City's earliest Presbyterian congregation, organized in 1716. The church, constructed in 1845, was modeled after Magdalen College in Oxford, England.

A casual observer might not have seen the tension they were sharing, unless he overheard the biting whisper that forced its way through Watson's clenched mouth. "Too late. Everything I'm doing is too fuckin' late."

Reilly knew words would be useless. She held his hand tightly, and stroked the back of his neck, not breaking physical contact for even a single second. When they returned to her apartment, still she didn't speak. She simply disrobed, turned off the light, and lay in her bed. After a few minutes, Watson joined her, and they lay naked together, intertwined, not making love, but sharing love more intensely than she had ever known.

Just before they fell asleep, she leaned close to his ear. "You're a good man, Bob. You made mistakes. We all do. But we're going to make it right. We're going to get him out." She anticipated his rebuttal and placed her finger over his mouth so he couldn't speak. "I don't know how," she said. "But we'll do it."

As soon as her regular Sunday brunch with her friends was finished, Teri Scanlon hurried to the *Daily News* offices on West 33rd Street to concentrate on a letter she had been writing for weeks and couldn't seem to finish. Alone and uninterrupted, this time it flowed. First, she referenced the *Chicago Tribune* series. She said she was writing a story to explore the comparable situation in New York, and she ended her letter with three questions:

1. The *Chicago Tribune* reported that for two decades an average of one murder conviction per month was set aside in Cook County because the courts found improper conduct by prosecutors. What is the comparable rate for the Manhattan DA's Office?

2. The *Tribune* reported withholding of evidence in violation of *Brady* obligations as the major form of prosecutorial misconduct which resulted in these murder convictions being overturned. What are the policies of the Manhattan DA's office with regard to turning over evidence to the defense? What procedures are in place to assure these policies are followed?

3. In the cases the *Tribune* reviewed, even when prosecutorial misconduct resulted in a murder conviction being reversed, the prosecutor involved was never punished. The paper concluded it was this lack of accountability which encourages such behavior, or at least does not discourage it. What sort of punishment does the Manhattan DA's Office exact on prosecutors who are found to have secured murder convictions by misconduct such as withholding evidence?

Scanlon printed out her letter, took a deep breath, signed it, and posted it to Manhattan District Attorney Harold Markman.

TWENTY-THREE

"I'm sorry it took so long between visits," Darlene says, as I take my place across from her in the large visitor room. It's been seven weeks since her first visit to Sing Sing. So much has happened.

"No apologies needed," I manage to say, and then I choke up. "... I'm so lucky to ... have you for a friend ... It's just ..."

"What is it, Josh?"

How can I answer her question? I certainly can't tell her about Spider and the Aryan Brotherhood. Fortunately, Darlene waits patiently until I regain my composure, and doesn't push for an answer. When I do speak, I tell her about Hector and my new class.

"There are three students. We write, and we talk about what we write. Hector wrote a story when we were at Rikers, only one paragraph but it was powerful. He described how his little brother Pacho was killed in a drive-by shooting."

"How horrible."

"The lives these people live are beyond our comprehension. Drugs, violence, betrayal." I thought how closely my own new life matched what Hector and the others had known all their lives. "Hector took his one paragraph and expanded it into a thirty page story describing what his brother meant to him when he was alive, and how everything changed in his family after he was killed. It's really excellent, both the physical depictions and the way he's able to write about his emotions."

"What's happening with your case?" Darlene asks.

"I told you a lawyer came to see me. Maureen Reilly. A few days later, Detective Watson came, the one I wrote to."

"And they're going to help?"

"That's what they said. Larry Mullin called to tell me they were working on it. But it's been over a month since Watson was here and I haven't heard anything specific." I tell Darlene about Angel Martinez and the unmatched fingerprints. When I mention the name of the fingerprint expert, she practically jumps out of her chair.

"I know Frank Grabowsky! He's the one who sent Roger Claiborne to me."

"You know it bothers me," I say stupidly, as if I'm in any position to judge her.

"Don't even think about it," she says, adding offhandedly, "It's just business." A fierce glow comes to her eyes. "But this is great news. I can really help you now."

"This could get nasty."

"It already is nasty, or didn't you notice where you're living these days." We smile together. "Listen, Josh," she says, serious again, "I want to help. You always show me respect. You don't make fun of me, like my other friends do, when I talk about college and my goals for the future. Your respect is more important to me than you can possibly know."

"So how is college?" I ask, sidestepping the emotion her words have evoked.

"I got two A's this semester," she says. "Intro to economics and European history."

"Wow. I'm impressed. Better grades than I got."

So we talk about Europe in the twentieth century and I remember my conversation with Alejandro at Rikers, eons ago, when I told him how World War One began. "Life in prison is such an illusion," I tell Darlene. "Time seems to drip by, but then, suddenly, months have passed." This conversation is a great interlude for me, a semblance of real life. But it can't last. It's almost time for Darlene to leave. There's something I have to tell her.

"I told Detective Watson about you and Claiborne, but I didn't say your name."

Darlene chuckles, and I wonder what's funny. "He's a detective, Josh, an NYPD homicide detective. If he wants to know my name, it won't be a problem for him. I'm sure he already knows."

"I'm sorry," I say, flooded with guilt.

"Don't worry about it," she says with a bright smile. "He's helping you. I'm helping you. So we're on the same team." She draws herself up, proudly, and announces with a little flourish, "We're both on the Blake Team."

I feel a surge of optimism. There's a whole team working on my behalf. "Will you talk to Ms. Reilly and tell her what you know about Frank Grabowsky?"

"I'll call as soon as I get back to the City."

Two days later, Maureen Reilly returns, and we're back in the claustrophobic attorney interview room. "So what's up," I ask as soon as the guard leaves the room. It would have been better to say hello, to make some small talk, but I'm bursting with impatience. "Have you made any progress?"

"Some," Reilly says, but her tone says otherwise.

"Did you find Angel Martinez?"

"Not yet."

"What about the unidentified fingerprints? Who's the third person? Did you find him?"

"Not yet."

I don't say what I'm feeling, which is that nothing is happening, and nothing is likely to happen. Reilly and Watson have good intentions, but that just doesn't cut it.

"These things take time," Reilly says, to break the silence. Perhaps she senses my unspoken thoughts.

"Easy for you to say," I finally explode. "I don't have time. Every day here is another day in hell."

"I know," Reilly says, and I can tell she does. "Larry Mullin has filed the direct appeal in a timely fashion."

"Any chance of that succeeding?" I ask.

"No, not much," is Reilly's honest response. But she goes on, "What we're working on now - Mullin, Watson and me - is to prepare a motion to overturn the verdict based on new evidence that was not presented at trial. There's no time restriction at all on that kind of motion.

"So I can sit here forever?" I say.

"That's not what I meant. We'll file as soon as we think we can win."

I keep telling myself not to fight Reilly. She's the one hope I have. "I'm sorry. It's just so frustrating for me."

"I understand, Josh, I really do." She smiles and adds, "You can take it out on me."

"Nothing but getting out of here will make me feel better. Has my friend Darlene contacted you?"

"She called and we're going to meet on Friday. What's it about?"

"When she was here two days ago, she told me something."

Reilly looks at me expectantly. Actually, she looks desperate to hear something positive.

"Darlene has other clients, besides Roger Claiborne," I say. "One of them is Frank Grabowsky."

"Will wonders never cease?" Reilly says, and her face muscles visibly relax. "So there's an out-of-court connection between Grabowsky and Claiborne."

"You'll ask Darlene to help? I mean, since she sees both of them."

"If she would," says Reilly. "It could be dangerous."

"I told her. But she wants to do it."

Since I've been in prison, I frequently have moments when the enormity of my situation just overcomes me. They seem to be coming more frequently. With Darlene the other day. Now again. I struggle to get my emotions under control. Reilly is so good. She just waits.

"It's so bad here," I say finally. Reilly no doubt thinks I'm referring to the threat of violence and rape, the horrible living conditions. Actually, I'm thinking about my new house of horrors as Spider's *consigliore*. I don't want her to ever know, but she will, and it terrifies me. She looks at me sadly, and I feel her compassion, which I no longer feel I deserve. Gradually I settle down. "I'm sorry," I say. "Please don't give up on me."

"We're not giving up," Reilly says, placing her hand over mine. "But you need to hang in there, too. Don't do anything stupid. I know it's hard."

"You can't possibly know," I say, as much to myself as to her.

"You're right." Reilly says, shaking her head. "Being in this place upsets me, and I can leave. I can't possibly feel how you feel. But don't give up."

"I promised Detective Watson I wouldn't crack," I say, "and I won't."

There's a lull in our conversation and I remember something I wanted to ask her. "I've been thinking about something. There are other innocent guys in prison. Maybe if I could read some of their stories, especially if there's some who got out, I would feel there's hope for me."

"Good idea. I'll talk to Barry Scheck and get you things to read."

"I've heard of him. In the O.J. trial. You know him?"

"I've been a volunteer at the Innocence Project for years." She pauses. "I just had another thought," she says. "There's an old case, but it's actually still going on, and there's been a lot written about it. It might be depressing for you to read about it, but maybe it'll help you be patient."

"What case?"

"The guy's name is Jeffrey MacDonald. He was a Green Beret, a medical doctor, who was convicted of killing his wife and two young daughters. He said it was intruders, kooks on drugs having some kind of ceremony with candles, and there was evidence of someone else in the house, but this evidence never came out during the trial, just like the extra fingerprints in your case. MacDonald's been in prison for twenty, twenty-five years."

"This is going to make me feel better?" I ask.

Reilly laughs out loud, so do I, and we giggle together for a precious moment.

"See, it's working already," Reilly says when she stops laughing. "I'll send you the book that describes how Jeffrey MacDonald got shafted. At least you'll know you're not the only one."

"It's heartbreaking, being with him," Reilly began, as soon as Watson answered his cell phone.

"How're his spirits?" Watson asked.

"Better than ours. He's on the edge, but way more composed than I would be in his place, with the progress we haven't made. I'm sending him some books, so he can read about others who've been victims of prosecutorial abuse."

"That's sure to cheer him up."

"Funny," Reilly said, "it's just what Josh said, and we had our first good laugh together. By the way, he had more information."

"He's our best detective. How does he do this in prison? Who does he know?"

"It's the hooker."

"He told us about her before," said Watson. "Her and Claiborne. By the way, her name is Darlene Brantley."

"He told me. You're going to love this. She not only sees Claiborne, she also sees Grabowsky."

"Can we set something up?" Watson asked, his face bright with anticipation for the first time in weeks.

"I'm meeting with her Friday."

Watson hated it whenever he had to see or speak with ADA Roger Claiborne, but he had no choice.

Claiborne had called in connection with the Washington Heights shooting case, which had, as evidenced by the DEA and FBI presence on the scene, turned out to be part of a much larger picture. The victim, a low level criminal named Anthony Marone, had been a member of a crime family which was at war with the rival crime family of the shooter. The two families were each planning an assault on the Washington Heights drug distribution business then controlled by Dominican gangs. This feud had law enforcement at every level on serious edge.

"We're going to delay the prosecution," Claiborne said.

"Why?" Watson asked. "You have enough evidence to nail him."

"There are other developments. DEA business," Claiborne said, his tone implying that such things were known to him but not to a lowly homicide detective. Watson, anxious to end the conversation and not wanting to give Claiborne the satisfaction of explaining anything to him, didn't ask.

"I called to postpone our meeting for tomorrow," Claiborne said. "Probably for at least a few months would be my guess."

"Fine with me," Watson said. Maybe, he thought, I'll have your ass nailed to the wall before we ever have to talk again.

"About the Blake case," Claiborne said, and Watson was shocked he had brought it up. Maybe Grabowsky did talk to Claiborne.

"The Blake case is over," Claiborne's words penetrated Watson's racing mind. "Let it go."

"Fuck you, Roger," Watson said, slowly hanging up the phone. Maybe not smart, he thought, but very satisfying.

Darlene Brantley didn't look like a hooker. Oh, she was good looking and very sexy, but there was an unexpected freshness to her. Reilly had defended many prostitutes, but none like this. Darlene was dressed like a co-ed, in jeans and a Ralph Loren polo, with her blonde hair pulled back in a pony tail.

"Josh said you're going to college," Reilly said, after they were comfortable in her conference room.

"Over a year now. City College."

"What courses?" Reilly asked, still a little off kilter from Darlene's unexpectedly wholesome appearance.

"Normal freshman distribution, American novels, intro to political systems, economics, European history. This summer I'm taking an art survey course."

"I love the Impressionists," Reilly said. "Have you been to the Met?"

No, she had not, and for the next ten minutes they talked about Renoir, Matisse, Van Gogh, and Picasso.

"How did you meet Josh?" Reilly asked, back on message.

"At the Broadway Big Apple Hotel. He stayed there his first couple of nights in New York." Darlene paused, a sad look on her face. "After he was arrested, I saw his picture in the paper, and I went to visit him on Rikers."

This is a good woman, Reilly thought, and she really cares about Josh. Why on earth is she a hooker?

Darlene said, "I can see the question on your face."

"I don't want to pry," Reilly said.

"I figure maybe one more year. By then I'll have enough put aside to finish college full time. It's not bad. I don't do drugs.

Annabelle and me are probably the only hookers in Manhattan who don't."

"Be careful," Reilly said. "I'm sorry. You obviously know how to take care of yourself."

"Thanks for caring," Darlene said.

"Tell me about Frank Grabowsky."

"He's a pathetic sort of guy. Not a bad person, but sex at home doesn't work for him. His Polish wife isn't much of a conversationalist either. Of course, I only hear his side of the story."

"He told you his real name?"

"Nobody said he was smart. After I recognized Claiborne, I re-read the newspapers. Grabowsky's name popped up and I made the connection. I hadn't seen him, though, at trial. He must have testified the one day I missed."

"You went to the trial?"

"Almost every day." They chatted about Darlene's impressions of the testimony she had seen. Then, a wicked smile crossing her face, Darlene asked, "So exactly how are we going to recruit Detective Frank Grabowsky to the Blake Team?"

"We got some major shit comin' down on this one, Cap."

Lieutenant Brian Kerrigan had reached the final item in his weekly informal update with his boss, Captain Ignacio Munoz, head of Major Crimes for the Manhattan North Borough Command. The meeting, as always, was held in Munoz's office at Command Headquarters, housed in the Two-four Precinct on West 100th Street in Harlem.

Kerrigan had asked Detective Watson to prepare a short memo summarizing what they knew and suspected about the Blake case, and the investigative steps currently underway. He had delayed for several weeks, hoping to have more to report, but there had been no progress finding Angel Martinez, and no new leads had developed. Kerrigan couldn't delay any longer, so he handed Watson's report to Munoz.

"What's your take?" the Captain asked when he finished reading, his face professionally inscrutable.

"If we knew then what we know now this kid would never have been charged, let alone convicted," Kerrigan said.

"Do you think it was purposeful?"

"To a moral certainty. The brass had gone public, ditto the Mayor and the DA. Everybody was committed to Blake as the perp and nobody wanted to hear anything different. So they didn't."

"Can you prove it?"

"Not yet. But we will."

"Roadblocks?" asked Munoz.

"Somebody called Detective Watson, after he confronted Grabowsky at Latents. Friendly advice to back off."

"Is it us?" Munoz asked, referring to NYPD.

"Could be. The ADA is the most likely culprit, but he may have had help."

"Is Watson solid?"

"He feels terrible, like it was his fault it happened."

"Was it?"

"There's enough blame to go around. He caught the case at CPP and could have done more at the beginning, but he's not the one who tanked the evidence."

"Time for a 'heads up' to the DA?"

"Too soon."

Captain Munoz agreed. He added, "I'll fill the Inspector in. Harry can decide whether to go downtown." Inspector Harry K. Martin was the Manhattan North Borough Chief of Detectives, Munoz's boss.

Kerrigan started to leave, but Munoz held him with a stare. "Brian, no surprises. Let me know 'forthwith' if anything changes."

Watson received the first note the day after Lieutenant Kerrigan reported to Captain Munoz. Written on a scrap of paper folded several times, the message was childishly clear. "What's with you and Blake?"

Two more notes, one each on the next two days, expanded the message. "Blake was a good conviction ... Don't fuck up a good conviction ... Doesn't your lawyer girl friend have enough paying clients?"

"Two were left on my windshield, one on my desk," Watson related to Kerrigan.

"Shit," said Kerrigan. "Somebody here."

"Could be someone who helped Claiborne hide the exculpatory evidence," said Watson, looking up for permission to proceed. "Claiborne knows we're working on the Blake case."

"Talk to me," Kerrigan said.

"Claiborne mentioned Blake to me last week, when we were talking about the DEA thing. Then I get warning notes. It's not a coincidence."

"Or it could be someone else who just doesn't want the squad embarrassed," said Kerrigan, and then, when Watson's eyebrows raised, he added, "Not likely, eh?"

"Could be some other connection we don't know about yet," said Watson.

"Keep the notes," Kerrigan said. "Eventually, they'll slip up, and we'll nail 'em."

As upset as he was, Watson knew Kerrigan was even more disturbed. Somebody in his command was probably part of the cover-up, and maybe also involved in the original hiding of evidence. This had all the makings of a horrible black eye for Manhattan North Homicide and the NYPD, as well as for the Manhattan DA's Office. The Commissioner, the Mayor, and the DA were all going to feel the impact personally, and whatever happened would surely come down on Lieutenant Brian Kerrigan. It couldn't be worse, but, so far at least, Kerrigan showed no signs of backing off.

"What the fuck do you think you're doing down there, he said. I wasn't even sure who it was. Inspector? I asked in my most innocent tone. He expressed his great pleasure I recognized his voice, and then he got to his point, something about blowing the lid off the whole fuckin' borough command, and how the Commissioner and the Mayor were in his face and it was my fault."

"This was about the Blake case?" Watson asked after listening to Kerrigan's monologue, but it wasn't really a question.

"Good guess," said Kerrigan. "Inspector Harry K. Martin, Chief of Detectives for Manhattan North Borough, and, may I remind you, my boss, is definitely not pleased."

So this is the price, Watson thought. Everybody's pissed. Cops hate me. Bosses don't trust me. And Joshua Blake is going to rot at Sing Sing for at least twenty years.

"Anything new about the case?" Kerrigan asked.

"Not since we talked this morning," Watson answered.

"What's your gut tell you?" Kerrigan asked.

"Blake is innocent but we're going to have one hell of a time getting enough hard evidence so any judge will give him a new trial."

"About what I told Martin," Kerrigan said, "whenever I managed to get a word in edgewise."

It suddenly came to Watson that Kerrigan was not upset. He was recounting Martin's anger, but he himself was totally calm. He didn't appear at all discouraged. As Watson was coming to this realization, a sly smile emerged on Kerrigan's face.

"I bought us one week," Kerrigan said. "Give me something good by next Friday."

Lewis M. Weinstein

TWENTY-FOUR

"The man is awesome," Reilly said after Watson related his conversation with Kerrigan. "But it sounds like there's some serious opposition at very high levels."

"I told you the department wouldn't want this case re-opened. If it turns out Josh is proven innocent, a lot of very important people are going to be seriously embarrassed."

"Josh *is* innocent," Reilly said.

"I mean if we prove he's innocent," said Watson.

They were standing in a light drizzle, waiting to begin a four mile race organized by The New York Roadrunners to celebrate the club's forty-fifth anniversary. Reilly, training for her first New York City Marathon, had run six miles before the race, and now Watson, with thousands of other runners, had joined her at the starting line. He was running regularly now, entering the almost weekly races that made New York the best place in the world for a runner, and he found it easier to keep up with her, although he suspected she still slowed her pace so as not to embarrass him.

Watson told Reilly about the warning notes he had received, and Kerrigan's reaction. "Also," he said, "Claiborne brought up the Blake case when he called about the DEA case. I think Grabowsky must have told him I came to see him."

"We're touching some open wounds," said Reilly, not at all flustered.

"Kerrigan said we have a week to produce something he can use to convince the brass. You know what we have to do," Watson said.

"When can you be ready?" Reilly asked.

"Monday."

"I'll call Darlene," said Reilly, as the gun went off. "See ya," she said, sprinting off. Watson tried to follow, couldn't keep up, and soon settled into his normal pace.

Enchanted by her art survey course, Darlene went to the Metropolitan Museum of Art on Fifth Avenue and wandered around in a state of overwhelming confusion, until she arrived in a roomful of paintings by Pablo Picasso. She gulped in each painting like a drowning swimmer in sight of the beach sucking for air. She sat on a bench in the center of the room, her heart racing, staring for over an hour. This man, Pablo Picasso, so famous throughout the world, was talking to her. Pablo Picasso was talking to Darlene Brantley!

Absorbing Picasso in the quiet museum, letting her mind wander, she found herself thinking about Josh. She had only met him briefly at the hotel before he was arrested, not enough to know much about him. What made her care so much? The answer was what she had told him. He had shown respect. Sure, he looked at her tits. Who didn't? She stuck them out there for public view. But right from the beginning, Josh had talked to her, shared his own plans, listened to what she had to say as if it mattered. When she told him about her college courses, he had been pleased and supportive. He made it clear he didn't like what she did, and also he was afraid for her, which was really touching, but he never lectured her. In return, she was prepared to do whatever she could for him, regardless of the risks.

She went to the bookstore at the Met and found a book on Picasso's early years. She squeezed it to her chest all the way home, ordered a pizza, and devoured both the pizza and the entire Picasso book, finally turning off her light at 2:00 am.

Darlene caught herself just as she was about to ask him what he thought about Picasso. Frank Grabowsky was a gentle man. He was always considerate with her. It was a shame a man like this wasn't able to enjoy satisfying sex with his wife, about whom he obviously cared. He talked about his wife often, and Darlene would make sure he did so on this visit as well. "As many details as possible," Detective Watson had said when he installed the microphone and miniature recording device in her "work" apartment on West 53rd Street. "We could probably prove his identity with just a voice print," he said, "but names and events will be so much better."

So Darlene encouraged Grabowsky to talk even more than usual. It wasn't hard. He liked talking to her. As she listened, she wondered what he thought of her. We're not going to be best buddies when this business is all over. She made a point of discussing the price and the new fifty dollar bills Grabowsky used to pay her. In bed, she performed all the acts and positions he particularly liked, discussing each one explicitly and getting him to contribute to the verbal record of their couplings.

Finally, all talked out, and all sexed out, Grabowsky left, well within the two hour limit on the mini-tape. Darlene removed the cassette and carefully labeled it.

From Bethesda Fountain, one of Central Park's great vistas, Darlene could see a few couples rowing slowly around the small lake on a lazy summer day. Nowhere to go, just enjoying life. What a concept! Darlene had not had such luxury in a long time. She directed her steps toward the nearby Boat House, which, like so many City landmarks, is both a tourist destination and a place real

New Yorkers enjoy. The mini-cassette was secure in her jeans pocket and Detective Watson was waiting.

Watson waved and she saw Maureen Reilly standing next to him. Watson led them to a sunlit table overlooking the lake. Darlene struggled to remove the tape from her tight jeans and she finally had to stand up to get it out. "I think you'll be pleased," she said, handing it to Watson. "How are you going to use it?"

"Privately," Reilly said emphatically.

"Whatever you have to do is okay with me," Darlene said. "It doesn't matter."

"Yes it does, Darlene," Reilly said. "I'm not going to compromise you."

"If you have to, don't hesitate a second," Darlene insisted.

"We won't have to," Watson said. "Who's going to confront Grabowsky on this?"

Reilly raised her hand. "Please let me have the pleasure."

"I'll log the tape into the record and have a copy to you before the end of the day," Watson said.

Reilly had an appointment and excused herself after one cup of coffee, leaving Watson and Darlene alone. Darlene considered the irony of dining with a cop, but enjoyed Watson's company nevertheless. They talked about Josh, their only common point of interest. Watson paid for the late breakfast, and as they left the Boat House, asked if she had seen the spot where Mrs. Cooke had been attacked.

"It's only a few minutes from here," he said, "and I have to walk by there anyway." Watson pointed out landmarks along the way – the carved King Kong hedge at Tavern on the Green, the statue of Fred LeBow, who had founded the New York City Marathon. Darlene was surprised at the number of cars whizzing by on the outer road.

"Cars are allowed during commuting hours, Monday to Friday," Watson said. "Otherwise, it's runners' paradise, along with bikers, boarders and walkers." They reached the short path to the west side exit at 63rd Street and stood respectfully at the place where Mrs. Cooke had died.

"Why?" Darlene asked. "In this peaceful spot, with people all around? Why did she die here?"

"If we knew the answer to that question, Josh would be on his way out of Sing Sing," Watson said. "Grabowsky is the key. We need to know who those extra fingerprints belong to and why the defense never knew about them. Our hope is Maureen can use your tape to convince him to step up."

"You don't think an appeal to his higher nature and sense of justice will be enough?" Darlene asked.

"We tried," Watson said. "It didn't work."

Reilly called Grabowsky as soon as she listened to the tape. "Detective Grabowsky is in a meeting." She got the same result later in the afternoon and again the next morning. Enough of this, she said to herself, and practically ran over to One Police Plaza and barged into Grabowsky's small office. He was alone, and she stood silently, glaring at him. She closed the door behind her.

"Who are you, and what are you doing here?" Grabowsky asked.

"My name is Maureen Reilly. I'm an attorney representing Joshua Blake."

"I think you should leave, counselor," Grabowsky said, starting to stand.

"You goin' home tonight, Frank?" Reilly asked. He stared at her, uncomprehending. "You goin' to play with your kids, make love to your wife, take a shit in a warm room with a door? Joshua Blake isn't going to do any of those things tonight, or maybe any other night for the rest of his life. You did that to him, Frank."

Grabowsky responded angrily, "I did my job."

"That's bullshit, Frank, and you know it. You let Roger Claiborne hide the evidence, and you lied for him in court. You're getting on with your comfortable life and you forgot all about the kid who's dying at Sing Sing."

"I didn't lie," Grabowsky said. He avoided Reilly's eyes, but his defiance was waning. She was determined to keep pushing until he broke.

"You didn't tell the truth. You knew there were more latents on the pocketbook. But the DA's theory didn't have room for another perp. Blake touched it and that was all Claiborne wanted anybody to know. Josh was the suspect you had in custody, and Claiborne, the DA and the Mayor had already paraded his arrest all over the media. You let Claiborne tank the evidence. He knew he could rely on you to keep quiet or he wouldn't have had the guts to do it. You and Claiborne sent an innocent kid to Sing Sing."

Grabowsky hung his head, but he didn't answer. She waited, but it was clear he wasn't going to answer.

"By the way, Frank, I have regards for you." He didn't react. "For your wife, too." Grabowsky looked confused, but still said nothing.

"Darlene says hello. You remember Darlene, don't you? Darlene's hoping maybe you'll invite her to dinner one night. You know, one of those special Polish meals your wife cooks. Red beet soup with dumplings. What did you call the pork loin, Frank? *Pieczen*? Did I get it right? You described everything so well."

"What the fuck are you talking about?"

"Not me, Frank. It's what you talked about. All on tape. Very graphic, I must say." Reilly waited for Grabowsky to absorb his new situation. "You decide," she said. "You talk to Detective Watson, today, this very afternoon, or we talk to Aleksandra. And, Frank, do remember not to mention anything to Roger dear about this little conversation."

An hour later, Detective Frank Grabowsky walked into Watson's office, closed the door, and whispered, "I re-ran the prints. It's a kid named Anthony Marone. Lives in Brooklyn. A few weeks after the Cooke murder, he was arrested on a burglary in the Seventy-fifth Precinct."

Watson was speechless, his mind racing. Was this the same Anthony Marone who was killed in his Washington Heights DEA case? Was Marone part of a crime family? Could the murder of Mrs. Cooke have been gang-related? Is the Blake case related to the Washington Heights shooting? Then something clicked. Roger Claiborne was the ADA in both cases. What does Claiborne know about Marone? When did he know it?

"Frank," Watson said, "I want you to take everything and turn it over to Kerrigan."

"I can't do it today. Tomorrow."

"First thing tomorrow morning." Watson said. Grabowsky nodded. Watson waited.

"Can I have the tape now?" Grabowsky asked.

"The very day you testify, you bastard," Watson said, finally permitting himself the smile he had been suppressing.

Grabowsky left without another word. Watson punched his right hand in the air. "Yes," he said, reaching for the phone.

His first call was to Reilly. The second was to the Seventy-fifth Precinct, where he worked for years before his transfer to Central Park. He left a message for his friend Detective Christine Parker. Watson's final call was to Kerrigan, who immediately arranged an update meeting for the two of them and John Banyon.

Spider has initiated his plan to take over the Sing Sing drug trade from the Cali Columbians. These are sophisticated, powerful, and politically connected criminals who were vicious enough to displace Pedro Escobar and the Medellin cartel. They are not going to welcome intruders onto any piece of their turf. Spider knows violence is the only way and he's preparing for battle.

The first thing he says to me, though, is, "Did you get tattooed yet?"

"I haven't had a chance."

"You're fuckin' with me, Josh. What's keeping you so busy? Teaching every illiterate in this prison how to read?"

"If they can read, they can work, and then you can make more money off them."

Spider looked at me as harshly as he ever had, and I thought he was going to hit me. Instead he laughs and says, "You are the fuckin' hardest case in this prison."

"Not likely," I say.

"You are. You have your own mind. If I thought you were fuckin' with me because you wanted to be in business for yourself, I'd have to kill you. You know what I'm sayin'?"

"I know."

"But you're not. You hate all this stuff, don't you, even though you need the protection."

"Did you set up the attack on me when I was in keeplock?" Once out, the question can't be taken back. I hold my breath and prepare to be pummeled.

Spider raises his eyebrows and a huge smile plays across his ugly face. It seems my question had increased his respect for me. I think it's a good time to return the favor before he changes his mind.

"I'll get that thing done tonight," I say.

Spider nods his approval. "It's coming," he says. "We're talkin' and getting' no where. Somebody's going to have to get hurt. We're goin' to have to stick together."

"Do you think the guys will?" I ask.

"I think they will. What do you think?"

I give Spider a rundown on every key player in B-block. Who could be counted on, who needed to be watched, and why. He listens attentively and never interrupts.

"I knew there was a reason to tolerate your shit," he says. "How do you know so much?"

"I talk to my students, and they talk to everyone else in this cell block."

"You've nodded hello to more than twenty guys just while we've been walking."

"I didn't think you'd noticed, o' hallowed leader."

"Fuck you, Josh," he says, laughing out loud.

That night I had double lightning bolts tattooed onto my right bicep.

The thundering crescendos of Beethoven's Seventh Symphony, played to perfection by the Philadelphia Orchestra under the baton of Ricardo Muti, filled every corner of his apartment. Roger Claiborne was congratulating himself over just how good his life had become, when a familiar voice on the phone jarred him back to a harsher reality.

"Bad news, Roger."

"I thought the investigation was over," Claiborne said, his heart pounding.

"Well it's not. Kerrigan gave the okay to keep going."

"What happened?"

"They know who belongs to the third prints from the old lady's bag."

Claiborne's heart spiked, but he was immediately comforted by the realization it was too late for anyone to learn anything from Anthony Marone.

The phone clicked, and Claiborne was left with his dark thoughts. He had no illusions about how much trouble he was in. What he didn't understand was how Joshua Blake, a kid from Baltimore with no resources and no friends in New York, all alone in his prison cell at Sing Sing, had managed to instigate such a furious firestorm.

TWENTY-FIVE

"So, you still on the straight and narrow?"

"Yes, Christine," Watson said. "Last thing I need is to incur your wrath again."

Watson had seen Detective Christine Parker and others from the 7-5 many times since they had ripped into him at the previous year's Fourth of July party, and of course she knew about his transfer to Homicide. They exchanged more small talk, and then Watson asked if she knew who handled the Anthony Marone case.

"That was mine, such as it was. Two punks and a candy store."

"Marone is dead. I need to learn everything I can about him."

"He's dead?" Parker asked.

"Killed in a shooting in Washington Heights two months ago," Watson said. "It looks like it was a gang killing."

"Really? He never showed up for trial, not a word since."

"Marone jumped bail?" Watson asked. "What about the other guy, Picollo?"

"You've done your homework," Parker said. "Anyway, Picollo got sixty days. What's your interest in this, Bob? This is penny ante stuff for you guys."

"Marone's prints turned up in a case I'm working on," Watson said. "What do you know about him? Who was he mixed up with?"

"Street talk was he suddenly started talking tough, maybe got hooked up with some bad guys."

"Did you look for him?"

"Not really," said Parker. "We gave it a dusting. You know how it is."

"What about Picollo? Was he with the same bad guys?"

"I don't think so. He's back here, by the way. No problems, even has a job."

Teri Scanlon shows up the day after I get my tattoo, but I cover it with my shirt. I didn't know she was coming, and didn't even recognize her. When she tells me her name, I remember she had written about my case. In fact, she was one of the few people who seemed to have any real doubts about my guilt. When I last saw her on Rikers, she was chubby and sort of scruffy, with a jeans and rumpled sweater look. But now! She's lost weight, and her hair, which had been long and wild, is short and styled. She's dressed professionally and she looks terrific.

"Looks like it's been a good year for you," I say, my eyes complimenting her appearance.

"Thank you," she says, blushing. She looks at me in a way that signals she couldn't say the same for me, which made me think about how I must look to someone who hasn't seen me in a while. I'm thirty pounds heavier, really bulked up, with muscles straining against my prison t-shirt. It's been a week since my last shave, who knows how long since my last haircut. Maybe I still have that macho look that so disturbed Tom. Whatever, I don't look much like the innocent college kid who arrived in New York City a year ago.

"I've been thinking about you recently," Scanlon says.

"Why is that?" I ask.

"The Chicago Tribune published a five-part series about people who were wrongly convicted. They call their series *How Prosecutors Sacrifice Justice To Win*. Actually, they published it a while ago, but I just read it recently."

My defensive antenna go on full alert. Does she know about my case, or is she just guessing? I remember Detective Watson's admonition. Don't say anything to anybody. On the other hand, Teri Scanlon has been sympathetic, and maybe she could help.

"What did those prosecutors do?" I ask, not quite achieving the innocent tone I was seeking.

"Some of them concealed evidence which might have proven innocence," she says, and I'm afraid my facial reaction tells her she is right on target.

"This happened a lot?"

"The Trib identified 381 defendants whose homicide convictions were later thrown out when it was learned prosecutors had withheld evidence or presented false evidence. And they claim this is only the tip of the iceberg."

"How do they get away with it?"

"My question exactly," she said. "Why don't prosecutors get caught more often? Why don't they get punished when they do get caught?"

"They don't get punished?"

Teri consults her notes. "Here it is," she says. "Not one of the prosecutors in those 381 cases was ever convicted of a crime. Not one was barred from practicing law. None received a public sanction. Instead, many saw their careers advance. Some became judges or district attorneys. One became a congressman."

"You think stuff like that happens here?"

"I don't know, Josh. Does it?"

"I wouldn't be surprised," I say.

A Good Conviction   253

"Is that all you want to say?"

"For now."

Teri removes a flat manila envelope from her bag and gives it to me. "Maybe after you read these articles we can talk again. If something like this happened to you, I'd like to write about it. Maybe I could help you. Even if the prosecutors don't get punished, you'll see in these stories a fair amount of convictions are overturned."

"I've decided to write my own story," I tell her. "I've been scribbling notes for the past few weeks."

"Really? Can I see what you've written?"

"Not yet," I say. "Maybe when it's ready."

"Josh, I think you have something important to say. My guess is you're working on an appeal and you've been told by your attorney not to say anything."

She waits for an answer, but I don't give her one.

"You don't have to confirm it," she says, "but if it's true, maybe you want to discuss my interest in your case with your lawyer, and see if he thinks I could be of any help to you."

I say nothing.

"I understand, Josh. Here's my card. Two cards, just in case you want to give one to someone else."

"What are you and your cop boyfriend up to?"

Roger Claiborne had seen Maureen Reilly in court and asked her to come up to his new office on the sixth floor of 80 Centre Street. He leaned back in his new leather chair, smug and arrogant. "The Blake case is over. The guy got twenty years to life. It was a good conviction. It's done."

Reilly, still standing, leaned across Claiborne's desk, and put her face as close to his as she could get. She spoke quietly and in control. "You're a no good bastard, Roger. You needed a conviction so much you couldn't admit you might have arrested the wrong person. You hid evidence and you let Joshua Blake go down. Martinez, the additional fingerprints, the ballgame video, all exculpatory. You knowingly violated the law when you didn't give it to the defense."

"Sit down, counselor," Claiborne said. Reilly remained standing. Claiborne waited until it was embarrassing and then continued. His voice had a slight quiver. "It doesn't mean Blake didn't do the crime. Besides, Mullin could have interviewed Martinez."

"You weren't actually worried about that, were you? You knew Martinez was gone. Tell me, Roger, what did you know about the additional fingerprints?"

254   Lewis M. Weinstein

"Didn't mean a thing," Claiborne said with an oily smile, although his eyes were twitching. "Those prints had not been identified."

Claiborne's use of the past tense made Reilly think he knew the prints had now been identified. Did Grabowsky tell him? A chill went through her. Did Claiborne also know how they had turned Grabowsky? Was he aware of Darlene's connection to Josh? If he knew the prints had been identified, he might also know they belonged to Marone. And surely, since he was the ADA on the shooting case, he would know Marone was dead.

All those thoughts passed in a flash. Then Reilly snapped, "The prints would have been identified, if you'd kept looking."

"The jury would have ignored them," Claiborne insisted. "Same with the videotape. You'll never convince an appeals judge otherwise."

Reilly felt a flush of excitement. Claiborne, focused on the fingerprints, had just slipped, revealing he knew about Josh's videotape. That meant there must have been an NYPD report, and thus another piece of exculpatory evidence withheld from the defense.

"It should have been up to the jury to decide, not you," Reilly said, her voice rising. "You made sure the jurors never saw the evidence that proved Josh's innocence."

"This is bullshit, Reilly. Let it go."

"Let it go?" She was hollering now. "Joshua Blake is in Sing Sing. You ruined his life and you want to just let it go. How do you sleep at night?"

"So file your motion," Claiborne said, shrugging his hands and smiling. "You don't have the goods to win, and you know it."

Reilly stormed out of Claiborne's office, but she knew he was right about one thing. They did not have enough to overturn the verdict, or even to get a hearing. Not yet.

"What was that all about?" George Henson had poked his head into Claiborne's office seconds after Reilly left. "Maureen sure sounded upset."

Claiborne didn't know how much Henson had heard. He calculated the risk of telling at least part of the truth was less than the risk of lying to his best friend in the DA's office. And, since Henson knew Reilly from her days as an ADA, he would likely find out anyway.

"It had to do with the Blake case," Claiborne said. "She thinks the kid is innocent and she's working on an appeal."

"No news there," said Henson. "Everybody in the Office knows that. But what made her so upset?"

"She thinks there was evidence the defense didn't get," Claiborne said. He quickly added, "It's not true. They got everything."

"Are they going to file *Brady*?" Henson asked.

Claiborne expected Reilly and Mullin would, if they got enough proof, indeed file a *Brady* motion, alleging he had withheld exculpatory information. He knew he had covered himself legally, but he also knew District Attorney Harold Markman took it very personally whenever anyone had the temerity to suggest his Office had done anything wrong. A *Brady* motion would infuriate him.

"No," Claiborne lied, rationalizing there was no need to raise a very unpleasant issue sooner than necessary, "there's no basis for *Brady*."

After Henson left, Claiborne closed his door and tried to calm down. He was on the verge of losing the enhanced professional and social status he had gained by convicting Joshua Blake. He had to stop Reilly and Watson. The warning notes had obviously not worked. He remembered that Kerrigan was also part of his problem, and Kerrigan hated him.

Now there was another issue – Marone. Watson would put together, if he hadn't already, that the Anthony Marone who was killed in Washington Heights was the same person whose fingerprints were on Mrs. Cooke's pocketbook. What would he do with that information? A good detective, and Claiborne grudgingly admitted Watson was an excellent detective, would wonder if Marone's crime connections, revealed by the way he was killed, had anything to do with the earlier attack on Mrs. Cooke. Sooner or later, Watson might construct a credible story explaining Marone's presence in Central Park. And such a story, Claiborne realized with a shudder, would have nothing whatever to do with Joshua Blake.

Claiborne considered his potential allies. Clearly the Mayor, the DA, and the Police Commissioner would be embarrassed if what he had done in the Blake case became known. But they wouldn't help. In fact, they would drop him like three day old fish in order to save their own asses.

But there had been others who knew and said nothing.

Frank Grabowsky had flipped. How had they squeezed him to get him to reveal Marone's prints? Whatever it was, Grabowsky was no longer on his side, and the others knew it, which would add to their own reluctance to get in any deeper. Nevertheless, he had to get somebody's help to stop this damn Blake investigation.

It occurred to him that the DEA had an interest. Exposing Marone in the Cooke killing might compromise DEA's ongoing investigation of the crime families' war to control drug distribution in Manhattan, of which Marone's killing was but a small part. DEA would not want anything about Marone to become public knowledge. Maybe, crazy as it sounded, somebody at DEA would help him keep a lid on the Blake case, at least for a while.

Claiborne took out a yellow pad and started to write names, connections, and things he might do to stop the Blake case. In his confused and rattled state of mind, he didn't get far. He picked up the phone and put it back down several times. Eventually, he put the pad back in his drawer and tried to concentrate on the day's prosecutorial work, also without much success.

"I just got another call from my boss," Kerrigan began. He did not sound happy.

"I thought they were okay with this," Watson asked, holding his breath.

"They were *never* happy. I bought one week."

"But look what we produced. We have proof of the third fingerprints and we know who it was."

"They were impressed for about a minute," said Kerrigan with an ironic smile.

"What happened?"

"Somebody's convinced the department will be embarrassed if this case is re-opened," Kerrigan said, his eyes unable to hold Watson's. "They're shaking in their boots."

Watson couldn't believe what he was hearing.

"It was the ADA who hid the evidence," he said, "not the department."

"My bosses don't care about Claiborne, or DA Markman either. But Claiborne had to have help to hide the evidence, help that probably came from somebody in the NYPD."

"An innocent kid is rotting his life away in Sing Sing."

"They don't care about him either," said Kerrigan. "They care about their jobs, their reputations, and most of all, their pensions. Nobody's goin' to fall on a sword for Joshua Blake."

"Who got to them?" Watson asked.

"I don't know."

"Why are you telling me this? Are we done with this?"

"You want to quit?" Kerrigan asked.

"Of course not." But Watson knew it was over if Kerrigan ordered him to stop.

"Neither do I," said Kerrigan. "But it'll have to be different now. Quiet. Nobody else involved. Nobody else knows anything."

"Have you been told to stop the investigation?" Watson asked, amazing himself with his audacity.

"They're too smart to give a direct order," said Kerrigan, taking no offense. "But the message was clear."

"Nobody else involved?" Watson paused, debated with himself, and decided to ask straight out. "What about Banyon?"

"Do you trust him?" Kerrigan asked.

"That's the second time you've asked me. Why?"

"Because he loses, whatever happens. Maybe he didn't actually do anything. Maybe he turned away and let it go down. Or maybe he didn't even know what Claiborne was doing. But any way it goes down, his ass is on the line. He was responsible. If this case ever gets back to court, it could be a career killer for him. The NYPD bosses will need eyes and ears, and they'll reach out for Banyon. He's at risk, so he'll have to respond. He can't know anything more."

It occurred to Watson there was another way for Banyon. If Kerrigan believed he was clean, he could bring him in, let him help set things straight. It spoke volumes that Kerrigan was not going that way.

"How will I investigate anything if I can't talk to anyone? We know it was Marone's fingerprints on the pocketbook, and then Marone was wiped out in what looks like a drug killing. I need to find out if there's a connection between the two cases. Why was Marone in Central Park? This is complex. DEA and who knows who else is involved. How can I do all this myself?"

"Calm down. You won't be by yourself." Kerrigan said.

"What do you mean?"

"I'll be your partner on Blake. You'll still be Banyon's partner on everything else, but I'll tell him the Blake case is done. You and I will work it off hours. Nobody else will know."

"How high does this go?"

"You know the chain of command," said Kerrigan.

"Has it gone to Police Plaza?" asked Watson, by which he meant the NYPD Chief of Detectives and the Police Commissioner. The very thought of coming to their attention in this case terrified him. What have I got myself into? I'm acting directly in opposition to downtown's expressed wishes. Who do I think I am?

"I don't know," Kerrigan said, an answer that did nothing for Watson's fragile state of mind.

Reilly and Watson drove with the windows open on a glorious June morning. Watson explained how he and Kerrigan were now going to secretly investigate the Blake case, Tony Marone, and a possible link between the Blake and DEA cases.

"It won't work," Reilly said. "You can't keep people from finding out what you're doing. This is going to be big trouble for you."

Watson put his hand over hers. "It's okay," he said.

"No it's not. I pushed you into this."

"I made my own decision," Watson said, "and I don't regret it. It'll work out." They exchanged a quick smile and drove in silence for another mile.

"I think Claiborne knew about Marone's fingerprints when he called me into his office the other day," Reilly said.

"Did Grabowsky tell him?"

"I called Grabowsky as soon as I left Claiborne's office," Reilly said. "He swore he hadn't spoken to Claiborne."

"You believe him?" Watson asked.

"I don't know. He seemed terrified Claiborne knew, which increases the chances his wife will learn about Darlene. I told him if we ever found out he said anything to Claiborne, he was dead meat."

"It might have been Banyon," Watson said, and again, they drove for awhile in silence.

"Here's something strange," Watson said. "Kerrigan never asked what we had done to convince Grabowsky to cooperate. I wonder if he knows."

"You worried about Kerrigan now?" Reilly asked.

"No. It's just strange. I don't know what drives him. Anyway, what do you think Claiborne will do?"

"Everything possible to impede the investigation. He'll be desperate now."

"You think he's behind the pressure from the NYPD brass to stop working on the Blake case?" Watson asked.

"Nobody would listen to Claiborne," Reilly said. "It had to be Markman."

"You think Claiborne went to Markman?"

"It's possible. Same as NYPD needs to cover their ass, Markman may feel a need to cover his. Even if he had nothing to do with Claiborne's withholding of evidence, it happened on his watch, and he's got an election coming up."

The high grey walls of Sing Sing came into view and Watson was left with his increasingly morbid thoughts. They had made so little progress even without any active opposition. Now it would be much harder.

"I'm not looking forward to this meeting," Watson said.

"Me neither," said Reilly.

"This is some occasion," I say. "It's the first time I've ever seen the two of you together." Actually, I'm surprised Reilly and Watson even got into the prison. Tensions are incredibly high and this place is about to explode. But I'm thrilled they did. Finally, after two months of calls from Mullin saying they're working on it, I'll find out what they've been doing.

They take no time for pleasantries.

"We know whose fingerprints were on Mrs. Cooke's pocketbook," Reilly says, and all of a sudden, I'm wildly excited. Thoughts go through my head in a flash, simple things like walking down the street, eating in a restaurant, taking a shower all by myself.

"It's a guy named Tony Marone," says Watson, but then his head drops, and he adds, "He's dead."

"So what," I say, unwilling to be deflated. "Even if the guy is dead, if the court knows who touched Mrs. Cooke's pocketbook, won't that be enough to get another trial?"

"Of course we'll include what we know about Marone in our appeal," Reilly says, "and it will make a difference, certainly at the hearing. But at the trial itself, it's not the same as if he was indicted and available to testify, so we could prove you had nothing to do with him."

Watson jumps in. "Marone had an accomplice in the candy store robbery, a guy named Marco Picollo. Maybe he'll have something useful to say."

I ask if we're almost ready to file the appeal.

"We know a lot," Reilly says, "but so far, we can't prove much of what we know."

"Please explain that to me," I say. "I really don't get it."

"Detective Grabowsky will testify there were more latent fingerprints, and that this information was known to the prosecution. He'll testify the prints belong to Anthony Marone, which is enough to implicate Marone, but not necessarily to exonerate you. Claiborne will argue it was both of you, so we still need Angel Martinez to tell a jury where you were at 8:00 o'clock that night. Bob is doing everything he can to find him."

"This really stinks," I say.

"I'd like to try something," Watson says. "I think I've found people who know Angel, but they won't talk to me. I want you to write an open letter to Angel, ask for his help."

"Where will I mail it?"

Watson laughs. "You won't. I'll be your postman. You give the letter to me. I'll make copies and get them out in the neighborhoods."

"You're hoping somebody will give Angel the letter and he'll come forward?"

"Exactly."

"I'll work on it tonight."

We sit silently for what seems like hours, each of us lost in our own thoughts. Finally, Reilly says, "We wouldn't have gotten Grabowsky to tell us about Marone without Darlene."

"What did she do?" I ask. "She promised she wouldn't take risks."

"She tape recorded Grabowsky," Reilly says.

"What? You can't use that without ..." I stop myself before I say without admitting Darlene is a prostitute.

"It's not for court," Reilly says. "I just let Grabowsky know what we had."

"They're going to hurt Darlene."

"There are risks," Reilly says. "I won't deny it."

Now I'm the one who feels rotten. I'm yelling at them and they're working so hard and taking all these risks for me. I keep thinking what would happen if they found out I was an Aryan Brotherhood criminal. And it isn't *if* they find out, but *when*. My stomach ties in knots and I take a series of quick short breaths. I really have become an emotional mess.

Reilly puts her hand on mine and flashes her great Irish smile that seems to wipe away the world's problems, even here. I choke up more, fighting back tears. "We understand the pressure you're under," she says. "I'm sorry."

"You have nothing to apologize for," I manage to say. "You're doing this for me. Nobody's making you."

"We're not going to give up, Josh," Watson says. "We're going to get there, whatever it takes."

I think he's pretending to be more optimistic than he really is, but I don't object. Lord knows I can stand some optimism. But I can't ever again allow myself to get excited, even for a single second. I just have to accept the idea that I'll stay here the rest of my life.

Maybe I'll become a *capo* in the Aryan Brotherhood! Now there's a life to look forward to!

Reilly is talking, although I barely hear her through the clutter in my head. Something about how terrific Larry Mullin has been.

"After you file, what then?" I ask.

"The prosecution gets to submit their brief, opposing our motion. Then the court will schedule oral arguments."

"If we win, do I go free?"

"No," Reilly said. "You get another trial. But that trial, Joshua Blake, you will win."

Despite my resolve not to be overly optimistic, Reilly's confidence is actually exhilarating. I think she really believes if we can ever get to a trial, we'll win. I ask the question which frightens me most. "Suppose the appeals court turns us down and we don't get a new trial?"

"We can appeal one more level."

"How long will it take?"

"It could be years," says Reilly.

We all sit silently with this sobering thought. Then I remember Scanlon.

"I had a visitor," I say. "Teri Scanlon from the *Daily News*."

"She wrote about your case," Reilly said.

"She wants to help. She's working on a big story about prosecutorial abuse."

"She wants a Pulitzer," Reilly said.

"That too, but I think she really wants to help me."

"You do have an interesting effect on people," Reilly said, her great smile re-appearing. "Do you trust her?"

"I do."

"She'd have to hold back, make her story secondary to the needs of our appeal."

"I think she will," I say.

"We can use all the help we can get," Reilly says. "I'll call her."

After Reilly and Watson leave, I walk slowly back to my cell. My head is swimming, part depressed and part optimistic, and I guess I'm not concentrating as closely as I should be, given the battle status that has engulfed the prison. Or maybe my attackers are just really good.

The whole thing takes only a few seconds. I'm surrounded on the bridge between the visiting area and B Block. My arms are forced behind me in an iron grip. I'm jerked backwards, down to my knees. I feel the knife go through my left cheek and into my mouth. I feel the slice across my throat. I feel my own warm blood. Then nothing.

"Roger, your friend in Ossining was attacked today. Stabbed pretty bad."

"Will he die?" Claiborne asked.

"That would solve a lot of problems, wouldn't it?"

TWENTY-SIX

"All right, let's review," said Larry Mullin, checklist in hand. "What do we know? What do we need to know?"

Mullin, Watson, Reilly and Darlene were assembled around Reilly's conference table. It was Sunday morning, and Reilly had laid out bagels, cream cheese, and Swiss cheese. The coffee pot was beginning to gurgle.

Watson and Reilly went through their update, including the identification of Anthony Marone and the fact that he was dead. When they finished, Mullin said, "Let's move on to what do we need to know."

"We need to find Angel," Reilly said. "We need to know what Marone was doing in Central Park."

Watson had his head into some papers he had brought with him, and suddenly he looked up with a start. "I've got something here," he said, clearly excited, drawing everybody's attention. "At the beginning of the investigation, we got a list from the MTA of all the Metro Cards used at Columbus Circle between 7:50 and 8:10 on the night of May 29, 2003. Some of those Metro Cards were purchased by credit card, and we were looking up the names." He cut off abruptly, his hands clenching the table. "We stopped looking when Josh was arrested."

"And now?" Reilly asked, seeking to relieve his embarrassment.

"I finished the list a couple weeks ago, but this is the first time I've looked at it since Marone's name surfaced." He pointed to an item on the list, shook his head slowly as if in disbelief. "Anthony M. Marone entered the Columbus Circle station at 8:03 pm on the night of May 29, 2003." The room erupted in cheers.

"Joshua Blake's card isn't on the list," Watson said. "He must have entered the subway after 8:10."

"Can you expand the list to show later times?" Mullin asked.

"Unfortunately, no," said Watson, looking away. "MTA doesn't have the records any more."

"I think there's another aspect of this we should discuss," said Reilly, jumping in quickly. "Our little investigation is beginning to be noticed, and we're getting a reaction. Bob got a warning call after he talked with Grabowsky, and then three nasty notes were left at Homicide, presumably by a cop. Also, Claiborne invited me to his office on Friday to holler at me for not letting the Blake case stay dead."

"We're making people nervous," said Mullin.

"It'll get worse," said Watson, relating the gist but not the details of Lieutenant Kerrigan's problems with the NYPD brass. "We've got some room to work for now," he said, "but the leash is tightening."

"Then I think we should get a tape of Claiborne while we still can." It was the first time Darlene had spoken, and her words prompted utter silence in the room. Everybody knew what she had to do to get the tape.

"It's too risky," said Watson finally. "Claiborne may have spoken to Grabowsky."

"I don't think Grabowsky told Claiborne anything about Darlene's tape," said Reilly. "Frank and I had a little conversation after my blowup with Claiborne. Grabowsky is terrified Aleksandra will learn about Darlene. Grabowsky may have told Claiborne Marone had been identified, but not about Darlene."

"Sooner or later Claiborne will ask Grabowsky what led him to re-run the fingerprints," said Watson. "How will Grabowsky answer?"

They all thought for several moments, then Watson answered his own question. "He'll have to blame Kerrigan. Lieu's the only one with the power to move him."

"Do you think Grabowsky will testify?" Mullin asked.

"Yes, but nothing is certain," said Watson.

"So let's get Claiborne taped while we still can," Darlene repeated.

Reilly wondered why Darlene was so insistent, but saw no reason to veto the request. "Bob, when can you have the gear?" she asked.

"Next week, maybe Tuesday," he said, and they all nodded.

The phone rang, and Reilly went out of the room to answer, while the others went to work on the bagels. Reilly returned, her face ashen.

"It's Josh," she said. "He's been stabbed. He's in the hospital at Sing Sing."

"Josh, we're here."

"The docs say you're going to be all right."

I was too groggy to see them. But their voices – Maureen Reilly, Bob Watson, Larry Mullin, Darlene Brantley – were the best music I had ever heard. I raised my hand in a feeble greeting and they took turns hugging me as I drifted back to sleep.

Later, I learned Hector and several other of my "students" had rushed to my aid and immediately staunched the flow of blood, long before any medical support reached the scene. It's almost as if they had been waiting in the wings to help me. I also learned Spider was attacked within minutes of the attack on me. His jugular was sliced clean through, and he bled to death in a matter of seconds. No inmate was ever charged with either attack, and the war to control the distribution of drugs in B-block was over.

They rode in silence for the first ten minutes, all of them still pretty much in shock.

Watson spoke first. "One of the COs told me we were lucky to visit today because there's a war going on for control of the drug trade in the prison. The prison is on the way to a complete lockdown. He also said Josh's friend Spider was the Aryan Brotherhood boss in B-block and he was trying to take over the drug trade."

"Pretty ambitious," said Mullin.

"He won't succeed," said Watson. "Spider was killed yesterday. Exact same time Josh was attacked."

"Was there a connection?" asked Reilly.

Before Watson could answer, Darlene spoke. "Did any of you see the tattoo?" she asked.

"What tattoo?" Mullin asked.

"When Josh raised his hand, I saw it on his arm." Darlene hesitated. She had been upset since she saw it, and she knew it would change everything.

"It was lightning bolts. An Aryan Brotherhood symbol."

"Oh shit," said Reilly. "He was part of it."

Nobody said a word for the rest of the thirty minute drive into the City, each enveloped in their private thoughts. But when Watson pulled over to drop off Darlene, she said, "Before I get out of this car, I want to make it clear I still believe in Josh Blake. Whatever he's got himself into up there, he didn't kill that lady in Central Park."

"Yes, but ...," Reilly said, turning to face Darlene and Mullin in the back seat.

"There's no buts, Maureen," said Darlene. "He's a good person. I've seen him change over the last couple of months. He's gotten much tougher. But what else could he do? He had to survive. How can we judge him?"

"That's very nice to say, Darlene," Watson said, "and we might all agree with you. But if Josh committed a crime, and if the authorities at Sing Sing know about it, he could have a real problem. They could prosecute and add years to his sentence, years that would have nothing to do with any appeal on the original conviction."

"It'd make our appeal even more difficult," Reilly said. "The courts would take Josh's prison behavior into consideration."

"They shouldn't, because it has nothing to do with the original conviction, but they well might," said Mullin. "And even if they didn't, and we won the appeal, Josh would still have the years to serve for the second crime."

"First crime," insisted Darlene. "And aren't we jumping to conclusions here? How do we know if Josh did anything wrong?"

There was another long silence, which Darlene broke. "So what do we do?" she asked.

"Maybe Josh isn't linked to whatever went on," said Watson. "I could ask around."

"Making inquiries could suggest a connection they're not yet aware of," said Reilly. "Especially if Claiborne got wind of it. I think it's better to do nothing and see what happens."

They left it there, but Darlene couldn't help wondering if the enthusiasm of the Blake Team would be diminished by what they had learned. She regretted saying anything about the tattoo. She was terrified both by what Josh might have done and by the possibility he would be caught. She cared so much, and it all seemed so futile.

Darlene didn't like Roger Claiborne, never had. In her view, there was nothing to like, even if he hadn't done what he did to Josh. He was a sour man, unhappy to the core, and his new-found social success, played out on the upper east side of New York and in fancy places like Newport and the Hamptons, hadn't seemed to overcome his fundamental insecurities or bring him any real satisfaction. Good, you bastard, Darlene thought behind her most charming smile, you don't deserve any satisfaction.

While Claiborne took off his clothes, Darlene concluded Reilly was right. Claiborne wouldn't be there if he knew about the Grabowsky tape.

Removing her own clothes, she also reflected on the significance of the occasion. This is the last time I'm ever going to fuck anyone for money. I've been so lucky, no drugs, no AIDS, no beatings. Annabelle is going to miss me, but maybe she'll get out as well.

Her thoughts were interrupted by Claiborne's hand moving up her thigh. Usually, he wanted to sit together naked while he looked at her and got excited. She would bend and stretch, and show him what he needed to get going. But this time he was ready and he wanted sex right away. Darlene worried there might not be anything useful to record.

Her fears turned out to be unfounded. After they fucked, which lasted less than a minute, Claiborne was not in a hurry to leave. In fact, he wanted to brag about his newly enhanced sex life, and Darlene showed great interest, drawing him out. Stupidly, she thought, he gave her lots of names. Detective Watson will be very pleased to learn every detail of each of your conquests.

Talking about it got Claiborne excited again, but Darlene told him she had another appointment and he left. She closed the door behind him, threw the bolt, and experienced an emotion which exceeded even her most profound expectations. Her career as a prostitute was officially concluded. Now she could let herself think about Josh, her studies, and a future she could be proud of.

Detective Bob Watson and his new partner Lieutenant Brian Kerrigan approached Tony Marone's home in Brooklyn's Flatbush section with low expectations. Watson rang the bell and was greeted by a woman who he assumed was Tony's mother. He identified Kerrigan and himself as police officers and she let them in. Very politely, she asked them to sit. They shared a sofa behind which hung a small crucifix.

"Mrs. Marone," Watson said, "we're here to talk about your son Anthony."

A look of long-suffering concern passed over the woman's face. Watson saw a photograph on the table next to her. The boy in the picture didn't look exactly like Josh, but close enough to account for the eyewitness testimony. "Is that him?" he asked.

"Yes, that is Anthony," said Mrs. Marone. "You know he is dead?"

"Yes, we know," Watson said, catching his breath. "We're very sorry for your loss, but we have to ask you some questions."

Mrs. Marone nodded and Watson asked, "Did Anthony ever mention a Mrs. Cooke?"

"No."

"Mrs. Cooke was murdered in Central Park a little over a year ago."

"Why are you asking me this? My son is not a murderer."

"Mrs. Marone, his fingerprints were on the lady's pocketbook. The pocketbook was discarded at the Fort Hamilton Parkway subway station, which is not very far from here."

"No. My Anthony is not a murderer. He's gone. Let him alone."

"I understand this is upsetting to you," Watson said, "but there's another boy, about the same age as your son."

Watson had a college photograph of Josh, and he showed it to Mrs. Marone.

"This boy was found guilty of murdering Mrs. Cooke and now he's in Sing Sing. I don't think he did it."

"You think my Anthony did?"

"He might have," Watson said.

Mrs. Marone sat very still, her world even worse than it had been before. Her eyes revealed a sadness that must have afflicted her often with respect to this child.

"He never mentioned any of this to you?" asked Watson.

"No," Mrs. Marone answered. "He never said anything." She paused, remembering something and trying to decide whether to say it. Watson could feel her pain as she made her decision. "But he was very interested in this case," she said. "He read the papers about this case. He watched the news whenever it came on. I asked him once why he was so interested, but he didn't say." She paused, remembering, and then added so softly she could barely be heard, "There's so much he didn't tell me."

"Might he have told anyone else?" This was the first time Kerrigan had spoken, and Mrs. Marone seemed surprised by the new voice, as if she had forgotten he was there.

"About something like this? About a murder? I don't think so."

Watson tried to be as delicate and understanding as he could. "There is a way," he said, "to determine if your son was involved in this crime or not."

"What way?" Mrs. Marone asked.

"If there was any contact between Anthony and Mrs. Cooke, it's possible there might be some of her DNA on his clothes." He waited while the woman absorbed this information. "Do you still have any of his clothes here?"

"Yes," Mrs. Marone said. "His clothes are here. But everything has been washed. Wouldn't the ... what did you call it?"

"The DNA," Watson said.

"Yes, wouldn't it be washed off?"

"Maybe not," Watson said, thinking of the blood stains Concolita Jones had seen. "Could we look?"

Mrs. Marone was so saddened by this request Watson found himself wishing there were some other way. But she sighed and asked them to follow her to Anthony's room. At the door, she motioned them to enter, but she herself walked away. Watson and Kerrigan went through the drawers and closet, putting everything back exactly as they had found it. All of the clothes had been washed and neatly folded. There were no bloody jeans.

"Should we take anything to the lab?" Watson asked.

"There's no point," said Kerrigan. "Like she said, everything's been washed. And if we go to the lab, our secret investigation will be blown sky high."

A few minutes later, Watson and Kerrigan left. They had driven about a mile when Kerrigan pointed and said, "Look at that church. It's a beauty. Reminds me of my old neighborhood in the Bronx."

"Mr. Claiborne called last night," Annabelle said, a distinct lilt in her voice.

Darlene was thrilled. "How did it go?"

"Just like we planned," said Annabelle. "I told him you weren't in 'the life' any more."

"And ..."

"He went ballistic. 'What do you mean,' he said, 'she's been a hooker for years. What happened? She hit the lottery?'"

Darlene could hear Annabelle laughing at the other end of the phone. "I told him that would be your business," Annabelle said. She paused. "Then he asked me if I was available." Another pause, which Darlene chose not to interrupt. "I told him he wasn't my type."

"You did good, Annabelle. Thank you so much."

"You know I'm going to miss you, partner," Annabelle said. "Are you sure you're goin' to stay retired."

"Absolutely. I'm a college girl now. I've got enough set aside to pay for my education. I don't want to fuck any more. At least not for money. By the way, I want to remove our web site. I'll make one just for you if you'd like."

"Does that darling boy have anything to do with it?"

Darlene debated how to answer. She wasn't sure herself how she felt about Josh. No, she thought, of course I know how I feel. I just don't want to say, when it seems so impossible anything will come of it. Maybe he'll never get out of prison. Even if he does, what could he want with a whore like me.

"You think? Don't be absurd, Annabelle. He's a friend, that's all."

TWENTY-SEVEN

I'm released from the prison infirmary, my face covered with bandages and my body full of antibiotics to prevent infection. Cell Block B is very strange in some respects and unchanged in others. Spider is gone, but the enterprises he initiated seem to be performing without a hitch, under new management, as it were. Francisco Franco and Cutter have retained their positions. It isn't clear to me who the new CEO is, and I make no effort to find out. This is no longer my business. It's as if I've been offered early retirement from my position as *consigliore*, and I'm thrilled to be alive to take it. Maybe the tattoo will fade.

It's awkward when I see Hector, who has managed to get himself transferred into B Block. I believe he knew I was going to be attacked. Maybe he negotiated the less-than-lethal nature of the attack, and clearly, he and the others were on the spot in a flash, with bandages that must have been at the ready. I decide never to ask, and he doesn't volunteer. Maybe some day a clue will show up in one of his stories.

I'm part of the story Hector brings to our next class, but the setting is Rikers, not Sing Sing. He describes our Rikers class from the viewpoint of the students, and I'm really moved by what they had to say. Writing is the first chance most of these guys have ever had to express any emotion other than anger. They're very conscious of wasting their lives, and frustrated by not knowing how to change their dismal expectations. They're afraid to try, afraid of being ridiculed, afraid of failure. This is very different from physical courage, of which they have plenty.

I've learned much about broken families, drugs, poor education, lack of employment, and all of the other conditions that lead men like this to crime and prison. It has nothing to do with a lack of intelligence or even lack of ambition. They just don't know how to succeed, and I feel their tragedies in the stories they write.

My students' stories have also influenced how I'm writing my own story. At first, my journal was little more than a terse compilation of dates and events. Now I've begun to write how I feel about what's happened and the people who are helping me.

I want to write about Darlene, but so far I can't do it. It's unsettling her body is for sale, or rent, because I really like her. What does she think about when she's having sex with some stranger? How will I feel if I ever get the chance to make love to her? I remember coming in my pants when she first visited at Sing Sing, and I always get an erection when I think about her. But it's more than sex. I'm more attracted to her than I've been willing to admit to myself.

"I'd like to write a story about the differences between Rikers and Sing Sing," Hector announces, and I realize I've been floating off while the class has been discussing Hector's story about his brother.

"What are the differences?" I ask, awakening to my teacher role, and this kicks off an intense discussion that lasts for thirty minutes.

Tom Kaplan arrives, concerned about the knifing. Of course he assumes it's connected to what I told him before, but he can't begin to imagine what's happened since then. I have to tell someone, so I begin to explain about Spider's "businesses."

"You took over the prison rackets?" he asks. "How ..."

"It's a long story," I say, and I tell him pretty much everything. This is very cathartic for me. There's not a hint of this in my journal. How could there be? What if it was confiscated?

"But it's over," I conclude. Tom looks dazed.

"Your students protected you by allowing you to be stabbed?" he asks.

"Strange but true. I'm alive. Spider's not."

"How can you be sure it's over?"

"Maybe 'sure' is the wrong word. I think it's over. Whoever's in charge now has no need of my services. I'm sure – there's that word again – they don't trust me either."

"I'm going to have nightmares about this," Tom says. "Don't you?" He doesn't wait for an answer, but instead asks, "How's the appeal coming?" More material for nightmares.

"Lots of unanswered questions," I say. "Not enough hard evidence, yet, for Maureen and Larry to feel confident about filing."

Tom won't ask the obvious question, so I volunteer an answer. "At the moment, I'm not optimistic, but good people are working hard on my behalf, so maybe it'll change." I tell him about Teri Scanlon.

"Do you think she'll write about your case?"

"Yes. But first she needs to meet with my lawyers."

"The press could make a huge difference."

"Scanlon has a broader interest," I say. "Apparently what happened to me is not so uncommon. She gave me newspaper clippings about what went on in Chicago. It's sickening how many innocent people have been convicted by rotten prosecutors who lie and distort the evidence. I think Scanlon is truly disturbed at the perversion of the justice system. Good reporters hope their stories will change the world.

"Meanwhile," Tom says, "Roger Claiborne is out there, enjoying his life."

"You're right," I say. "Claiborne is the one who should be behind bars. Sometimes I dream about shoving a shank in his gut and twisting it until his internal organs are mush."

Tom looks at me like he's never seen me before, and maybe he never has.

"She seems to be enjoying herself."

"Maureen has a way of fitting in," Watson said.

"Montclair is a very special place for us," Professor Watson said. "but it's so different from Manhattan. Has she ever been here before?"

"I don't think she's ever been in New Jersey before. Except to drive through."

Watson and his father had been watching Maureen Reilly as she circulated through the Fourth of July assemblage of friends and relatives, eating a hot dog and drinking a beer. She talked with both of Watson's brothers, and to some long-time friends from his Montclair high school days. Now Watson's mother had joined her and the two of them seemed deep into a serious conversation.

"I wonder what they're talking about," Watson said.

"They'll tell us if they want us to know. My advice would be not to ask."

Just then, as if she knew they were being discussed, Reilly looked up, found Watson across the lawn, and blew a kiss. At the same time, Mrs. Watson nodded to her husband.

"They know things in ways we'll never understand," said Professor Watson. "Are you going to stay for the fireworks?"

"Wouldn't miss it for anything."

"How's it going with that boy in prison?" Professor Watson asked. "It's been a couple of months since we discussed that case."

"Not nearly enough progress. There's an important witness we haven't found. Somebody scared him real good. There's also fingerprints but the person they belong to has also disappeared. I don't know if we're going to get what we need."

Watson held back, not wanting to frighten his father.

"What is it?"

"I can never hide anything from you, can I?"

"I hope not. What is it?"

"I've been threatened," Watson said. "Once on the phone, and several notes. I'm pretty sure it's other cops."

"Why?"

"Something about the Blake case was very wrong, but opening the wound will be embarrassing. Careers could be in jeopardy."

"Do people ever learn? How many times has the cover-up been worse than the original crime?"

"Watergate?"

"History is replete with examples," said Professor Watson. "What are you going to do?"

"I'm in this to the end."

Watson received the look of pride from his father he had expected and desired.

"Is your boss with you?"

"He is. He's furious at what was done to this kid. At least Blake didn't get a death sentence. Speaking of which, did I tell you about the play Maureen took me to? *The Exonerated*?"

"I've heard about it."

"You and Mom would like it. True stories of innocent people on death row, the lucky ones who didn't get executed."

"Do I hear a cop who's opposed to the death penalty?"

"Growing up with you, are you surprised?"

"Those people who are opposing you," Professor Watson said, fingers at his chin in his distinctive contemplative mode, "... any chance of going directly at them, raising the pressure a bit ... maybe pushing them to make a mistake?"

"They like you," Watson said in the car on the way back to Manhattan.

"And this surprises you?" Reilly asked.

"Not one little bit. You're terrific." He rubbed her thigh. "And hot."

"Your mother was asking me about the Blake case," Reilly said.

"Same with Dad. They must have planned it."

"They're very proud of you."

"My father had a suggestion. He thinks we should push harder, smoke out the opposition, see if we can get somebody to make a mistake."

"I agree," Reilly said. "We need to squeeze everyone. Claiborne, Grabowsky, whoever was involved in withholding evidence at the trial stage or stopping the investigation now. We're not making enough progress. What's your plan?"

"So far, I have options. When I meet with Kerrigan, we'll make a plan."

"Tell me the options."

Watson laid out his ideas and Reilly criticized. She offered suggestions which he tore apart. This went on until they turned off West Side Drive and maneuvered to Reilly's apartment on West 13th Street where the miracle of a parking spot awaited them.

"You have such a refreshing way of letting me know when you think I'm full of shit." Watson smiled. He turned the motor off and placed his hand back on her thigh, squeezing gently. "You know, my parents and both brothers each told me what a handful you'd be."

"Sound advice from obviously intelligent and perceptive people," Reilly said. With a lascivious laugh, she added, "You can have your hands full of me any time you want. How 'bout now?"

Roger Claiborne, the new darling of the East Side, was hob-knobbing in the Hamptons with the likes of Alec Baldwin, P-Diddy, Candace Bushnell, and Nathan Lane. Of course he didn't actually meet any of those people, or even see them, but he was in the Hamptons when they were, so he felt free to drop their names.

Each summer, from Memorial Day to Labor Day, the collection of villages and farms at the eastern tip of Long Island, becomes a playground for the super rich and the merely very-well-to-do. Some argue the Hamptons is more than cocktail parties, Porches and Lamborghinis, but nobody takes such declarations seriously. A 350 year history that includes native Americans, early English settlers, a role in the American revolution, whaling, and some of the nation's first railroads, is largely ignored.

Claiborne had rented a small place for the summer at three thousand per week, and he was there every weekend, from Thursday night to Monday morning. His sister Gwendolyn provided a steady flow of party invitations and attractive women anxious to meet him, and Claiborne was well into the absolute best summer, or best anytime, of his life. His success in the Blake case, and in other high profile cases which followed, had made him one of the stars in the Hamptons' sky, a lesser star than others perhaps, but still a brilliant contrast with the total non-entity he had been all his life.

On occasion, though, he was joined by colleagues from the District Attorney's office, invited to be impressed, and their growing speculations about the possible re-opening of the Blake case were inserting serious angst into Claiborne's still fledgling and decidedly insecure comfort.

"The rumor is they're not quitting," said George Henson, spoiling what had otherwise been a perfect Fourth of July weekend. "Whatever you told Maureen Reilly, it hasn't worked."

"Pain in the ass, she is," Claiborne responded. "She was when she was in the Office, and she still is."

"That may be," Henson said, "but Watson's the real problem. Without him, Reilly would get nowhere. Does Markman know what's going on?"

This was a question Roger Claiborne did not want to answer. In fact, he had spoken to his Bureau Chief Sam Monti, and to Harold Markman, the Manhattan District Attorney, several weeks before, and had assured them there was no basis for a Brady motion in the Blake case. Based on these representations, Markman had so advised New York City Mayor Raymond Gardino. The word to leave the case alone, he was told, had found its way from the Mayor's office to One Police Plaza and down the chain of command to Lieutenant Kerrigan. But, as Claiborne already knew, something had gone seriously awry. Whatever that meant, he was not about to discuss it with Henson.

"Markman knows everything," Claiborne answered, quickly switching the conversation to the upcoming Republican Convention and preparations for the Hamptons International Film Festival in October. But no matter what they talked about, he could not stifle the panic rising in his gut.

As soon as Henson left, Claiborne dug out his yellow notepad. He added a note that Blake was still alive, another about Watson and Kerrigan's visit to Mrs. Marone. That was a close call, he thought. They didn't find anything, but they were closing in on the truth.

The Village of Ossining puts on an impressive fireworks display. We see the highest skyrockets rising above the Hudson River and we hear every thunderclap. But inside the prison walls, it's just like every other day until I purposely make it different.

From my fountain of useless knowledge, I report to my students that the French traveler and social critic Alexis de Tocqueville visited what was then the new Sing Sing penitentiary in June and July of 1831, and observed and wrote about Independence Day celebrations. This leads to an assignment to write about America - what is good about our country, what is bad? – and launches a spirited discussion encompassing 9/11, the failure to catch Osama bin Laden, and the tragedy of the Iraq War. I'm surprised at the level of knowledge and sophistication displayed by my students. You don't often think about criminals as citizens, people with views, people who care about America.

When I return to my cell, my eyes seek out the picture of my parents, the one I brought from Baltimore to my apartment in Greenwich Village, and Larry Mullin later brought to Rikers. That too was a Fourth of July, and it brought back a whole flood of memories. It's painful to have happy thoughts when you're alone in a six foot by nine foot cell. I place the photo in a drawer.

I think about Roger Claiborne. I wonder what he's doing this Fourth of July and hope he's having a miserable time. I think about Bob Watson and Maureen Reilly. It's obvious they really care for each other. Will I ever again have the opportunity to care for a woman? I try to read, but tonight it doesn't work. I cry myself to sleep, quietly, so no one hears my sobs.

TWENTY-EIGHT

"We're going to step it up, push harder." Reilly had called Nana as soon as Watson left. "I'm meeting later this morning with a reporter for the *Daily News*."

"Nobody ever accused my granddaughter of being timid," Nana said. Reilly always appreciated that Nana never put a "but" at those kinds of sentences.

"It's risky," Reilly said.

"Of course it is, dear. How is that young man doing in prison?"

"Exactly," Reilly said. Nana had nailed it again, as she always did.

"Keep me informed," Nana said. "This is better than Law and Order."

I see the fear in Darlene's face as she stares at my bandages. I tell her I'm all right, but of course I can't tell her about Spider or the Aryan Brotherhood or my own role in Spider's criminal activities. I can't tell her, but it turns out she already knows.

"I saw your tattoo," she says. "We talked about it."

"Who talked about it?" I ask, panicked.

"All of us – Bob, Maureen, Larry."

I hang my head. Now they'll abandon me. My own stupidity has destroyed the best chance I would ever have. Then I realize Darlene is here with me. She hasn't abandoned me. I look at her, not daring to hope.

She touches my hand across the table, quickly removes her fingers before the guard can admonish her. "We understand living in prison requires some ... accommodation."

"Who's we?"

"All of us. We had some conversation about it."

I can imagine how the conversation must have gone, and I also imagine Darlene was the one defending me.

"But you do understand what could happen if ..."

Her voice trails off, and the anguish in her face is painful for me to see, but also joyful. This woman, this beautiful person, really cares about me.

"I know. Listen, maybe you think what I did was stupid, but I didn't have any choice. I was attacked and Spider was my only source of protection."

"You don't have to explain a thing to me," Darlene said. "Look at the things I've done in my life. Do you think I'm proud?" She paused. "We learn. We go forward. We become the best people we can be. You've always accepted who and what I am, or was. It would be … ungracious … of me not to do the same for you. I understand. We all understand. But, Josh, is it really over?"

I'm not a Catholic, but I feel what it must be like to go to confession and be forgiven. We look deeply at each other and I whisper "Thank you" in a voice barely free of tears.

Then something dawns on me. "You said was."

She bites her lip, holding back, then finally breaks into the most glorious smile I have ever seen.

"Was is right. I'm a college student now, nothing else."

"No more …?"

"No more. And you?"

"No more. I'm retired. I teach now, nothing else."

"So you're a teacher and I'm a student," Darlene says. "We make a good pair."

My heart leaps, and I finally say what I've been holding back. "Yes we do make a good pair … I … care about you … so much. "

"Me too," she says.

I'm sure Darlene understands, as I do, how unlikely it is anything can come of the feelings we've just expressed. But I can always hope. As I return to my cell, there's a spring in my step that's been absent for more than a year.

Maureen Reilly called Teri Scanlon and arranged to meet at the Metropolitan Museum of Art on Fifth Avenue. "What got you interested in the Blake case?" Reilly asked as they entered the Impressionist wing, her favorite section.

"I happened to be in arraignment court when Josh was brought in," Scanlon replied, "and then at the press conference the Mayor and prosecutor held right after the arraignment. I followed up on the story and interviewed Josh on Rikers, with his first lawyer, Larry Mullin."

"Good story, that one," Reilly interjected. "By the way, I was in arraignment court the same morning. Strange coincidence."

"It is strange, both of us there on a Sunday morning," Scanlon said. "Anyway, I've interviewed enough people to know when someone is lying. I believed Blake was telling the truth, and my gut was screaming to me Joshua Blake was not the kind of kid who would attack an old woman. So I covered the trial. I don't blame the jury for their decision, based on what they heard. But I've always felt there was more."

Scanlon waited, and even though she hadn't asked a question, Reilly felt compelled to answer. This is a good reporter, she thought to herself as she said, "You were right. There's a lot more."

They had stopped in front of Renoir's *Madame Charpentier and Her Daughters*, Reilly's favorite painting at the Met, an old friend she visited whenever she could.

"Do you like Renoir?" Reilly asked, trolling for time, processing what she wanted to say, not quite ready to trust Scanlon.

"Yes, of course," Scanlon said, from which Reilly concluded the reporter could take Renoir or leave him. Well, nobody's perfect. They walked on, silent, amidst one of the greatest collections of Impressionist paintings in the world.

"Your story will have to wait, Teri."

"Will I get everything and will it be exclusive?"

"As long as you agree to hold off until I say it's time to go public."

"That day will eventually come?"

"Yes."

"Then we're on," Scanlon said, reaching out her hand.

"It's Claiborne, you know, at the heart of it" Reilly said.

"I've never liked that snotty bastard," Scanlon responded. "Always had the feeling he would do anything to get a conviction he really needed. But he couldn't have done it himself."

Barely noticing the masterpieces that usually fascinated her, Reilly described the doctoring of Angel Martinez' interview report, the failure to disclose the unidentified fingerprints, and Josh's videotape.

"This is great stuff," Scanlon said. "Is it enough?"

"I wish," Reilly said, shaking her head sadly, "but this is a motion to overturn a conviction, not a trial. This stuff at trial creates reasonable doubt in the jurors' minds, and very likely, a 'not guilty' verdict. But on a motion, before a judge who really doesn't want to see any conviction thrown out, we're not there yet."

"Let me show you something," Scanlon said, taking several folded papers from her shoulder tote.

Reilly read the letter Scanlon had written to District Attorney Markman. "Do you think he'll answer? Your article about the Palladium case is likely to have raised some hackles."

"That's my job, raising hackles." Scanlon laughed. "What the hell is a hackle anyway?"

"Damned if I know."

"I think he'll answer," Scanlon said. "If there are problems in the DA's office, I'd be willing to bet the DA himself isn't part of it."

"It's a big office and it's tough to control everything. I used to work there, you know."

"I know."

"Of course you know. You do your homework."

"Where do we go from here?" Scanlon asked, ignoring the compliment.

"We share what we know," Reilly said, pausing for emphasis. "Everything ... facts, guesses ... sources. Both ways. All in confidence. Sooner or later, you can go public."

"Before or after you file your motion?"

"I don't know yet. It depends on what we learn."

Scanlon continued, "You have other people working on this? Besides you and Mullin?"

"How do you know?"

"Just a guess," Scanlon said with a smile, and then added, "Bob Watson?"

Reilly continued to be amazed at what Scanlon knew. Her investigative skills were impressive and she would be a powerful addition to their team. "Bob got the original catch," she said, "and he was the one who actually arrested Josh. But he always had problems with the case." Reilly paused, finally looked at the Van Gogh they were passing. "Here's your first piece of confidential information. Bob told Claiborne from the very beginning the case was weak. Claiborne blew him off. 'Don't fuck up a good conviction,' he said."

"And Darlene Brantley?" Scanlon asked. Reilly was no longer surprised, as Scanlon explained, "Visitor logs at Rikers and Sing Sing."

"She's been Josh's friend since the first day he arrived in the Big Apple."

"She's a ..."

"... student at City College," Reilly finished the sentence.

"Got it," said Scanlon.

"One more thing," said Reilly.

"Just like Colombo," Scanlon said, and her mouth dropped open when Reilly told her what she had in mind. "I'm being set up," Scanlon said when Reilly was through.

"I guess you could put it that way," said Reilly.

"I love it," said Scanlon.

"You called this meeting, Bob. What's the agenda?"

It was the Tuesday morning after the Fourth of July holiday, and Detective Watson and Lieutenant Kerrigan had just ordered their pre-dawn breakfast at a diner on Amsterdam Avenue in the seventies.

"The attorneys say if we go with what we have now, there's zero chance to win an appeal, so we have a lot of work to do. However, we're hampered by having to do it secretly, just the two of us. It's also becoming clear there's powerful opposition to any re-opening of the case from persons currently unknown to us, who may have excellent reasons, their own careers for example, to want to keep this case forever in the tank."

"So ..." Kerrigan said.

"I think it's time to get more aggressive, ratchet up the investigative side, see if we can provoke a self-destructive response from the opposition."

"I surely do like your laid back style, detective," Kerrigan said. "Do you have a plan?"

"I would not be so bold, sir, to devise a plan without consulting with you," Watson said. Then, in response to Kerrigan's raised eyebrows, he added, "but I do have some options to suggest."

The eggs arrived. Watson took a quick forkful, expecting they might be cold before he had another. "I see three leads to pursue on the investigative side," he said as soon as he had swallowed. "First is Angel Martinez. We've got to find him, confirm his testimony, and learn who scared him away."

"One of ours?"

"Could be."

"Number two?"

"The videotape. It was in the evidence file here at MNH, but there was no report with it. Somebody must have watched it and prepared a report. Who? And what happened to the report? Who kept it from the defense?"

"How do you know anybody watched it?"

"Claiborne knew about it."

"And you know that because ...?"

"He slipped when he was yelling at Reilly."

"Do you think Banyon was part of it?" Kerrigan asked.

"Maybe. But it could have been Claiborne alone or somebody else from the DA's office."

"Yes," said Kerrigan, "and then there's the fascinating question of what the legendary Mr. Harold Markman knew and when he knew it."

Watson chose to sidestep Kerrigan's reference to the DA, the very thinnest of thin ice, terror for another day. "Third is Marone. What's the connection, if any, between the Blake case and his murder in the DEA case? Marone's accomplice on the candy store robbery might know something."

"There's a fourth direction," Kerrigan said, and Watson allowed himself to hope this meant he had accepted the first three. "Mrs. Cooke," Kerrigan said. "Everybody has assumed this was a random robbery gone wrong, but has anybody ever really looked into her story. Who was she? Who were her friends? Did she go to the park often? Why was she there the night she was attacked? What had she planned to do later? Maybe we can find a motive for the attack to lead us to the perp."

"Good," said Watson. "So we have four leads, and there'll be more as we get into it. But we can't do any of this without attracting attention."

"I gather you have some thoughts."

They ate in silence for several minutes, finishing their plates, and calling for more coffee.

"This is delicate," Watson said, and Kerrigan let loose a laugh that attracted eyes from every nearby table.

"Delicate, is it?" Kerrigan said, lowering his voice. "The word from on high says the Blake case is not the best use of the department's time, even after Marone's fingerprints are identified and the guy has turned up dead, and you think it might be delicate to proceed anyway? It's delicate to ignore the Chief of Detectives, the Commissioner, and hizzoner?"

"Actually," Watson said, "I don't think we should proceed without approval from the brass."

"That's not going to happen, so you think we should quit?" Kerrigan asked.

"Not at all. I think we can get permission. We should take what we have and walk it up the chain until we find someone with balls enough to authorize the investigation."

"Ah, an idealist of the first order. Appeal to their higher values, should we? Let them see the light of reason?"

"No idealism at all," Watson said. "We simply explain the dangers of being exposed on the wrong side of this one."

"You would threaten ..."

"No threats," Watson said. "The argument would be that proceeding with the investigation is the best way, in fact the only way, to minimize the department's embarrassment."

"Explain."

Watson replayed in his mind the exact words of his telephone conversation with Maureen Reilly the previous night and carefully began to execute the plan they had agreed upon. "Let's assume the press already knows something about this case, and is likely to learn more. Whoever is already tainted may or may not burn. Their choices are limited. Higher levels, assuming they are so far uninformed non-participants, can still choose. They can be on the side of the cover-up, or they can be on the side of the angels. You might remind them of Richard Nixon."

"The press already knows?"

"Yes."

"Who?"

"Teri Scanlon," Watson said. "The *Daily News*."

Watson and Reilly had debated how to use Scanlon's involvement to leverage the NYPD and the DA. They understood that without Brian Kerrigan's help, and the Lieutenant's willingness to take his own significant risks, there was no way Joshua Blake would ever again see the light of day outside the walls of Sing Sing. But Kerrigan had to be unleashed by his superiors, so Kerrigan had to know about Scanlon. Reilly had set it up with her meeting with Scanlon. Now they would see if it worked.

"Have you spoken to her?"

"No, but Josh has, and so has Maureen Reilly."

"So she knows exculpatory evidence was suppressed?"

"Yes."

"Will she wait to get the whole story?"

"As long as she doesn't think she's being jerked around. Josh trusts her, and she apparently is highly motivated to help him. Blowing the story too soon won't help Josh, so I think she'll wait."

Kerrigan leaned back, nodded his head and smiled. "This kid Joshua Blake," he said, rubbing his hand together. "He's in Sing Sing, on a life with twenty. No family. Hardly any friends. No hope. No money, I assume." Watson nodded. "And somehow," Kerrigan continued, "from nothing, without ever leaving his cell, he's got you, and Maureen Reilly, and this Teri ... he's got this whole team of people working for him."

Watson thought maybe this was not the best time to mention Darlene Brantley, although he knew that time was coming. Kerrigan continued, "I think you're right we can't do this *sub rosa*. We'll both get our dicks caught in a wringer if we try. We've got to go up the chain. But before we do, I want to meet this kid."

"Same thing I did," Watson said. "I think Josh is out of the hospital by now. When do you want to go?"

"Hospital?" Kerrigan asked.

"He was slashed. It was a warning. His former cellmate wasn't so lucky, bled to death."

"Related?"

"I think so," Watson said. "The cellmate, a guy named Spider Johnson, was organizing a number of prison rackets behind the façade of the Aryan Brotherhood. Apparently, Josh was ... assisting him."

"Muscle?"

"More like a senior management assistant. Actually, the word *consigliore* was used."

Kerrigan exploded. "Jesus Christ! An innocent college kid, my ass. And you still want to help this guy?"

"He shouldn't be there at all, Lieu," Watson said, his voice rising. "Joshua Blake never committed a crime in his life, and he got sent to prison for something we know he didn't do. But once he's there, he's got to survive. He can't hide in a corner and read books. Whatever he did with Spider Johnson, he's got no charges pending, and none are anticipated. There's still time for him to get out clean." Watson's tone softened. "But not much time."

"And to think what trouble it took to get you transferred to Homicide," Kerrigan said, picking up the check and standing to leave. "Leave the tip. We'll go up there this afternoon."

Darlene had been to visit the day before, so I'm surprised when I'm again told to strip, in preparation for two visitors. I'm back in the classy conference room where I first met Detective Watson. While saying hello to Watson, I try to size up the big man with him.

"This is Lieutenant Brian Kerrigan," Watson says, "my boss at Manhattan North Homicide."

"How're you feeling, Josh," were the first words out of Kerrigan's mouth. He points to the bandages on my face and neck.

"I'm okay," I say, but I'm not at all okay. Questions about how and why I was slashed will lead to Spider, the Aryan Brotherhood, my role in criminal activities, and the end of the effort to re-open my case. All this flashes in front of me, and I don't know what to do. Watson, a blank look on his face, is no help.

"Your friend, the one who was killed. Can you tell us about him?" Kerrigan again.

"Spider was my cellmate the first few weeks I was here. Then we got our own cells."

"Why was he killed?" Kerrigan asks.

I look to Watson, who gives me nothing. It's my decision.

A Good Conviction   285

"He was into some prison businesses," I say. "Some other people didn't appreciate the competition."

"What businesses?"

I give Kerrigan a list of Spider's activities – laundry, food, telephones, everything. "But it wasn't those things got him killed. He was getting into drugs."

"What was your role in this?"

I stare straight into Kerrigan's eyes, which are totally expressionless. Does he know? Darlene said Watson knew, but she never told me what he knew. I should have asked. If they know and I lie, I'm done. If they don't know and I tell them, then what? I think it's more likely they already know, and I'm a lousy liar anyway, so I describe what I was doing for Spider before he got killed.

When I'm finished, Kerrigan asks, "Why weren't you killed?"

"My friends bought me another chance."

"What friends?"

"The guys I teach. My students." Kerrigan waited, so I explained how I had begun teaching reading and writing at Rikers, and now continued at Sing Sing. "When I was cut, they were right there, with antiseptics and bandages. They couldn't keep it from happening, but it seems they made a deal. I wouldn't be killed, and they were there to help me." I paused. "But you knew all this already, didn't you?"

"Yes," said Watson, finally breaking his silence.

"It was a test?" I ask.

"If we decide to help you, we're going to go way out on a limb," Kerrigan says, "and we need to know what kind of guy you are. What's your current status in all this?"

"I'm retired," I say. I've noticed throughout this interrogation that Kerrigan has not asked me about anybody else, except Spider, who's dead. He's not asking me to rat on anyone.

"Will they let you stay out?" Kerrigan asks. His question tells me he understands exactly how things work in prison.

"I think so," I say.

"You know someone named Teri Scanlon?" Kerrigan asks.

"She's a reporter who wrote about my case." I realize this is not enough, and I go on. "She was here a couple weeks ago. She wants to write about prosecutorial abuse."

"She thinks that's what your case is about?"

"Yes."

"What does she know?"

"She knows I had no reason to attack Mrs. Cooke. I don't know what else."

"What did you tell her?"

286   Lewis M. Weinstein

"Nothing. I told Ms. Reilly that Teri was here, and what she wanted. She was going to call her. I don't know if she did."

Kerrigan nods to Watson. It's his turn in their tightly scripted scenario.

"Josh," Watson says, "we knew everything you've told us. Darlene saw the tattoo and that led to the rest. I want you to know there are no charges pending against you. None will be brought. But you've got to stay totally clean from now on. We can't help you if you don't."

"Sometimes you have to fight," I say. "If you don't, they'll kill you." From someplace, out of the terror that fills every pore of my body, I find a smile. "Nobody can help me if I'm dead." Watson and Kerrigan exchange a look. "I'm not looking for any trouble," I say. "Spider's dead. Nobody's pushing me any more. But if you're a wimp here, they destroy you."

"We understand you have to protect yourself. I don't think we can ask for more than that," Kerrigan says, and a huge weight lifts. The three of us look at each other. I'm trying to process the last few minutes. Maybe they are too.

"I'm ready," Kerrigan says to Watson, and I don't have a clue what he's ready to do. Help me? Leave?

"There are people who don't want your case re-opened," Watson says. "We need to figure out how to deal with them."

There are questions I don't dare ask. Who doesn't want the case re-opened? What are Watson and Kerrigan going to do next? What are my chances?

"Either Maureen or I will be back to you soon," Watson says, and they both get up. Watson extends his hand and we shake. I look at Kerrigan, extend my hand.

"We're in this with you," Kerrigan says, taking my hand. "I don't know where it's going, but we're in it."

Kerrigan seemed content on the ride back to Manhattan, repeating his favorable impression of Blake, discussing what their next steps might be, even talking about the Yankees, all the while leaning back with his eyes closed. But Kerrigan never missed anything, so Watson wasn't surprised when he asked, "Who's Darlene?"

"A friend of Josh's. She was with us when we rushed up to Sing Sing after Josh was cut."

Kerrigan, his eyes still closed, waited.

"She's a hooker," Watson said. "At least she used to be. Josh met her at the Broadway Big Apple when he first came to New York."

Kerrigan looked over at Watson, crinkling eyes morphing into a smile that spread across his face. Still, he said nothing.

"She visited him on Rikers, came to the trial." Watson paused. There was no response from Kerrigan. "Do you always get the whole story with one question?" Kerrigan's smile was now complete.

"She had two very interesting clients." Kerrigan didn't bite, but there was no holding back now. "Frank Grabowsky and Roger Claiborne," Watson said. "We have both of them on audiotape."

"Nice work, detective," Kerrigan finally broke his silence. "Is there anything else I should know?"

"I think that's just about everything."

"Good," Kerrigan said, reclining the car seat and closing his eyes. This time, Watson thought, he actually fell asleep.

Roger Claiborne was unable to control his shaking hands. At 7:00 am on Tuesday morning, all he could think about was Joshua Blake. He sweat and shivered at the same time. He barked at his secretary and Helen discretely closed his door. He stared obsessively at the scribbles he had made in Southampton over the weekend.

Grabowsky. Mackey. Banyon. He drew arrows connecting the names, added comments and questions along the arrows. Why did Grabowsky give them Marone? What else did he tell them? They must know the fingerprint report was altered. Did he tell them when we first knew about Marone?

He wrote the names of the NYPD brass, drew more lines in what was becoming a vast jumble. Monti told me the word had been delivered. Why didn't it work? He thought about his history with Kerrigan and shuddered. How long would that man bear a grudge? And for what? It really wasn't that big a deal.

Claiborne took a red felt-tipped pen and added more notes. Possible actions. Things he could do instead of sitting alone in his office shivering like a coward. He thought about his Hamptons rental, with seven or eight weekends to go, and felt his wonderful new life slipping away. Disgraced. Ridiculed. Arrested.

Nonsense. No prosecutor is ever arrested. Maybe a conviction is overturned and it's embarrassing, but arrest the prosecutor? Never. That made him feel better, and the chills subsided. He would survive this, maybe not even get hurt. He circled two of his red notes, put the pad in his middle drawer.

But still he avoided his considerable workload. His thoughts returned to Frank Grabowsky. He hadn't seen Frank much recently, since they both started frequenting the same whore. Now she's retired. I wonder who Frank is fucking now.

The light dawned. He whispered "that bitch," and made two phone calls, one to Rikers and one to Sing Sing. Then he added Darlene Brantley's name to his list.

Tom Kaplan brings my friend M.J. Martini with him, and M.J. is totally blown away by Sing Sing. He's horrified, but also fascinated.

"This is a scary place to be," M.J. says, "even to visit."

I look at him and laugh, like, tell me something I don't know. I tell them about the recent visit from Detective Watson and Lieutenant Kerrigan, although I don't mention Kerrigan's name, and we share the excitement over this very positive development. M.J. asks questions about Darlene, which make it clear Tom has never told him she's a prostitute. Was a prostitute, I say to myself.

"She's a very special person," I say. "She's been visiting me almost from the day I was arrested."

They wait, expecting me to say more, and I do. "I really care about her. If I ever get out of here ..."

They met in Reilly's office. Mullin and Reilly had been there for hours when Watson and Kerrigan arrived. Kerrigan had asked for the briefing, telling Watson he wanted to know everything about the case, and everyone he was working with, before he approached his superiors and started what might become a major confrontation. Watson made the introductions.

"So this is the Irish demon who does killer cross-examinations," Kerrigan said.

"Is that what they say about me?" Reilly asked.

"Among other things."

"Well, I've heard good things about you, too," said Reilly, with a broad smile.

"I'll bet," Kerrigan said, casting a sideways glance at Watson. Then his face lost the smile and he was ready to begin. "What have we got here?" he said, addressing the lawyers. "I need to know what you know, what you think, what you can prove. Then I need to know about Teri Scanlon."

"Teri's here," said Reilly. "So is Darlene Brantley. The whole Blake team has been assembled for your edification, Lieutenant."

Kerrigan was visibly surprised. He turned to Watson. "I didn't know," Watson said.

"Well, as long as they're here, bring them in," said Kerrigan.

Reilly left and returned a moment later, with Teri Scanlon and Darlene Brantley in tow. Teri looked at ease, but Darlene was visibly nervous, and Kerrigan got right to it.

"Ms. Brantley," Kerrigan said, looking her straight in the eye, "I work in homicide, not vice. I'm here because Bob Watson has convinced me Joshua Blake got a very raw deal. I understand you're an important part of the effort to rectify that situation, so we're on the same side, and that's the only interest I have in you."

Darlene visibly relaxed. She glanced around the table, her eyes finding Reilly's in an unspoken thank you. She sat up ramrod straight and said to Kerrigan, "Well, then, call me Darlene, and let's get started."

"Larry," said Reilly, "why don't you summarize the legal situation."

Mullin, as always, had piles of documents all around him, on the table, on the floor, everywhere, but he spoke without reference to any.

"There are two completely different legal procedures," Mullin began. "First is the direct appeal to the Appellate court, based on technical errors in the trial. We filed that appeal some time ago, but we expect to lose it.

"Then, there's a second approach, based on motions allowed under Criminal Procedure Law Section 440.10, to bring before the original trial court relevant matters that were not part of the trial record. We plan to file two motions.

"The first will present new evidence, discovered after completion of the original trial. The second will show that the prosecutor failed to turn over to the defense evidence that tends to prove Josh's innocence or is at variance with the prosecution's stated theory of the case. Either of these motions, if we can prove what we think we know, can get Josh a new trial.

"There are at least three important pieces of newly discovered evidence. One, the full report of Detective Mackey's interview with Angel Martinez. Two, the unidentified latent fingerprints on Mrs. Cooke's pocketbook. And three, the videotape taken from Josh's apartment. There may be more.

"Clearly, if I had received this evidence, I would have called different witnesses and presented a very different case. I would have been able to argue Josh could not have been in Central Park when Mrs. Cooke was attacked and could not have been in Brooklyn when Concolita Jones saw someone else throw Mrs. Cooke's pocketbook into a trash barrel. The fingerprints on Mrs. Cooke's pocketbook would have pointed to the real perp. This newly discovered evidence is the basis for a motion under Criminal Procedure Law, paragraph 440.10, subparagraph (g).

"ADA Claiborne knew all this evidence existed and failed to turn it over to us. The U.S. Supreme Court, in the case of *Brady v. Maryland*, established the basic doctrine that the rights of due process and equal protection provided by the Fourteenth Amendment of the U.S. Constitution are violated when the government achieves a conviction by withholding evidence clearly supportive of a claim of innocence. When ADA Claiborne failed to turn over exculpatory evidence, especially if we can prove he withheld such evidence purposely, he deprived Joshua Blake of his constitutional right to due process and a fair trial. This is the basis for a motion under Criminal Procedure Law, paragraph 440.10, subparagraph (h)."

"Very impressive, Mr. Mullin," Kerrigan said. "It sounds like you have a great case. Why do you need more?"

"Because we can't prove what we think we know. We only get one shot at this. Newly discovered evidence is only new once. We have to be sure we can get a new trial, and can then win that trial. To be sure, we need Angel Martinez to corroborate Josh's alibi and we need to make a better case against Anthony Marone as the real killer."

Teri Scanlon interjected, speaking quickly and with obvious passion. "If the full story of the Blake case comes out, public sympathy will favor a young man with no criminal record and his whole life ahead of him. The DA's office will pay a huge price for withholding evidence. Heads will roll. There's always an election coming up and DA Markman might not be as invulnerable as he thinks. This means there will be intense pressure from the DA's Office to keep the Blake case closed."

"And I take it you intend for all of this to become known," Kerrigan said, addressing Scanlon.

"In due course," Scanlon said.

"Why haven't you published yet?"

"I think there's a better story coming," Scanlon said. "And I don't want to do anything to interfere with getting Josh out of that hellhole. And Maureen made me promise not to." She looked directly at Kerrigan. Her challenge couldn't have been more blatant. "But at the end of the day, if this is all there is, this is what I'll publish."

"And no doubt add that NYPD did nothing to help."

"If that's the way it turns out."

"What are you going to do with Darlene's audio tapes?" Kerrigan asked, jarring everyone at the table, although they all knew Watson had told Kerrigan of their existence.

"That's how we learned about Anthony Marone," said Reilly.

"And the other tape?" Kerrigan asked.

"I think we'll wait a while on that one, see what develops," Reilly answered.

"Tell me what Claiborne said to you," said Kerrigan to Reilly.

"He said this was all bullshit, that I should let the Blake case go. He said it didn't matter if we filed an appeal, we didn't have the goods. By the way, he was right about that."

Kerrigan turned to Watson. "You told Claiborne, before the trial, you thought there were holes in the case?"

"Yes."

"How did Claiborne react?"

"He told me Blake was going down and I shouldn't be the one to fuck up a good conviction."

"So Claiborne is the bad guy here," said Kerrigan, looking around the table. "But none of you believe he did it by himself, do you?"

"Not likely," said Watson. Mullin, Reilly and Scanlon agreed.

"So NYPD may have a problem, too?"

"Right now," said Reilly, "it's a small problem. Try to cover it up, it could turn out to be something bigger."

"Judiciously said, counselor," Kerrigan said.

Nobody had anything more to add, and after they looked at each other silently for a few more seconds, Kerrigan rose.

"Thank you for this meeting," he said. "The ball is in my court now." He walked out of the room. Watson followed.

"That is one smart dude," Scanlon said.

"Let's hope he's got the courage to go with the brains," said Reilly, "because he's headed straight into the lion's den."

A few minutes after Kerrigan and Watson left, Tom Kaplan and M.J. Martini arrived, having trained down from their morning visit with Josh at Sing Sing. Larry Mullin had invited them to meet the rest of the Blake Team, and he introduced them to Maureen Reilly and Teri Scanlon. They had already met Darlene.

First they discussed the legal and investigative aspects of the case, with Mullin repeating much of what he had just told Kerrigan. Then the discussion turned to Josh. Scanlon, always the reporter, wanted to know more about Josh's life before he came to New York. Tom and M.J. obliged with stories about school, parties, girls, baseball, friends helping each other, and the fact that Josh was just an overall nice guy.

"But he's changed," Tom said. "Underneath, he's still the same good guy, but he's got a tough exterior now that nobody who knew him in Baltimore would recognize."

"We talked about this on the train," M.J. said. "Josh is really just an ordinary person. A great guy, maybe a little smarter than most of us, but not really macho or tough. So now this regular guy gets dealt this terribly unfair, devastating blow, and he's dumped into an environment he could never have imagined. He knows if he's soft, he'll be destroyed, so he does what he has to do to survive. He gets tough, at least a whole lot tougher than he was."

"The question is whether this is a permanent change," Tom said. "If he gets out of prison, what kind of person will he be?"

"He'll be a wonderful person," Darlene said. "A loving, caring, sensitive man, just like he was before. Just like he still is now."

"I sure hope you're right," Mullin said.

"Our job is to give him the chance," Reilly said. Addressing Tom and M.J., she added, "Welcome to the Blake Team."

Watson never learned who Kerrigan spoke to, or with what result. He didn't know if the NYPD brass signaled a go-ahead, or if Kerrigan decided to proceed without it. All he knew was the following Monday, his Lieutenant appeared and said, "Let's go. This is now a normal investigation."

John Banyon was back on the team. Kerrigan never told Watson why Banyon was back in the loop, but Watson guessed it was better to have him close and involved. Trust him? That was still an open question.

TWENTY-NINE

Detectives Watson and Banyon worked their way through some of the worst parts of the South Bronx and Spanish Harlem, distributing Josh's open letter to Angel Martinez. They started with the latest address they had for Angel, going door to door. Nobody admitted they knew where he was. In fact, no one admitted they knew him, although several had a look in their eye suggesting otherwise.

"What is this about?" an elderly woman asked when she answered the door and Watson showed her his badge.

"It's all in this letter," Watson said, giving her the page which had the letter in both English and Spanish, and Josh's picture.

The woman looked at the picture and read the letter.

"Why you trying to get someone out of jail?"

"He didn't do it."

The woman snorted. "Lot of people didn't do it." She slammed the door.

The letter distribution went on for a week, as the detectives were directed from one neighborhood to another, never knowing if these were helpful leads or purposely false trails intended to waste their time. Finally, they had done all they could. They would just have to hope Angel, wherever he was, would come forward.

Although they didn't use any precinct officers or detectives in the canvass, they had made no effort to be secretive, and other cops knew what they were doing. Some were curious, some seemed angry, and nobody was helpful. As the week went on, it seemed to Watson that the mood among at least some of the cops was increasingly ugly.

With Banyon back in the picture, they met in Kerrigan's office and Watson asked Banyon what he knew about the videotape taken from Josh's apartment.

"What videotape?" Banyon asked.

Watson answered angrily. "The videotape that proves Josh was in Greenwich Village at 8:28 pm on the night Mrs. Cooke was murdered," he said. "The one that was taken from his apartment. The one I found in the evidence file here at Homicide."

"I don't know what you're talking about," Banyon said. "There was no tape."

"Is it on the inventory from the warrant search?" Kerrigan asked.

Banyon went to retrieve the inventory. When he returned, his face was chalk white. "It's not on the inventory."

Kerrigan's head jerked up and his eyes bore into Banyon's. "So how did the videotape get into our evidence file if it wasn't picked up in the warrant search?"

Nobody had any suggestions. Kerrigan picked up the phone and dialed an internal extension. "Blake case," he said. "Tell me every person who went into the kid's apartment." There was a pause. "That's right. From the first time until it was no longer a crime scene." A longer pause, and then Kerrigan hung up.

"Roger Claiborne was there on July 4, 2003. He's the only one who was in the apartment after the warrant search."

"But if he found the tape, we would have watched it and prepared a DD5," said Banyon.

Kerrigan just looked at him.

"He never turned it in," said Banyon.

"Later," said Watson. "Much later, when he was sure it wouldn't be noticed."

Teri Scanlon found plenty to write about without mentioning the Blake case. Her initial research produced more than enough for her editor to allow her considerable freedom to pursue the topic of prosecutorial abuse. He was even going to introduce her followup story on the Palladium case as the first in a promised series. Teri did a final proof over coffee.

> The long-awaited appeal in the 1990 Palladium murder case was filed yesterday, alleging that newly discovered evidence and the withholding of some of that evidence by the office of the Manhattan District Attorney warrants overturning the convictions gained against two defendants in 1993.

Teri skipped over her summary of the background of the Palladium case and statements by the lawyers who had filed the appeal.

The more serious question raised by this filing, however, is whether the Manhattan DA's Office withheld evidence it is obligated by law to provide. Although DA Markman has never admitted a single case of purposeful withholding of evidence by any of his ADAs, there is ample evidence from other jurisdictions that this is not as rare an event as we might all like to believe. Consider ...

... The Chicago Tribune reports that, since 1963, at least 381 murder convictions have been reversed because of police or prosecutorial misconduct. The Tribune also found that not one of the prosecutors who broke the law was ever convicted or disbarred, and most were not even disciplined.

... A recent Columbia Law School study provides a long list of cases illustrating what they termed "chronic prosecutorial suppression of evidence of innocence."

... Barry Scheck, Peter Neufeld and Jim Dwyer, in their landmark publication, Actual Innocence, state that prosecutorial misconduct was a factor in 26 of 62 cases cited, and that in 43% of cases involving prosecutorial misconduct, there was suppression by the prosecution of known exculpatory evidence.

... The website of the organization Truth in Justice summarizes a study of prosecutorial misconduct which states that, since 1970, individual judges and appellate court panels have cited prosecutorial misconduct as a factor in at least 2,017 cases.

These publications cite case after case in numbing detail, and unless you're a lawyer, books like these are hard to read.

But what if you were the one accused of a crime you didn't commit? What if the prosecutor had evidence that would prove your innocence and kept this evidence hidden in his files?

Does withholding of evidence happen in the office of the Manhattan DA? We'll be following the Palladium case, and other cases, and we'll let you know what we learn.

Teri felt good about her story, but her joy was tempered by the fact that Joshua Blake was still in Sing Sing. She closed her eyes, visualized Josh in his cell, and said softly, "Soon, Josh, soon." She hoped it was true.

It didn't take long for Detective Christine Parker to locate Marco Picollo, observe his comings and goings, and develop a plan to confront him that would take him by surprise and minimize the chances their meeting would be observed. On a humid, rainy Sunday in late July, Watson, Kerrigan and Parker parked their unmarked on a side street and walked three blocks to the Hill Diner on Court Street, where Marco Picollo was sitting alone at the counter.

"Good morning, Marco," Parker said from behind him.

When Picollo saw Detective Parker, who had arrested him for the candy store robbery, along with two large men who looked like cops, he was terrified. "What do you want?" he sputtered.

"Let's sit where we can be more private," Parker said.

Picollo didn't move.

Kerrigan laid his huge hand on Picollo's shoulder. Picollo looked up at the burly Irishman, grabbed his coffee cup, and followed Parker to a corner booth near the rear of the diner. Picollo slid in and Kerrigan sat next to him, blocking his exit.

Picollo's eyes flitted warily among the three detectives. "What's this about?" he asked. "I didn't do anything."

"Nobody says you did," said Parker. "This is about someone else. We came here to talk to you in a quiet way that won't be seen by anybody you might have reason to be afraid of. We want to have a short conversation nobody ever needs to know about."

When Picollo didn't respond, Parker said more firmly, "If you don't talk to us here, we'll put you in a squad car and take you to the precinct, and then everybody in Brooklyn will know you've been questioned. It's your choice."

Picollo looked around, perhaps confirming that whoever he might be worried about wasn't there. "Okay. What do you want?"

Watson, as they had planned, did the questioning. "A little over a year ago, you and a guy named Tony Marone robbed a candy store."

"So what? I did the time. It's over."

"You know Marone was killed?"

Picollo nodded.

"Who did bail for Marone?"

"I don't know."

"Not good, Marco," Watson said. "I don't believe you. Who did the bail? Who was Marone running with? Why was he killed?"

Marco looked down, looked all around, and didn't answer. Now it was Kerrigan's turn. "Let's go to the station," he said, grabbing Picollo's shoulder. Picollo squirmed, and Kerrigan smiled and squeezed hard enough to make it hurt.

"There was a guy named Sonny Durante. That's all I know. Can I go now?"

"Not just yet," Kerrigan said, but he did loosen his grip.

Five minutes later, Kerrigan slid aside and allowed Picollo to escape.

Watson and Banyon set out to learn what they could about Mrs. Cooke. They interviewed her daughter, neighbors in the apartment building where she had lived, and nearby shopkeepers. Even though it was more than a year since her murder, people remembered, but their stories weren't helpful. There was nothing to suggest Mrs. Cooke wasn't exactly what she seemed, a nice elderly lady, starting to get a little frail, who often took after-dinner walks. She adored her grandchildren, and had many friends and no enemies. Of course there was no police blotter.

"I never saw it coming."

These were Watson's first words when Brian Kerrigan came into his room at Columbia Presbyterian Hospital, twelve hours after Watson had been brutally beaten. His wounds showed he had been cracked once in the head with a blunt object, punched in the body, and kicked multiple times in the legs and back, but his assailants had carefully avoided serious damage to internal organs or his face, and did not break any bones.

The beating had taken place in a high rise tenement building on Wadsworth Avenue near 175th Street in Washington Heights. Watson and Banyon had gone to the Heights again to look for Angel Martinez, a task they undertook whenever they had spare time. Once inside the building, they had split up. Watson started from the top floor, Banyon from below. There had been a dark corridor, and then the sudden beating. Watson did not lose consciousness and he radioed for help. Banyon arrived almost immediately and the medics soon after. The assailants had fled and were not apprehended.

"Was it a setup?" Kerrigan asked.

"It was very professional," Watson said. "They knew exactly what they were doing.

"Where was Banyon?" Kerrigan asked.

"We split, like we usually did. I went above, he went below."

Their doleful silence was interrupted by the arrival of Professor and Mrs. Watson, along with Maureen Reilly. They had all been there for hours but had gone out for coffee and had not seen Kerrigan arrive. Reilly nodded to Kerrigan and they went into the hall.

"You know this is connected, don't you," she said.

"I don't know anything, counselor, but you can be sure I'll do everything possible to find out," Kerrigan said.

"It was Claiborne," Reilly said.

"Claiborne doesn't have this kind of juice," Kerrigan said, his sadness so profound Reilly didn't say another word. They were still standing there, silently contemplating the horrible meaning of Kerrigan's conclusion, when Larry Mullin, Darlene Brantley and Teri Scanlon arrived.

When Maureen Reilly returned to her office that night, she found it thoroughly ransacked, drawers emptied, files thrown about, her computer screen smashed.

On top of the largest pile of disarrayed papers, carefully and prominently displayed, was a photo of Maureen and Bob Watson, taken in front of the fountain at Lincoln Center. The photo had been on top of the bookcase facing her desk. The glass was broken and the frame appeared to have been stomped on.

"Did they get the tape?" Watson asked when she told him what had happened.

"No," Reilly answered.

Darlene's visits have become magical. For the hour she's here, I'm in a special world. There are no prisoners and no guards. It isn't noisy, it doesn't smell, and nobody is lurking around the corner to stab me. It's just the two of us, talking quietly, learning more about each other.

We try to resist speculating about any possible future together, but it creeps in nevertheless. Once we start, we can't stop, even though we know we're setting ourselves up for huge disappointment.

When we're apart, we dream about what might be, and when we're together, we share those dreams. When there's a setback in the progress of my case, we share the pain of knowing how unlikely it is our dreams will ever come true.

"Bob Watson was beaten, and there was a break-in at Maureen's office, both on the same day," Darlene reports. She assures me Detective Watson is okay, but we can't ignore the reality that powerful forces don't want my case to ever come to light again.

"How did I get to be so important?"

"It's not you, honey," she says. "They don't care even a little bit about you. They care about themselves. ADA Claiborne, and maybe some others, did wrong, and they don't want to be caught. And their bosses don't want to be embarrassed."

"Watson is really risking a lot for me, isn't he? And paying a big price."

"Lieutenant Kerrigan too," Darlene says.

"Why do they do it?"

"Partly they care about justice and doing their jobs. But it's Maureen too. She pushes Bob, and he responds because he loves her. Then he pushes Kerrigan. Teri, of course, wants to be a star investigative reporter and win a Pulitzer prize.

"But it's more than that ... for all of them. They care about you, Josh. You're a good guy who got blindsided by a corrupt prosecutor."

"That's a whole lot to live up to," I say.

"If we get you out of here, you'll have a long time to prove it was worth the effort."

The internal investigation showed John Banyon had followed all proper police procedures when he and Watson entered the building. They were not looking for a criminal and there had been no apparent danger. It was routine to have such an inquiry after an officer was attacked, and Banyon gave no indication he took any offense at all. On Watson's first day back at Homicide, he had been welcomed with enthusiasm and concern. He was alert to find an evasive or hostile look, but had seen none.

"It was a message," said Watson when he met with Kerrigan. "We know why, but not who. Any comment from above?"

"Just concern for your health," Kerrigan said. "Nobody mentioned the Blake case."

"Any new directives?"

Kerrigan shook his head.

"I had a call from Angel Martinez," Watson said, "I found the message on my phone this morning."

"Here?" Kerrigan asked.

"Yeah," said Watson. "The guy said, 'This is Angel. If you can't protect yourself, how could you protect me?'"

"At least we know he's out there."

"I don't think it was really him."

"Somebody trying to discourage us?" suggested Kerrigan.

"Trying real hard, I would say,"

Watson, still hurting from his beating, had been assigned to desk duty for a few days. He took a fresh pad and started writing, in no particular order, the unanswered questions related to the Blake case. Then he sorted the questions into several categories. Two hours later, he reviewed his discouragingly long list:

Attack on Mrs. Cooke

1. Why was Mrs. Cooke attacked?
2. Was it a random robbery?
3. Any connection between the Mrs. Cooke attack and Marone's murder?

Original Hiding of Evidence

4. Who altered Mackey's Martinez report? How and when?
5. Who altered Grabowsky's fingerprint report? How and when?
6. Were any NYPD officers (in addition to Grabowsky) part of the original hiding of the evidence? If so, who (Banyon? Mackey? somebody else?) and why?
7. Did anyone else in the DA's office know what Claiborne did? Before or after the fact?

Recent (Cover up?) Events

8. Who warned Watson (phone call, notes)?
9. Who beat Watson? (ACTIVE NYPD INVESTIGATION)
10. Was the beating connected to the Blake case? If so, who ordered it?
11. Who broke into Reilly's office? (ACTIVE NYPD INVESTIGATION)
12. Was the break-in related to the Blake case? If so, who ordered it?
13. Does Claiborne know about Darlene's tape?
14. Was somebody looking for that tape in Reilly's office?
15. Was it really Angel who called Watson?

Who is fighting us?

16. What does Markman know and what role is he playing?
17. Which NYPD brass are trying to scuttle the investigation?
18. Do any NYPD brass support the investigation?
19. Is NYPD meeting at high levels to discuss this?
20. Is Mayor Gardino aware of any of this?
21. Has there been any conversation on this matter between Gardino and Markman?

22. Have NYPD and the DA's office discussed this matter at any level? Who? When?

How could this case have become so complicated? Watson had solved hundreds of cases, often in a few days, and while it was true some cases were never solved, this one was extraordinary. Part of it was the delay in beginning the investigation. Time never worked in your favor. Leads got cold and memories hazy. But there was more to this case than the passage of time. Most criminals were stupid, and they made mistakes which led to their capture. The bad guys in this case, however, were ADA Claiborne, maybe other ADAs, and probably cops ... plus whatever higher-ups were now part of the cover-up. All of these bad guys understood evidence very well, and none of them were stupid.

He thought back to his initial reluctance to risk his career on this case. Part of the reason had always been the likelihood of failure. He had known it would be difficult to prove who doctored the evidence. Getting a judge to act on whatever they learned would be even more daunting. It was looking increasingly doubtful they would even get to a court.

"Here we are, the four of us, just like *Sex in the City*, except nobody's getting any but Maureen. How is your hot detective anyway?"

Joan Peterson, not unlike Nana, always hit it exactly right, except Joanie was funnier. Suzanne Dixon and Elyse Letterman, with Maureen, always made a great audience. They had assembled for their weekly dinner, this time at The Cafeteria, one of their low cost but still chic favorites, on Seventh Avenue in Chelsea.

"You're not smiling, Maureen," said Joan. "What's the matter?"

"Bob Watson was beaten last week. The same night, my office was broken into."

"What's going on?" said Suzanne.

"How's Bob?" asked Joan.

"He's okay. He's out of the hospital."

"Hospital doesn't sound okay to me," Suzanne said.

"No, really, he's all right. No broken bones. It was actually an almost clinical beating."

"Cops?" asked Joan.

"Maybe. I haven't wanted to tell you, because it might involve the Office."

"Friendship comes first," said Elyse.

A Good Conviction

"Confidentiality counts too," said Reilly. "I don't want to put any of you in an awkward situation."

"We're discrete," said Joan.

Reilly decided. "You remember the elderly woman who was killed in central Park?" she said. They all nodded. "A kid named Joshua Blake was convicted."

"Roger's launching pad," said Joan. "That case made him the toast of Broadway."

"Bob was the arresting officer," Reilly began, and she related how Josh had written to Watson and what they had done and learned so far.

"That shit Claiborne," said Elyse. "Do you think he had anything to do with the beating or the break-in?"

"It's possible. He's got a lot to hide and we're starting to get close to provable truth. It won't be pretty."

"Do you think the boss knows?" asked Suzanne, referring to District Attorney Markman.

"I hope not, but I'm not sure," said Reilly.

"That's awful," Elyse said. "How can we help?"

"I wouldn't ask," said Reilly.

"You'd better ask," said Joan.

"Did we live together all those years for nothing?" added Suzanne, and everyone nodded. "Okay. It's unanimous. What can we do?"

Reilly was thrilled, and who knew, they might learn something useful, although Markman was legendary for keeping things close to the vest and insisting others do the same. She asked her friends to be alert for any out-of-the-ordinary interactions between Markman and Claiborne, or any talk at all about the Blake case.

"Did you notice we haven't asked you how you're doing with the case?" Elyse said.

"Don't know, can't say," Joan added. "When you're ready, you tell us."

"I appreciate it, I really do, and I don't want you to do anything that might get you in trouble."

"Sure you do, you just don't want to ask," said Elyse, "and you don't have to ask. We're all big girls."

"Some of us are bigger than others," Joan added.

With that, they flew into the rest of their usual repertoire without delay. When they were leaving, Suzanne, who often ran with Reilly, confirmed they would meet at Tavern on the Green at 8:00 am the next morning, Saturday.

THIRTY

The New York City Marathon attracts world class runners. It also attracts average runners, slow runners, handicapped runners, even walkers, over thirty thousand in all. Marathons are the only sporting events where any participant can compete on the same course in the same event with the world record holder. Everybody who finishes gets the same medal.

The decision to run a marathon must be made months in advance. For one thing, you have to register and get in. Reilly had been lucky in the marathon lottery and she had her number. Now all she had to do was get prepared. There are several training regimens, and many running clubs in New York. Reilly had joined the New York Flyers, the largest running team affiliated with the New York Road Runners Club, with members ranging in age from teens to those in their sixties and above. She ran at least four times per week, gradually building up, over the prescribed eighteen week training period, to a target of forty miles per week.

Reilly was diligent, and she had completed three of the Road Runner sponsored half marathons, in Brooklyn, Queens, and the Bronx. The Manhattan half was coming up soon, then an eighteen miler, then a twenty mile training run. Reilly met Suzanne as planned.

Before they had run a quarter mile, Suzanne asked, "Did I ever mention that the woman who found the body is a friend of mine?"

"You know Kim Scott?" asked Reilly, stopping in mid-stride.

"She belongs to a running club with some other runners I know.

"I'd like to meet her," Reilly said.

"I'll set it up. How's next Saturday?"

"This is my ... first marathon," Reilly said to Kim Scott as they cruised past ten miles. "How many ... have you run?"

"Twenty eight," said Scott.

"Been running ... all your life?"

"No. About ten years."

"There's a whole club of ... women like you?" asked Reilly.

"The Mercury Masters have thirty five members," Scott replied.

"And you all run marathons?"

"Most of us. Together, we've run over three hundred marathons."

Reilly felt totally inadequate in the face of these incredible accomplishments by women almost twice her age. Suzanne Moore had been laughing through the whole conversation, although she also struggled to keep up with Scott, who ran with a light stride that made it seem like her feet didn't touch the ground. By comparison, Reilly and Suzanne pounded along beside her.

They had begun on the outer loop, diverted to take two laps around the reservoir and a mile or two on the bridal paths, a brisk twelve miles. When they finished on the east side of the park, Suzanne left, and Reilly and Scott walked a few blocks to the Jackson Hole restaurant on Madison Avenue in the eighties.

They ordered breakfast and Reilly began, "I guess Suzanne told you I'm representing Joshua Blake. We're trying to develop a basis for appealing his conviction. I don't think he had anything to do with the attack on Mrs. Cooke."

"I saw him in court when I testified," said Scott. "He didn't look like someone who would hurt an old lady, but I guess you never know. You weren't his attorney then."

"No. Larry Mullin was his attorney at trial. We're working together on the appeal."

"How did you get involved?" Scott asked.

"Josh wrote a letter to one of the detectives on the case, who I happen to be dating. We talked about it, and one thing led to another."

"How can I help?" Scott asked.

"I'm not sure," Reilly said. "I'm pursuing every possible avenue. Can we go over your testimony at trial?" Scott nodded and Reilly continued. "You said you heard Mrs. Cooke say her assailant seemed like a nice young man. 'He helped me and then he robbed me' was the quote. Do you remember?"

"I'll never forget it," Scott said. "It was such a horrible moment."

"Did you think Mrs. Cooke recognized her assailant?"

"Yes, I think she did."

"Let's assume for the moment she may have thought she recognized the person, but it wasn't Josh," Reilly said. "Because I know it wasn't."

"How can you know it wasn't? The jury heard the evidence and they concluded he was guilty."

"They didn't hear all the evidence," Reilly said.

"What do you mean?" Scott asked.

"There was evidence they should have heard but didn't," Reilly said. "Evidence that proved Josh was somewhere else when the crime was committed."

"Wow. Why didn't Josh's lawyer present that evidence?" Scott asked.

"He didn't know about it then," Reilly said. Then she hesitated, unsure how much to share with Scott. "Can I trust you?" she asked.

"Why do you need to trust me?"

"Because the reason the jury didn't know about the evidence that would have acquitted Josh involves some nasty and illegal acts on the part of the prosecutor, and I don't want him to know how close we're getting to proving what he did."

"You're talking about the prosecutor at the trial?" asked Scott. "The one who questioned me?"

"Yes, Roger Claiborne."

"I never did like that guy," Scott said. "Something 'off' about him."

"You've got good instincts, Kim," Reilly said, breathing a sigh of relief.

"Okay, let me think more about Mrs. Cooke. I told everything I knew to the police, and then again at the trial." Scott screwed her face in thought, visibly straining to remember.

"Anything, Kim," Reilly said. "I'm grasping at straws. I've got a kid rotting away in Sing Sing for a crime he didn't do, and I've got to get him out of there while he still has a chance to get back to a normal life."

Scott sat very still, and closed her eyes. She didn't move a muscle for several minutes. She started to speak, then stopped.

"What?" asked Reilly.

"Wrong woman," she whispered.

"Wrong woman?"

"Yes. Mrs. Cooke mumbled the words 'wrong woman' just before she died."

"What did she mean?"

Scott shook her head and raised her hands in a questioning motion. "I don't know. I guess it didn't make any sense to me. I didn't remember it when I testified. I didn't remember it at all until just now when you made me think about it again. Is it important? Did I do wrong not to mention it before?"

Later that same Saturday afternoon, Reilly convened an emergency meeting of the Blake Team. Bob Watson, Larry Mullin, Teri Scanlon and Darlene Brantley were assembled in Reilly's office.

"I talked to Kim Scott this morning," Reilly began.

"The one who found Mrs. Cooke's body?" Mullin asked.

"Yes. She's a runner. Runs marathons, of all things," said Reilly. "Imagine."

"She testified a six mile run was a short run," Mullin said. "The courtroom was amused."

"She told me something this morning that wasn't in her trial testimony. Said she'd forgotten it completely until today." Reilly paused until everyone's attention was riveted. "Just before she died, Mrs. Cooke said the words 'wrong woman.' "

"What did she mean?" Darlene asked.

Reilly shook her head. "Don't know. I'm hoping we can figure it out. It must mean something, the last words Mrs. Cooke ever uttered."

Watson got up and walked to the window, his back to the rest of the group. He sorted through everything he knew, wondering how far to leap, how silly he would sound if he was wrong. He could feel everyone's eyes on him. When he returned to the table, he remained standing and spoke in sharp police-talk mode.

"Here's a possible scenario," he said. "The bad guys Anthony Marone is hanging with send him to steal a pocketbook from a woman in Central Park. Marone attacks the wrong woman. He realizes his mistake, and says 'wrong woman' aloud, maybe to himself in frustration, before he runs off with the pocketbook. Mrs. Cooke hears him say 'wrong woman' and repeats it to Kim Scott.

"If this is true, then the attack on Mrs. Cooke wasn't a random robbery, and it had nothing to do with Josh or her fall on Broadway earlier in the evening."

Watson paused, and the others waited.

"Let's take this line of thought a little further," Watson said. "After Marone screws up by attacking the wrong woman, he compounds his mistake by taking the pocketbook, since, if it was the wrong woman, he should no longer have any interest in the bag. Dummy that he is, he takes it anyway."

Watson's confidence grew as he put each subsequent piece in place.

"Then Marone screws up again by getting caught in a candy store robbery with Marco Picollo. When he's arrested, his bad guy friends panic. They're afraid he's too stupid to be trusted in police hands, that he'll spill the beans on whatever was really going on in Central Park. They make bail for him, send him away, or he gets away, and nobody sees him again until he's killed in Washington Heights by a shooter from a rival criminal family. Maybe it's a set up to get rid of him permanently."

Utter silence followed Watson's monologue. Mullin and Reilly looked at each other. Darlene just looked stunned.

Lewis M. Weinstein

"Well, what do you think?" Watson asked.

Reilly spoke first. "When I was in the prosecutor's office, preparing for my first trial, my Irish grandmother told me I had to tell the jury a story. It didn't have to be a true story, Nana said, just make it sound like it could be true. Wise lady, my nana."

"So you think my story could be true?" Watson asked.

"The basic idea hangs together," said Mullin. "Maybe *both* Josh and Mrs. Cooke just happened to be in the wrong place at the wrong time."

"It would be nice to have just one scrap of real evidence to support it," Reilly said.

"What evidence can there be?" Watson asked. "Mrs. Cooke can't testify. Marone is dead. Maybe we'll learn something from Sonny Durante, the guy Marco Picollo said Marone was hanging with, but that's a long shot. So far, Parker hasn't been able to make any contact with him."

Darlene raised her hand.

"You don't need permission to speak," Reilly said.

"Well," Darlene began, still tentative, "if Mrs. Cooke was the wrong woman, who was the right one? What we need to do is find Lady X."

"I can't say this to anyone else, but it's really starting to look hopeless. I'm the one who has to keep everyone else focused, but right now I'm having trouble keeping myself going. We have so little proof of anything. Bob made a long list of unanswered questions. We'll get laughed out of court on what we have so far."

Nana listened to Reilly's lament without saying a word, and gradually Reilly ran out of steam. For several long moments, there was silence on the line.

"Do you remember, Maureen, when you said you wanted to be an attorney, and your parents wanted you to be a teacher, and you didn't have any money?"

"I didn't give up then, did I?"

"And why didn't you quit?"

"I dreamed I could make a difference in this world."

"And you have, dear, you have. Do you think that boy still has dreams?"

Reilly didn't answer. As she often did, she envisioned where Josh might be at this very moment, who he might be with, what he might be thinking, whether he had any real hope, what it would mean for him if he gave up hope. Then she thought how much Josh's hopes were depending on her.

"Thanks, Nana," she said.

"What were you talking about with my father?" Reilly asked.

"He wanted to know if it was dangerous being a homicide detective," Watson said.

"My parents live in isolation. They're good people, but their view of the world is restricted, and they're very timid about anything outside their own narrow experience."

"And I'm outside their experience?"

"Like another planet," Reilly said.

This intriguing conversation was abruptly interrupted by the appearance of a small, elderly lady wearing a full length skirt and a bright fluffy blouse.

"When are you going to introduce me to your friend, Maureen?" the lady said.

"Where have you been? I've been looking all over for you," Reilly sputtered. "Nana, this is Bob Watson. Bob, this is my Nana."

Without another word, Nana took Bob's arm and directed him across the lawn, leaving a stunned Maureen standing alone. She was immediately surrounded by cousins and family friends she hadn't seen in months, all assembled for the traditional Hennessey family Labor Day picnic in Prospect Park.

"Look at her," Nana said to Watson. "She can hardly talk to anyone, looking around to see where I've taken you, worried what I'm telling you."

"What *are* you telling me?" Watson asked, more than a little surprised. Maureen had of course mentioned her grandmother, but Nana had always been a bit of a mystery. He knew she was an important part of Maureen's life, but he was missing all the details, and detectives always need to know the details.

"You're the best thing to happen to Maureen in a long time," Nana said, "and I want to make sure you appreciate how much she cares about you."

"Maureen said you were rather direct," Watson said, smiling, but Nana, waiting for his answer, ignored his comment. "I know she cares," Watson said, "and I care about her. Something very good is happening with us. She's a good and strong woman."

"Do you love her?"

Watson was amazed Nana would ask such a question within minutes of meeting him, but he didn't hesitate. "Yes, I do," he said. "Very much."

310   Lewis M. Weinstein

"Good. Don't hurt her."

Watson towered over the little woman, but he had no doubt who would win in a contest of wills.

"I won't."

"I told Maureen not to dare give up on that boy in Sing Sing. You, too. You must succeed, not just for him, but for both of you as well. Your future lives, and your life together, depend on it."

"You're right," he said. "But you know what a mountain we still have to climb."

"Have you ever seen Crough Patrick Mountain near Westport, in Ireland? Every year, pilgrims climb the mountain on their knees. I've climbed that mountain on my knees. Don't tell me about mountains. Just keep climbing."

Reilly had broken loose from her relatives.

"Do you need to be rescued?" she asked.

"I think we're doing just fine, dear," Nana said.

"Why does this frighten me?" Reilly asked.

"No, it's good," Watson said, smiling conspiratorially at Nana. "We're talking about Irish mountains."

THIRTY-ONE

"Detective Watson has a new theory." Darlene has just arrived, and she's excited about her news. She tells me how Reilly met Kim Scott, how Mrs. Cooke said "wrong woman," and how Watson put it together from there.

"But it would be like finding a needle in a haystack," I say.

"Maybe, maybe not," Darlene says. I ask what she means but she won't say any more.

Darlene left the City College campus at 4:30 pm and caught the downtown A-train. As she had done many times in the past two weeks, she exited at 59th Street, Columbus Circle. The leaves were beginning to change color. This would be the second fall Josh had spent in prison.

She walked up Central Park West and entered the park at 63rd Street, pausing as she always did at the site of the attack on Mrs. Cooke. She walked past Sheep's Meadow, closed and empty, beautiful in the late afternoon sun. She stood with her back resting on the parapet overlooking Bethesda Fountain, staring blankly.

It would be hard to say when she first saw the old lady. By the time it became a conscious thought, the woman had been within her scope of vision for several minutes. Once registered, however, she was struck with the resemblance of this woman to the photograph of Mrs. Cooke she had seen at Josh's trial. Same small frail shape, same gray hair. Of course lots of women might fit that description, but this woman sent Darlene's antenna buzzing.

At first, she felt fear for the old lady. It would soon be dark, unsafe for a woman walking alone in the park, old or young. The same tragedy that happened to Mrs. Cooke could happen to this lady. But then she got the feeling this woman was not just out for a stroll. She wasn't hurrying, although she was moving with definite purpose. The buzzing intensified.

The woman passed Darlene, heading from the east side of the park to the west side, then veered off on a small path toward Literary Walk. Darlene waited until she was perhaps fifty yards away before she followed.

As the woman walked under a canopy of trees, Darlene's attention was drawn to the statue of Christopher Columbus which dominates the far end of Literary Walk. She thought she saw the shadow of a man standing next to the statue.

Lady X – as Darlene was now calling her - walked up to the man in the shadows. There didn't seem to be any conversation. Lady X discretely handed her pocketbook to the man, receiving in return what looked like an identical pocketbook, which the man had extracted from a satchel. The woman, who never broke stride, proceeded to the outer road, heading to the west side of the park. The man put the lady's pocketbook in his satchel, waited perhaps thirty seconds, then walked off in the opposite direction.

Darlene followed Lady X along the small path to the 63rd Street exit on Central Park West, past the very spot where Mrs. Cooke had met her fate.

"She did what?" Watson asked, after Darlene had described the old woman's walk in the park and the pocketbook exchange.

"It's Lady X," Darlene said. "I'm sure."

"Marone was supposed to steal Lady X's pocketbook," said Watson. "We need to find out who those people are and what's in the pocketbook. "Are you busy tomorrow afternoon? Maybe lightning will strike twice."

"I'm available," said Darlene.

The Blake Team came together in Maureen Reilly's conference room. Reilly, beginning to panic, wanted another recap and a new plan.

"Going to the Stadium tonight?" Mullin was asking Watson when Reilly walked into the room, trailed by Teri Scanlon and Darlene Brantley.

"Wouldn't miss it for the world," Watson said. "Time to put those guys away."

"Are you sure, Bob?" Reilly jumped in. "This could be the Red Sox year."

"No way."

Mullin, although he had started the baseball talk, abruptly changed gears. "We're all here now. Let's review where we are."

"Right now," Mullin said, "our direct appeal is a loser, and we're not confident a CPL 440 motion would be any more successful."

"We need more," said Reilly.

"We may have something useful," Watson said. "Darlene, tell them."

"I went for a walk in the park a couple of days ago," Darlene said. "I saw an elderly woman who met a man, exchanged pocketbooks with him, and then left the park exactly where Mrs. Cooke was attacked. I think it was Lady X, Tony Marone's intended victim."

"Darlene and I were in the park last night and again tonight, before we came here," Watson said. "So far, Lady X hasn't reappeared, but we'll keep looking."

Teri Scanlon raised her hand.

"Speak up, Teri," Reilly said. "You don't need permission."

"I have another suggestion," Scanlon said. "The last time you pushed Claiborne, Maureen, he made a big mistake, about the videotape. Suppose we push him again and see what happens."

"What do you have in mind?" Reilly asked.

"You know I'm working on a story about prosecutorial abuse. I've written to District Attorney Markman, asking questions about the extent of the problem in Manhattan, and what his office does to prevent it. It's been a long time, and he hasn't answered yet. Maybe he never will. But suppose I go to Claiborne, show him the letter, and ask him the same questions. I'll focus on prosecutors who've been caught hiding exculpatory evidence, and I'll mention the Blake case. Try to scare the shit out of him."

Everybody looked at everyone else, but nobody said anything.

"Well, what do you think?" Scanlon asked.

"Desperation breeds desperate measures," Reilly said. "I say go for it."

The crowd in the TV room at Sing Sing is mostly Yankee fans, but there are some red hats, and here, violence is always a possibility.

The Sox score four runs, all they would get, in the fourth inning, and the Yankees threaten but don't ever overcome the deficit.

When the game ends, the TV camera pans over to Mayor Gardino, and I'm horrified to see ADA Roger Claiborne, big as life, standing next to the mayor.

THIRTY-TWO

"Thank you, Mr. Claiborne, for agreeing to meet with me."

"Anything to accommodate the press," Claiborne said, oozing an oily unctuousness that turned Scanlon's stomach.

"Well, I appreciate it," Scanlon said. "You've become quite a figure in the DA's office, a regular New York hero." Actually, she was surprised he had agreed to see her. Well, she thought, it's been a while since I wrote the article about prosecutorial abuse. Maybe he's forgotten it.

Claiborne smiled, completely missing Scanlon's intended sarcasm.

"I saw you on television the other night," she added. "At the Stadium."

Claiborne beamed. "Too bad they lost."

"Well, sometimes the underdog does win," Scanlon said, meaning Joshua Blake and not the Boston Red Sox. Then, tiring of small talk with someone she disliked intensely, she got to the purpose of her visit. "Did you happen to read a series in the Chicago Tribune a few years ago about prosecutorial abuse?"

Claiborne looked up sharply, his smile evaporated. "No," he said. "But I did read your articles about the Palladium case. Is this some sort of cause for you?"

Scanlon ignored his question. "It's actually quite a series," she said. "Hundreds of murder convictions were overturned when it was later found that prosecutors had failed to turn over exculpatory evidence as required by law. I'll send you a copy." Scanlon watched the color rise in Claiborne's face. This was fun!

"I'm working on a story comparing Manhattan's experience to Chicago's. You know, do prosecutors here hide exculpatory evidence like they do in Chicago? How many Manhattan convictions have been overturned on *Brady* violations?"

Claiborne blanched, and Scanlon could see clear signs of growing panic. She drove the wedge deeper. "I'm particularly interested in how the Manhattan DA's office deals with prosecutorial abuse when it happens. What happens to prosecutors who bend the law?"

And now for the final thrust. "I wrote to Mr. Markman," she said, handing a copy of her letter to Claiborne. She watched as Claiborne read, fingers tightening, eyes darting, looking anywhere but at her.

"He didn't answer yet," Scanlon said. "Do you think he will?"

A Good Conviction

"I think this interview is over," Claiborne said.

"Not quite, Mr. Claiborne, sir," Scanlon said, emphasizing the sir. "Maybe you could comment first on your meeting a while back with Maureen Reilly. I'm sure you remember. Do you think the Blake case might fit into my story?"

"Fuck you, Scanlon," Claiborne spat out. "Get out of here."

"Ooh, a little testy, are we? Well, anyway, thanks for the quote. That would be f-u-c-k, right?" Scanlon smiled sweetly as she got up to leave. Within minutes, she called Reilly to tell her the hook was in.

For six consecutive nights, Detective Watson and Darlene Brantley had haunted Central Park in the hour just before dusk, but Lady X had not reappeared. They were giving it one more try, positioned again on a bench about fifty yards west of Literary Walk. They had been there for forty minutes, and were about to give up, when Darlene suddenly grabbed Watson's arm and pointed with her eyes.

As before, the old lady moved slowly along the path from the east side of the park heading west. Glancing quickly towards the end of Literary Walk, Darlene said, "And there's her friend!"

"Let's split," Watson said. "Now, before she passes. You loop ahead so you can follow the woman. Stay with her when she leaves the park, but far enough behind not to be noticed." Watson put his hand on Darlene's arm. "Be careful."

"I'll follow the man," Watson said, already moving to cross Literary Walk ahead of the man's anticipated path. It was then he realized the pattern. It's Thursday night. Same night Darlene saw Lady X last week. Same night Mrs. Cooke was attacked. Whatever this is about, it happens on Thursday nights.

Watson watched the transfer of the pocketbooks, exactly as Darlene had described. Lady X walked away, and through the trees, Watson saw Darlene in place to follow her. The man waited a few seconds, then walked in the other direction. Watson followed him out of the park and across Fifth Avenue east on 59th Street. Just past Madison, the man entered a red Chrysler convertible. Watson wrote the license plate number in his spiral notebook.

Kerrigan's light was still on. Watson knocked and was invited to enter.

"You're going to love this," Watson said, relating what Darlene had seen a week before and how that sighting led to this day's events. He added Lady X's address, which Darlene had phoned him excitedly to report.

"The Chrysler is registered to one Joseph F. Baldini," Watson said, "aka Joey Bald. Baldini is known to be a soldier in the same crime family as the shooter who killed Anthony Marone in Washington Heights.

"Marco Picollo, Marone's partner in the candy store robbery, linked Marone to Sonny Durante. If we can prove it was Durante or someone else in his family who sent Marone to Central Park, then we'll know Marone's reason for being there."

"And that would be something related to the feud between the families, having nothing whatever to do with either Mrs. Cooke or Joshua Blake," Kerrigan said.

"Exactly," said Watson. "My guess is there's a transfer of some kind between Baldini and this Lady X on a regular basis, maybe every Thursday night, and Durante sent Marone to steal whatever it was they were transferring. When we learn more about those transfers, we'll have some real facts to support our theory."

"And maybe," Kerrigan said, "we can solve both murders, Mrs. Cooke and Anthony Marone. I'll put some people on it."

"Four days after Teri Scanlon scared the shit out of Roger Claiborne, I get a new cellmate. Now I haven't had a cellmate for months, so right away it's suspicious. Jason LaRue arrives at eleven in the morning, and by the time lunch is over, at least twelve inmates have told me the guy is a snitch. That afternoon, an invitation-only meeting is convened.

Two of my students lead LaRue into the most remote section of the yard. One by one, they're joined by others, including me, until there's a tight circle of maybe twenty guys, with LaRue in the middle. He does not look comfortable.

"So, switched to B-block? Who sent you?" asks Hector Rodriquez. Subtlety is not high on Hector's list of virtues, but loyalty is, and I am truly moved by what's happening. Most of the group surrounding LaRue are my students, plus friends of theirs who I don't know. Imported muscle.

"Nobody sent me," says LaRue.

"We don't fuckin' believe you. You've been a snitch before."

"Let's just suppose you really don't want to begin your experience on B-block with a lie, and you start over."

"A mulligan! He gets a mulligan!" I'm surprised somebody knows that golf term.

"Only get one, fucker, better use it wisely."

There's a period of silence. The men are respectful of the decision LaRue has to make, but they won't wait long.

"You ain't got all day."

"Whatever deal you were offered, we got a better one."

LaRue is wilting noticeably within the circle of hostile stares.

"Under our deal, you get to live."

LaRue capitulated. "Okay," he said. "I was sent."

"Who sent you?" Hector asks. The question is put forward so softly and so politely that a less savvy inmate might have missed the ferocity. LaRue doesn't miss it. He now looks one small step removed from shitting his pants.

"I don't know," he says, and the funny thing is we believe him.

I speak for the first time. "I have a good idea who sent you to spy on me, but we're going to need your help to prove it. And you're not going to tell anybody else what you're doing." I see the fear in LaRue's eyes, and add, "You okay with that? No problems?"

"I'm good," LaRue whispers, looking at the group which still surrounds him. "Whatever you say."

"Excellent," I say, placing my arm around his shoulder and moving him out of the group, quite aware we have attracted the attention of the guards and that they're about to break us up anyway.

"Let's you and I get better acquainted," I say as we walk off. "It's good for cellmates to know each other, don't you think?"

I call Reilly and let Jason LaRue know he will soon have a visitor. Detective Watson shows up two days later. I learn this when LaRue returns to our cell, his face white, trembling.

"A problem, Jason?" I ask in my most solicitous manner.

"Fuckin' NYPD homicide detective came to see me," he mutters.

"I told you to expect a visitor. What did he want?"

"You didn't say nothin' about no detective. How did I ever get involved in this shit?" LaRue asks.

"Life consists of choices," I say. "You made a bad choice." I pause to let this sink in. "Fortunately for you, you've been given a chance to make better choices." Pause again, watching him squirm. "It's up to you, my man."

"This is fuckin' unbelievable," LaRue says.

"Actually, it's exactly that. Are you going to cooperate?"

"What choice do I have?"

"Let's start out with the Brooklyn situation," Scanlon said, "and see how far we get before you throw me out like your charming assistant did last week."

318   Lewis M. Weinstein

"He wasn't amused," District Attorney Harold Markman said.

It was the first time Scanlon has been in Markman's office, and she was impressed. Contrary to the drab nature of most of 100 Centre Street, Markman's enclave is richly wooded and quite elegant. The walls are covered with photos of the great man with other great men, the public record of a long and distinguished career.

"There's nothing amusing about hiding evidence in the Blake case," Scanlon said.

"Those are serious charges, young lady. Can you prove them?"

Scanlon noted that Markman had not automatically jumped to Claiborne's defense. "I guess we'll know in due time," she said, looking straight into Markman's eyes, seeing concern but not hostility.

"Reilly's good," Markman said. "Used to work here, you know." He shook his head in a gesture of approval and perhaps even fondness. "I don't know Mullin."

"Can we talk about Brooklyn?" Scanlon asked, thinking Markman must know exactly where she was going and why. If he lets me get there, it won't be by accident. "Well, first I should thank you for agreeing to see me."

"You have fifteen minutes."

"Perhaps you're familiar with the case, even though it's not your jurisdiction. There was an article in the *New York Times* last December. The City settled a wrongful prosecution case for $5 million after an appellate judge found the trial prosecutor had withheld evidence that would have exonerated him."

"So there was a bad apple in Brooklyn."

"Seventy-two bad apples, apparently, at least so claimed by the defense attorney. Seventy-two cases where judges cited prosecutors for misconduct."

"Over a twenty year period," said Markman, displaying no discomfort with Scanlon's line of questioning and great familiarity with the facts, which didn't surprise her.

"Only one of those prosecutors was disciplined. The others all seemed to get merit raises and bonuses. Sounds like the City didn't really care what they did, as long as they got convictions."

No response from Markman, so Scanlon continued, "If the civil suit had gone to trial, it might have revealed a practice of misconduct in the Brooklyn DA's office. The City settled the case so it wouldn't go to court. It sounds to me like they didn't want the publicity of a trial that would expose their practices and policies."

"Cases are often settled," Markman said, but Scanlon detected just the slightest tension in his neck, just the smallest evidence of sweat on his forehead.

"So what's the policy in Manhattan?"

"Don't tolerate it," said Markman. "We follow *Brady* here. Any exculpatory evidence must be turned over to the defense. No exceptions."

"Has it happened? Maybe in the Palladium case?"

"No comment."

"How does Manhattan compare to Chicago? Did you see the articles I sent?"

"I saw the articles when they were written five years ago. Also saw *The Exonerated*. And read Barry Scheck's book. We follow the law here, but we don't keep a scorecard."

"What do you do when one of your prosecutors gets a conviction by withholding evidence?"

"If such a thing ever happened, it would be very disturbing, and not the policy of this office. We run a tight ship here. We choose the best and most dedicated attorneys to become prosecutors. People like Maureen Reilly. We motivate them. We teach them to do the job right. We watch them to make sure they do."

"And if one of them fails to turn over evidence favorable for the defense?"

"It has to be material," Markman said. "The evidence is material only if there's a reasonable probability that, had it been disclosed to the jury, the trial result would have been different."

"Any examples you'd care to share?"

"That would be confidential. Personnel matters, you know."

The words "right to know laws" were on the tip of Scanlon's tongue, but she decided to hold that for another day. She was amazed when Markman's office had called the day after the blowup with Claiborne to set up the meeting. Now she had a solid interview, with useful threads to follow. Her intuition told her Markman didn't like Claiborne and wouldn't be totally sorry if things turned badly for him, as long as Markman himself could emerge unscathed. Score a big one for our side.

"Time's up, young lady." Markman stood. His gray suit was impeccably pressed, and his manner, as always, was elegant, courtly almost.

Scanlon wondered if he would be appalled when he fully understood what Claiborne had done. But why doesn't he already know? Is he part of the cover-up? Despite Markman's statement about appropriate action, Scanlon knew the City had never brought criminal charges against a prosecutor. Was Markman saying they would?

"Thank you again," she said, rising and offering her hand.

He shook her hand. It was a firm dry handshake. "If you happen to see Maureen, please give her my regards."

"Do you think he knows?"

The question posed by Teri Scanlon had been disturbing Reilly for a long time. She respected and liked DA Markman.

"I wish I knew," Reilly said, picking up her phone to get off the speaker.

"Markman knew every detail about the Brooklyn case. Isn't it logical to assume he's interrogated Claiborne on Josh's matter? Why did he meet with me after all this time? It had to be my confrontation with Claiborne. Maybe he wanted to know what I know."

"Those are good questions. What's your intuition?" Reilly asked.

"I think he knows, but I don't think he knew at the time," Scanlon said. "I also think he doesn't like Claiborne and that he's very upset about the Blake case."

"But not upset enough to take the initiative to vacate the conviction? He could make a motion to Judge Berman on his own authority, today, without any motions from us, or he could agree to concur in our motion."

This is what bothered Reilly the most. If Markman knew, and Markman cared about the integrity of his office, why didn't he do something?

"Maybe he doesn't know," Reilly mused. "Maybe Claiborne still has him fooled."

"Do you really believe that?" Scanlon asked.

"No."

After she hung up, Reilly silently cursed Markman as well as Claiborne for prolonging Josh's agony. She shivered as she imagined all the horrible things that could happen to Josh each additional day he spent at Sing Sing.

THIRTY-THREE

On the day of the New York City Marathon, Watson, carrying a step stool, met Darlene and Teri in Manhattan and boarded Brooklyn bound R-train. They rode for almost an hour, to 95th Street, Bay Ridge.

"This way," said Watson. He led his group to a small street at the foot of the Verrazzano-Narrows Bridge, where they took up positions along the roadway, behind police barriers, just a few feet from where the runners would come off the bridge.

"This is mile two," Watson said. He opened his step stool and offered it to the ladies as a seat. He had spent hours in the days before the marathon making his plan.

"Here come the wheelchairs," Teri shouted, pointing.

"That's incredible," said Darlene, as the wheelchairs sped by. Some were sleek, sophisticated racing machines, and others looked like they had been stolen from a hospital emergency room. "Twenty six miles in that thing? Wow!"

Next were the elite women runners, and ten minutes later, the main body of women runners came pounding off the bridge and around the corner. Watson mounted his step stool and they all waved their signs, trying to pick out the few runners they knew from the mass of humanity racing past.

"How are we ever going to see Maureen?" Darlene asked.

"She'll see us," Watson answered. "Runners' left at mile two. On the stool."

Sure enough, after thousands more women had passed, there was Maureen Reilly, wearing a broad smile and waving like crazy. Watson felt an intense surge of pride. With Maureen were Suzanne Dixon and Kim Scott.

"How are you doing, honey," Watson asked Reilly, leaning down for a kiss. "You look great!"

"It was unbelievable. All those runners on the bridge. Ships in the harbor shooting red, white and blue streams of water into the air. Here, take my sweatshirt. It's getting warm."

Several photographs, another quick kiss, and she was gone, part of the thundering herd.

"Okay, let's move," said Watson, folding his stool. "Got to hurry."

Watson, Darlene and Teri retraced their steps to the subway and boarded the northbound R-train.

At their next stop, 4th Avenue and 9th Street, thousands of runners hooted and hollered, creating a raucous, joyous, thrilling sound as they ran along Fourth Avenue in Brooklyn.

"We're just past mile six. Maureen will be here in ten minutes," Watson said, consulting his watch and a sheet of paper on which he had calculated exactly when she would reach each mile marker.

They stood silently, watching one of the great scenes in all of sports. To their left, thousands of runners were moving away, up Fourth Avenue through Brooklyn toward Queens, seven miles away. To their right, thousands more were coming at them in a seemingly endless procession. Spectators called out the runner's names which were written on their shirts. It was a huge moving block party involving thirty-six thousand runners and two million spectators.

Almost precisely when predicted, Darlene, on the stool, saw Maureen a hundred yards away, waving at them. More photos and kisses, and again she disappeared into the mob. Watson, now that Maureen had passed, relaxed and watched the other runners, and the crowd, both groups in constant flux. The movement of so many people and the joyous rising noise combined to form a scene more thrilling than he could have imagined.

A man standing near him looked familiar, but Watson couldn't quite place him. Then he spoke.

"Some race, isn't it Sonny?"

It was Marco Picollo. Could 'Sonny' be Sonny Durante? Picollo had given them Durante's name at the diner in Brooklyn, but Durante had been out of town since then. Now it appeared he was back.

"Here comes your sister," Picollo yelled.

While Picollo and Sonny were focused on the runners, Watson pulled his cap down over his eyes and oriented his digital camera. He took several shots straight on, including the sister when she arrived. Durante's sister ran on, and Marco and Sonny walked away.

Watson whispered to Darlene and Teri, "Got to go. I'll try to meet you on First Avenue," but as he started to follow the two men, he noticed Teri and Darlene right behind him. Watson had already keyed in Detective Christine Parker's cell number. Christine answered on the second ring.

"I'm following Marco Picollo and a guy who may be Sonny Durante."

"Where are you?"

"Fourth Avenue at Tenth, heading north."

"Can you stay with them?"

"Not for long without being spotted. Picollo knows me."

"I'll send a team. Hang in there as long as you can."

By now, Darlene and Teri had figured out what was happening, and Watson recruited them into the surveillance. He directed Darlene to cross Fourth Avenue and maintain contact from the other side. He kept Teri with him, awaiting a new development. They all had cell phones. Picollo and Durante stayed on Fourth for several blocks, then crossed the street. Darlene stayed ahead, looking back from time to time, with Watson and Teri behind.

Watson's phone rang. "Where are you?" Christine hollered in his ear. "My team is on Fourth at Twelfth."

Watson gave directions and soon spotted a raggedy looking kid trying to get his attention. He nodded to the kid, and then toward Picollo and Durante. The kid nodded back. His cell rang again. "Okay, we've got 'em," said Christine. "Go watch the race."

"Not yet, Chris" Watson said. "I've got pictures."

"I'll send a car."

Twenty minutes later, Watson, with an incredulous Darlene and Teri still in tow, had been to the Seventy-fifth Precinct and downloaded the photos. The three of them were back in a patrol car, headed for the subway farther north on Fourth Avenue.

Exiting the subway at 59th Street and Lexington Avenue, they walked to O'Flanagan's Irish Pub at First Avenue and 65th Street.

"How are we going to see anything?" Teri asked, pointing to the six deep crowd along the curb.

"Not a problem," said Watson. "We still have about forty minutes until Maureen gets here. The people in front will leave when their runners come by, and we'll move up. Who wants to keep watch on the stool?"

Teri climbed up. "What a view," she exclaimed. "The runners are coming out of the sun. It's packed all across First Avenue. There's a TV camera." Just as Watson had predicted, they moved up as others left, and they were soon in the front of the spectator pack along the curb.

"There's Suzanne," screamed Darlene.

"Maureen's right behind me," Suzanne hollered as she passed, and sure enough, in another minute, Maureen arrived. She came over to Watson. "I can't tell you how great it is you're here. Actually, you're everywhere, and it really means a lot to me to look forward to seeing you all, cheering me on. I love you, guy."

"And you are one beautiful sweaty woman," Bob said, hugging her tightly. "You still okay?"

"I'm fine."

"By the way, we found Sonny Durante at Fourth Avenue. Christine Parker's probably questioning him by now." Reilly's mouth dropped open. "I'll explain later," said Watson. Maureen, looking a little dumbfounded, ran off. Watson watched her running along First Avenue and experienced again the tingling pride he had been feeling all day. Too soon to celebrate, though. Ten more miles to go.

"The runners turn into the park here," Watson said when they reached Columbus Circle. "We have to go around." The route to Central Park West was blocked, but Watson flashed his badge and they were allowed though. They walked north on Central Park West and into the park at 63rd Street.

"This is the place," Darlene said, showing Teri where Mrs. Cooke had been attacked, and the joyous mood turned somber. "Josh said he was planning to watch the race," Darlene said. "Wouldn't it be great if he could see Maureen on television."

"This way," said Watson, leading them across the grass to a spot near the roadway, just before the large Mile 26 sign high up on a street lamp pole. Again, there was a crowd along the curb line, and again, they moved up as others left. Cobblestones made it difficult to set the stool firmly, but Watson got it placed and climbed up.

"The looks on these runners faces are something," he said. "Some look ecstatic, some look almost dead."

"Does everybody finish?" Teri asked.

"Most of them," Watson said. "The New York City Marathon has one of the highest finishing percentages. The runners say it's the crowds, which are like no other. The crowds keep the runners going."

"How long until Maureen gets here," Darlene asked.

Watson consulted his paper and his watch. "Thirty two minutes," he said.

"Yeah, right," Darlene scoffed.

Music blared and a voice on a loudspeaker encouraged the runners. It was over four hours into the race. The winners had long since finished, but in many ways this was the real New York City Marathon, what it was all about. The pace was not fast, although occasionally, someone decided to put on a burst to the finish. Some were clearly struggling. Several disabled runners passed, each with an accompanying guide, and each time, Watson was thrilled by the effort of the handicapped runners, some of whom were blind.

"Well, look who's here," Teri said, and Watson turned to see Larry Mullin.

"Thanks for telling me about this," Mullin said. "All these years a New Yorker, I never saw a marathon. This is fantastic! Did Maureen get here yet."

"Another fifteen minutes," Watson said. "She'll be glad to see you, Larry."

Watson thought he would burst when he saw Maureen coming up the hill toward him. He could not keep the tears of pride from his eyes. What an achievement, he thought. What a great woman.

She was running with Suzanne and Kim, the three of them holding hands and dancing along like it was a lark in the park. Maureen came over to hug Darlene and Teri. She saw Mullin and hugged him too. Watson stayed on the stool, looking down, his heart filled with joy at Maureen's accomplishment. Maureen looked up and their eyes met. He gave her a thumbs up and she beamed, pointing to the clock, which read 4:26:25.

"You can still break four and a half hours," Watson hollered. "Go get it!"

After the Marathon, everyone went to a party in an apartment just off Central Park West, the home of a friend of Suzanne Dixon's. As they walked from the finish line to the apartment, Suzanne spoke to Reilly.

"I've been wanting to talk to you all day, but we were never alone," she said. "All hell broke loose on Friday, right after a reporter interviewed Markman."

"That reporter was with Bob all day, cheering you on," Reilly said. "Her name is Teri Scanlon. She'll be at the party."

"You knew," said Suzanne. "You're working together?"

"Yes."

"I don't want to talk with her," Suzanne said. "I'll just tell you and then you do what you need to do."

"I understand."

"So, Scanlon interviewed Markman. As soon as she left, Markman sent for Monti and Claiborne, and I'm told it was a brutal meeting. The old man never raises his voice, but he sure did this time. When Monti and Claiborne left, they were beyond distraught."

"Do you know what Markman said?"

"No. But there will be gossip next week for sure."

"Thanks, Suzanne. I never heard it from you."

At the party a few minutes later, Reilly beckoned Watson, Scanlon, Mullin and Darlene to the adjoining bedroom. She closed the door.

Lewis M. Weinstein

"Our plan is working," she said. "The shit has hit the fan." Reilly repeated what she had just learned.

"Well, he knows now," Scanlon said, referring back to her conversation with Reilly over what Markman knew.

"Maybe," said Reilly, not yet willing to admit that Markman might be complicit with Claiborne. "Roger could still be lying to him."

"Not likely," said Scanlon. "But even if Claiborne tries to stonewall him, Markman can learn the truth if he really wants to know."

I watch every minute of NBC's marathon coverage, including the aerial views of the start at the Verrazzano Bridge, with Mayor Gardino starting the race. A lot of attention is focused on the women's race. The American and the Brit from the Olympics are the leaders. The Brit wins, redemption is hers, and I hope this is an omen for me. I tell every inmate in the room my attorney is running, and I strain to see her in the crowds of runners, but I never do.

THIRTY-FOUR

"I haven't spoken to her in three days," Reilly said as soon as Watson came on the line. "Something's happened."

"What could happen? She's not in 'the life' any more."

"Bob, I'm telling you I'm scared. We were supposed to have breakfast and she didn't show, which is not like her at all. Please find her."

Watson called Darlene's number, got her answering machine, and rushed over to her apartment. Nothing. He went from there to the Broadway Big Apple Hotel and sat at the dismal hotel bar. He was on his second beer when a woman entered, ignored several empty stools, and sat next to him. She looked Hispanic, and was just a tad overweight.

"Hi, honey," she said. "I'm Annabelle. What's your name?" Watson didn't answer.

"You here for a reason?" she asked.

He nodded.

"You look like a cop to me," she said.

"You're right," he said. He smiled at the amazed look on the hooker's face. She had clearly been expecting a denial. "My name's Robert Watson. I'm a detective at Manhattan North Homicide. I work homicide, not vice, and I'm not looking to hassle anyone here. I'm looking for a woman named Darlene Brantley."

"What do you want with Darlene?" Annabelle said, and her concern, even fear, was obvious.

"She knows a young man named Joshua Blake."

"He's at Sing Sing."

"I know. I'm trying to help get him out."

"Why should I believe you?" Annabelle asked.

"Because cops never lie," said Watson, unable to keep a straight face.

"You can do better than that, honey," she said, also laughing.

"Darlene was supposed to meet with a friend of mine. She missed the meeting. Nobody's heard from her in three days, and we're worried sick something may have happened to her."

Hookers are hard-boiled. They have to be. But Watson could see the emotion on Annabelle's face, and the tears beginning to form in the corners of her eyes.

"Darlene is my best friend and I've been worried sick about her. She stopped in here to see me on Sunday, but I was out. She left a note and I keep calling, but she's not home."

"You don't think she just left town for awhile?"

"She wouldn't go away without telling me." She raised her hand to her mouth, shook her head.

"I'll check the hospitals. Is Darlene Brantley her real name? Does she use any others?"

"That's her name."

Watson used his cell phone to begin the hospital search.

"Let's talk about her clients. Any problems? Anybody angry with her?"

"She's not in the life anymore," Annabelle said. She called to the bartender, "Daryl, come over here."

Daryl ambled three steps from one end of the bar to the other. He looked tense and wary. He must also have made Watson for a cop.

"This cop is going to help us find Darlene," Annabelle said. "Answer his questions. No bullshit, you hear?"

"Did you see her Sunday night?" Watson asked.

Daryl looked down, and Annabelle clarified his choices for him. "Answer the man, you motherfucker, or I'll rip off your dick and shove it down your throat."

"She was here," Daryl mumbled, still not looking at Watson.

"Did she work?" Annabelle asked. "And mind your manners. Look up when you talk."

"No," Daryl said. "She was waiting for you."

"Did she talk to anybody? Daryl, you tell me what happened. Don't make me drag it out of you."

"A guy came in and talked to her. I heard him say he got her name from somebody at that college she goes to."

"Did she go with him?" Watson asked.

"I think so," Daryl said.

Annabelle popped in. "That makes no sense. She was so proud of going to City College. She wouldn't tell anyone there about this."

"Maybe someone recognized her," Watson suggested.

"I guess it's possible," Annabelle said.

"What did he look like?" Watson asked Daryl.

"Light skinned. Maybe white, maybe Hispanic. Thin face. Dark hair. Tall guy, maybe six feet, maybe more."

A Good Conviction

Not bad Daryl, Watson thought. Turning to Annabelle, he asked, "What do you know about Darlene's friends at college?"

Annabelle rambled on about Darlene's college experience, and Watson got two names, Marilyn Jones and Henry Campbell.

The City College of the City University of New York, known as CUNY, was founded in 1847. It describes itself as the flagship institution of public education in America. The campus along Amsterdam Avenue, beginning at 135th Street and stretching several blocks north, serves over 10,000 students.

Watson went to the Registrar's office and got class schedules for Marilyn Jones and Henry Campbell, along with photographs of each. He found Marilyn first. She had noticed Darlene's absence from classes, but had no useful information.

Henry Campbell knew more. Watson found him coming out of a class in Wingate Hall on Convent Avenue. Campbell was nervous and began sweating as soon as Watson introduced himself and the purpose of his visit.

"Where can we get a cup of coffee?" Watson asked.

"The student lounge," Campbell answered, "but I really don't have time."

"Make time," said Watson. "I'll write you a note."

They found a small table away from the other students. Watson purchased two cups of coffee.

"Talk to me, Henry," Watson said.

"Is Darlene in trouble? Did she do something?"

"What do you know, Henry? I don't have time to waste."

Campbell took a napkin and wiped his wet face. Watson drummed the table. "There was another student," Campbell said. "He recognized her, said she was a whore. Said he fucked her about a year ago."

"Name?"

"Richard Smith."

"For real? Don't fuck with me."

"That's his name."

"Did you tell anyone what Smith told you?"

Campbell hesitated. "I told Charles Coburn."

"Anybody else?"

"No."

"I need to talk with Richard Smith and Charles Coburn right away. Where can I find them."

"They're both in the class I'm supposed to be in."

"Let's go."

They waited in the hallway until the class let out. As the students exited, Campbell nodded. "There's Smith," he said, indicating a short heavy-set guy with blond hair. Several seconds later, Campbell pointed at a tall, thin, dark-haired student. "That's Charles."

"Thanks. Don't tell anyone anything," Watson said, already on the move.

Coburn walked quickly. Watson followed. There were enough people on the street to keep Watson from being obvious.

Coburn headed north and west. Watson had to be more discrete as the crowds thinned out, and once he panicked when he thought he had lost him. He spotted him again just as Coburn entered a six story apartment building on West 141st Street. Watson called for backup and followed Coburn into what had once been a fine building. Now abandoned, it was home for drug addicts and low level dealers, and eyes stared from the darkness. Watson slipped on a missing step, losing his balance and almost falling. Patches of light came from broken windows and holes in the exterior walls. Watson's feet crunched on discarded needles, slipped in what he guessed was human waste.

He could hear Coburn above him on the dark steps. Watson drew his Smith & Wesson 38 caliber revolver and moved silently up the stairs. He heard a key turn, a door open, then close and lock. When he reached the floor, only one door showed light within. He pounded on it. "Police. Open up."

Darlene screamed, "He's got a gun," and Watson dropped down as two shots came through the door at chest height. Laying low, he kicked in the door and rolled into the room as another shot passed by, also high. He fired twice, and then it was quiet. Sirens screamed in the street outside.

"More help," said Watson, gently untying Darlene and covering her nakedness with a blanket just as the room filled with cops. EMTs followed shortly. Coburn was placed in the first stretcher and wheeled away. Darlene followed on a second stretcher.

"Darlene's at Harlem Hospital."

"What happened?" Reilly asked.

"She was kidnapped," Watson said. "She's scared and close to starved. She's been raped and badly beaten, but it doesn't seem to be life threatening."

"Who did this?"

"The guy's name is Charles Coburn. He's at Columbia Presbyterian. Two gunshot wounds."

"Any connection to the Blake case?"

"Don't know. He'll be interrogated after he comes out of surgery."

"Are you okay?"

"Took you long enough."

"Oh, Bob, I'm sorry. I'm so sorry."

"I'm fine. Three shots in my direction all missed. Darlene hollered and warned me."

"Can I see her?"

"I'll meet you at the hospital," Bob said. "Better yet, I'll pick you up. Twenty minutes."

"It's too far out of your way. I'll take the subway. Meet me at One twenty-five and Central Park West."

"Above One-ten it's called St. Nicholas. Call me when you get there."

Twenty-five minutes later, Reilly emerged from the subway into the mid-morning sun. Watson was waiting, and he had more news about Coburn.

"He may have done this before," Watson said as Reilly fastened her seat belt. "Same M.O. The last hooker he abducted wasn't so lucky."

"Thank God you found her."

Watson left his car in a No Parking zone beside the main door at Harlem Hospital, and they took the elevator to the eight floor. Watson showed his badge and they walked to Darlene's room. She was sitting up sipping orange juice.

"My hero," she gushed as soon as she saw Watson. Reilly rushed over and Darlene reached to hug her. Watson came over and kissed Darlene gently on the forehead.

"Are you all right?" Reilly asked.

"I think he was going to kill me," Darlene said. "You got there just in time."

"Tell us what happened," Watson said. "Everything you can remember."

"It was Sunday night. The guy came into the hotel asking for me."

Darlene took a sip of juice, and Reilly, looking closer, flinched at the bruises on her face.

"You know I'm not working anymore. I went to spend some time with Annabelle. But even when I was working, I never went out of the hotel with someone I didn't know, and I wasn't going with this guy either. He was very polite, and he seemed so forlorn. Said he wanted to take me to the Plaza. Imagine, the Plaza! All night, and brunch the next morning. I stepped outside with him, just to get a breath of fresh air, and to sort of let him down easy. As soon as we were away from Daryl, he shoved a gun against my side. There was a car parked on 38th Street, near the hotel. He shoved me in and hand-cuffed me."

"He had hand cuffs?" Watson exclaimed.

"He had it all worked out, like he had done it before," Darlene said. "He cuffed me to some kind of bolt in the car. He drove me to a place in Harlem. Or maybe it's Washington Heights. I'm not sure. He stuffed a slimy gag in my mouth and took me up the stairs, gun in my back. The building seemed to be abandoned, except for druggies lying on the floor. There was only one room that even had a door. He tied me to a bed and turned on a battery lamp. He ripped my clothes off and raped me."

Darlene's voice was flat as she described her ordeal. Watson knew how hard it must be for her to keep from breaking up. "Did he say anything to you?" he asked.

"He kept calling me a worthless whore, a blight on society. Deserved to die."

"Where did he go when he left the room?"

"I don't know. He put the gag in and left. IIe turned off the light and it was pitch black. I could hear people walking and talking, moaning, fighting. I could hear rats in the walls. I thought he locked the door, but I wasn't sure.

"Did he bring any food or water?" Reilly asked

"A bag of fries and a Big Mac. Two small bottles of water in four days. He beat me. I was sure he was going to kill me. The last time, when he came in the room, he looked scared. He said, 'They're looking for you.' Then I heard you at the door. How did you find me?"

Watson described how he had found Coburn and followed him. " I didn't think he spotted me, but I guess he did."

"I didn't know he was a student."

"I think his college days are over," Watson said.

Kerrigan's first question after Watson reported what had happened was whether it was related to the Blake case.

"I don't know," Watson said. "Maybe if Claiborne found out about the tape …"

"Why did you go in yourself? You know better."

"When he went into the building, I thought Darlene was in mortal danger. I think she was."

"All this before your shift even started," Kerrigan said, his eyes sparkling. "Remarkable."

Watson couldn't tell whether Kerrigan was jerking his chain or if he was upset. "The perp turns out to be someone we were looking for," Watson said. "Abducted and killed a woman three months ago."

"A hooker," Kerrigan said. Of course, Watson thought, he already knows everything I've just told him. Watson made a mental note never to underestimate Kerrigan again.

The phone rang and Kerrigan listened for a moment.

"Coburn died. They never got to talk to him."

THIRTY-FIVE

Detective Watson confirmed that Josh's new cellmate, Jason LaRue, had indeed been planted by Roger Claiborne to get information about Joshua Blake. He also learned Claiborne had followed the correct procedures for establishing a confidential informant. But then, before any further contact could be made, LaRue was suddenly transferred to Attica State Prison, near Buffalo at the other end of the state.

Darlene is subdued and tentative, and obviously upset.

"I had a very bad experience," she says, and my heart begins to pound.

"I was kidnapped and held for four days until Detective Watson rescued me."

"Oh my God," I say. "Are you all right?"

"Now I am."

She tells me what happened. I can't imagine how terrified she must have been, all alone, never knowing if help would ever come. It was even worse than prison.

"We should stop right now," I say. "I couldn't bear it if you got killed because of me. I'd rather finish my twenty years."

"Don't be silly," she says. "We don't think this has anything to do with your case,.

"But you're not sure?"

"No. We can't be sure. Bob shot the guy and he died before the police could question him."

"Bob killed him?"

"The other guy shot first."

"Was Bob ...?"

"No. He wasn't hit."

"This is so bad," I say. "It's a horror story with no end."

"There is an end," Darlene says, "the day you walk out of this prison. Nobody's backing off. Don't even think it. You are going to get out of here."

The direct appeal is rejected.

Reilly and Mullin make the trip to Ossining to show me the terse written decision ... *the jury's verdict was amply supported by the evidence ... the court's instructions were entirely proper ... the trial court judgment of conviction is unanimously upheld.*

Roger Claiborne has won again.

We have but one chance left, the CPL 440 motions based on new evidence discovered since the trial and the failure of ADA Claiborne to turn over evidence he had before or during the trial. But Mullin explains that since you get only one opportunity to submit each piece of new evidence, we don't dare file until we're sure we have enough to win.

Of course, there's no guarantee we'll ever get to that point, because every aspect of the re-investigation of my case has now hit a dead end.

I watch as ADA Claiborne is interviewed on the evening news. He is visibly triumphant as he explains how his victory at the trial level has been confirmed by the Appellate Division.

Mayor Gardino praises Claiborne and his boss, District Attorney Harold Markman. "We're all pleased with the appellate decision," the mayor says. "Joshua Blake is guilty and he should stay right where he is."

I think the mayor will get his wish. I have nothing to look forward to except an endless procession of ever more dangerous days with no hope. Get killed? Kill somebody? What does it matter? Watson, Reilly, Mullin, Darlene, Kerrigan, Tom Kaplan and the other guys, Mrs. O'Neil, Teri Scanlon. They all tried. As the years go by, maybe they'll occasionally think of me, but eventually, like the rest of the world outside of Sing Sing, they'll forget I ever existed.

Father Michael O'Hanahan was distracted by a voice from a television he could not see. A newscaster was saying "and so twenty-three year old Joshua Blake will remain at Sing Sing for at least nineteen more years. Blake was convicted of the May 2003 Central Park murder of Mrs. Sarah Cooke and today, his appeal of that conviction was denied by the Appellate Division. Assistant District Attorney Roger Claiborne, who prosecuted the matter originally, had the last word today."

The priest got close enough to see Claiborne's face set in a smug smile.

"This spurious appeal was always unfounded and should never have been brought," Claiborne said. "A jury found Joshua Blake guilty of the murder of Mrs. Sarah Cooke and he is being appropriately punished for his crime. Justice has prevailed."

Father O'Hanahan stood frozen to the spot, not moving a single muscle for the entire thirteen minutes it took for the New York TV1 news cycle to repeat itself. This time, he watched the entire clip.

Then he took out his gold pen and carefully printed Maureen Reilly's name in his little notebook.

"Tom, I have a problem. There's a case, a murder, perhaps you've heard of it. An elderly woman was robbed and killed in Central Park several years ago."

Tom was Monsignor Thomas Sheehan, a confidant of the Cardinal and thus a very important figure in the New York diocese, and very knowledgeable in church law from his years of study in Rome. They sat in Sheehan's elegant study, absorbing the rich smells of wood and leather, sharing a cup of hot tea on a rainy April afternoon. Sheehan was a handsome man, tall with gray hair, slim, well tailored, all that Father O'Hanahan was not. They were not social friends, but for years the monsignor had been the person to whom the younger priest took all of his difficult decisions.

"I don't remember the case," Sheehan said.

"Shortly after it happened," O'Hanahan continued, "a young boy came to me and told me he was the one who committed the crime, but someone else, an innocent person, had been arrested and charged."

"I see."

"The boy who was convicted appealed, but the appeal was denied. The denial was reported on the television last night. They showed a photograph of the boy who was convicted, and it's not the one who came to me."

Father O'Hanahan choked back his tears, and when he finally managed to speak, he blurted out, "The boy in Sing Sing is innocent."

"The one who came to see you, where is he now?" asked Monsignor Sheehan.

"I don't know."

"Have you tried to contact him?"

"I don't know his name. He ran away before I could ask. For a while, I was hoping he would come back, so I could convince him to go to the police. But I never saw him again, and I'm ashamed to say I forgot all about it."

Father O'Hanahan stopped. He buried his face in his hands. When he looked up, his face reflected his anguish. "When I read about the trial, I should have come forward then."

"Why didn't you?" Monsignor Sheehan asked.

"I had promised not to tell. He made me promise before he confessed."

A Good Conviction   337

There was a long silence, which Father O'Hanahan broke, "I was wrong not to help that innocent boy. I don't want him to stay in Sing Sing for another nineteen years."

The Monsignor took his time formulating his next question. He looked carefully at Father O'Hanahan, and finally asked, "Did the boy in church think he was under the seal of confession?"

"No. I asked if he wanted to confess, and he specifically refused to go into the confessional."

"Do you think he was telling the truth?"

"Yes."

"Do you want to break your promise?"

"I'm haunted by the thought of this innocent boy in prison."

"Do you want me to give you permission to break your promise?"

"I know you can't do that," Father O'Hanahan said softly.

"No, Michael, you must decide for yourself. But it is a matter of conscience for you, not a matter of sacrament. You didn't learn this information in the confessional, even though you made a promise not to reveal it. You must decide which is the greater good, to keep your word to the boy who committed the murder, or to help the one who is wrongfully imprisoned."

"Can you give me guidance?"

"I already have," replied the gentle voice. "Now you must pray. God will help you decide. I too will pray you make the right decision."

"Maureen, there's a priest on the line. He says it's important."

Reilly picked up the phone. "This is Maureen Reilly, Father. How can I help you?"

"I may be able to help you. It's about Joshua Blake. Can I see you?"

"Of course. Can you come to my office?"

"It would be better if you came here."

"What is this about, Father?" Maureen's heart was in her throat.

"I know your client is innocent."

"How ... ?"

"I'll explain when I see you." He gave Reilly directions.

It took Reilly an exasperating hour to clear her schedule, retrieve her car, and drive to the Holy Cross Catholic Church in Brooklyn. Forcing herself to be calm, she entered the imposing building. The priest was waiting for her in a pew near the rear of the church.

"I'm Maureen Reilly," she said.

"Father Michael O'Hanahan. Please sit."

Reilly thought it was unusual to meet with the priest in the open church rather than in his office.

"He sat where you're sitting now. He told me he had done a terrible thing. That it was unintended, an accident, that he was sorry."

"This was the murder of Mrs. Cooke?"

"Yes."

"When did he tell you this?"

"It was before the trial."

Reilly sat very still. She was furious. This priest had known Josh was innocent for almost a year and a half. He had remained silent while Josh went to trial. He said nothing when Josh was sentenced to life in prison. Reilly struggled to compose herself.

"You're angry with me," Father O'Hanahan said. "I don't blame you."

Reilly took a deep breath, and waited.

"I don't know his name."

Still Reilly waited, afraid to trust her voice.

"Is this helpful to you?"

"Last week would have been more helpful. Our appeal was denied."

"Yes, I saw the prosecutor on television. That's what prompted me to call. But now, you can appeal again. There's a new suspect. The police can find this other boy and arrest him."

"He was killed over a year ago," Reilly said quietly.

Father O'Hanahan was stunned. "He's dead?"

Reilly had no patience for the priest's belated feelings. She showed him Marone's photograph.

"He's the one," O'Hanahan said.

"His fingerprints were on the victim's pocketbook," Reilly said, "but we didn't know until after the trial. When we finally found out who he was, he was already dead."

Try as she might, and knowing the futility of it all, Reilly couldn't restrain herself.

"Father," she said, "why couldn't you have said something before?"

"I can't even think about telling Josh," Reilly said, calling

Watson from her cell phone as she drove back from Brooklyn. "All this time, he never said a word."

"But it's good, even now," Watson said. "He recognized Marone's picture?"

"Yes."

"Good. By the way, I had another thought. DNA."

"You tried that before," Reilly said. "Marone's clothes have been washed."

"Not his clothes. Hers. Her clothes haven't been touched." Watson said.

"His DNA on her?" Reilly asked.

"Nobody ever looked. It's worth a shot."

"But we don't have Marone's DNA," said Reilly.

"Let's see if we can get it."

Watson asked Detective Christine Parker to call Mrs. Marone to set up the meeting, and Reilly suggested bringing Father O'Hanahan. The four of them were seated in the Marone living room.

"This is the first time a priest has been in this house in many years," Mrs. Marone said.

Father O'Hanahan looked at the photograph on the side table.

"Did you know my Anthony?" Mrs. Marone asked.

"I met him once," the priest answered. Father O'Hanahan looked to Mrs. Marone, silently asking permission to proceed. She nodded and he said, "It's hard for me to tell you this."

"Please say it, Father."

"Anthony came to Holy Cross shortly after Joshua Blake was arrested. He told me someone else had been charged with a crime he had committed. It was an accident, he said. He hadn't meant to hurt the woman. I believe he was telling the truth and that he was truly contrite."

"Why ...?" Mrs. Marone asked.

"He didn't tell me why he did it," O'Hanahan said.

"But the lady died," whispered Mrs. Marone.

"And an innocent young man is in prison," the priest said.

Mrs. Marone buried her head in her hands. Father O'Hanahan took her hands and they sat quietly for several minutes.

"Why are you here again?" Mrs. Marone said to Watson when she regained control. "The detective said I could help. What can I do?"

340   Lewis M. Weinstein

Watson explained. "If we can prove Anthony was with Mrs. Cooke in the park, it will help Joshua Blake get a new trial. We need to find evidence of Mrs. Cooke on Anthony's clothes, or evidence of him on her clothes."

"Is this about DNA?" Mrs. Marone asked. "Anthony is gone. How will you find DNA?"

Watson asked gently, "Is his toothbrush still here?"

"You want his toothbrush?"

Father O'Hanahan interjected, "There's a chance it could help, Mrs. Marone."

Mrs. Marone nodded to the priest. "Follow me."

"Let the detectives look," O'Hanahan said.

Detectives Parker and Watson followed Mrs. Marone to the back of the house, while Reilly and O'Hanahan waited in the living room. Soon Mrs. Marone returned, and the three of them sat in silence.

Watson returned, and they looked up expectedly. He carried a plastic bag in which was a toothbrush, a hairbrush, and something else they could not identify. Reilly sighed. This was really grasping at straws.

Then Detective Parker walked into the room. She had nothing with her, but the look on her face brought them all to attention.

"What?" asked Reilly, not daring to hope.

"I found Anthony's jeans," said Parker, "and there's blood all over them." Parker explained she had pulled Marone's dresser away from the wall. "There was a supermarket bag taped to the back of the dresser, three more plastic bags, one inside the other, and the jeans."

Mrs. Marone crumpled into the sofa, shaking her head, sobbing quietly.

"I'm sorry," said Reilly.

THIRTY-SIX

Two sections of New York State Criminal Procedure Law apply to me, one dealing with what is called "newly discovered evidence" and the other with the failure of the prosecutor to turn over to the defense exculpatory information in his possession. These sections provide the opportunity to file the CPL 440 motions which are my last chance.

Newly discovered evidence is defined as evidence not known to the defense before or during the trial. It must be important enough that it would probably have resulted in a different verdict if known to the jurors, and it must also have been undiscoverable by what the law calls "due diligence" on the part of the defense. If the information was readily available, but the defense failed to look for it, it doesn't count as newly discovered evidence for the purpose of a CPL 440 motion.

There are other requirements. The new evidence must not be cumulative, and it must not merely impeach or contradict the trial evidence. Each of these terms are ambiguous – nuances I expected to learn in law school but have difficulty understanding now – and they will allow Judge Berman considerable flexibility of interpretation, which can be dangerous.

"Courts don't want to overturn any conviction," Mullin repeats, "so they'll look for any reason not to. The burden of proof, which was on the prosecutor at the trial, switches to the defense. In order to win our arguments we must prevail on every single point."

Thus instructed on the importance of every word, we read the motion together.

First is the new evidence implicating Anthony Marone as the person who attacked Mrs. Cooke - his fingerprints on her pocketbook, her blood on his jeans, the fact that Marone's Metro Card was used at the Columbus Circle station, and Marone's confession to Father O'Hanahan.

Anthony Marone's subsequent murder and his alleged criminal connections are also mentioned. This information might not be admissible in a trial, unless we can find a witness to link it to the Cooke murder, but it may be useful in convincing Judge Berman that Marone is a plausible alternate suspect.

Next is the alibi evidence which proves I couldn't have been the one who attacked Mrs. Cooke - Detective Mackey's report that Angel Martinez said I was with him at 8:00 pm, and the videotape which proves I was in my apartment before 8:30 pm. We hope we can get Mackey's testimony admitted this time. Of course it's a problem that Angel never had a chance to actually say it was me he was talking to.

"Any jury hearing this evidence would surely vote to acquit," I say.

"Remember you're only hearing one side," says Reilly.

"But it's the truth," I insist.

"We know," Mullin says, "but believe me, the prosecutor will argue differently. I'm not saying his arguments will prevail, but you can be sure he'll make our case seem less certain than it does when viewed unopposed. These motions, by the way, go to the original trial judge, Judge Berman, not to the Appellate court."

"Will she be upset that we criticized her in the direct appeal?" I ask.

"I think not," says Mullin. "CPL 440 motions don't criticize the trial judge at all. In fact, it says she was as much in the dark as the jury, unable to reach a just decision because they didn't have all the facts."

"If we can win on the newly discovered evidence alone, why even file the Brady motion?" I ask.

"A question Maureen and I have debated at length," says Mullin.

"Part of it is tactical leverage," says Reilly. "The DA hates it when anyone criticizes him or his office."

Mullin adds, "We think filing on *Brady* grounds will make it easier for Judge Berman to vacate the conviction and dismiss the indictment on the new evidence alone."

"So it's a threat?" I ask.

"I guess you could say that," Reilly says. "We don't care if we succeed on the *Brady* violations. All we care about is getting you out of prison."

"Not to punish Claiborne for what he did?" I ask.

"It's not going to happen. Don't even think about it," says Mullin. "Markman doesn't want to be embarrassed by any publicity about possible prosecutorial abuse, not with an election coming up in the fall."

"But won't Teri write about what Claiborne did?"

"Teri will write," says Reilly. "But if the court overturns based solely on newly discovered evidence and ignores *Brady*, any criticism of Markman's office will be considerably muted. You can't really fault the prosecutor if new evidence shows up."

"So the bastard will get away with it," I say.

"Probably," says Mullin.

"And other prosecutors who're weak and unprincipled like Claiborne will be further emboldened to do the same thing."

"Probably," Reilly concurs.

We read the second part of our motion.

It begins with a legal summary of the prosecutor's obligations to turn over evidence to the defense, established in 1963 by the United States Supreme Court, in the landmark decision known as *Brady v. Maryland*. It doesn't even matter if the failure is inadvertent. If the withheld evidence would likely have resulted in a different jury decision, the jury's verdict must be vacated.

We specifically argue that Claiborne knew about the additional fingerprints, knew Martinez provided an 8:00 pm alibi, knew about the videotape, and failed to provide any of this information to the defense.

"It's really powerful stuff," I say, when we had completed our read-through.

"Ready to go," says Mullin. "We can file tomorrow."

Reilly is unusually quiet. Several times, she starts to speak and holds her tongue. Finally, she says, "I want to take this to Markman and give him a chance to drop the charges and avoid the embarrassment."

"He won't do it," Mullin says. "What would he say?"

"He would figure it out," Reilly says to Mullin. "You keep telling me our goal is to get Josh out of prison, not to punish Claiborne, and you're right. There's no downside to waiting another day or two to file these motions."

"Before you leave," I say, "I want to say something. You guys are terrific. You're doing all this for me."

Reilly starts to say something, but I don't let her. "No, let me get this out. I've been thinking about it for a long time, and I want to say it. You both know I've wanted to be a lawyer for a long time. Then this happened, and I began to think, why would I ever want to be a part of something as corrupt as this? But now ... your efforts, your dedication ... and Detective Watson too ... I was wrong to hate the whole legal profession for what a few bad apples have done."

"Thank you, Josh," Mullin said. "I've felt from the beginning that the system failed you. But, maybe when we get to the end of this path, it will redeem itself."

"Well, if I ever get out of here, I still want to be a lawyer. That's something."

"Keep that dream in your mind," Reilly said. "We're finally getting closer to making it come true."

"It's always a pleasure to see one of my favorite former employees," DA Markman said, standing as Maureen came into his office.

"I hope you still feel so friendly when I leave," Reilly said.

Markman came around his desk and offered his hand. He indicated two easy chairs away from his desk.

"Is this about the Blake case?" Markman asked.

"We're ready to file our CPL 440 motions, but I wanted to talk with you first. There are some very serious *Brady* violations." Reilly handed the documents to Markman and waited patiently while he read.

"You think you can prove these allegations?"

"Yes, sir, I do," Reilly said, looking him straight in the eye. Markman gave no indication he was upset, but Reilly knew he had to be seething.

"Why are you here?" he asked.

"You have a really bad apple in your Office, Mr. Markman, and I know how that must pain you. I have the greatest respect for you, and also concern for the reputation of your Office."

Reilly knew she sounded pompous, but she just couldn't relax.

"Perhaps you'd prefer to deal with Roger Claiborne in your own manner rather than having his deplorable actions publicized as they will be if we file the *Brady* motion."

"What's your proposal?"

"We won't file *Brady* if you agree to drop the charges based on the newly discovered evidence."

"Drop the charges?" Markman asked. "Not just agree to a new trial, but drop the charges completely? Blake walks?"

"We would also request a complete expungement."

Markman smiled, but it wasn't a particularly friendly smile. "You expect me to reverse everything this Office has said in this case for the past two years?"

"Everything you've said has been wrong. If all the evidence had been known, you would never have charged Joshua Blake. He's completely innocent, and Roger Claiborne has violated the law and all sense of professional ethics to send him to prison. I'm asking you to do what's right."

For a brief second, Reilly thought Markman was actually going to do what she asked. But then the look on his face hardened. It would be excruciating to admit his Office had done what she was alleging, even privately to her. And there was always the chance Claiborne had convinced him their motions would fail.

"Just because you think it's right, Maureen, doesn't make it right," Markman said. "You have every right to take your shot, but this Office will oppose your motion, and I suspect in the end ... we will prevail."

"It's always a very unequal battle, sir," Reilly said, "but you're riding a very bad horse in this one. He won't make it to the finish line."

Markman rose. The meeting was over. Reilly felt something very sad had happened between her and a man she had respected. It would never be the same between them.

As she was leaving, Markman gave her back the envelope containing the motion documents. Both motions were filed that afternoon in the court of Judge Phyllis Berman.

"Mr. Claiborne, you gave me your assurance there would be no *Brady* motion, and yet here it is."

Whenever District Attorney Harold Markman addressed one of his staff as mister, this was a sign he was upset. He turned to Sam Monti, Chief of Trial Bureau 20 and Roger Claiborne's boss, to make clear he too was included in the circle of anger.

"Mr. Monti, what do you have to say?"

"We didn't think they would do it," Monti said. "There were no *Brady* violations. Roger gave them all the material."

"Some light, Roger?" Markman asked.

"They're simply not telling the truth," Claiborne answered. "As Sam said, all of the potentially exculpatory material was given to Larry Mullin before the trial."

"You think Maureen Reilly is lying?"

"The papers do not tell the truth. She may believe they do, but she's wrong."

"Did you know about the videotape taken from Blake's apartment? Were you the one who took it?

"No to both questions."

"There's also new evidence unrelated to your disclosures," Markman said. "The videotape, the bloody jeans."

"Yes, that is new ...," Claiborne said, and then he hesitated.

Here was a way out, Claiborne thought. Perhaps he should just agree that the uncontested new evidence was enough, and the weight of the evidence now pointed to Marone as the sole perpetrator. Marone was dead, there would be no trial, Blake would go free, and no allegations of prosecutorial wrongdoing would ever surface. If he just let it all go, right now, he would avoid all risk of being destroyed.

346   Lewis M. Weinstein

Of course he would no longer be a star. His status in the DA's Office would plummet even faster than it had risen. His uncertainty was amplified because he didn't know how much Markman knew. Was the old man laying a trap? He had to make a decision on the spot. All these thoughts went through his mind in a split second, but the deciding image as he finished his sentence was his memory of summer evenings in the Hamptons.

"It's new," Claiborne repeated. Then he added, "... but it's not exculpatory. Blake is still guilty."

"Explain," said Markman.

"Our case will present two perpetrators, Blake and Marone, committing the crimes together."

"It's a completely new theory," said Markman.

"We'll present it as a modification, within the scope of the original theory," Claiborne countered.

"That's a real stretch," Markman said, looking at Monti.

"It could be sellable," Monti said. "Berman won't want to overturn."

Markman nodded. The CPL 440 motions would be opposed. Joshua Blake would remain at Sing Sing.

THIRTY-SEVEN

Claiborne's response to our motions hits with the thundering impact of a sledgehammer. What had seemed so clear and unassailable to us had been turned completely around. When I read Claiborne's answer, all of my fragile optimism went slithering into renewed despair.

"First," Claiborne stated, "we can quickly dispose of the alleged *Brady* violations. This Office has more than fulfilled all of the disclosure obligations imposed by law. Every single piece of evidence which the defense so blithely accuses the People of withholding was in fact made available to the defense, as required, prior to commencement of the trial. Proof of such service is attached herewith. The People submit that defendant's motion as regards *Brady* material should be summarily denied."

"What is he talking about?" I scream at Mullin, panic in my voice. The look on Mullin's face frightens me to my very marrow. He glances quickly at Reilly, but she has nothing to say. This is his issue to address.

"On the day the jury was finally selected, the day before opening statements, I received three large cartons from the DA's Office. They came in sometime after 6:00 pm. The cover note said they had found another set of the discovery materials previously forwarded and, since they had no use for them, they were sending them to me."

Mullin's mouth continues to move but no words emerge. Finally, speaking in a voice choked with emotion, he says, "I was up all night re-working my opening statement and preparing for the first prosecution witnesses. I thumbed through the files quickly, but it didn't look like anything new. I never looked at them again, until yesterday."

I wait, dreading what Mullin's expression told me must come next. Reilly, avoiding both me and Mullin, stares at the table.

"When we received the People's response yesterday, I looked at those files again," Mullin says. "Both of the documents we claimed never to have received were in the package delivered that night - the complete fingerprint report and the complete Martinez interview. Josh, I'm so sorry."

Mullin drops his head into his hands and looks like he's about to cry. Reilly places her hand gently on his shoulder, and I stare at the stained walls around me, thinking how close I had come to never seeing, hearing or smelling the inside of Sing Sing prison.

"I looked at those files this morning," Reilly says. "The bastard was devilishly clever. The first page of the fingerprint report and the Martinez interview look exactly the same as the copies delivered earlier, but both documents include additional pages which were not part of the first transmittal. Larry had no way to know the documents were different."

"Except by reading them," I say quietly.

"Claiborne obviously intended to deceive the defense," Reilly says, letting my remark pass, "both in the timing of the delivery and in the manner the documents were presented. He was covering his ass just in case anybody later learned what he had previously withheld, which of course he never expected to happen."

I pound the table, one fist, then the other, slowly, gently almost, struggling to control my anger. The prosecutor had purposely screwed me, and now I learn my own attorney had let our best opportunity to stop him slip through his fingers.

"This last-minute production of documents is actually proof he purposely withheld them before," Reilly says, but her voice barely penetrates the walls of my gloom. "He won't get away with it."

"He did get away with it!" I scream. "Where do you think I've been for the past two years? And why would you think Judge Berman will come down on him now? He'll say it was an honest mistake, and she'll accept his explanation."

Reilly doesn't argue and Mullin can't. We all know how unlikely it is Claiborne will ever be held accountable for his unspeakable actions.

There's more bad news in the People's response.

Claiborne argued that even if all the known evidence had been presented at trial, there was no reason to believe the verdict would have been any different. "This is not an either/or proposition," he wrote. "The fact that Mr. Marone may have participated in the attack on Mrs. Cooke does not exculpate Mr. Blake.

"Based on the admittedly new evidence of the blood on Anthony Marone's jeans, it may well have been Mr. Marone who ran to the subway and dropped Mrs. Cooke's pocketbook in Brooklyn, but there is every reason to believe Mr. Blake was also part of the attack in Central Park, after which he may have walked quietly the other way, perhaps even spoken to Mr. Martinez as he alleges, and then gone to his apartment in Greenwich Village.

"Blake and Marone were in it together," Claiborne went on, "and each is equally guilty. The new evidence, far from exonerating the defendant, would rather lead an impartial jury to conclude that Blake and Marone were accomplices. Furthermore, the court is aware that the People are not required to prove which participant committed which acts. Both are equally guilty.

"Since there were no *Brady* violations," Claiborne concluded, "and since the evidence which is actually newly discovered does not exculpate Mr. Blake, the defendant has failed to establish any probability of a more favorable verdict. Thus there is no basis to vacate the judgment of conviction. The People believe this conclusion is so straightforward that the court can reach its determination on the papers submitted, without the necessity of holding a hearing on the matter."

"No hearing," I whisper. I'm totally deflated, and I think Mullin is too.

Reilly, however, is as feisty as ever. "He's got balls, and he's incredibly arrogant," she says, "and by suggesting no hearing is needed, he's inviting the court to take the easy path. But he won't get away with it. *Brady* material must be provided in a usable form, and the People cannot simply construct a new theory of the case and apply it to the old trial. This is not a problem for us."

I look up and shake my head, unable to make myself even hope Reilly might be correct. Claiborne has won. Overturning the People's "good conviction" is something the justice system has no predisposition to do. Admitting that Claiborne had violated disclosure rules to get a conviction would be hugely embarrassing, and judges do not like to embarrass District Attorneys, especially DAs as prestigious as Harold Markman.

Was there any conceivable likelihood Judge Berman would have the courage to go against the Manhattan DA, the NYPD top brass, and the Mayor of the City of New York, all of whom have publicly trumpeted my conviction as evidence of their own crime-fighting prowess? I'm certain we won't even get a hearing, let alone a new trial.

Fortunately, it's Reilly who undertakes to prepare our next broadside, and she never wavers, dragging me and a dispirited Mullin along in her considerable wake.

In a few sentences, she blows to smithereens the prosecutor's new theory of the case. The presence of both fingerprints on Mrs. Cooke's pocketbook, she writes, was a result of unrelated incidents. I helped Mrs. Cooke, and later, in a totally unconnected action, Anthony Marone killed her. The People have established absolutely no link between me and Marone.

"At trial, the People advanced a specific theory of the case," she writes, "and now they are stuck with the consequences of having argued that theory. Evidence at odds with the People's stated theory, or supporting an alternative theory, is sufficient grounds for overturning the judgment of conviction. We remind the court that new evidence need not fully exonerate defendants or completely discredit People's theory, but merely needs to support an alternative theory. Surely the newly discovered presence of Marone's role in this crime would have raised reasonable doubt in the minds of the jurors as to whether Joshua Blake was involved in this crime at all."

Fury and passion run through her words like a roaring fire. "The People's argument is patently ridiculous on its face and demonstrates a seriously misguided understanding of how our Constitution guarantees a fair trial. The People's efforts to change their theory in the face of new evidence, after the trial is over, is deceitful as well as impermissible. That the prosecutor even advances a new theory of the case is reason enough, all by itself, to grant a new trial."

Mullin writes a section dealing with whether our new evidence qualifies as newly discovered evidence. "It is unconscionable," he writes, "for an officer of the court, sworn to uphold justice, to provide critical evidence in such an underhanded, scurrilous manner."

To show the differences, Mullin prepares side-by-side exhibits of three versions of the Martinez and fingerprint reports, the reports originally provided to the defense, the reports provided to the defense at the last minute, and most devastating to the People's case, copies of the incomplete reports taken from the files of Manhattan North Homicide. This proves it couldn't have been Larry Mullin who altered those reports.

I think what Mullin and Reilly have written is powerful, and the depression I felt after reading Claiborne's submission is fully gone, despite Mullin's repeated admonitions that the future is still uncertain. Our response is submitted to Judge Berman one week after receiving Claiborne's bombshell.

Claiborne, fighting for his life, responds with equal fervor. The People, he argues, have no obligation to prove a pre-existing relationship between Blake and Marone. Marone's involvement in no way exonerates Blake. Again and again he pounds at Mullin's failure to use information he had in his possession. If Mullin needed testimony from Angel Martinez, he should have asked for a subpoena and demanded the police go find him. He should have asked Detective Mackey what Martinez said. Had he asked Detective Grabowsky the right questions, he would have learned about the third set of latent fingerprints. He should have learned about the videotape from his client and made his own analysis of it.

None of these assertions are untrue, and reading them gives me pause. On these issues, given what we assume is an underlying predilection to support the prosecutor, Judge Berman could well find fault with Mullin rather than blaming Claiborne.

Then Claiborne fires an even more insidious shot. "The People," he writes, "caution your honor that giving credence to false *Brady* claims may serve to undermine public confidence in the justice process and the Office of the Manhattan District Attorney, with dire consequences for the citizens of New York."

What a sleazy way to put the reputation of the prosecutor above the faithful administration of justice. Yet, as both Mullin and Reilly repeatedly remind me, it's essentially the same argument we use when we invite Judge Berman to vacate my conviction on newly discovered evidence alone, without addressing the *Brady* claims. We know we must give Judge Berman a way to set me free without forcing her to engage in open warfare with the Manhattan DA.

Reilly's response also defends Mullin. "The prosecutor's vicious attack," she writes, "is in part designed to discourage any defense attorney who would dare allege wrongdoing on the part of the prosecutor. The People tricked Attorney Mullin and now seek to blame the victim for being tricked, a preposterous argument given the facts of this case. These arguments lower the DA's office to a level of deceit that, if permitted to succeed, will spread a numbing chill over the entire criminal justice system."

Freedom beckons.

A white shrouded woman waves from just beyond an open set of wrought iron gates, also white. I struggle toward her, my feet slogging through a thick morass of heavy paper, continually fed by men in blue pin-striped suits, gold cufflinks, and red ties. Others try to sweep the paper away, to clear a path between me and the white gates. Their efforts are sincere and valiant, but they're unable to keep up with the flow.

Each step is harder than the one before. I slip, catch myself, fall. Floundering forward, I begin to crawl. The gate is closing. From either side, men dressed in gray prisoner uniforms slide into view. Several flourish shanks, others spit razor blades from their mouths. Behind them, prison guards watch, their faces void of expression. I'm approaching the gate. It's still open.

I strain to reach the lady's hand, now only inches away. A razor slashes my outstretched wrist. A shank is buried in my side. The men in the blue pin-striped suits laugh and throw more crumpled paper in my path.

My blood turns everything near me bright red. The gates of freedom are now closed. The shrouded lady cries from the other side, no longer visible, and I collapse, a dying figure sinking in a churning mass of paper.

As I do every morning, I wake with a start, my bed soaked with sweat, a vile taste in my mouth. I will myself to summon every fiber of my being for the strength to face another day in prison.

"The gods of crime and punishment have smiled upon us."

The note on Detective Watson's desk was unsigned, but as soon as he arrived at 7:30 am, he hurried to Kerrigan's office.

"What's up, Lieu?"

"Sonny Durante was arrested last night. The Feds picked him up in a drug bust in Brooklyn. This is doubly good, because a Brooklyn arrest won't automatically come to the attention of Roger Claiborne or anyone else in the Manhattan DA's Office."

"Can we talk to him?" Watson asked.

"I'll work on it," Kerrigan said. "They won't let us at him until they get everything they need, and they might resist even then, but I'll see what I can do. This may give us the opening to make the deal we need on Blake."

Oral arguments are anti-climactic after the fury of the written papers. Judge Berman asks Claiborne what he gave the defense and when. She asks Mullin what he asked for and when he received it. Her questions reveal little about how she might be leaning.

We have assembled to hear Judge Berman's decision. At 9:00 am sharp, she emerges from her chambers. I can barely breathe. Maureen Reilly and Larry Mullin sit on either side of me. Bob Watson, Teri Scanlon, Tom Kaplan, and Darlene Brantley are nearby in the spectator seats.

Judge Berman reads in a calm and unhurried voice, and it makes me even more nervous, if that's possible, when I can't pick up any clues to her intent. My anxiety must be affecting my hearing as well as my concentration, because I only get snatches of what she's saying. She reads an interminable list of affirmations, transcripts, motions, and memoranda of law. I almost faint when she says "defendant's claims were found to be without merit," until I realize she's referring to the direct appeal, which of course had been denied months before.

It is excruciating to listen to what I already know when all I care about is the decision. Finally, after what I'm later told was only ten minutes but seemed like ten years, Judge Berman pauses and clears her throat. She is ready to pronounce her decision. A look of deep gravity comes over her. Reilly takes my hand and Mullin, on the other side, places his hand on my arm. We are all at a peak of tension and anxiety.

For some unfathomable reason, at that moment I look at ADA Roger Claiborne. It makes me furious to see him totally composed and confident. But then I have the indescribable pleasure, as we learn Judge Berman's decision, of seeing Claiborne's face collapse in shocked dismay.

"The court concludes," the judge states, "there are questions of fact that require a hearing to resolve. This applies to both the newly discovered evidence and the *Brady* claims. Accordingly, the parties are directed to prepare their witnesses and evidence regarding both grounds."

"Yes!" I hear Darlene Brantley exclaim.

It's as if I've crawled out of a long dark tunnel, emerging suddenly into blinding light when, seconds before, only the scantest pale glimmer could be seen. There will be a hearing!

Tears roll down my cheeks. Reilly hugs me, and so does Mullin.

"The judge had more courage than I dared to hope," Mullin whispers.

"She must be really pissed at Claiborne," says Reilly.

Detective Watson shakes his fist in triumph, and behind him, I see the large figure of Lieutenant Kerrigan, smiling broadly. Teri Scanlon flashes a thumbs up.

Darlene stands behind the railing. Her smile is radiant. We stare at each other, throbbing energy passing between us. I long to hug her. This woman has become more important to me than anyone else I have ever known. Improbably, impossibly, against all common sense, I am in love.

THIRTY-EIGHT

Nobody has a greater sense of relief than Larry Mullin. He had been in terrible doldrums for three months, since learning about the evidence he had failed to see. We all told him it wasn't his fault, but he refused to be consoled until Judge Berman confirmed our opinion. The next time I see him, he's a different person, able to feed off Reilly's energy and generate more than a little heat of his own. He and Reilly are fully enmeshed in preparing for the upcoming hearing. Reilly, with no time to train, has decided to skip the 2005 New York City Marathon, deferring her acceptance to the following year.

We still don't know why Lieutenant Brian Kerrigan hates Claiborne, but he's clearly thrilled at the ADA's discomfort and new dilemmas. "I hope they cut off his balls," is the verbatim report from Watson.

Teri Scanlon writes a good story in the *Daily News*, but we're all disappointed by the other newspapers, which barely cover the story. There's no TV coverage at all.

Despite the exuberance of the Blake Team, we all know it's way too soon to celebrate. True, we have a hearing, but there's no guarantee Judge Berman will vacate my conviction, and even if she does, we might still have to face the uncertainties of a second trial. We expect Claiborne has more arrows in his quiver, and there's always the question of whether Judge Berman can sustain her courage in the face of the withering peer pressure about to engulf her. So the tension in my gut does not abate. In fact, getting a step closer may have made me even more anxious.

"Didn't expect to lose, did you Mr. Claiborne?" Harold Markman asked. The DA's question did not call for an answer and Claiborne waited for Markman to continue.

"What do you think, Sam," Markman asked, addressing Sam Monti. "Any chance the Office will prevail at the hearing?"

Claiborne jumped in, not giving Monti a chance to answer. "Of course we'll win," he said. "We have powerful arguments."

"You do?" said Markman, raising his eyebrows. "What else are you going to present beyond what has so far failed to keep Judge Berman from granting a hearing?"

When Claiborne didn't answer, the DA became more adamant. "We are not going to allow a *Brady* violation to besmirch this Office. If there's any chance of that outcome, I'll throw in the towel. Am I perfectly clear, Mr. Claiborne?"

"There weren't any *Brady* violations," Claiborne said.

"Have we had enough of this bullshit, Mr. Claiborne?" Markman had never spoken to Claiborne that way, and it terrified him. "Delivering papers the night before a trial is not the way we meet our *Brady* obligations in this Office. And what are you going to say about two versions of the same document? Do you really expect Judge Berman to believe it was just an accident?"

"Do you want to withdraw?" Claiborne asked, regretting he had not taken the opportunity earlier, when the price would have been so much less.

Markman's expression registered doubt, but only for a short moment.

"No," he said.

Then Markman abruptly dismissed Claiborne. "You can go now," he said, "and there'll be no need for us to meet again. Sam will keep me in the loop."

Dismissed and disgraced, Claiborne dragged himself back to his office. He plopped in his chair and stared out the window, ignoring the files piled before him. The phone did not ring. He sat undisturbed, except for his own thoughts, for at least fifteen minutes.

"May I see you, sir?"

It was Claiborne's secretary, speaking quietly from the door.

Claiborne nodded. Helen came in and closed the door. She stood before his desk, working her mouth and wringing her hands. Finally, she looked at Claiborne and began what was obviously a prepared speech. "I read the pleadings in the Blake hearing."

Helen O'Rourke had been a loyal assistant to Claiborne for eight years. Even before she spoke again, he knew their relationship had irrevocably changed.

"I want you to know I won't volunteer any information, but if I'm ever asked about it or called to testify, I will tell the truth." She looked down, then back at Claiborne. "Well, that's all I had to say. I thought you should know."

"Harold, what the fuck is going on with the Blake case?"

"And it's my pleasure to talk with you as well, Ray."

"What happened? Who was involved?" Mayor Gardino asked.

"I don't know all the details yet," DA Markman responded.

"Why am I skeptical?" Gardino said. "I need to know if I have a problem," he added, making clear his distinction between what was obviously Markman's problem and what might possibly be his. "You know, more times than not, the cover-up turns out to cause more trouble than the deed itself."

"You didn't need to remind me," Markman said.

"The Mayor wants to see you. Right now."

Police Commissioner Troncone arrived exactly seven minutes later.

"What do you know about the Blake case?" Gardino asked before Troncone was even seated.

"We were told by Markman's office it was a good conviction, and we put a little pressure on the Manhattan North Homicide Commander, a Lieutenant named Brian Kerrigan, to let it alone."

"But he didn't."

"No, he didn't. He asked for a little time, which, given who he is, we gave him, and what he soon learned is that it was anything but a good conviction. At a minimum, it seems the ADA failed to turn over evidence and sent a kid away who never killed anybody. At worst, it might have been purposeful."

"Markman says he doesn't know all the details yet."

"With respect, your honor, that's a crock," Troncone said.

"I wouldn't be surprised. Is anybody at NYPD culpable?"

"It's possible. The ADA couldn't have done it by himself. And there's been some overt resistance, not to Kerrigan but to a detective named Robert Watson."

"Tell me about Watson," the mayor said.

"One of our rising stars," the Commissioner said. "Started in patrol the Seventy-fifth Precinct in Brooklyn, worked undercover, got the gold badge a little ahead of schedule. Kerrigan was interested, but he had Watson sent to Central Park for awhile, which is where he caught the Blake case. Transferred to Homicide almost two years ago. Well thought of."

"What do you mean by resistance?" the mayor asked.

"Watson received several warnings, then somebody gave him quite a beating."

"You think this is connected to the Blake case?"

"One might think so, but no proof so far," the Commissioner said.

"What are you doing to find out?" Gardino asked.

"We're continuing to investigate. It's in Kerrigan's hands and he's been told he's free to go for it, let the chips fall where they may. If he gets proof of criminal behavior, we'll act."

"Good. Keep me informed."

A Good Conviction

"There's something else you should know," Troncone said.

Gardino looked up sharply. Anything prefaced like that was never good news.

"There's another suspect in the Blake case, name of Anthony Marone," the Commissioner said. "Marone is probably the one who actually attacked the woman in the park. He was murdered about a year and a half ago. We caught the shooter. Actually it was Detective Watson who caught the guy, with an open field tackle that was talked about for weeks. Anyway, the deceased Marone was a low level operative caught in the middle of a very high level war between two Italian families seeking control of drug distribution in northern Manhattan. The prosecution on Marone's murder is still being kept under wraps to protect an ongoing DEA investigation and possible significant arrests."

"So re-opening the Blake case will unleash a whole can of worms?" Gardino asked.

"It might, if the connection to the other case comes out," said Troncone.

Troncone smiled, prompting the mayor to ask, "What else?"

"Roger Claiborne was the ADA in both cases."

After Troncone had left, Gardino wondered if his Police Commissioner had told him the entire truth. Letting the chips fall where they may was not Troncone's style, never would be. He would control everything, if he could, and he wouldn't hesitate to crush Kerrigan or anyone else if he felt himself threatened.

Gardino moved from that troubling thought to a consideration of the political implications of a possible scandal. His next re-election campaign was two years away, an eternity in politics, but DA Markman's term was up next year. Markman could be hurt, but that wasn't the mayor's problem.

The police, however, were very much his problem. Cops and mayors are criticized when crime goes up. Neither the press nor the voters seem to get upset if somebody gets convicted who might've been innocent. Must have been guilty of something, they think, or he wouldn't have been arrested in the first place. It's a shame but true.

So maybe it's not such a big problem, the mayor thought, as he went on to other matters on his busy agenda.

On the way back to his office, Commissioner Troncone stopped to see his Chief of Staff, Inspector Ralph Burns. It was Burns he often turned to when he had something serious to discuss privately.

"You hear about the Blake case?" the Commissioner asked, parking himself on the arm of Burns' leather sofa.

"I heard," Burns said. "We got trouble?"

"I just spoke to Gardino. Seems like he's been talking to the DA. Hizzoner asked if the department was involved."

"What'd you tell him?" Burns asked.

"I told him 'maybe.' I also told him about Watson's beating. Figured he knew or would know soon anyway."

"Are you going to have Kerrigan back off?"

"Way too late for that," the Commissioner said. "But somebody helped Claiborne, and I want to know if it was anybody here."

"This case has a whole lot of spotlight potential," Burns said. "One of Blake's lawyers is Maureen Reilly, and the word is that Teri Scanlon from the *Daily News* is also involved."

"Scanlon?"

"She's written several stories about prosecutor abuse and now it seems like a crusade with her. The word is she pushed Claiborne pretty hard in an interview. She's also been seen with Reilly, which means she probably has a line to Watson."

Troncone looked up, questioning, so Burns added, "Watson is screwing Reilly."

The PC snorted. "We should have a departmental policy against cops fucking defense attorneys."

"Exactly which part of the Constitution do you think is violated by such acts?"

Troncone considered this for a moment. "Okay," he said, "we'll leave that one alone. But we need to know what happened, who did it, and whether the department has culpability."

"Maybe Kerrigan knows more than he's saying," Burns said. "Do you trust him?"

"Wrong question," the Commissioner said. "Does he trust me? Will he pass on everything he knows?"

"I would have asked it that way if I had more courage," said Burns, laughing.

"Detective Watson was beaten pretty bad?"

"It was apparently a very careful beating," Burns answered. "Painful enough to send a message, but no permanent damage."

"Do we know who did it ... who ordered it?"

"I don't," said Burns.

The Commissioner decided to leave it there, wondering if Inspector Burns was telling him everything he knew. How did you ever know in this business who really knew what and whose ass was being covered? He loved most aspects of running a huge paramilitary organization like the NYPD, but there were times he would have preferred the small town police department familiarity he had experienced three decades earlier. You knew everybody, and you could be pretty sure who was being straight with you. In the bureaucratic complex of the world's largest municipal police force, you could never be certain, and often you were most at risk when you thought you did know.

"One last question. What's DEA's take on this?" Troncone asked.

"They obviously don't want a public airing of Marone's connection to the family feud and their case. Otherwise, they don't care.

What began with a 7:30 am phone call from Mayor Gardino to District Attorney Markman ended at a 6:00 pm meeting between Lieutenant Brian Kerrigan and Detective Robert Watson. It was perhaps an NYPD record for moving down the chain of command.

Kerrigan recapitulated the sequence of events for Watson. After hearing from the Mayor, the PC had called the NYPD Chief of Detectives, who called the Manhattan North Borough Chief of Detectives, who called Captain Ignacio Munoz, the commander of the Manhattan North Major Crimes unit and Kerrigan's boss.

"The Captain requested my presence in his office forthwith," Kerrigan said with a wry smile. "He was clearly pissed."

Watson waited to learn if their efforts to free Joshua Blake were about to come crashing down. It just couldn't be! Not on the heels of the great triumph in Judge Berman's court. But maybe that was just the smoke and the real truth was still hidden.

"There is great concern in the department that this affair may result in a significant embarrassment," said Kerrigan.

"And well it should," said Watson, "if one of ours was complicit."

"Yes. Well, that's not the way they see it. There are careers, and pensions, and perhaps even criminal charges. Their first concern is to cover their own asses. There's also pressure from DEA not to blow their investigation."

"Does anybody care about Josh?" Watson asked.

"Actually, he wasn't mentioned."

"So where are we?" Watson asked, afraid to know.

"I used the same argument you used with me."

"Teri Scanlon?"

"Indeed. Better not to cover-up if she already knows. Keep it contained at a low level. Best for the bosses to take the high road and do what's right."

"And did it work?"

Lewis M. Weinstein

"Remains to be seen. These complex and troubling thoughts will percolate in the chain of command for the next several days. Eventually, the Commissioner will consider the spin with the DCPI. Then he'll talk to the mayor again." Kerrigan paused, and a malicious smile came over his face. "One good thing is nobody likes Claiborne."

"Including you," Watson ventured.

"Yes, including me. Nobody at NYPD will take a fall for that bastard," Kerrigan volunteered no more and Watson didn't ask.

"They're concerned you're the source for Scanlon," Kerrigan said. "I told Captain Munoz it was Reilly, plus what Scanlon learned on her own and by talking with Josh."

"Did the Captain believe you?" Watson asked.

"I doubt it. They know about you and Reilly."

"Who's going to read our stories when you go home?"

This is the first comment from my class when I tell them about Judge Berman's decision.

"Not so fast," I say. "It's only a hearing. After the hearing, maybe I'll get a new trial. If I get a trial, maybe I'll be found not guilty. So you're stuck with me for a while yet."

"What are your chances if you get to trial?" Hector asks, in the serious formal manner he sometimes adopts.

"My attorneys think we have a chance, but it's not certain. There's a witness named Angel Martinez, worked at a newsstand on Columbus Avenue. We can't find him, and we need his testimony."

Hector's eyes open wide. He asks, "Why is this Angel guy important?"

"The murder in Central Park took place at 8:00 pm on May 29, 2003. At that exact time, I was talking to Angel Martinez at his newsstand, and we both heard sirens heading to the park. Having him to corroborate my story might be enough to persuade the jury."

"That would do it for you?" Hector asks.

"I think it would."

"Since you're still here, Mr. Josh, can we discuss my story?" This from Jose Alioto, a relative newcomer to our class who has just written his first story and is very anxious for feedback. Everybody laughs and the class begins.

Kerrigan and Watson never learned what the police bosses would have decided, because a week or so after Judge Berman's decision to grant a hearing, Larry Mullin received a letter. The name in the return address was vaguely familiar, but he didn't place it until he read the letter. Then he called Margaret White and arranged a meeting in Maureen Reilly's office.

Margaret White was the jury foreman at my trial almost two years before.

"I read in the *Daily News* about new evidence in the Blake case," White explained to Mullin and Reilly. "I did a Google search and read all of Teri Scanlon's articles. It sounds like there's a lot we didn't know."

White listened attentively while Mullin and Reilly took turns describing the evidence that had come to light after the trial.

"Well, this surely does change things," White said when they concluded.

"There's more," Reilly said. "The ADA knew most of what we just told you. He knew before the trial, but he didn't tell Larry."

"I read that," White said, "but it was confusing to me. Is the prosecutor supposed to tell even when it would hurt his case."

"A prosecutor is required by law to tell the defense anything suggesting the innocence of the defendant. He's supposed to seek justice, not just convictions."

White considered for a long moment, then said, "I never did like that guy."

"There's a long list," Reilly said.

"What can I do to help," White asked.

The *affidavit* sent to Judge Berman a day later dramatically changed the public perception of the case. "Based on the evidence presented at trial," White's *affidavit* stated, "the jury believed Joshua Blake was guilty. But it now seems we did not know all the facts. Had I seen the evidence which is now available, I would have voted to acquit Mr. Blake."

Teri Scanlon wrote a great story about Margaret White's turnaround, but now she was not alone. The headline above the fold in the *New York Time*'s Metro Section read "Juror Changes Mind in Central Park Slaying." NBC's *Dateline* called for interviews.

And, most important, Captain Ignacio Munoz called Lieutenant Kerrigan.

"It's all yours, Brian," the Captain said. "Chips fall where they may."

"But not too high?"

"That would be good."

Sonny Durante was finally sucked dry of everything the Feds thought they could get, and the DEA gave Lieutenant Kerrigan and Detective Watson an hour.

It was a productive hour. With immunity, Durante stated that Anthony Marone had been sent to steal a pocketbook from an elderly woman in the park and had attacked the wrong woman by mistake. He had no comment on Marone's subsequent murder. Durante also said he never heard of Joshua Blake.

The Feds agreed Durante could testify privately before Judge Berman in the upcoming hearing, but they would not say he'd be available to testify at a public trial.

THIRTY-NINE

Now that the media is enamored with my case, we're suddenly providing legal theater for New Yorkers and indeed for the entire country. The press is out in force. *Dateline* has cameras on site. Court TV plans to record the entire hearing, stockpiling video in the event they later decide to televise the trial. All of this creates a circus atmosphere which will try Judge Berman's patience.

A hearing is like a trial, but different. The biggest difference is there's no jury. There are witnesses, and evidence is presented, but the rules are far more flexible. Since the defense has brought the motion to overturn a previous conviction, the normal trial roles are reversed, and the defense bears the burden of proving its case with the prosecution placed in the normal defense position. The judge can run the hearing pretty much any way she wants, allowing questions that might be considered inappropriate at trial, asking her own questions, and, most important, deciding that certain witnesses should testify.

So it comes to be that ADA Roger Claiborne finds himself uncomfortably seated in the witness chair. Claiborne objected strenuously, but Judge Berman is adamant and in the end, in the full glare of the New York media, he has no choice. His assistant in the second chair, a young woman named Deborah Dishler, acts as his attorney. Reilly does the interrogation, pacing back and forth like the lioness she is. As she is about to ask her first question, there's a brief flurry in the courtroom. Lieutenant Brian Kerrigan, in full dress uniform, takes a seat in the first row of the spectator section. Reilly smiles at Kerrigan and turns back to Claiborne like he was raw meat.

"Do you remember a conversation you had with Detective Robert Watson regarding the Blake case?" Reilly asks.

"I had many conversations with Detective Watson about this case," Claiborne responds, in the haughty patrician tone I hate so much.

"Perhaps this will refresh your memory," Reilly says, handing Claiborne a copy of Watson's *affidavit*. "You've seen this before?"

Claiborne reads the document, then looks up, stone-faced, furious, silent.

"Will your honor please ask the witness to respond," Reilly says.

"Answer the question, Mr. Claiborne," Judge Berman says.

"Yes," Claiborne says.

Reilly takes two steps closer to Claiborne. She is getting in his face. "The conversation I'm referring to took place in the first floor hallway of 100 Center Street, on Friday, June 6, 2003 at approximately 10:00 am. Would you please read the sections of Detective Watson's *affidavit* I've highlighted?"

Claiborne looks to Judge Berman, silently pleading, but she nods for him to proceed. He reads aloud Watson's statement that there were "holes in the Blake case." Then he stops, and all of us on the defense side know why.

"Please go on," Reilly says, and Judge Berman nods without being asked.

Claiborne's voice is barely audible as he reads Watson's words. "ADA Claiborne then said I should back off and not fuck up a good conviction." Court TV must have loved it.

"What exactly did you mean?" Reilly asks, as disingenuously as she can.

"I never said it," Claiborne says.

"You're calling Detective Watson a liar?"

"I never said those words."

Reilly smiles, but lets it go and moves on. She produces Mullin's side by side exhibits and shows them to Claiborne, pointing out the three versions of the reports prepared by Detective Mackey on his interview with Angel Martinez and Detective Grabowsky on the fingerprints found on Mrs. Cooke's pocketbook.

"How do you account for these differences?"

"I have no idea. Perhaps defense counsel altered the reports on the left."

"Yes, you would say that," Reilly sneers.

"Your honor." The third voice was startling. It's Deborah Dishler, and Judge Berman responds to her unspoken plea. "Counselor," she says, addressing Reilly, "please continue your questioning without editorial comment."

"Yes, your honor. Sorry," says Reilly, but I don't think she's sorry at all.

"So we're all clear, you're saying you sent the complete reports to defense counsel Mullin and he altered them?"

"I sent the complete reports. It's possible he altered them."

"That's quite an accusation. Do you have any proof?"

"Proof of what?"

"Proof you sent the full reports the first time, as required by law." Reilly's voice rises just slightly, but enough to ratchet the tension in the courtroom even higher. "Like maybe a transmittal sheet with copies attached, signed as received by attorney Mullin? Anything like that, Mr. Claiborne?"

"I'm sure it exists," says Claiborne, "but I don't have it here with me."

Reilly addresses Judge Berman. "Will your honor please direct the prosecutor to find and produce the documents he says must exist?"

"So directed," says the judge.

"Thank you, your honor," Reilly says. "Mr. Claiborne, you claim, in your papers and here today, that all of this evidence was in attorney Mullin's hands before the trial. Is that right?"

"Yes."

"So you knew it as well?"

Claiborne immediately sees the trap, but it's far too late to stop her. Since he doesn't immediately answer, Reilly repeats the question. Claiborne looks at Judge Berman, who seems a little exasperated as she again nods for him to answer. Finally, ADA Roger Claiborne whispers "Yes."

"Why didn't you investigate?" Reilly asks, as if this question has just occurred to her.

"Investigate what?" Claiborne answers, as if he didn't know.

"Investigate who really killed Mrs. Cooke."

"We knew who killed Mrs. Cooke."

"So you say," Reilly says, practically leaping at him. Claiborne recoils. "But you also knew, Mr. Claiborne, there was evidence Joshua Blake was with Angel Martinez at the time of the murder, evidence he was in his apartment in Greenwich Village when Mrs. Cooke's pocketbook was thrown into a trash receptacle in Brooklyn, evidence ..."

"Objection, you honor," says Ms. Dishler. "Counsel is making a speech."

"Is there a question?" Judge Berman asks.

"Almost there, your honor," says Reilly.

"Continue."

"We were going over what you knew, Mr. Claiborne, and I was about to say you knew there were more latent fingerprints on Mrs. Cooke's pocketbook. You did know about those fingerprints, didn't you?"

Claiborne is trapped. He can't possibly deny he knew precisely what he's insisting he had transmitted to Mullin. Again his "yes" is barely audible.

"And you knew about the report prepared by Detective Mackey?"

"Yes."

"And you also knew about Josh's videotape of the Yankee game?"

"Yes."

"So if you knew there was another suspect and also knew Joshua Blake had an alibi, why didn't you investigate the possibility it was the other suspect who attacked Mrs. Cooke?"

"At the time, we believed that Joshua Blake was the sole perpetrator."

Reilly almost jumps with joy at Claiborne's slip. "We," she says. Who is we? Who else did you discuss this with?"

"Other attorneys in the Office. You know how it works, counselor, you were an ADA."

"Yes, I was," Reilly says, "and I went to meetings where cases were discussed. Can you please tell the court which other attorneys were involved in the meetings where the Blake case was discussed?"

"Not without referring to records."

"Your honor?"

"So directed."

Judge Berman is leaning forward, an intense look on her face. Perhaps she's remembering how Claiborne misrepresented to her, in chambers during the earlier hearing, about Detective Mackey's possible testimony. Perhaps she's making sure she will not again be made the fool. I don't think Claiborne will get any breaks from Judge Berman.

"Now," says Reilly, unleashing her final thrust, "when you had these meetings, did everyone else at those meetings know Mr. Blake had an alibi and there were other fingerprints on Mrs. Cooke's pocketbook?"

"I'm sure they did," Claiborne answers. Reilly cannot suppress a triumphant smile.

"So when we learn who was at those meetings, and bring each one of them here to testify, they'll all say they knew about the exculpatory evidence?"

Claiborne doesn't answer, and Reilly doesn't push it. She knows Claiborne has just lied under oath. She also knows DA Markman will do virtually anything to avoid having Sam Monti and all the ADAs of Trial Bureau 20 come to court to testify. She has significantly ratcheted her leverage.

Nor is she done with ADA Claiborne. "Let me go on to the question of your investigative procedure in this case," she says. "For instance, did you personally question Angel Martinez?"

"No. I never met Mr. Martinez."

"I understand the third set of fingerprints did not initially produce a match. Is that correct?"

"Yes."

"How often did you request Detective Grabowsky to process the prints again, to see if a match had turned up?"

"I don't remember."

"Did you ask him even once?"

"I don't remember."

"You are aware, are you not, that ultimately there was a match?"

"Yes."

"The prints were identified as belonging to Anthony Marone?"

"Yes."

"When did you first learn about Mr. Marone?"

"I don't remember."

"The defense learned the additional latent fingerprints belonged to Mr. Marone in June 2004. Would it be fair to say you learned around that same time, or maybe before?"

"I don't remember."

"When you did learn about Mr. Marone, whenever that was, did you cause an investigation to be made, to see if perhaps he was the one who killed Mrs. Cooke?"

"No."

"Why not?"

"The trial was over. Mr. Blake was already in prison and Mr. Marone was dead. What was the point?"

Reilly shakes her head and walks away from the witness chair. She stops at the defense table, smiles at me, turns back to Claiborne.

"Justice, Mr. Claiborne," she says. "The point would have been justice. If you had investigated Mr. Marone, ..."

"Objection," Ms. Dishler shouts.

"Is there a question, counselor?" Judge Berman says.

Reilly walks across the room to stand behind me. She places her hands on my shoulders.

"Do you think, Mr. Claiborne," she says, "that maybe the reason you didn't pursue an investigation of Mr. Marone was because, if you had, it would have been perfectly obvious to everyone that Joshua Blake had nothing whatever to do with Mrs. Cooke's death?"

Dishler does not object, and Claiborne does not answer. Reilly doesn't expect or need an answer. It is a perfect moment, and Court TV has recorded it all.

"I have no further questions," Reilly says, and Judge Berman excuses the witness.

A few seconds later, the moment gets even more perfect, if there is such a thing. Claiborne rises slowly from the witness chair, ashen from the beating Reilly has administered. As he steps down, he glances toward the spectator section.

I have never seen such terror on a man's face. I follow his eyes, and there is Darlene Brantley, sitting next to Tom Kaplan and looking directly at Claiborne. She raises her hand and gives a little wave, and it occurs to me that Claiborne might drop dead on the spot.

The next day, in a private session of Judge Berman's court, with no spectators or press in the room, Sonny Durante tells what he knows about Anthony Marone, and also swears under oath I had nothing whatever to do with Marone or the attack on Mrs. Cooke. Nobody asks him about Marone's murder or what was in the pocketbook.

It's still not certain whether Durante will testify in open court, if we get to trial, but that is a matter for another day. Meanwhile, Judge Berman can decide if she believes him. If she does, this will surely increase the chances of having a second trial.

Teri Scanlon's article the next day is scathing.

Simple fairness
demands a new trial
By Teri Scanlon

Joshua Blake is in Sing Sing prison, convicted of the murder of Sarah Cooke, a tragic event that took place in Central Park in May of 2003. His attorneys have petitioned for a new trial and there is every reason to believe he deserves it.

A hearing this week made public for the first time

significant new information that was not available to the jurors who convicted Mr. Blake, including two alibis which, if true, would have made it impossible for Mr. Blake to have committed the crime. In addition, it was revealed that Mrs. Cooke's pocketbook contained the fingerprints of another man, who Assistant District Attorney Roger Claiborne now admits was probably the one who actually killed Mrs. Cooke, although Mr. Claiborne still insists that Mr. Blake was an equally guilty accomplice.

Lawrence Mullin and Maureen Reilly, Blake's attorneys, are seeking to have his conviction vacated. Mr. Claiborne, on behalf of Manhattan DA Harold Markman, is opposing their motion. When a legal reversal is sought in a murder case, the bar is properly set very high, which automatically favors the district attorney's position. Mr. Markman's office has expended considerable resources and energy in an effort to persuade the courts not to vacate the verdict.

It seems, however, that the new evidence is compelling, so persuasive that one of the jurors who convicted Mr. Blake has now come forward to state that if she had known the evidence now available, she would have voted to acquit. Of course this newly discovered evidence should be submitted to the give and take of a trial, with witnesses subjected to cross-examination under oath, but simple fairness suggests that there should be such a trial.

It's time for District Attorney Markman to concede that the questions raised over the guilt of Mr. Blake are too serious to be dismissed. He should drop his objections and give Mr. Blake his day in court.

Some days I feel totally confident. Maureen Reilly absolutely destroyed Roger Claiborne on the stand. Sonny Durante said I wasn't involved. Of course Judge Berman will overturn the conviction.

Then there are other days, when I'm perhaps more realistic. Judge Berman is part of the judicial system, normally an ally of the DA, perhaps even a personal friend. Will she have the courage to act against his interests?

I think about astronauts in space, knowing their craft has been damaged, not knowing if it can sustain the rigors of re-entry. Or miners stuck far below the earth, their air supply dwindling. Forced to deal with these enormous uncertainties, they probably believe they'll be saved, perhaps until the very moment they cease to breathe.

I still have my nightmare, almost every night.

The courtroom is packed with press and TV reporters, eager to hear Judge Berman's decision. Dateline is there, Court TV, Darlene of course, Tom Kaplan, Detective Watson, and again, Lieutenant Brian Kerrigan. I think I appreciate Kerrigan's interest as much as any. We would never have reached this point without his dogged and courageous struggles to convince the NYPD brass to do the right thing.

Early in her decision, Judge Berman rejects the prosecutor's argument that the defense has shown a lack of due diligence. "There is nothing on the record to indicate the defendant's failure to acquire the evidence before trial was unreasonable." She makes no reference to Claiborne's sneaky last-minute delivery of exculpatory material, as if it had never happened, and this is the first indication she has found a way to make decisions favorable to me while minimizing embarrassment for the DA's office. This is encouraging, but will the pattern continue? Or will the horrible word "however" precede a change in the judge's direction that will doom my life forever?

Judge Berman next expresses her conclusion that the evidence defense has presented is in fact "newly discovered" as defined by the law. This is crucial, especially since the law is ambiguous enough to leave considerable discretion to the judge. My head is buzzing, and I start to squirm. Reilly signals me to calm down and listen.

"The newly discovered evidence," Judge Berman says, "would have significantly eviscerated the scenario presented by the People while allowing the defense to present a viable alternate theory of the case. This evidence creates, in the court's view, a substantial probability that, had such evidence been received at trial, the verdict would have been more favorable to defendant."

All she has to do now was say the final words. I hold my breath. Please, I pray, don't say 'however.'

"Accordingly ...," the judge says, and my prayer is answered.

"Accordingly, defendant's motion to vacate the judgment of conviction is granted and the indictment is reinstated."

Granted! I remember how disconsolate I was when we read Claiborne's response to our motion, and how Reilly refused to give up, how she fought like a lion. Tears are pouring down my face as I turn to her and she hugs me. I have a new chance, a new trial. Reilly said we would win a new trial and I believe her. It's only a matter of time until I can leave Sing Sing and resume my life.

Around me, the courtroom is buzzing, ignoring Judge Berman's gavel. Reporters run. Cameras flash. The judge bangs her gavel repeatedly and eventually restores order. Claiborne sits ramrod stiff, his face expressionless. Only a slight twitch in his cheek betrays how hard he's working to control his emotions at this moment of defeat. Suffer, you bastard!

"Say nothing," Mullin tells me. Court has been adjourned, and the media are approaching. "Let Maureen handle the press."

"Will there be a second trial?" A microphone is thrust in Reilly's face.

"That's up to the prosecutor," she says. "We would hope the DA will realize Mr. Blake's innocence and drop the charges. That would be the right thing to do. But, if not, I have no doubt a new jury, knowing all of the facts, will find Mr. Blake not guilty."

"Did ADA Claiborne withhold evidence?"

"No comment."

"Why didn't Judge Berman rule on the alleged withholding of evidence?"

"It wasn't necessary. The new evidence itself was sufficient to vacate the conviction, so it didn't matter why that evidence wasn't available to the first jury."

Mention of the first jury turns everyone's eyes to Margaret White, standing shyly away from the camera lights. Reilly invites her to come forward.

"Were you pleased with the decision today?"

"I now believe Joshua Blake did not attack Mrs. Cooke," White says, "so I'm very pleased he'll be getting a new trial."

The reporters and TV cameras turn to me, but Reilly touches my arm and says I will have no comment. It isn't until then that I realize I'm not yet a free man. The uniformed court officers, although they haven't shackled or even held me, have never left my side, and I will soon be back inside a cell.

"Will you ask for bail so Mr. Blake can leave prison?"

"Yes," Reilly says. "Judge Berman has scheduled a bail hearing for Wednesday."

"Will the DA oppose bail?"

"You'll have to ask him."

"He's left the courtroom."

"He'll be back," Reilly says, finally allowing herself a triumphant smile.

With the indictment reinstated, the DA's Office has the choice of whether to bring a second trial or drop the charges. When we meet at the Tombs, we discuss whether the DA's Office will voluntarily drop the charges.

It will be Markman's decision, Reilly points out, and we try to see it from the DA's point of view. If he drops the charges, he can walk away with his Office's reputation reasonably well intact. Judge Berman has completely ignored the *Brady* charges, so any public criticism will be muted. Mullin in particular thinks this was Judge Berman's intent.

Reilly counters that prosecutors who've achieved a guilty verdict in court are not likely to admit they were wrong. She rattles off a string of examples where it seemed obvious a second trial was a pointless cruelty to impose on a wrongly convicted defendant, and an unnecessary expense for the State, but the prosecutor had gone ahead anyway, losing them all.

We're also forced to admit it's not certain we would win the case if it comes to trial again, and that the DA knows this as well as we do. Reilly reminds us we still don't have Angel Martinez, and it's possible Claiborne might find a jury more receptive to his Blake-Marone conspiracy theory than had been Judge Berman.

Claiborne would also surely challenge Father O'Hanahan's testimony on cross-examination, and no one could predict what kind of witness the priest might make under pressure.

I hadn't thought we could still lose. It seemed inconceivable in the euphoria of Judge Berman's decision, but you never know what will ultimately impact a jury, and Claiborne might pull it off. His risk, if Markman let him try the case, was the possibility of greater public humiliation, since the accusation he suppressed evidence would become more widely known.

On the other hand, Claiborne felt secure he would never be censured and punished. Prosecutors almost never suffer official consequences for their misdeeds, no matter how egregious. Wasn't this the essence of Scanlon's articles, the *Chicago Tribune* series, and a hundred other articles and opinion pieces?

Nobody is surprised when, later in the day, the DA's office issues a press release announcing they will bring the Blake case to a second trial.

"Joshua Blake has been incarcerated for over two years," Mullin argues. "There is now substantial evidence which proves he had nothing to do with Mrs. Cooke's death. We request reasonable bail be set so Mr. Blake can assist in preparing his defense from outside prison walls."

We're back in Judge Berman's court, and the media had returned with us. My case is now a continuing saga on a national scale. DA Markman and the Office of the Manhattan District Attorney are icons of the criminal justice system, and the press likes nothing so much as tarring an icon. Their swords are poised.

"Mr. Blake is more of a flight risk now than he was before, when your honor refused bail," Claiborne counters, his patrician manner in full flower.

"Not at all," responds Mullin. "Josh expects to be acquitted at the upcoming trial, and it's inconceivable he would do anything to jeopardize his one opportunity to clear his name and get on with the rest of his life."

Judge Berman seems deeply concerned, and more than a little conflicted. In the final analysis, as Reilly puts it, it seems she has done all she is going to do to antagonize DA Markman. She denies bail, but she sets a very rapid trial date. I have at least two more months to try to avoid being killed in the Sing Sing Correctional Facility.

But it will not be an uneventful two months. My twenty-third birthday arrives a week later, and with it, Darlene and Tom. Tom brings more drawings from Katie.

"My cell is Katie's personal gallery."

"Did you see the one of Eeyore?" Tom asks. I hadn't, but careful looking and generous interpretation reveals the donkey's sad image.

Tom and Darlene share a conspiratorial look.

"What are you two up to?" I ask, and for the next fifteen minutes, they describe their plan to take advantage of the favorable publicity we are finally receiving. If it works, it will surely increase the pressure on DA Markman, although it remains to be seen whether this will lead him to drop the charges, or make him dig his heels in even more.

No sooner have Tom and Darlene left than I'm collared by three of my students. My friends have arranged a birthday party. Looking at them, I think how inconceivable it was, two years ago, that I would ever know any of them. My last party of any kind was pizza around the table in Mom's house, all my old friends gathered for one last time. That is now ancient history, featuring someone who is no longer me.

Most of those at the party are my students. I've worked with each of them repeatedly, some on their reading, others, more advanced, on what we call creative writing. Some of the writing is outlandishly creative, and some of it is quite good. Hector Rodriquez stands out. I've known Hector since my early days on Rikers. When you critique someone's writing, you can sometimes get pretty close to what makes them tick. Hector is angry, but also resigned. There are forces in the world he doesn't understand and can't hope to defeat. He has come to understand, however, that he has to make his way with what he has. My goal has been to help him see among his assets an extraordinary gift of expression. At its best, his writing allows you to feel the pain of his frustration and the glory of his success, sometimes in the same sentence.

"How did you get this cake?" I ask, after it's been fully consumed in a matter of seconds and we're walking back to our cells.

"Jose's friend works in the kitchen," Hector says.

In the process of our collaboration, Hector has come to know a lot about me. He knows about my nightmare and how I'm terrified an inmate's shank or a correction officer's club might take my life just as I reach the very threshold of freedom.

"Any change in your case?" Hector asks.

"It's better," I say, "but you can never tell. Powerful forces don't want me to win."

"I know all about powerful forces," says Hector. "They been beating on me all my life."

"The problem is you can never predict what a jury will believe," I add. "Jurors tend to accept what they're told by the prosecutor and police. You're supposed to be innocent until proven guilty, but it's actually the other way around. If you've been arrested, jurors think you must be a bad guy. You have to prove you're not."

"Two and a half strikes when you come to the plate," Hector says.

"A guy named Anthony Marone is the one who actually attacked Mrs. Cooke. I think it'll be clear to the new jury, based on evidence the jury in my first trial never saw."

"So what's the problem?"

"The prosecutor is going to argue we were in it together."

"So you really need this Angel guy," Hector says.

"I'm surprised you remember. It's been a long time since we talked about him."

"I remember."

FORTY

The plan devised by Darlene and Tom is in full swing. Darlene has created a web site, which she calls www.setjoshfree.org. Tom makes the first posting, and immediately calls *Dateline*. A few days later, *Dateline* does a five minute segment featuring Margaret White, Larry Mullin and Maureen Reilly. Postings on the web site peak at more than a thousand per day.

Tom then organizes a candlelight march outside the walls of Sing Sing. Three hundred people solemnly chant "Set Josh free!" NBC News covers it live. Inside, watching on TV, I see Tom and Darlene at the head of the crowd. Right behind them are M.J., Steve and Sean.

The day after the candlelight march, Teri Scanlon is contacted by a major New York City publisher and offered a significant advance to write a book about the now famous "Blake Case".

"We could write it together." These are her first excited words when I pick up the phone.

"I'd be thrilled," I tell her.

"There's a problem, though," Teri says. "You can't get any money unless you're acquitted. You're not allowed to profit from your crime."

"Alleged crime."

"Yes, that one."

The time waiting for my trial passes surprisingly quickly. I thought it would be excruciating and interminable, but it isn't. My students take much of my time, and I'm pushing them hard.

Teri Scanlon is a regular visitor and we work diligently on our manuscript. She also writes a perceptive article, analyzing Judge Berman's decision. Why, she asks, did the court totally ignore ADA Claiborne's obvious *Brady* violations? She points out there has never been an admitted *Brady* violation in the entire history of the Manhattan DA's Office. Can it be there have actually been no violations, or have they just been ignored and buried? What does it mean, she asks, if a prosecutor knows he will never be held accountable if he himself violates the law?

"Do you ever think you're blowing in the wind?" I ask Teri one day.

"Perhaps," she answers, "but if enough of us blow hard enough, somebody might pay attention. Look at what Barry Scheck and

Peter Neufeld have done with DNA evidence. That whole line of inquiry didn't exist a few years ago, and now it's everywhere."

One night we have a special treat. Teri managed to get a copy of Court TV's video of Maureen Reilly's interrogation of ADA Roger Claiborne. All of my students gather to watch.

"Oh man, how nice it is to see that scum prosecutor suffer."

"The asshole really did hide evidence."

It is an indescribably delicious moment. We play the tape three times and nobody leaves the room.

Mullin and Reilly are scrambling furiously to prepare the case for trial. The defense witness list is of course substantially stronger than it had been in the first trial. New witnesses include Father O'Hanahan, Anthony Marone's mother, and Detective Christine Parker. Tipped off by one of Reilly's friends in the District Attorney's Office, they add Claiborne's secretary Helen O'Rourke. NYPD detectives Grabowsky and Banyon will offer vastly different testimony than they had before. They hope to get Mackey's testimony admitted this time, at least as to the altering of his report on the Martinez interview. Maybe Sonny Durante will testify, and maybe someone will believe him.

But still there's no Angel Martinez. "Without Angel," Reilly says to me when we meet in mid-February, "we're leaving an opening for jurors to make a leap. Claiborne will allege you and Marone were in cahoots, and we need to corroborate your alibi to prove you couldn't have been in the park. I'm not going to be comfortable without Martinez."

Watson is still searching for Martinez, circulating my letter throughout Washington Heights, Harlem and the Bronx, but so far, not a trace. Somebody really scared the shit out of him, or killed him.

At one of our meetings, Mullin says how unusual and wonderful it is to be working on the same side with Lieutenant Brian Kerrigan.

"Did I ever tell you the story of Kerrigan and Claiborne?" Reilly asks.

Mullin shrugs his hands to prompt her, and Reilly begins.

"According to Suzanne Dixon, it happened in 1989. Kerrigan had been on the force for fourteen years. He'd received his gold detective's badge and a promotion to sergeant, and was heading up a small team of detectives in the 19th Precinct on the Upper East Side of Manhattan. Claiborne had been in the Manhattan DA's Office about two years.

"It should have been a simple drug case involving a long term informant. A detective named Kevin Murphy, in Kerrigan's unit, was in charge. Murphy used an informant despite knowing the DA's Office thought he was unreliable. To get around the objections, he didn't properly register the informant as required by NYPD regulations. Claiborne, in one of the first cases he ever handled as a lead prosecutor, found out about it.

"Kerrigan told Claiborne he would handle it, disciplining Murphy informally, and it would never happen again, but Claiborne would have none of it. Kerrigan told Claiborne the informant would be at considerable risk if his identity was revealed. Claiborne didn't care. The short of it is Claiborne blew the cover on the informant, and the poor guy's body was found in a dumpster a few weeks later.

"Claiborne also made a stink about Murphy that led to him leaving the department with no pension. Murphy's wife was terminally ill at the time, and she died a year later. Kevin Murphy, now an old man, works as a security guard in a warehouse somewhere in the Bronx. Kerrigan still feels responsible for the guy, visits him on occasion. He's never forgiven Claiborne."

"If I was Claiborne, I would not want Brian Kerrigan for an enemy," Mullin says.

In the offices of the Manhattan District Attorney a few blocks away, Roger Claiborne was deep into the most crucial struggle of his life. If he failed to convince a second jury that Blake and Marone had committed the attack on Mrs. Cooke together, his brief place in the sun would be over forever.

Claiborne's boss Sam Monti monitored his progress regularly, but DA Harold Markman was unapproachable. "He's disgusted with you," Monti said.

Claiborne understood that losing this case would mean no more good cases leading to public recognition. He would not be officially punished, but he would be severely ostracized and eventually, he would probably have to leave the Office. Meanwhile, he had no allies. Deborah Dishler, assigned as second chair, was there only to report to Monti.

"How do you want to handle the Grabowsky testimony?" Dishler asked, and Claiborne had not been able to develop a coherent plan. Whatever leverage he had, Reilly had more.

The mention of Grabowsky led him to think about Darlene Brantley. He felt pretty certain the hooker had taped Grabowsky, and probably him too, another sword swinging over his head. Reilly had no scruples. Who knew how she would use the tape, if there was one. He shivered at the thought that people in the DA's Office, and even his family, might find out what he had done. Images of Darlene, naked and provocative, were replaced by his memory of her in court. That blond whore had the gall to wave at me!

Claiborne watched Mayor Gardino on TV. "We all thought that Blake was guilty. Now there's apparently new evidence, and we'll just have to wait and see what a new jury decides." There would be no more invitations to the mayor's box at Yankee Stadium.

With it all, Claiborne and Dishler proceeded with their only hope, the two perpetrator scenario. "A jury could find it credible," Dishler said after one long strategy session. It occurred to Claiborne she would like to add, "even if I don't."

But she was right. A jury could be led to believe the two-perp scenario. Both fingerprints were on the pocketbook, and Blake's story about Mrs. Cooke falling down was uncorroborated. As long as Angel Martinez stayed disappeared, he could still win this case.

Claiborne drove himself hard. He convinced himself that a second victory, this time against the odds, would actually enhance his reputation and career, and the spoils of victory would once again be his. He thought longingly of summer sunsets in the Hamptons, and this brought new energy to his preparations.

Claiborne interviewed Father Michael O'Hanahan and was excited to learn how easy it would be to destroy his testimony. He was sure he could get the priest to admit, after all this time, he didn't remember Marone's exact words, that maybe he and Blake were in it together, and that Marone was really feeling guilty because Blake had been caught and he hadn't.

"Claiborne knew!" Reilly screamed.

Detective Watson had joined Mullin and Reilly in Reilly's office, and had repeated what he had just learned from Lieutenant Kerrigan. Grabowsky had run the prints again, after he testified, but while Josh's trial was still ongoing. He had identified Marone and told Claiborne.

"Claiborne lied under oath," Mullin said. "You asked him why he didn't begin an investigation when he learned who the third fingerprints belonged to. Do you remember what he said?"

"Tell me," said Reilly, once again amazed at Mullin's nearly total recall.

"Claiborne said by the time he learned, the trial was over, Mr. Blake was already in prison and Mr. Marone was dead."

"But actually Josh was still on trial and Marone was still alive," said Watson.

"Exactly," said Reilly. "This is perjury, and we should charge him."

380   Lewis M. Weinstein

"The time will come," said Mullin.

Watson wasn't done. "Grabowsky told Claiborne one of Marone's fingerprints was partially on top of one of Josh's, although both could still be identified. So Claiborne knew Marone had touched the bag after Josh.

"An hour and a half later," said Reilly.

Mullin said. "At long last, Anthony Marone testifies from his grave."

"Kerrigan had more," Watson added, and when he was done speaking, Reilly added the name of Sonny Durante to her list of defense witnesses.

"Should we drop the charges?"

Sam Monti surprised himself with the question he had just asked DA Harold Markman. Markman had never admitted a *Brady* violation in his Office, but it now seemed incontrovertible to both of them that Claiborne had purposely withheld evidence in the Blake case.

"Go over this again for me, Sam," Markman said. The DA's face was contorted by anger, and also, Monti could not help observing, fear.

When Monti was through, Markman held his head in his hands and said, "That bastard should be fired."

Monti wanted to agree, but he knew that admitting Claiborne's blatant prosecutorial misconduct would injure the reputation of the entire Office, to say nothing of the impending re-election campaign of DA Harold Markman.

"Yes," he said. "But Claiborne could still win the case."

FORTY-ONE

Court TV is going to televise the trial, and the night before, they play the videotape of Maureen Reilly's devastating interrogation of ADA Roger Claiborne. Dateline runs another story, although none of the attorneys on either side will make new comments. The media thinks we can't lose. But the media is not the jury, and no one can ever predict what a jury will do. A desperate Roger Claiborne might still have a trick or two up his sleeve.

Claiborne doesn't look like a beaten man. It may have taken an enormous effort, but he's projecting the same arrogant, patrician air so evident at the first trial. His opening statement, of course, will present a very different case than he argued before, but the new jurors will be hearing it for the first time, so they won't know it's different.

The prosecutor goes first, and therefore has the first chance to set the way the jurors will think. Some court observers think many jurors actually make up their minds during opening arguments, before a single witness has testified.

"Mr. Claiborne, are you ready," Judge Berman says, and Claiborne gets right to the main thrust of his new case.

"Joshua Blake and Anthony Marone," he says, "collaborated in the attack which caused the death of Mrs. Sarah Cooke. Mr. Blake is on trial here today. Mr. Marone, unfortunately, has died. Otherwise, we would be prosecuting him as well.

"Both Marone and Blake had Mrs. Cooke's blood on their clothes. Both Marone's and Blake's fingerprints were found on Mrs. Cooke's pocketbook.

"We don't know which man actually pushed Mrs. Cooke to her death, but that doesn't matter. They committed the crime together and they are equally guilty."

He provides an overview of the State's intended witnesses and what the jury will learn from their testimony. Claiborne's opening statement takes an hour.

Maureen Reilly replaces Claiborne on center stage. She has a commanding presence that draws every eye in the courtroom. She manages to hide her anger, projecting a completely professional demeanor. Her only goal is to tell a compelling story in a straightforward manner that will be easy for jurors to understand and believe.

"The People are claiming Joshua Blake and Anthony Marone together planned and committed the attack on Mrs. Sarah Cooke that caused her death.

"But the People will not offer a single shred of evidence to prove these two men even knew each other, let alone were partners in crime. They won't offer such evidence because it doesn't exist. Joshua Blake never met or knew or even laid eyes on Anthony Marone.

"The People will also provide no evidence to tell you why they believe Joshua Blake would commit such a terrible crime. They will not offer such evidence because it doesn't exist. The simple truth is this - Joshua Blake had no conceivable motive to commit any crime.

"With these huge deficiencies, the People's case will fall on its own lack of merit.

"When it is our turn, however, the defense will tell you who Joshua Blake is, why he came to New York City, and how his life was totally blown apart by an unfortunate coincidence."

Reilly describes my life in Baltimore, graduation from college, anticipation of law school at NYU, and the events of the fateful week in May of 2003.

"Joshua Blake helped an elderly woman who had fallen in the street. He retrieved the pocketbook she had dropped.

"That's it. That was the only time Joshua Blake ever saw Mrs. Sarah Cooke. He went his way and she went hers.

"Unfortunately, Mrs. Cooke's path led to Anthony Marone and death.

"Joshua Blake was blocks away when Anthony Marone killed Mrs. Cooke in Central Park.

"Joshua Blake was miles away when Anthony Marone dumped Mrs. Cooke's pocketbook in a trash barrel in a Brooklyn subway station.

"Josh himself will describe for you every step he took that night, and when you hear his story you will find it totally credible, because it's a description of what actually happened.

"When you combine Josh's testimony with the evidence of Anthony Marone's guilt, you will know Joshua Blake is innocent.

"Joshua Blake was tried before on these same charges, and he was found guilty. Why then, should you find differently this time?

"First, you should know that the prior conviction was, after an extensive court hearing, overturned. That conviction no longer exists. You start from scratch.

"You will hear compelling evidence of Josh's innocence, none of which was presented to the first jury. It was the *absence* of this

A Good Conviction 383

evidence at Josh's first trial that led to his conviction. It was the *discovery* of this evidence that led Judge Berman to overturn that conviction. It will be the *presence* of that evidence at this trial that leads you to find Joshua Blake not guilty.

"Anthony Marone entered the subway station at Columbus Circle moments after Mrs. Cooke was attacked in Central Park a few blocks away.

"Anthony Marone's jeans were covered with Mrs. Cooke's blood, and this blood was observed by the subway attendant in Brooklyn where Mr. Marone exited the train he had entered in Manhattan.

"At the same time Anthony Marone was discarding Mrs. Cooke's pocketbook in Brooklyn, Joshua Blake was in his apartment in Greenwich Village, turning off his VCR.

"None of this was known to the first jury.

"You will learn, as the first jury did not, that Anthony Marone, after reading in the newspaper that Joshua Blake had been arrested for a crime which he himself had committed, took himself to the Holy Cross Catholic Church in Brooklyn, where his mother had often taken him when he was a child.

"Mr. Marone sat alone with his thoughts in a pew in that church until he was approached by Father Michael O'Hanahan. Then he poured his heart out.

"'That kid didn't do it,' Marone told Father O'Hanahan. 'It was me,' he said. It was Anthony Marone. Not Joshua Blake.

"Father O'Hanahan's testimony was not known to the first jury.

"Why did Anthony Marone attack Mrs. Cooke, a woman he had never met and a woman, it turns out, he had no desire to hurt?

"You will learn from an ongoing police investigation that Anthony Marone made a fatal mistake that night. He had been sent to Central Park for a criminal purpose that had nothing to do with Mrs. Cooke or with Joshua Blake.

"But he attacked the wrong woman.

"None of this was known to the first jury.

"Joshua Blake did not know Anthony Marone ... the only thing that links the two men is they both met Mrs. Sarah Cooke on the night of May 29, 2003.

"Joshua Blake was a Good Samaritan. He helped Mrs. Cooke when she fell in the street.

"An hour and a half later, in Central Park, Anthony Marone killed her."

Reilly walks to the defense table and stands as close to me as she can get. As we had planned, I look each juror directly in the eyes.

"Joshua Blake has been behind bars for a total of two years, ten months, and eighteen days ... for a crime he certainly did not commit.

"Imagine how horrible it must be to be incarcerated for a crime you did not commit.

"When you have heard all the evidence, you will not send Joshua Blake back to Sing Sing for a single additional minute.

"You will find Joshua Blake not guilty, and you will set him free."

"Claiborne says new evidence does not exonerate Blake." That's the headline in the *New York Times*. The ensuing article carefully explains the ADA's new theory of the case, and when I read it in my cell at the Tombs, it terrifies me. Could it be, after everything we now know, and all the new evidence which will be presented to the jury, they might still find me guilty?

The *Times*, apparently, still believes it's possible.

"I read the paper this morning, so I call you."

"Who is this?" Detective Watson asked. He had received the call at his desk at Manhattan North Homicide, where he had stopped prior to going downtown for the second day of the trial.

"You lookin' for me, and now I'm here, you don't know who I am?"

"Is this Angel?" Watson gasped, remembering the earlier call, which he was sure was *not* Angel.

"I'm Angel."

"Where are you?"

"That doesn't matter. I come to you."

"Not here," Watson said. "Meet me at 100 Centre Street, in the court building, by the newsstand. You can get there?"

"I meet you in forty-five minutes."

Watson left a note for Kerrigan and was in his car and on the phone to Reilly, all within seconds.

"Why now?" Reilly asked.

"He said he read the paper. Call Larry."

Watson, Reilly and Mullin waited impatiently near the newsstand at 100 Center Street, but there was no Angel. Was this another false alarm? Had he changed his mind? Then, a slight elderly Hispanic man, wearing an old but well pressed suit, approached them.

"My name is Angel Martinez," the man said very formally. "Are you Detective Robert Watson?"

"Yes. This is Larry Mullin and Maureen Reilly. They're Joshua Blake's attorneys."

The four of them retreated to a small conference room Mullin had arranged. Watson brought coffee and doughnuts.

Angel, not waiting for anybody to ask a question, said, "My cousin Hector Rodriquez say I must come here today. He say if I let Joshua Blake, who don't murder nobody, stay in prison, maybe die in prison, he do terrible things to me."

"Hector is one of Josh's students at Sing Sing," said Reilly.

"They were at Rikers together too," said Mullin.

"That's right," said Angel. "Hector say Josh teaches him. And respects him."

Watson, Reilly and Mullin all contemplated just how close they finally were to the end of the incredible trail that started with Josh's letter to Watson so long ago. Watson saw Reilly, tough combative Reilly, with tears welling in her eyes. He thought how, once again, against all reasonable expectations, it was Joshua Blake himself who had provided the impetus to their efforts.

"So what do you want?" Angel asked, breaking the silence.

They talked for ten minutes, and then Reilly said, "Larry, let's go see Mr. Markman. Bob, will you get Mr. Martinez some breakfast?"

"Is Mr. Markman in?" Reilly asked.

"Do you have an appointment?"

"Please, just tell him it's Maureen Reilly and Larry Mullin. It's very important."

The receptionist, whose job it was to keep unscheduled people away from the District Attorney, left with a skeptical look, but returned quickly to invite them into Markman's office.

"Well, Maureen, here we are again," Markman said, smiling. "Nice to meet you, Mr. Mullin."

Without waiting to be seated, Reilly said, "We have Angel Martinez."

"And he has something interesting to say?" Markman said, motioning them to his mahogany conference table.

"Yes, sir, he does," said Reilly. "He corroborates Josh's statement about where he was at 8:00 pm on the night of the attack on Mrs. Cooke. He remembers they were together when sirens passed on the way to Central Park."

"That will help your case," said Markman, a strangely bemused expression on his face. "But I know you well enough, Maureen, to guess you have something else you want me to know."

"It's very hard to put anything over on you," Reilly said, instantly regretting her choice of words, since it was obvious Roger Claiborne had done exactly that.

"It can be done," Markman admitted. "Not often though. So what is it?"

"You know Angel Martinez was not available to testify at the first trial. It turns out he had left New York and was living in the Dominican Republic."

Reilly paused, reluctant even then to tell Markman what he had to know, but there was no choice. "He was chased," she said. "Someone threatened to have U.S. Immigration deport him and his entire family. But if he did leave New York immediately, his family could stay."

Again she stopped, but Markman motioned for her to continue. He had to know what was coming.

"It was Claiborne who threatened him. Angel described him perfectly. Claiborne came to Angel's newsstand shortly after he read Detective Mackey's report, the complete report I might add. By the time Larry Mullin tried to talk to him, he was gone."

Markman looked appalled. "You believe you can prove the *Brady* charges?" he asked.

"I do, sir," Reilly said, as softly as she could.

"And now this," Markman said, more to himself than to her. "You know, I've studied your case pretty carefully. The priest would make a good witness."

Reilly picked up the "would" and it terrified her. They were so close. What further disaster could possibly happen now?

"You know it would be embarrassing for the Church if he testified."

"It wasn't a confession," Reilly said.

"I know, I know. But the Cardinal would be embarrassed anyway."

The Cardinal, Reilly thought, it's gone that high.

"So it might be best if Father O'Hanahan was not put in a position where he could incur the wrath of his superiors," Markman said. Reilly couldn't believe her ears. Markman was going to allow the Cardinal to make one of their key witnesses disappear.

"Well, thank you very much, Maureen, Mr. Mullin." Markman stood, dismissing them. "I believe you need to get to court now," he said with a rather wan smile. "Mustn't keep Judge Berman waiting."

A Good Conviction   387

I watch Mullin and Reilly troop into Judge Berman's court and be soundly chastised by the judge for being five minutes late. They look disheartened and confused. Then Judge Berman gets a message and returns to her chambers. Soon after, someone comes into the courtroom and whispers to Roger Claiborne, and he leaves as well.

With the break in the proceedings, Reilly explains what had happened in Markman's office, and how they had no idea what would happen next. Angel Martinez is here? Hector Rodriquez is his cousin? I look around for Angel, but he's not in the courtroom. I don't think I would recognize him anyway. It's been almost three years.

We wait for almost two hours, while Reilly and Mullin dodge questions from the press. Suddenly, there's a flurry at the back of the courtroom, and we're startled to see District Attorney Harold Markman stride into the room and take a seat at the prosecution table. Second chair Deborah Dishler joins him. Roger Claiborne is nowhere to be seen.

A minute or so later, the court clerk announces Judge Berman. The courtroom is now filled well beyond its legal capacity. The judge takes her seat and bangs her gavel. Court is in session.

"Attorneys approach," the judge says, and the four attorneys rise to her bidding. They stand before her bench and listen as she speaks. None of the attorneys says a word. No one else in the silent courtroom can hear.

The attorneys return to their seats. I have no chance to ask what's going on before Judge Berman announces, "For the record, District Attorney Harold Markman has replaced Assistant District Attorney Roger Claiborne as attorney of record in this case. Mr. Markman, you wish to address the court in the matter of *People v. Blake*?"

"Yes, your honor, thank you," Markman says, and he advances slowly to the well below the judge's bench. He speaks in the dignified tone New Yorkers have come to know so well. "This case has been ongoing for over two years and the defendant has been incarcerated all that time. This second trial was granted on the basis of newly discovered evidence, correctly assessed by your honor as meeting the high standards of New York's Criminal Procedure Law. Today, my office received even more new evidence, which has not yet been presented to this court."

Markman turns to face me. "Mr. Blake, you have been through hell. Unjustified hell. Based on what our office now knows, you should never have been convicted. In fact, you should never have been charged. I apologize to you, and I hope the day will come, perhaps when your justified anger has subsided, when you will be able to accept my apology. It is heartfelt, I assure you."

Turning back to face Judge Berman, Markman continues, "The People herewith drop all charges against Joshua Blake in the matter of the murder of Mrs. Sarah Cooke. We will not prosecute this case any further."

Judge Berman's gavel rings the erupting courtroom to silence. "Will the defendant please rise," she says. Reilly and Mullin stand with me.

The judge waits for Markman to take his seat, then says, "All charges against the defendant Joshua Blake having been dropped, this case is dismissed."

She looks at me and smiles. "Mr. Blake, you are free to go."

EPILOGUE

We all went to Reilly's office, and the afternoon was a blizzard of press interviews and TV tapings. Dateline called to schedule a segment, and the Today Show wanted us for the following morning. The Abrams Report taped an interview.

"Larry and I agreed long ago to take you to dinner at a little bistro," Reilly said as the afternoon waned, "but there's way too many of us. Besides, you should pick. Where would you like to go?"

"John's Pizza," I said without any hesitation, and soon we were off. When we got there, however, we found the restaurant was no longer there. Watson, who knew the neighborhood well from his college days at nearby John Jay College, suggested the City Grill, a few blocks north on Columbus. He found the owner, Danny Hickey, who promptly offered us a private side room.

Everyone was there: Maureen Reilly and Larry Mullin, Bob Watson of course. Lieutenant Brian Kerrigan. Tom Kaplan and Barb arrived with Katie, who squealed and gave me the best hug ever. With them were M.J., Steve, and Sean. Boy was it great to see them again, and actually be able to talk with them.

Kim Scott, the runner who remembered the "other woman," sat quietly in a corner with her friend Suzanne Dixon. Reilly introduced me to Suzanne, and to Joan Peterson and Elyse Letterman, also from the DA's office. Darlene re-acquainted me with her friend Annabelle. The jury foreman from my first trial, Margaret White, came up to me and gave me a hug.

Angel Martinez, who I truthfully didn't recognize, sat quietly, looking with uncertain eyes at detectives Watson and Kerrigan, despite assurances that Claiborne had frightened him with nonsense and neither he nor his family was in any danger of being deported. Teri Scanlon found Angel and I saw her taking notes.

"I'm Father Michael O'Hanahan," the priest said. "I'm sorry, Josh. I waited so long."

"Father, you did the right thing," I said, and I meant it. "The prosecutor is to blame, not you. Thank you for coming forward when you did. You made a huge difference."

It was time to sit down to dinner.

Darlene Brantley had been standing near me all this time, but we had barely spoken. I wondered if she was afraid, now that I was free, that our relationship might no longer have the same meaning. I took her hand and led her to the seat next to mine. We continued to hold hands throughout the entire meal.

"

Josh, you can stay at my place tonight," Watson said when dinner was over. "You can stay until you get yourself settled."

"I really appreciate your offer, Bob," I said, "but I already have a place to go."

Annabelle, standing nearby, heard what I said and came close to whisper in Darlene's ear, loud enough for me to hear.

"Congratulations, honey. You've been wantin' to fuck that boy for almost two years now."

Reilly and Mullin filed charges against Roger Claiborne with the disciplinary board of the Appellate Division, as did Judge Berman, but it'll be years before those accusations are resolved.

DA Harold Markman, however, acted much more quickly. The day after the trial ended, Claiborne took an extended unpaid leave, and no one thought he would ever return to the DA's Office.

A few days later, Reilly and I had a conversation about the DA.

"I really appreciate what Mr. Markman said in court," I said.

"I used to think a lot of Mr. Markman myself," Reilly said.

We walked another few steps before Maureen stopped suddenly, her face dark with distress.

"You know," she said, "Markman colluded with the Cardinal so Father O'Hanahan wouldn't testify."

I nodded. "Larry told me."

Maureen looked away, upset at her thoughts.

"There's no way Markman would have caved," she said, "if Angel hadn't shown up. Markman still thought Claiborne could win, and he might have been right. Without Father O'Hanahan, and without Angel, it would've been a toss up."

She paused and the last words were barely audible.

"Markman didn't really care about Claiborne's abuses and lies. And he didn't care about you."

"But his apology..."

"A coldly cynical political calculation," Maureen said, "offered only after he had no better choice."

Further evidence of Markman's political acumen came soon after. Reilly called one morning, obviously excited.

"Two things, Josh," she said. "First, the DA's Office called. They expect us to file a lawsuit for damages, and they want us to know they'll be willing to negotiate once we do."

We had discussed the possibility of seeking compensation, but both Reilly and Mullin had emphasized how much it would cost to litigate, how long it would take, and the very real likelihood of getting nothing. This sounded a whole lot better than nothing.

"You said two things?" I asked.

"Can you come with me this afternoon?" Reilly asked. "There's someone I'd like you to meet."

"Sure. Who is it?"

"Meet me at Washington Square at 1:30?"

Reilly could scarcely contain her smile when she joined me under the arch and led me across the park to the administrative offices of NYU Law School.

"You're a little late for class, Josh," Dean David Rogers said when we entered his office. "But one of our favorite alumna has explained that you've been otherwise engaged."

We all laughed and I still wondered what was up.

"Are you still interested in law school?" Dean Rogers asked.

"I sure am. I'm going to submit an application for the fall semester."

"I don't think that will be necessary. You were admitted before. We'll just call it a deferred admission."

"Thank you, Dean."

"And Josh, there will also be a full scholarship. Tuition, books, room, board, the whole works. We'll be proud to have you."

Without a pause, the dean turned to Reilly. "Have you started the paperwork yet on Josh's expungement?"

When we left Dean Roger's office, Reilly showed me her ring. She and Bob Watson had become engaged the night before. "We're having a party this weekend. I can't wait until my Nana meets Bob's father. I think they'll have a lot to talk about. Will you and Darlene come?"

"Of course we'll be there. How are things at Manhattan North?" I asked as soon as I had congratulated her.

"They seem okay," Reilly said. "Bob says Kerrigan is headed for greater things, maybe Munoz' job as Manhattan North Head of Major Crimes, when Munoz retires next year.

"How is Bob?"

"He's getting the mysteries, and he couldn't be happier, although he's still upset with the unanswered questions. Who gave him that awful beating? Who broke into my office? Who was helping Claiborne? Did Roger Claiborne have anything to do with Charles Coburn and Darlene? There's a lot we never learned."

"He'll get the answers some day," I said.

"Maybe," Reilly said, "or maybe he'll just move on to other things."

"I'm going to Sing Sing on Monday," I said.

Reilly blanched. "I guess I'm not surprised," she said. "Going to see Hector?"

Darlene and I took the train together to Ossining, but she chose not to enter the prison. I have to admit I felt a chill when I passed through the gates and heard those awful clangs again. I knew exactly where to sit when I got to the visitor's room, but it was very strange to be on the other side of the table.

When Hector came in, he saw me, but he didn't come over.

He stood rigid for a moment, and then started to clap, one slow clap after another breaking the silence. Slowly, one after another of the inmates joined in, until a crescendo of rhythmic clapping filled the room. I looked slowly around me. The room was filled with my students, every one of them.

I looked at the COs, wondering how long they would allow this obvious breach of regulations to continue. As my head pivoted around the room, I was amazed to see each one of the COs also standing, each one slowly clapping.

I couldn't help myself and I cried like a baby.

Finally, the clapping stopped and Hector came over to sit with me. He gave me a thin manila envelop. In it was a short story.

The title was "Josh Gave Us Respect."

Acknowledgements

There are many real life cases where innocent people have been convicted of crimes, including murder, and were subsequently exonerated, including those recounted in the play *The Exonerated*, the book *In Spite of Innocence*, the film *After Innocence,* and through the monumental work of the Innocence Project headed by attorneys Barry Scheck and Peter Neufield. All of these were an inspiration for my novel, as was the Chicago Tribune series titled *Trial and Error, How Prosecutors Sacrifice Justice to Win*, by Ken Armstrong and Maurice Possley.

As I was writing *A Good Conviction*, a column in the New York Times by Bob Herbert, another in *New Yorker* by Jeffrey Toobin, and *Dateline NBC* programs by Stone Phillips and Dan Slepian, all served to provide new insights and keep me focused on the real-world parallels of my story.

Much of this publicity concerned two 1990 murders committed at the Palladium Club in New York City. Justice in this case was finally achieved by a former Federal prosecutor, Steven M. Cohen, and a former New York City detective, Robert Addolorato, who would not rest until the new evidence they had obtained led to the overturn of the convictions of two men wrongly imprisoned for a decade. The Manhattan DA's office fought them all the way.

Paul A. Sarmousakis, a former Federal prosecutor, made an excruciatingly careful read of an early draft of *A Good Conviction* and we spent five hours one day going over his comments and observations. Nicholas E. Tishler, a practicing appeals attorney in New York State, read my draft as if it were a document he planned to use in court, and his numerous corrections regarding the appeals process were invaluable. I cannot fully express how much I appreciate Paul and Nick's careful and patient reads. Former NJ Judge Richard S. Hyland also made numerous helpful suggestions, for which I am deeply appreciative.

Of course I take full responsibility for any errors which may remain.

I was fortunate to have Linda Bernstein and Kerry Lenny read ... and re-read ... and re-read ... the ever-evolving versions of various scenes. Their suggestions, and often significant corrections, are very much appreciated. Each could be professional editors any author would be lucky to have.

When the book was done, my friends Bill Workman, Rose Mo

orse, and Norma Klein, and my sons Joshua and Jonathan Weinstein each read a galley copy and found numerous typos as well as some substantive errors. Anyone who has ever written a novel knows how difficult it is to find your own typos, no matter how diligent you try to be, and I truly appreciate their work and enthusiasm. Any typos still lurking in the printed pages are of course my sole responsibility.

Very early in the writing process, I was fortunate to meet Linda Fairstein, internationally acclaimed author and former Assistant District Attorney in Manhattan, and Linda was very gracious in suggesting certain approaches and directing me to resources regarding prosecutor experience and attitudes. Linda, of course, bears no responsibility for my fictional portrayal of the Manhattan DA's office.

There were several NYPD officers who provided valuable background information, including Police Officer Joseph Badalamente and Detective Christine Beck, now both retired. I truly appreciate the time and interest they each took in my then-developing story. Neither, however, bears any responsibility for my fictional portrayal of their department.

There would be no *A Good Conviction* without my wife Patricia Lenny. I am deeply appreciative of her encouragement to write the book in the first place and her considerable support over the years it took to complete. In addition, her experience as an attorney was invaluable in structuring certain scenes.

Finally, I named the lead character in *A Good Conviction* after my son Joshua Blake Weinstein. I did this so that every line I wrote would be influenced by a pervading personal dread that something so horrible could happen to someone I love. Thank you, Josh, for being the kind of son who could evoke the strong feelings which guided my writing.

For my other children, Jon and Marissa, I love you just as much, but you'll have to wait for your own book.

Annotated References

Prosecutorial Abuse

Trial and Error, How Prosecutors Sacrifice Justice to Win, a Chicago Tribune five part series by Ken Armstrong and Maurice Possley ... 381 defendants had homicide convictions thrown out because prosecutors concealed evidence suggesting innocence or presented evidence they knew to be false.

Actual Innocence: When Justice Goes Wrong and How to Make it Right, Barry Scheck, Peter Neufeld and Jim Dwyer ... the work of the Innocence Project.

After Innocence, Jessica Sanders and Marc Simon ... the stories of seven innocent men wrongfully imprisoned for decades.

Exonerations in the United States 1989 through 2003. Journal of Criminal Law and Criminology - January 1, 2005. Samuel R. Gross ... exonerations of falsely convicted defendants.

The Exonerated. by Jessica Blank and Erik Jensen ... the words of six innocent men and women who, after years in jail, emerged from death row.

In Spite Of Innocence: Erroneous Convictions in Capital Cases, Michael L. Radelet, Hugo Adam Bedau, Constance E. Putnam ... 400 cases of persons wrongly convicted of crimes carrying the death penalty.

Prosecutors Not Penalized, Lawyer Says, Andrea Elliott, New York Times, December 17, 2003 ... dozens of cases of prosecutorial misconduct in the Bronx district attorney's office did not result in disciplinary action.

'Sorry' Isn't Enough, Bob Herbert, New York Times, May 17, 2001 ... Prosecutors tend to be far more interested in convictions than justice.

Fatal Justice: Reinvestigating the MacDonald Murders, Jerry Allen Potter and Fred Bost ... the prosecution mishandled crime-scene evidence, withheld potentially exculpatory material, and discounted confessions from other suspects.

Lewis M. Weinstein

The Palladium Case

The People of the State of New York v. David Lemus and Olmedo Hidalgo. Kronish Lieb Weiner & Hellman LLP., www.kronishlieb.com. ... law firm's web site contains full text of all pleadings and decisions.

January 3, 2005. *When the Weight of the Evidence Shifts*, Bob Herbert, New York Times ... despite serious questions about the (Palladium) case and new evidence which has emerged, prosecutors in the Manhattan district attorney's office continue to fight all efforts to have the convictions overturned.

January 31, 2005. *One More Chance to Overturn Their Murder Convictions*, Sabrina Tavernise, New York Times ... lawyers argued that (new) evidence shows the men were wrongfully convicted, but prosecutors say the new evidence is not strong enough to reverse the conviction

February 7, 2005. *Murder at the Palladium: Were two men wrongly convicted in New York nightclub case?* Stone Phillips and Dan Slepian, Dateline NBC ... It looks to be a case of faulty eyewitness evidence and prosecutorial withholding of evidence.

May 16, 2005. *The Upstart: Manhattan's legendary D.A. faces a tough challenger*, Jeffrey Toobin. New Yorker ... (former Federal) prosecutor Steven Cohen reported the confession to lawyers in the D.A.'s office, who said that they would look into it. Ten years later, the D.A.'s office is still looking into it. Cohen, who is now in private practice, says, "What the D.A. has done in this case is an outrage. They know these men are innocent, and yet they refuse even to give them a new trial."

October 20, 2005. *Free After 14 Years*, Anemona Hartocollis and Colin Moynihan, New York Times ... David Lemus, who spent the last 14 years in jail for the 1990 killing of a bouncer at the Palladium nightclub, walked out of State Supreme Court in Lower Manhattan yesterday a free man, hours after a judge overturned his conviction in the killing.

Lewis M. Weinstein

Lew began writing novels when he was 55 years of age, finally taking the advice of his high school English teacher, who said he should write.

The Pope's Conspiracy is his 4th novel, following The Heretic (2000), A Good Conviction (2007) and Case Closed (2009). He is currently working on a novel to be set in 20th century Germany and Poland.

After graduating from Princeton and the Harvard Business School, Lew enjoyed a long management career in the private, public and not-for-profit sectors, including his last position as CEO of a biomedical research institute focused on infectious disease research.

In 1980, He was a candidate for the U.S. Congress from New Jersey.

Lew is married and lives with his wife in Key West, FL.

Lew is available to appear at book clubs, either in person, or if that is not possible, via a Skype video connection.

Additional information about Lew and his novels can be found at his author blog ...

lewweinsteinauthorblog.com